THE HARVARD CLASSICS
SHELF OF FICTION

PUNCH OFFICE, LONDON.

PUNCH OFFICE, LONDON

THE HARVARD CLASSICS
SHELF OF FICTION
SELECTED BY CHARLES W ELIOT LL D

VANITY FAIR

VOLUME II

BY

WILLIAM MAKEPEACE
THACKERAY

EDITED WITH NOTES AND INTRODUCTIONS
BY WILLIAM ALLAN NEILSON Ph D

P F COLLIER & SON COMPANY
NEW YORK

CONTENTS

VANITY FAIR, A NOVEL WITHOUT A HERO

PART II

i

VANITY FAIR

PART II

CHAPTER I

How to Live Well on Nothing a-Year

I SUPPOSE there is no man in this Vanity Fair of ours so little observant as not to think sometimes about the worldly affairs of his acquaintances, or so extremely charitable as not to wonder how his neighbour Jones, or his neighbour Smith, can make both ends meet at the end of the year. With the utmost regard for the family, for instance (for I dine with them twice or thrice in the season), I cannot but own that the appearance of the Jenkinses in the Park, in the large barouche with the grenadier-footmen, will surprise and mystify me to my dying day: for though I know the equipage is only jobbed, and all the Jenkins people are on board wages, yet those three men and the carriage must represent an expense of six hundred a-year at the very least—and then there are the splendid dinners, the two boys at Eton, the prize governess and masters for the girls, the trip abroad, or to Eastbourne or Worthing, in the autumn, the annual ball with a supper from Gunter's (who, by the way, supplies most of the *first-rate* dinners which J. gives, as I know very well, having been invited to one of them to fill a vacant place, when I saw at once that these repasts are very superior to the *common* run of entertainments for which the *humbler* sort of J.'s acquaintances get cards)—who, I say, with the most good-natured feelings in the world, can help wondering how the Jenkinses make out matters? What *is* Jenkins? We all know—Commissioner of the Tape and Sealing Wax Office, with £1200 a-year for a salary. Had

3

his wife a private fortune? Pooh—Miss Flint—one of eleven children of a small squire in Buckinghamshire. All she ever gets from her family is a turkey at Christmas, in exchange for which she has to board two or three of her sisters in the off season; and lodge and feed her brothers when they come to town. How does Jenkins balance his income? I say, as every friend of his must say, How is it that he has not been outlawed long since; and that he ever came back (as he did to the surprise of everybody) last year from Boulogne?

"I" is here introduced to personify the world in general —the Mrs. Grundy of each respected reader's private circle —every one of whom can point to some families of his acquaintance who live nobody knows how. Many a glass of wine have we all of us drunk, I have very little doubt, hob-and-nobbing with the hospitable giver, and wondering how the deuce he paid for it.

Some three or four years after his stay in Paris, when Rawdon Crawley and his wife were established in a very small comfortable house in Curzon Street, May Fair, there was scarcely one of the numerous friends whom they enter-tained at dinner that did not ask the above question regard-ing them. The novelist, it has been said before, knows everything, and as I am in a situation to be able to tell the public how Crawley and his wife lived without any income, may I entreat the public newspapers which are in the habit of extracting portions of the various periodical works now published, *not* to reprint the following exact narrative and calculations—of which I ought, as the discoverer (and at some expense, too), to have the benefit? My son, I would say, were I blessed with a child—you may by deep inquiry and constant intercourse with him, learn how a man lives comfortably on nothing a-year. But it is best not to be intimate with gentlemen of this profession, and to take the calculations at second-hand, as you do logarithms, for to work them yourself, depend upon it, will cost you some-thing considerable.

On nothing per annum then, and during a course of some two or three years, of which we can afford to give but a very brief history, Crawley and his wife lived very hap-

pily and comfortably at Paris. It was in this period that
he quitted the Guards, and sold out of the army. When
we find him again, his mustachios and the title of Colonel
on his card are the only relics of his military profession.

It has been mentioned that Rebecca, soon after her arrival in Paris, took a very smart and leading position in
the society of that capital, and was welcomed at some of
the most distinguished houses of the restored French nobility. The English men of fashion in Paris courted her, too,
to the disgust of the ladies their wives, who could not bear
the parvenue. For some months the salons of the Faubourg
St. Germain, in which her place was secured, and the
splendours of the new Court, where she was received with
much distinction, delighted, and perhaps a little intoxicated
Mrs. Crawley, who may have been disposed during this
period of elation to slight the people—honest young military
men mostly—who formed her husband's chief society.

But the Colonel yawned sadly among the duchesses and
great ladies of the Court. The old women who played
écarté made such a noise about a five-franc piece, that it
was not worth Colonel Crawley's while to sit down at a
card-table. The wit of their conversation he could not appreciate, being ignorant of their language. And what good
could his wife get, he urged, by making curtsies every night
to a whole circle of Princesses? He left Rebecca presently to frequent these parties alone; resuming his own
simple pursuits and amusements amongst the amiable friends
of his own choice.

The truth is, when we say of a gentleman that he lives
elegantly on nothing a-year, we use the word "nothing"
to signify something unknown; meaning, simply, that we
don't know how the gentleman in question defrays the expenses of his establishment. Now, our friend the Colonel
had a great aptitude for all games of chance: and exercising himself, as he continually did, with the cards, the dice-
box, or the cue, it is natural to suppose that he attained
a much greater skill in the use of these articles than men
can possess who only occasionally handle them. To use a
cue at billiards well is like using a pencil, or a German
flute, or a small-sword—you cannot master any one of these

implements at first, and it is only by repeated study and perseverance, joined to a natural taste, that a man can excel in the handling of either. Now Crawley, from being only a brilliant amateur, had grown to be a consummate master of billiards. Like a great general, his genius used to rise with the danger, and when the luck had been unfavourable to him for a whole game, and the bets were consequently against him, he would, with consummate skill and boldness, make some prodigious hits which would restore the battle, and come in a victor at the end, to the astonishment of everybody—of everybody, that is, who was a stranger to his play. Those who were accustomed to see it were cautious how they staked their money against a man of such sudden resources, and brilliant and overpowering skill.

At games of cards he was equally skilful; for though he would constantly lose money at the commencement of an evening, playing so carelessly and making such blunders, that new comers were often inclined to think meanly of his talent; yet when roused to action, and awakened to caution by repeated small losses, it was remarked that Crawley's play became quite different, and that he was pretty sure of beating his enemy thoroughly before the night was over. Indeed, very few men could say that they ever had the better of him.

His successes were so repeated that no wonder the envious and the vanquished spoke sometimes with bitterness regarding them. And as the French say of the Duke of Wellington, who never suffered a defeat, that only an astonishing series of lucky accidents enabled him to be an invariable winner; yet even they allow that he cheated at Waterloo, and was enabled to win the last great trick:—so it was hinted at head-quarters in England, that some foul play must have taken place in order to account for the continuous successes of Colonel Crawley.

Though Frascati's and the Salon were open at that time in Paris, the mania for play was so widely spread, that the public gambling-rooms did not suffice for the general ardour, and gambling went on in private houses as much as if there had been no public means for gratifying the pas-

sion. At Crawley's charming little *réunions* of an evening
this fatal amusement commonly was practised—much to
good-natured little Mrs. Crawley's annoyance. She spoke
about her husband's passion for dice with the deepest
grief; she bewailed it to everybody who came to her house.
She besought the young fellows never, never to touch a
box; and when young Green, of the Rifles, lost a very
considerable sum of money, Rebecca passed a whole night
in tears, as the servant told the unfortunate young gentleman, and actually went on her knees to her husband to beseech him to remit the debt, and burn the acknowledgment.
How could he? He had lost just as much himself to
Blackstone of the Hussars, and Count Punter of the Han-
overian Cavalry. Green might have any decent time; but
pay?—of course he must pay; to talk of burning I O U's
was child's-play.

Other officers, chiefly young—for the young fellows
gathered round Mrs. Crawley—came from her parties with
long faces, having dropped more or less money at her fatal
card-tables. Her house began to have an unfortunate reputation. The old hands warned the less experienced of
their danger. Colonel O'Dowd, of the —th regiment, one
of those occupying in Paris, warned Lieutenant Spooney
of that corps. A loud and violent fracas took place between the infantry-colonel and his lady, who were dining
at the Café de Paris, and Colonel and Mrs. Crawley, who
were also taking their meal there. The ladies engaged on
both sides. Mrs. O'Dowd snapped her fingers in Mrs.
Crawley's face, and called her husband "no betther than
a black-leg." Colonel Crawley challenged Colonel O'Dowd,
C.B. The Commander-in-Chief hearing of the dispute sent
for Colonel Crawley, who was getting ready the same pis-
tols "which he shot Captain Marker," and had such a conversation with him that no duel took place. If Rebecca
had not gone on her knees to General Tufto, Crawley
would have been sent back to England; and he did not
play, except with civilians, for some weeks after.

But, in spite of Rawdon's undoubted skill and constant
successes, it became evident to Rebecca, considering these
things, that their position was but a precarious one, and

that, even although they paid scarcely anybody, their little capital would end one day by dwindling into zero. "Gambling," she would say, "dear, is good to help your income, but not as an income itself. Some day people may be tired of play, and then where are we?" Rawdon acquiesced in the justice of her opinion; and in truth he had remarked that after a few nights of his little suppers, &c., gentlemen *were* tired of play with him, and, in spite of Rebecca's charms, did not present themselves very eagerly.

Easy and pleasant as their life at Paris was, it was after all only an idle dalliance and amiable trifling; and Rebecca saw that she must push Rawdon's fortune in their own country. She must get him a place or appointment at home or in the colonies; and she determined to make a move upon England as soon as the way could be cleared for her. As a first step she had made Crawley sell out of the Guards, and go on half-pay. His function as aide-de-camp to General Tufto had ceased previously. Rebecca laughed in all companies at that officer, at his toupee (which he mounted on coming to Paris), at his waistband, at his false teeth, at his pretensions to be a lady-killer above all, and his absurd vanity in fancying every woman whom he came near was in love with him. It was to Mrs. Brent, the beetle-browed wife of Mr. Commissary Brent, to whom the General transferred his attentions now—his bouquets, his dinners at the restaurateurs', his opera-boxes, and his knick-knacks. Poor Mrs. Tufto was no more happy than before, and had still to pass long evenings alone with her daughters, knowing that her General was gone off scented and curled to stand behind Mrs. Brent's chair at the play. Becky had a dozen admirers in his place to be sure; and could cut her rival to pieces with her wit. But, as we have said, she was growing tired of this idle social life: opera-boxes and restaurateur-dinners palled upon her: nosegays could not be laid by a provision for future years: and she could not live upon knick-knacks, laced handkerchiefs, and kid gloves. She felt the frivolity of pleasure, and longed for more substantial benefits.

At this juncture news arrived which was spread among the many creditors of the Colonel at Paris, and which

caused them great satisfaction. Miss Crawley, the rich
aunt from whom he expected his immense inheritance, was
dying; the Colonel must haste to her bedside. Mrs. Crawley and her child would remain behind until he came to
reclaim them. He departed for Calais, and having reached
that place in safety, it might have been supposed that he
went to Dover; but instead he took the diligence to Dun-
kirk, and thence travelled to Brussels, for which place he
had a former predilection. The fact is, he owed more
money at London than at Paris; and he preferred the quiet
little Belgian city to either of the more noisy capitals.

Her aunt was dead. Mrs. Crawley ordered the most
intense mourning for herself and little Rawdon. The Colonel was busy arranging the affairs of the inheritance.
They could take the premier now, instead of the little entresol of the hotel which they occupied. Mrs. Crawley
and the landlord had a consultation about the new hangings, an amicable wrangle about the carpets, and a final
adjustment of everything except the bill. She went off in
one of his carriages; her French *bonne* with her; the child
by her side; the admirable landlord and landlady smiling
farewell to her from the gate. General Tufto was furious
when he heard she was gone, and Mrs. Brent furious with
him for being furious; Lieutenant Spooney was cut to the
heart; and the landlord got ready his best apartments previous to the return of the fascinating little woman and her
husband. He *serréd* the trunks which she left in his charge
with the greatest care. They had been especially recommended to him by Madame Crawley. They were not, however, found to be particularly valuable when opened some
time after.

But before she went to join her husband in the Belgic
capital, Mrs. Crawley made an expedition into England,
leaving behind her her little son upon the continent, under
the care of her French maid.

The parting between Rebecca and the little Rawdon did
not cause either party much pain. She had not, to say
truth, seen much of the young gentleman since his birth.
After the amiable fashion of French mothers, she had
placed him out at nurse in a village in the neighbourhood

10

of Paris, where little Rawdon passed the first months of
his life, not unhappily, with a numerous family of foster-
brothers in wooden shoes. His father would ride over
many a time to see him here, and the elder Rawdon's
paternal heart glowed to see him rosy and dirty, shouting
lustily, and happy in the making of mud-pies under the
superintendence of the gardener's wife, his nurse.

Rebecca did not care much to go and see the son and
heir. Once he spoiled a new dove-coloured pelisse of hers.
He preferred his nurse's caresses to his mamma's, and
when finally he quitted that jolly nurse and almost parent,
he cried loudly for hours. He was only consoled by his
mother's promise that he should return to his nurse the
next day; indeed the nurse herself, who probably would
have been pained at the parting too, was told that the child
would immediately be restored to her, and for some time
awaited quite anxiously his return.

In fact, our friends may be said to have been among the
first of that brood of hardy English adventurers who have
subsequently invaded the Continent, and swindled in all
the capitals of Europe. The respect in those happy days
of 1817-18 was very great for the wealth and honour of
Britons. They had not then learned, as I am told, to hag-
gle for bargains with the pertinacity which now distinguishes them. The great cities of Europe had not been as
yet open to the enterprise of our rascals. And whereas
there is now hardly a town of France or Italy in which you
shall not see some noble countryman of our own, with that
happy swagger and insolence of demeanour which we carry
everywhere, swindling inn-landlords, passing fictitious
cheques upon credulous bankers, robbing coach-makers of
their carriage, goldsmiths of their trinkets, easy travellers
of their money at cards,—even public libraries of their
books:—thirty years ago you needed but to be a Milor
Anglais, travelling in a private carriage, and credit was at
your hand wherever you chose to seek it, and gentlemen,
instead of cheating, were cheated. It was not for some
weeks after the Crawleys' departure that the landlord of
the hotel which they occupied during their residence at
Paris, found out the losses which he had sustained; not

until Madame Marabou, the milliner, made repeated visits, with her little bill for articles supplied to Madame Craw-ley; not until Monsieur Didelot from Boule d'Or in the Palais Royal had asked half-a-dozen times whether cette charmante Miladi who had bought watches and bracelets of him was de retour. It is a fact that even the poor gar-dener's wife, who had nursed Madame's child, was never paid after the first six months for that supply of the milk of human kindness with which she had furnished the lusty and healthy little Rawdon. No, not even the nurse was paid—the Crawleys were in too great a hurry to remember their trifling debt to her. As for the landlord of the hotel, his curses against the English nation were violent for the rest of his natural life. He asked all travellers whether they knew a certain Colonel Lor Crawley—avec sa femme —une petite dame, très spirituelle. *"Ah, Monsieur!"* he would add—*"ils m'ont affreusement volé."* It was melan-choly to hear his accents as he spoke of that catastrophe.

Rebecca's object in her journey to London was to effect a kind of compromise with her husband's numerous credi-tors, and by offering them a dividend of ninepence or a shilling in the pound, to secure a return for him into his own country. It does not become us to trace the steps which she took in the conduct of this most difficult negoti-ation; but, having shown them to their satisfaction, that the sum which she was empowered to offer was all her husband's available capital, and having convinced them that Colonel Crawley would prefer a perpetual retirement on the Continent to a residence in this country with his debts unsettled; having proved to them that there was no possibility of money accruing to him from other quarters, and no earthly chance of their getting a larger dividend than that which she was empowered to offer, she brought the Colonel's creditors unanimously to accept her proposals, and purchased with fifteen hundred pounds of ready money, more than ten times that amount of debts.

Mrs. Crawley employed no lawyer in the transaction. The matter was so simple, to have or to leave, as she justly observed, that she made the lawyers of the creditors them-selves do the business. And Mr. Lewis representing Mr.

CHAPTER II

The Subject Continued

IN the first place, and as a matter of the greatest necessity, we are bound to describe how a house may be got for nothing a-year. These mansions are to be had either unfurnished, where, if you have credit with Messrs. Gillows or Bantings, you can get them splendidly *montées* and decorated entirely according to your own fancy; or they are to be let furnished; a less troublesome and complicated arrangement to most parties. It was so that Crawley and his wife preferred to hire their house.

Before Mr. Bowls came to preside over Miss Crawley's house and cellar in Park Lane, that lady had had for a butler a Mr. Raggles, who was born on the family estate of Queen's Crawley, and indeed was a younger son of a gardener there. By good conduct, a handsome person and calves, and a grave demeanour, Raggles rose from the knife-board to the foot-board of the carriage; from the foot-board to the butler's pantry. When he had been a certain number of years at the head of Miss Crawley's establishment, where he had had good wages, fat perquisites, and plenty of opportunities of saving, he announced that he was about to contract a matrimonial alliance with a late cook of Miss Crawley's, who had subsisted in an honourable manner by the exercise of a mangle, and the keeping of a small greengrocer's shop in the neighbourhood. The truth is, that the ceremony had been clandestinely performed some years back; although the news of Mr. Raggles' marriage was first brought to Miss Crawley by a little boy and girl of seven and eight years of age, whose continual presence in the kitchen had attracted the attention of Miss Briggs.

Mr. Raggles then retired and personally undertook the superintendence of the small shop and the greens. He added milk and cream, eggs and country-fed pork to his

stores, contenting himself, whilst other retired butlers were
vending spirits in public-houses, by dealing in the simplest
country produce. And having a good connection amongst
the butlers in the neighbourhood, and a snug back parlour
where he and Mrs. Raggles received them, his milk, cream,
and eggs got to be adopted by many of the fraternity, and
his profits increased every year. Year after year he quietly
and modestly amassed money, and when at length that snug
and complete bachelor's residence at No. 201, Curzon Street,
May Fair, late the residence of the Honourable Frederick
Deuceace, gone abroad, with its rich and appropriate furniture by the first makers, was brought to the hammer, who
should go in and purchase the lease and furniture of the
house but Charles Raggles? A part of the money he borrowed, it is true, and at rather a high interest, from a brother
butler, but the chief part he paid down, and it was with no
small pride that Mrs. Raggles found herself sleeping in a bed
of carved mahogany, with silk curtains, with a prodigious
cheval glass opposite to her, and a wardrobe which would
contain her, and Raggles, and all the family.

Of course, they did not intend to occupy permanently an
apartment so splendid. It was in order to let the house again
that Raggles purchased it. As soon as a tenant was found he
subsided into the greengrocer's shop once more; but a happy
thing it was for him to walk out of that tenement and into
Curzon Street, and there survey his house—his own house—
with geraniums in the window and a carved bronze knocker.
The footman occasionally lounging at the area railing, treated
him with respect; the cook took her green stuff at his
house and called him Mr. Landlord; and there was not one
thing the tenants did, or one dish which they had for dinner,
that Raggles might not know of, if he liked.

He was a good man; good and happy. The house brought
him in so handsome a yearly income, that he was determined
to send his children to good schools, and accordingly, regardless of expense, Charles was sent to boarding at Dr. Swishtail's, Sugar-cane Lodge, and little Matilda to Miss Peck-
over's, Laurentinum House, Clapham.

Raggles loved and adored the Crawley family as the author
of all his prosperity in life. He had a silhouette of his mis-

tress in his back shop, and a drawing of the Porter's Lodge
at Queen's Crawley, done by that spinster herself in India
ink—and the only addition he made to the decorations of the
Curzon Street House was a print of Queen's Crawley in
Hampshire, the seat of Sir Walpole Crawley, Baronet, who
was represented in a gilded car drawn by six white horses,
and passing by a. lake covered with swans, and barges containing ladies in hoops, and musicians with flags and periwigs.
Indeed Raggles thought there was no such palace in all the
world and no such august family.

As luck would have it, Raggles' house in Curzon Street
was to let when Rawdon and his wife returned to London.
The Colonel knew it and its owner quite well; the latter's
connexion with the Crawley family had been kept up constantly, for Raggles helped Mr. Bowls whenever Miss Crawley received friends. And the old man not only let his house
to the Colonel, but officiated as his butler whenever he had
company; Mrs. Raggles operating in the kitchen below, and
sending up dinners of which old Miss Crawley herself might
have approved. This was· the way, then, Crawley got his
house for nothing; for though Raggles had to pay taxes and
rates, and the interest of the mortgage to the brother butler;
and the insurance of his life; and the charges for his children
at school; and the value of the meat and drink which his
own family—and for a time that of Colonel Crawley too—
consumed; and though the poor wretch was utterly ruined by
the transaction, his children being flung on the streets and
himself driven into the Fleet Prison; yet somebody must pay
even for gentlemen who live for nothing a-year—and so it
was this unlucky Raggles was made the representative of
Colonel Crawley's defective capital.

I wonder how many families are driven to roguery and to
ruin by great practitioners in Crawley's way?—how many
great noblemen rob their petty tradesmen, condescend to
swindle their poor retainers out of wretched little sums, and
cheat for a few shillings? When we read that a noble
nobleman has left for the Continent, or that another noble
nobleman has an execution in. his house—and that one or
other owes six or seven millions, the defeat seems glorious
even, and we respect the victim in the vastness of his ruin.

But who pities a poor barber who can't get his money for powdering the footman's heads; or a poor carpenter who has ruined himself by fixing up ornaments and pavilions for my lady's *déjeuner;* or the poor devil of a tailor whom the steward patronises, and who has pledged all he is worth, and more, to get the liveries ready, which my lord has done him the honour to bespeak?—When the great house tumbles down, these miserable wretches fall under it unnoticed: as they say in the old legends, before a man goes to the devil himself, he sends plenty of other souls thither.

Rawdon and his wife generously gave their patronage to all such of Miss Crawley's tradesmen and purveyors as chose to serve them. Some were willing enough, especially the poor ones. It was wonderful to see the pertinacity with which the washerwoman from Tooting brought the cart every Saturday, and her bills week after week. Mr. Raggles himself had to supply the greengroceries. The bill for servants' porter at the Fortune of War public-house is a curiosity in the chronicles of beer. Every servant also was owed the greater part of his wages, and thus kept up perforce an interest in the house. Nobody in fact was paid. Not the blacksmith who opened the lock; nor the glazier who mended the pane; nor the jobber who let the carriage; nor the groom who drove it; nor the butcher who provided the leg of mutton; nor the coals which roasted it; nor the cook who basted it; nor the servants who ate it; and this I am given to understand is not unfrequently the way in which people live elegantly on nothing a-year.

In a little town such things cannot be done without remark. We know there the quantity of milk our neighbour takes, and espy the joint or the fowls which are going in for his dinner. So, probably, 200 and 202 in Curzon Street might know what was going on in the house between them, the servants communicating through the area-railings; but Crawley and his wife and his friends did not know 200 and 202. When you came to 201 there was a hearty welcome, and a kind smile, a good dinner, and a jolly shake of the hand from the host and hostess there, just for all the world as if they had been undisputed masters of three or four thousand a-year—and so they were not in money, but in produce and labour—if they did not pay for the mutton, they had it: if they did not give bullion in exchange for their wine, how should we know? Never was better claret at any man's table than at honest Rawdon's; dinners more gay and neatly served. His drawing-rooms were the prettiest, little, modest salons conceivable: they were decorated with the greatest taste, and a thousand knick-knacks from Paris, by Rebecca: and when she sate at her piano trilling songs with a lightsome heart, the stranger voted himself in a little paradise of domestic comfort, and agreed that, if the husband was rather stupid, the wife was charming, and the dinners the pleasantest in the world.

Rebecca's wit, cleverness, and flippancy, made her speedily the vogue in London among a certain class. You saw demure chariots at her door, out of which stepped very great people. You beheld her carriage in the Park, surrounded by dandies of note. The little box in the third tier of the Opera was crowded with heads constantly changing; but it must be confessed that the ladies held aloof from her, and that their doors were shut to our little adventurer.

With regard to the world of female fashion and its customs, the present writer of course can only speak at second hand. A man can no more penetrate or understand those mysteries than he can know what the ladies talk about when they go upstairs after dinner. It is only by inquiry and perseverance, that one sometimes gets hints of those secrets; and by a similar diligence every person who treads the Pall Mall pavement and frequents the clubs of this metropolis, knows, either through his own experience or through some acquaintance with whom he plays at billiards or shares the joint, something about the genteel world of London, and how, as there are men (such as Rawdon Crawley, whose position we mentioned before), who cut a good figure to the eyes of the ignorant world and to the apprentices in the Park, who behold them consorting with the most notorious dandies there, so there are the ladies, who may be called men's women, being welcomed entirely by all the gentlemen, and cut or slighted by all their wives. Mrs. Firebrace is of this sort; the lady with the beautiful fair ringlets whom you see every day in Hyde Park, surrounded by the greatest and most

famous dandies of this empire. Mrs. Rockwood is another
whose parties are announced laboriously in the !fashionable
newspapers, and with whom you see that all sorts of ambassadors and great noblemen dine; and many more might be
mentioned had they to do with the history at present in hand.
But while simple folks who are out of the world, or country
people with a taste for the genteel, behold these ladies in
their seeming glory in public places, or envy them from afar
off, persons who are better instructed could inform them that
these envied ladies have no more chance of establishing themselves in "Society," than the benighted squire's wife in Somersetshire, who reads of their doings in the *Morning Post.*
Men living about London are aware of these awful truths.
You hear how pitilessly many ladies of seeming rank and
wealth are excluded from this "Society." The frantic efforts
which they make to enter this circle, the meannesses to which
they submit, the insults which they undergo, are matters of
wonder to those who take human or womankind for a study;
and the pursuit of fashion under difficulties would be a fine
theme for any very great person who had the wit, the leisure,
and the knowledge of the English language necessary for the
compiling of such a history.

Now the few female acquaintances whom Mrs. Crawley
had known abroad, not only declined to visit her when she
came to this side of the channel, but cut her severely when
they met in public places. It was curious to see how the great
ladies forgot her, and no doubt not altogether a pleasant study
to Rebecca. When Lady Bareacres met her in the waiting-
room at the Opera, she gathered her daughters about her as
if they would be contaminated by a touch of Becky, and retreating a step or two, placed herself in front of them, and
stared at her little enemy. To stare Becky out of countenance required a severer glance than even the frigid old Bareacres could shoot out of her dismal eyes. When Lady de la
Mole, who had ridden a score of times by Becky's side at
Brussels, met Mrs. Crawley's open carriage in Hyde Park,
her Ladyship was quite blind, and could not in the least recognise her former friend. Even Mrs. Blenkinsop, the banker's wife, cut her at church. Becky went regularly to church
now; it was edifying to see her enter there with Rawdon by

her side, carrying a couple of large gilt prayer-books, and afterwards going through the ceremony with the gravest resignation.

Rawdon at first felt very acutely the slights which were passed upon his wife, and was inclined to be gloomy and savage. He talked of calling out the husbands or brothers of every one of the insolent women who did not pay a proper respect to his wife; and it was only by the strongest commands and entreaties on her part, that he was brought into keeping a decent behaviour. "You can't shoot me into society," she said, good-naturedly. "Remember, my dear, that I was but a governess, and you, you poor silly old man, have the worst reputation for debt, and dice, and all sorts of wickedness. We shall get quite as many friends as we want by and by, and in the meanwhile you must be a good boy, and obey your schoolmistress in everything she tells you to do. When we heard that your aunt had left almost everything to Pitt and his wife, do you remember what a rage you were in? You would have told all Paris, if I had not made you keep your temper, and where would you have been now?—in prison at Ste. Pélagie for debt, and not established in London in a handsome house, with every comfort about you—you were in such a fury you were ready to murder your brother, you wicked Cain you, and what good would have come of remaining angry? All the rage in the world won't get us your aunt's money; and it is much better that we should be friends with your brother's family than enemies, as those foolish Butes are. When your father dies, Queen's Crawley will be a pleasant house for you and me to pass the winter in. If we are ruined, you can carve and take charge of the stable, and I can be a governess to Lady Jane's children. Ruined! fiddlededee! I will get you a good place before that; or Pitt and his little boy will die, and we will be Sir Rawdon and my lady. While there is life, there is hope, my dear, and I intend to make a man of you yet. Who sold your horses for you? Who paid your debts for you?" Rawdon was obliged to confess that he owed all these benefits to his wife, and to trust himself to her guidance for the future.

Indeed, when Miss Crawley quitted the world, and that money for which all her relatives had been fighting so eagerly was finally left to Pitt, Bute Crawley, who found that only five thousand pounds had been left to him instead of the twenty upon which he calculated, was in such a fury at his disappointment, that he vented it in savage abuse upon his nephew; and the quarrel always rankling between them ended in an utter breach of intercourse. Rawdon Crawley's conduct, on the other hand, who got but a hundred pounds, was such as to astonish his brother and delight his sister-in-law, who was disposed to look kindly upon all the members of her husband's family. He wrote to his brother a very frank, manly, good-humoured letter from Paris. He was aware, he said, that by his own marriage he had forfeited his aunt's favour; and though he did not disguise his disappointment that she should have been so entirely relentless towards him, he was glad that the money was still kept in their branch of the family, and heartily congratulated his brother on his good fortune. He sent his affectionate remembrances to his sister, and hoped to have her good-will for Mrs. Rawdon; and the letter concluded with a postscript to Pitt in the latter lady's own handwriting. She, too, begged to join in her husband's congratulations. She should ever remember Mr. Crawley's kindness to her in early days when she was a friendless orphan, the instructress of his little sisters, in whose welfare she still took the tenderest interest. She wished him every happiness in his married life, and, asking his permission to offer her remembrances to Lady Jane (of whose goodness all the world informed her), she hoped that one day she might be allowed to present her little boy to his uncle and aunt, and begged to bespeak for him their good-will and protection.

Pitt Crawley received this communication very graciously —more graciously than Miss Crawley had received some of Rebecca's previous compositions in Rawdon's handwriting; and as for Lady Jane, she was so charmed with the letter, that she expected her husband would instantly divide his aunt's legacy into two equal portions, and send off one-half to his brother at Paris.

To her ladyship's surprise, however, Pitt declined to accommodate his brother with a cheque for thirty thousand pounds. But he made Rawdon a handsome offer of his hand whenever the latter should come to England and choose to take it; and, thanking Mrs. Crawley for her good opinion of himself and Lady Jane, he graciously pronounced his willingness to take any opportunity to serve her little boy.

Thus an almost reconciliation was brought about between the brothers. When Rebecca came to town Pitt and his wife were not in London. Many a time she drove by the old door in Park Lane to see whether they had taken possession of Miss Crawley's house there. But the new family did not make its appearance; it was only through Raggles that she heard of their movements—how Miss Crawley's domestic had been dismissed with decent gratuities, and how Mr. Pitt had only once made his appearance in London, when he stopped for a few days at the house, did business with his lawyers there, and sold off all Miss Crawley's French novels to a bookseller out of Bond Street. Becky had reasons of her own which caused her to long for the arrival of her new relation. "When Lady Jane comes," thought she, "she shall be my sponsor in London society; and as for the women! bah! the women will ask me when they find the men want to see me."

An article as necessary to a lady in this position as her brougham or her bouquet, is her companion. I have always admired the way in which the tender creatures, who cannot exist without sympathy, hire an exceedingly plain friend of their own sex from whom they are almost inseparable. The sight of that inevitable woman in her faded gown seated behind her dear friend in the opera-box, or occupying the back seat of the barouche, is always a wholesome and moral one to me, as jolly as a reminder as that of the Death's-head which figured in the repasts of Egyptian *bon-vivants*, a strange sardonic memorial of Vanity Fair. What?—even battered, brazen, beautiful, conscienceless, heartless, Mrs. Firebrace, whose father died of her shame: even lovely, daring Mrs. Mantrap, who will ride at any

fence which any man in England will take, and who drives
her greys in the Park, while her mother keeps a huckster's
stall in Bath still;—even those who are so bold, one might
fancy they could face anything, dare not face the world
without a female friend. They must have somebody to
cling to, the affectionate creatures! And you will hardly
see them in any public place without a shabby companion
in a dyed silk, sitting somewhere in the shade close behind
them.

"Rawdon," said Becky, very late one night, as a party
of gentlemen were seated round her crackling drawing-
room fire (for the men came to her house to finish the
night; and she had ice and coffee for them, the best in
London): "I must have a sheep-dog."

"A what?" said Rawdon, looking up from an *écarté* table.

"A sheep-dog!" said young Lord Southdown. "My dear
Mrs. Crawley, what a fancy! Why not have a Danish
dog? I know of one as big as a camel-leopard, by Jove.
It would almost pull your brougham. Or a Persian greyhound, eh? (I propose, if you please) ; or a little pug that
would go into one of Lord Steyne's snuff-boxes. There's
a man at Bayswater got one with such a nose that you
might,—I mark the king and play,—that you might hang
your hat on it."

"I mark the trick," Rawdon gravely said. He attended
to his game commonly, and didn't much meddle with the
conversation except when it was about horses and betting.

"What *can* you want with a shepherd's dog?" the lively
little Southdown continued.

"I mean a *moral* shepherd's dog," said Becky, laughing,
and looking up at Lord Steyne.

"What the devil's that?" said his Lordship.

"A dog to keep the wolves off me," Rebecca continued.
"A companion."

"Dear little innocent lamb, you want one," said the
Marquis; and his jaw thrust out, and he began to grin
hideously, his little eyes leering towards Rebecca.

The great Lord Steyne was standing by the fire sipping
coffee. The fire crackled and blazed pleasantly. There
was a score of candles sparkling around the mantlepiece, in

all sorts of quaint sconces, of gilt and bronze and porcelain. They lighted up Rebecca's figure to admiration, as she sate on a sofa covered with a pattern of gaudy flowers. She was in a pink dress, that looked as fresh as a rose; her dazzling white arms and shoulders were half-covered with a thin hazy scarf through which they sparkled; her hair hung in curls round her neck; one of her little feet peeped out from the fresh crisp folds of the silk: the prettiest little foot in the prettiest little sandal in the finest silk stocking in the world.

The candles lighted up Lord Steyne's shining bald head, which was fringed with red hair. He had thick bushy eyebrows, with little twinkling bloodshot eyes, surrounded by a thousand wrinkles. His jaw was underhung, and when he laughed, two white buck-teeth protruded themselves and glistened savagely in the midst of the grin. He had been dining with royal personages, and wore his garter and ribbon. A short man was his Lordship, broad-chested, and bow-legged, but proud of the fineness of his foot and ancle, and always caressing his garter-knee.

"And so the Shepherd is not enough," said he, "to defend his lambkin?"

"The Shepherd is too fond of playing at cards and going to his clubs," answered Becky, laughing.

"'Gad, what a debauched Corydon!" said my lord—"what a mouth for a pipe!"

"I take your three to two," here said Rawdon, at the card-table.

"Hark at Melibœus," snarled the noble Marquis; "he's pastorally occupied too: he's shearing a Southdown. What an innocent mutton, hey? Damme, what a snowy fleece!"

Rebecca's eyes shot out gleams of scornful humour. "My lord," she said, "you are a knight of the Order." He had the collar round his neck, indeed—a gift of the restored Princes of Spain.

Lord Steyne in early life had been notorious for his daring and his success at play. He had sat up two days and two nights with Mr. Fox at hazard. He had won money of the most august personages of the realm: he had won his marquisate, it was said, at the gaming-table; but he did not like an allusion to those bygone *fredaines*. Rebecca saw the scowl gathering over his heavy brow.

She rose up from her sofa, and went and took his coffee cup out of his hand with a little curtsey. "Yes," she said, "I must get a watchdog. But he won't bark at *you*." And, going into the other drawing-room, she sate down to the piano, and began to sing little French songs in such a charming, thrilling voice, that the mollified nobleman speedily followed her into that chamber, and might be seen nodding his head and bowing time over her.

Rawdon and his friend meanwhile played *écarté* until they had enough. The Colonel won; but, say that he won ever so much and often, nights like these, which occurred many times in the week—his wife having all the talk and all the admiration, and he sitting silent without the circle, not comprehending a word of the jokes, the allusions, the mystical language within—must have been rather wearisome to the ex-dragoon.

"How is Mrs. Crawley's husband?" Lord Steyne used to say to him by way of a good day when they met: and indeed that was now his avocation in life. He was Colonel Crawley no more. He was Mrs. Crawley's husband.

About the little Rawdon, if nothing has been said all this while, it is because he is hidden upstairs in a garret somewhere, or has crawled below into the kitchen for companionship. His mother scarcely ever took notice of him.

He passed the days with his French *bonne* as long as that domestic remained in Mr. Crawley's family, and when the Frenchwoman went away, the little fellow, howling in the loneliness of the night, had compassion taken on him by a housemaid, who took him out of his solitary nursery into her bed in the garret hard by, and comforted him.

Rebecca, my Lord Steyne, and one or two more were in the drawing-room taking tea after the Opera, when this shouting was heard overhead. "It's my cherub crying for his nurse," she said. She did not offer to move to go and see the child. "Don't agitate your feelings by going to look for him," said Lord Steyne sardonically. "Bah!"

replied the other, with a sort of blush, "he'll cry himself to sleep;" and they fell to talking about the Opera.

Rawdon had stolen off though, to look after his son and heir; and came back to the company when he found that honest Dolly was consoling the child. The Colonel's dressing room was in those upper regions. He used to see the boy there in private. They had interviews together every morning when he shaved; Rawdon minor sitting on a box by his father's side and watching the operation with neverceasing pleasure. He and the sire were great friends. The father would bring him sweetmeats from the dessert, and hide them in a certain old epaulet box, where the child went to seek them, and laughed with joy on discovering the treasure; laughed, but not too loud: for mamma was below asleep and must not be disturbed. She did not go to rest till very late, and seldom rose till after noon.

Rawdon bought the boy plenty of picture-books, and crammed his nursery with toys. Its walls were covered with pictures pasted up by the father's own hand, and purchased by him for ready money. When he was off duty with Mrs. Rawdon in the Park, he would sit up here, passing hours with the boy; who rode on his chest, who pulled his great mustachios as if they were driving-reins, and spent days with him in indefatigable gambols. The room was a low room, and once, when the child was not five years old, his father, who was tossing him wildly up in his arms, hit the poor little chap's skull so violently against the ceiling that he almost dropped the child, so terrified was he at the disaster.

Rawdon minor had made up his face for a tremendous howl—the severity of the blow indeed authorized that indulgence; but just as he was going to begin, the father interposed.

"For God's sake, Rawdy, don't wake mamma," he cried. And the child, looking in a very hard and piteous way at his father, bit his lips, clenched his hands, and didn't cry a bit. Rawdon told that story at the clubs, at the mess, to everybody in town. "By Gad, sir," he explained to the public in general, "what a good plucked one that boy of mine is—what a trump he is! —I half sent his head through the ceiling, by Gad, and he wouldn't cry for fear of disturbing his mother."

Sometimes—once or twice in a week—that lady visited the upper regions in which the child lived. She came like a vivified figure out of the *Magasin des Modes*—blandly smiling in the most beautiful new clothes and little gloves and boots. Wonderful scarfs, laces, and jewels glittered about her. She had always a new bonnet on: and flowers bloomed perpetually in it: or else magnificent curling ostrich feathers, soft and snowy as camellias. She nodded twice or thrice patronisingly to the little boy, who looked up from his dinner or from the pictures of soldiers he was painting. When she left the room, an odour of rose, or some other magical fragrance, lingered about the nursery. She was an unearthly being in his eyes, superior to his father—to all the world: to be worshipped and admired at a distance.

To drive with that lady in the carriage was an awful rite: he sate up in the back seat, and did not dare to speak: he gazed with all his eyes at the beautifully dressed princess opposite to him. Gentlemen on splendid prancing horses came up and smiled and talked with her. How her eyes beamed upon all of them! Her hand used to quiver and wave gracefully as they passed. When he went out with her he had his new red dress on. His old brown holland was good enough when he stayed at home. Sometimes, when she was away, and Dolly his maid was making his bed, he came into his mother's room. It was as the abode of a fairy to him—a mystic chamber of splendour and delights. There in the wardrobe hung those wonderful robes—pink and blue, and many-tinted. There was the jewel-case, silver-clasped: and the wondrous bronze hand on the dressing-table, glistening all over with a hundred rings. There was the cheval-glass, that miracle of art, in which he could just see his own wondering head, and the reflection of Dolly (queerly distorted, and as if up in the ceiling), plumping and patting the pillows of the bed. O, thou poor lonely little benighted boy! Mother is the name for God in the lips and hearts of little children; and here was one who was worshipping a stone.

Now Rawdon Crawley, rascal as the Colonel was, had certain manly tendencies of affection in his heart, and could love a child and a woman still. For Rawdon minor he had a great secret tenderness then, which did not escape Rebecca, though she did not talk about it to her husband. It did not annoy her: she was too good-natured. It only increased her scorn for him. He felt somehow ashamed of this paternal softness, and hid it from his wife—only indulging in it when alone with the boy.

He used to take him out of mornings when they would go to the stables together and to the Park. Little Lord Southdown, the best-natured of men, who would make you a present of the hat from his head, and whose main occupation in life was to buy knick-knacks that he might give them away afterwards, bought the little chap a pony not much bigger than a large rat, the donor said, and on this little black Shetland pigmy young Rawdon's great father was pleased to mount the boy, and to walk by his side in the Park.

It pleased him to see his old quarters, and his old fellow-guardsmen at Knightsbridge: he had begun to think of his bachelorhood with something like regret. The old troopers were glad to recognize their ancient officer, and dandle the little Colonel. Colonel Crawley found dining at mess and with his brother-officers very pleasant. "Hang it, I ain't clever enough for her—I know it. She won't miss me," he used to say: and he was right, his wife did not miss him.

Rebecca was fond of her husband. She was always perfectly good-humoured and kind to him. She did not even show her scorn much for him; perhaps she liked him the better for being a fool. He was her upper servant and *maître d'hôtel*. He went on her errands: obeyed her orders without question: drove in the carriage in the ring with her without repining; took her to the Opera-box; solaced himself at his club during the performance, and came punctually back to fetch her when due. He would have liked her to be a little fonder of the boy: but even to that he reconciled himself. "Hang it, you know she's so clever," he said, "and I'm not literary and that, you know." For, as we have said before, it requires no great wisdom to be able to win at cards and billiards, and Rawdon made no pretensions to any other sort of skill.

When the companion came, his domestic duties became very light. His wife encouraged him to dine abroad: she would let him off duty at the Opera. "Don't stay and stupefy yourself at home to-night, my dear," she would say. "Some men are coming who will only bore you. I would not ask them, but you know it's for your good, and now I have a sheep-dog, I need not be afraid to be alone."

"A sheep-dog—a companion! Becky Sharp with a companion! Isn't it good fun?" thought Mrs. Crawley to herself. The notion tickled hugely her sense of humour.

One Sunday morning, as Rawdon Crawley, his little son, and the pony were taking their accustomed walk in the Park, they passed by an old acquaintance of the Colonel's, Corporal Clink, of the regiment, who was in conversation with a friend, an old gentleman, who held a boy in his arms about the age of little Rawdon. This other youngster had seized hold of the Waterloo medal which the Corporal wore, and was examining it with delight.

"Good morning, your honour," said Clink, in reply to the "How do, Clink?" of the Colonel. "This ere young gentleman is about the little Colonel's age, sir," continued the Corporal.

"His father was a Waterloo man, too," said the old gentleman, who carried the boy. "Wasn't he, Georgy?"

"Yes," said Georgy. He and the little chap on the pony were looking at each other with all their might—solemnly scanning each other as children do.

"In a line regiment," Clink said, with a patronising air.

"He was a Captain in the —th regiment," said the old gentleman rather pompously. "Captain George Osborne, sir—perhaps you knew him. He died the death of a hero, sir, fighting against the Corsican tyrant."

Colonel Crawley blushed quite red. "I knew him very well, sir," he said, "and his wife, his dear little wife, sir—how is she?"

"She is my daughter, sir," said the old gentleman, putting down the boy, and taking out a card with great solemnity, which he handed to the Colonel. On it was written—

"Mr. Sedley, Sole Agent for the Black Diamond and Anti-Cinder Coal Association, Bunker's Wharf, Thames Street, and Anna-Maria Cottages, Fulham Road West."

Little Georgy went up and looked at the Shetland pony.

"Should you like to have a ride?" said Rawdon minor from the saddle.

"Yes," said Georgy. The Colonel, who had been looking at him with some interest, took up the child and put him on the pony behind Rawdon minor.

"Take hold of him, Georgy," he said—"take my little boy round the waist—his name is Rawdon." And both the children began to laugh.

"You won't see a prettier pair, I think, *this* summer's day, sir," said the good-natured Corporal; and the Colonel, the Corporal, and old Mr. Sedley with his umbrella, walked by the side of the children.

CHAPTER III

A FAMILY IN A VERY SMALL WAY

WE must suppose little George Osborne has ridden from Knightsbridge towards Fulham, and will stop and make inquiries at that village regarding some friends whom we have left there. How is Mrs. Amelia after the storm of Waterloo? Is she living and thriving? What has come of Major Dobbin, whose cab was always hankering about her premises? and is there any news of the Collector of Boggley Wollah? The facts concerning the latter are briefly these:

Our worthy fat friend Joseph Sedley returned to India not long after his escape from Brussels. Either his furlough was up, or he dreaded to meet any witnesses of his Waterloo flight. However it might be, he went back to his duties in Bengal very soon after Napoleon had taken up his residence at St. Helena, where Jos saw the ex-Emperor. To hear Mr. Sedley talk on board ship you would have supposed that it was not the first time he and the Corsican had met, and that the civilian had bearded the French General at Mount St. John. He had a thousand anecdotes about the famous battles; he knew the position of every regiment, and the loss which each had incurred. He did not deny that he had been concerned in those victories—that he had been with the army, and carried despatches for the Duke of Wellington. And he described what the Duke did and said on every conceivable moment of the day of Waterloo, with such an accurate knowledge of his Grace's sentiments and proceedings, that it was clear he must have been by the conqueror's side throughout the day; though, as a non-combatant, his name was not mentioned in the public documents relative to the battle. Perhaps he actually worked himself up to believe that he had been engaged with the army; certain it is that he made a prodigious sensation for

30

some time at Calcutta, and was called Waterloo Sedley during the whole of his subsequent stay in Bengal.

The bills which Jos had given for the purchase of those unlucky horses were paid without question by him and his agents. He never was heard to allude to the bargain, and nobody knows for a certainty what became of the horses, or how he got rid of them, or of Isidor, his Belgian servant, who sold a grey horse, very like the one which Jos rode, at Valenciennes sometime during the autumn of 1815.

Jos's London agents had orders to pay one hundred and twenty pounds yearly to his parents at Fulham. It was the chief support of the old couple; for Mr. Sedley's speculations in life subsequent to his bankruptcy did not by any means retrieve the broken old gentleman's fortune. He tried to be a wine-merchant, a coal-merchant, a commission lottery agent, &c., &c. He sent round prospectuses to his friends whenever he took a new trade, and ordered a new brass plate for the door, and talked pompously about making his fortune still. But Fortune never came back to the feeble and stricken old man. One by one his friends dropped off, and were weary of buying dear coals and bad wine from him; and there was only his wife in all the world who fancied, when he tottered off to the City of a morning, that he was still doing any business there. At evening he crawled slowly back; and he used to go of nights to a little club at a tavern, where he disposed of the finances of the nation. It was wonderful to hear him talk about millions, and agios, and discounts, and what Rothschild was doing, and Baring Brothers. He talked of such vast sums that the gentlemen of the club (the apothecary, the undertaker, the great carpenter and builder, the parish clerk, who was allowed to come stealthily, and Mr. Clapp, our old acquaintance), respected the old gentleman. "I was better off once, sir," he did not fail to tell everybody who "used the room." "My son, sir, is at this minute chief magistrate of Ramgunge in the Presidency of Bengal, and touching his four thousand rupees per mensem. My daughter might be a Colonel's lady if she liked. I might draw upon my son, the first magistrate, sir, for two thousand pounds to-morrow, and Alexander would cash my bill, down

sir, down on the counter, sir. But the Sedleys were always
a proud family." You and I, my dear reader, may drop
into this condition one day: for have not many of our
friends attained it? Our luck may fail: our powers forsake
us: our place on the boards be taken by better and younger
mimes—the chance of life roll away and leave us shattered
and stranded. Then men will walk across the road when
they meet you—or, worse still, hold you out a couple of
fingers and patronise you in a pitying way—then you will
know, as soon as your back is turned, that your friend
begins with a "Poor devil, what imprudences he has committed, what chances *that* chap has thrown away!" Well,
well—a carriage and three thousand a year is not the summit
of the reward nor the end of God's judgment of men.
If quacks prosper as often as they go to the wall—if zanies
succeed and knaves arrive at fortune, and, *vice versâ*, shar-
ing ill luck and prosperity for all the world like the ablest
and most honest amongst us—I say, brother, the gifts and
pleasures of Vanity Fair cannot be held of any great account, and that it is probable . . . . but we are wandering out of the domain of the story.

Had Mrs. Sedley been a woman of energy, she would
have exerted it after her husband's ruin, and, occupying a
large house, would have taken in boarders. The broken
Sedley would have acted well as the boarding-house landlady's husband; the Munoz of private life; the titular lord
and master: the carver, house-steward, and humble husband of the occupier of the dingy throne. I have seen
men of good brains and breeding, and of good hopes and
vigour once, who feasted squires and kept hunters in their
youth, meekly cutting up legs of mutton for rancorous old
harridans, and pretending to preside over their dreary
tables—but Mrs. Sedley, we say, had not spirit enough to
bustle about for "a few select inmates to join a cheerful
musical family," such as one reads of in the *Times*. She
was content to lie on the shore where fortune had stranded
her— and you could see that the career of this old couple
was over.

I don't think they were unhappy. Perhaps they were a
little prouder in their downfall than in their prosperity.

Mrs. Sedley was always a great person for her landlady, Mrs. Clapp, when she descended and passed many hours with her in the basement or ornamented kitchen. The Irish maid Betty Flanagan's bonnets and ribbons, her sauciness, her idleness, her reckless prodigality of kitchen candles, her consumption of tea and sugar, and so forth, occupied and amused the old lady almost as much as the doings of her former household, when she had Sambo and the coachman, and a groom, and a footboy, and a housekeeper with a regiment of female domestics—her former household, about which the good lady talked a hundred times a day. And besides Betty Flanagan, Mrs. Sedley had all the maids-of-all-work in the street to superintend. She knew how each tenant of the cottages paid or owed his little rent. She stepped aside when Mrs. Rougemont the actress passed with her dubious family. She flung up her head when Mrs. Pestler, the apothecary's lady, drove by in her husband's professional one-horse chaise. She had colloquies with the greengrocer about the pennorth of turnips which Mr. Sedley loved: she kept an eye upon the milkman, and the baker's boy; and made visitations to the butcher, who sold hundreds of oxen very likely with less ado than was made about Mrs. Sedley's loin of mutton: and she counted the potatoes under the joint on Sundays, on which days, drest in her best, she went to church twice, and read Blair's Sermons in the evening.

On that day, for "business" prevented him on week days from taking such a pleasure, it was old Sedley's delight to take out his little grandson Georgy to the neighbouring Parks or Kensington Gardens, to see the soldiers or to feed the ducks. Georgy loved the red-coats, and his grandpapa told him how his father had been a famous soldier, and introduced him to many sergeants and others with Waterloo medals on their breasts, to whom the old grandfather pompously presented the child as the son of Captain Osborne of the —th, who died gloriously on the glorious eighteenth. He has been known to treat some of these non-commissioned gentlemen to a glass of porter, and, indeed, in their first Sunday walks was disposed to spoil little Georgy, sadly gorging the boy with apples and parliament, to the detriment of his health—until Amelia declared that George should never go out with his grandpapa, unless the latter promised solemnly, and on his honour, not to give the child any cakes, lollipops, or stall produce whatever.

Between Mrs. Sedley and her daughter there was a sort of coolness about this boy, and a secret jealousy—for one evening in George's very early days, Amelia, who had been seated at work in their little parlour scarcely remarking that the old lady had quitted the room, ran upstairs instinctively to the nursery at the cries of the child, who had been asleep until that moment—and there found Mrs. Sedley in the act of surreptitiously administering Daffy's Elixir to the infant. Amelia, the gentlest and sweetest of every-day mortals, when she found this meddling with her maternal authority, thrilled and trembled all over with anger. Her cheeks, ordinarily pale, now flushed up, until they were as red as they used to be when she was a child of twelve years old. She seized the baby out of her mother's arms, and then grasped at the bottle, leaving the old lady gaping at her, furious, and holding the guilty tea-spoon.

Amelia flung the bottle crashing into the fire-place. "I will *not* have baby poisoned, mamma," cried Emmy, rocking the infant about violently with both her arms round him, and turning with flashing eyes at her mother.

"Poisoned, Amelia!" said the old lady; "this language to me?"

"He shall not have any medicine but that which Mr. Pestler sends for him. He told me that Daffy's Elixir was poison."

"Very good: you think I'm a murderess, then," replied Mrs. Sedley. "This is the language you use to your mother. I have met with misfortunes: I have sunk low in life: I have kept my carriage, and now walk on foot: but I did not know I was a murderess before, and thank you for the *news.*"

"Mamma," said the poor girl, who was always ready for tears—"you shouldn't be hard upon me. I—I didn't mean —I mean, I did not wish to say you would do any wrong to this dear child: only—"

"O, no, my love,—only that I was a murderess; in which case, I had better go to the Old Bailey. Though I didn't

poison *you,* when you were a child; but gave you the best of
education, and the most expensive masters money could
procure. Yes; I've nursed five children, and buried three:
and the one I loved the best of all, and tended through
croup, and teething, and measles, and hooping-cough, and
brought up with foreign masters, regardless of expense, and
with accomplishments at Minerva House—which I never
had when I was a girl—when I was too glad to honour my
father and mother, that I might live long in the land, and
to be useful, and not to mope all day in my room and act
the fine lady—says I'm a murderess. Ah, Mrs. Osborne!
may *you* never nourish a viper in your bosom, that's *my*
prayer."

"Mamma, mamma!" cried the bewildered girl: and the
child in her arms set up a frantic chorus of shouts.

"A murderess, indeed! Go down on your knees and pray
to God to cleanse your wicked ungrateful heart, Amelia,
and may He forgive you as I do;" and Mrs. Sedley tossed
out of the room, hissing out the word poison, once more,
and so ending her charitable benediction.

Till the termination of her natural life, this breach between Mrs. Sedley and her daughter was never thoroughly
mended. The quarrel gave the elder lady numberless advantages which she did not fail to turn to account with
female ingenuity and perseverance. For instance, she
scarcely spoke to Amelia for many weeks afterwards. She
warned the domestics not to touch the child, as Mrs. Osborne might be offended. She asked her daughter to see
and satisfy herself that there was no poison prepared in the
little daily messes that were concocted for Georgy. When
neighbours asked after the boy's health, she referred them
pointedly to Mrs. Osborne. *She* never ventured to ask
whether the baby was well or not. *She* would not touch
the child, although he was her grandson, and own precious
darling, for she was not *used* to children, and might kill it.
And whenever Mr. Pestler came upon his healing inquisition,
she received the Doctor with such a sarcastic and scornful
demeanour, as made the surgeon declare that not Lady
Thistlewood herself, whom he had the honour of attending
professionally, could give herself greater airs than old Mrs.

Sedley, from whom he never took a fee. And very likely Emmy was jealous too, upon her own part, as what mother is not, of those who would manage her children for her, or become candidates for the first place in their affections? It is certain that when anybody nursed the child, she was uneasy, and that she would no more allow Mrs. Clapp or the domestic to dress or tend him, than she would have let them wash her husband's miniature which hung up over her little bed:—the same little bed from which the poor girl had gone to his; and to which she retired now for many long, silent, tearful, but happy years.

In this room was all Amelia's heart and treasure. Here it was that she tended her boy, and watched him through the many ills of childhood, with a constant passion of love. The elder George returned in him somehow, only improved, and as if come back from heaven. In a hundred little tones, looks, and movements, the child was so like his father, that the widow's heart thrilled as she held him to it; and he would often ask the cause of her tears. It was because of his likeness to his father, she did not scruple to tell him. She talked constantly to him about this dead father, and spoke of her love for George to the innocent and wondering child; much more than she ever had done to George himself, or to any confidante of her youth. To her parents she never talked about this matter; shrinking from baring her heart to them. Little George very likely could understand no better than they; but into his ears she poured her sentimental secrets unreservedly, and into his only.

The very joy of this woman was a sort of grief, or so tender, at least, that its expression was tears. Her sensibilities were so weak and tremulous, that perhaps they ought not to be talked about in a book. I was told by Dr. Pestler (now a most flourishing lady's physician, with a sumptuous dark green carriage, a prospect of speedy knighthood, and a house in Manchester Square), that her grief at weaning the child was a sight that would have unmanned a Herod. He was very soft-hearted many years ago, and, his wife was mortally jealous of Mrs. Amelia, then and long afterwards.

Perhaps the Doctor's lady had good reason for her jealousy: most women shared it, of those who formed the small circle of Amelia's acquaintance, and were quite angry at the enthusiasm with which the other sex regarded her. For almost all men who came near her loved her; though no doubt they would be at a loss to tell you why. She was not brilliant, nor witty, nor wise over much, nor extraordinarily handsome. But wherever she went she touched and charmed every one of the male sex, as invariably as she awakened the scorn and incredulity of her own sisterhood. I think it was her weakness which was her principal charm: —a kind of sweet submission and softness, which seemed to appeal to each man she met for his sympathy and protection. We have seen how in the regiment, though she spoke to but few of George's comrades there, all the swords of the young fellows at the mess-table would have leapt from their scabbards to fight round her; and so it was in the little narrow lodging-house and circle at Fulham, she interested and pleased everybody. If she had been Mrs. Mango herself, of the great house of Mango, Plantain, and Co., Crutched Friars, and the magnificent proprietress of the Pineries, Fulham, who gave summer *déjeuners* frequented by Dukes and Earls, and drove about the parish with magnificent yellow liveries and bay horses, such as the royal stables at Kensington themselves could not turn out —I say had she been Mrs. Mango herself, or her son's wife, Lady Mary Mango (daughter of the Earl of Castlemouldy, who condescended to marry the head of the firm), the tradesmen of the neighbourhood could not pay her more honour than they invariably showed to the gentle young widow, when she passed by their doors, or made her humble purchases at their shops.

Thus it was not only Mr. Pestler, the medical man, but Mr. Linton the young assistant, who doctored the servant maids and small tradesmen, and might be seen any day reading the *Times* in the surgery, who openly declared himself the slave of Mrs. Osborne. He was a personable young gentleman, more welcome at Mrs. Sedley's lodgings than his principal; and if anything went wrong with Georgy, he would drop in twice or thrice in the day, to see the little chap, and without so much as the thought of a fee. He would abstract lozenges, tamarinds, and other produce from the surgery-drawers for little Georgy's benefit, and compound draughts and mixtures for him of miraculous sweetness, so that it was quite a pleasure to the child to be ailing. He and Pestler, his chief, sat up two whole nights by the boy in that momentous and awful week when Georgy had the measles; and when you would have thought, from the mother's terror, that there had never been measles in the world before. Would they have done as much for other people? Did they sit up for the folks at the Pineries, when Ralph Plantagenet, and Gwendoline, and Guinever Mango had the same juvenile complaint? Did they sit up for little Mary Clapp, the landlord's daughter, who actually caught the disease of little Georgy? Truth compels one to say, no. They slept quite undisturbed, at least as far as she was concerned—pronounced hers to be a slight case, which would almost cure itself, sent her in a draught or two, and threw in bark when the child rallied, with perfect indifference, and just for form's sake.

Again, there was the little French chevalier opposite, who gave lessons in his native tongue at various schools in the neighbourhood, and who might be heard in his apartments of nights playing tremulous old gavottes and minuets, on a wheezy old fiddle. Whenever this powdered and courteous old man, who never missed a Sunday at the convent chapel at Hammersmith, and who was in all respects, thoughts, conduct, and bearing, utterly unlike the bearded savages of his nation, who curse perfidious Albion, and scowl at you from over their cigars, in the Quadrant arcades at the present day—whenever the old Chevalier de Talonrouge spoke of Mistress Osborne, he would first finish his pinch of snuff, flick away the remaining particles of dust with a graceful wave of his hand, gather up his fingers again into a bunch, and, bringing them up to his mouth, blow them open with a kiss, exclaiming, *Ah! la divine créature!* He vowed and protested that when Amelia walked in the Brompton Lanes flowers grew in profusion under her feet. He called little Georgy Cupid, and asked him news of Venus, his mamma; and told the astonished Betty Flanagan that she was one of the Graces, and the favourite attendant of the *Reines des Amours.*

Instances might be multiplied of this easily gained and unconscious popularity. Did not Mr. Binny, the mild and genteel curate of the district chapel, which the family attended, call assiduously upon the widow, dandle the little boy on his knee, and offer to teach him Latin, to the anger of the elderly virgin, his sister, who kept house for him? "There is nothing in her, Beilby," the latter lady would say. "When she comes to tea here she does not speak a word during the whole evening. She is but a poor lackadaisical creature, and it is my belief has no heart at all. It is only her pretty face which all you gentlemen admire so. Miss Grits, who has five thousand pounds, and expectations besides, has twice as much character, and a thousand times more agreeable to *my* taste; and if she were good-looking I know that you would think her perfection."

Very likely Miss Binny was right to a great extent. It *is* the pretty face which creates sympathy in the hearts of men, those wicked rogues. A woman may possess the wisdom and chastity of Minerva, and we give no heed to her, if she has a plain face.

What folly will not a pair of bright eyes make pardonable? What dullness may not red lips and sweet accents render pleasant? And so, with their usual sense of justice, ladies argue that because a woman is handsome, therefore she is a fool. Oh ladies, ladies! there are some of you who are neither handsome nor wise.

These are but trivial incidents to recount in the life of our heroine. Her tale does not deal in wonders, as the gentle reader has already no doubt perceived; and if a journal had been kept of her proceedings during the seven years after the birth of her son, there would be found few incidents more remarkable in it than that of the measles, recorded in the foregoing page. Yet, one day, and greatly to her wonder, the Reverend Mr. Binny, just mentioned, asked her to change her name of Osborne for his own; when, with deep blushes, and tears in her eyes and voice, she thanked him for his regard for her, expressed gratitude for his attentions to her and to her poor little boy, but said that she never,

never could think of any but—but the husband whom she had lost.

On the twenty-fifth of April, and the eighteenth of June, the days of marriage and widowhood, she kept her room entirely, consecrating them (and we do not know how many hours of solitary night-thought, her little boy sleeping in his crib by her bed-side) to the memory of that departed friend. During the day she was more active. She had to teach George to read and to write, and a little to draw. She read books, in order that she might tell him stories from them. As his eyes opened, and his mind expanded, under the influence of the outward nature round about him, she taught the child, to the best of her humble power, to acknowledge the Maker of all; and every night and every morning he and she—(in that awful and touching communion which I think must bring a thrill to the heart of every man who witnesses or who remembers it)—the mother and the little boy—prayed to Our Father together, the mother pleading with all her gentle heart, the child lisping after her as she spoke. And each time they prayed to God to bless dear papa, as if he were alive and in the room with them.

To wash and dress this young gentleman—to take him for a run of the mornings, before breakfast, and the retreat of grandpapa for "business"—to make for him the most wonderful and ingenious dresses, for which end the thrifty widow cut up and altered every available little bit of finery which she possessed out of her wardrobe during her marriage—for Mrs. Osborne herself (greatly to her mother's vexation, who preferred fine clothes, especially since her misfortunes) always wore a black gown, and a straw bonnet with a black ribbon—occupied her many hours of the day. Others she had to spare, at the service of her mother and her old father. She had taken the pains to learn, and used to play cribbage with this gentleman on the nights when he did not go to his club. She sang for him when he was so minded, and it was a good sign, for he invariably fell into a comfortable sleep during the music. She wrote out his numerous memorials, letters, prospectuses, and projects. It was in her handwriting that most of the old gentleman's former acquaintances were informed that he had become an agent for the Black Diamond and Anti-Cinder Coal Company, and could supply his friends and the public with the best coals at —s. per chaldron. All he did was to sign the circulars with his flourish and signature, and direct them in a shaky, clerk-like hand. One of these papers was sent to Major Dobbin, — Regt., care of Messrs. Cox and Greenwood; but the Major being in Madras at the time, had no particular call for coals. He knew, though, the hand which had written the prospectus. Good God! what would he not have given to hold it in his own! A second prospectus came out, informing the Major that J. Sedley and Company, having established agencies at Oporto, Bordeaux, and St. Mary's, were enabled to offer to their friends and the public generally, the finest and most celebrated growths of ports, sherries, and claret wines at reasonable prices, and under extraordinary advantages. Acting upon this hint, Dobbin furiously canvassed the governor, the commander-in-chief, the judges, the regiments, and everybody whom he knew in the Presidency, and sent home to Sedley and Co. orders for wine which perfectly astonished Mr. Sedley and Mr. Clapp, who was the Co. in the business. But no more orders came after that first burst of good fortune, on which poor old Sedley was about to build a house in the City, a regiment of clerks, a dock to himself, and correspondents all over the world. The old gentleman's former taste in wine had gone: the curses of the mess-room assailed Major Dobbin for the vile drinks he had been the means of introducing there; and he bought back a great quantity of the wine, and sold it at public outcry, at an enormous loss to himself. As for Jos, who was by this time promoted to a seat at the Revenue Board at Calcutta, he was wild with rage when the post brought him out a bundle of these Bacchanalian prospectuses, with a private note from his father, telling Jos that his senior counted upon him in this enterprise, and had consigned a quantity of select wines to him, as per invoice, drawing bills upon him for the amount of the same. Jos, who would no more have it supposed that his father, Jos Sedley's father, of the Board of Revenue, was a wine merchant asking for orders, than that he was Jack Ketch, refused the bills with scorn, wrote back contumeliously to the old gentleman, bidding him to mind his own affairs; and the protested paper coming back, Sedley and Co. had to take it up, with the profits which they had made out of the Madras venture, and with a little portion of Emmy's savings.

Besides her pension of fifty pounds a-year, there had been five hundred pounds, as her husband's executor stated, left in the agent's hands at the time of Osborne's demise, which sum, as George's guardian, Dobbin proposed to put out at 8 per cent. in an Indian house of agency. Mr. Sedley, who thought the Major had some roguish intentions of his own about the money, was strongly against this plan; and he went to the agents to protest personally against the employment of the money in question, when he learned, to his surprise, that there had been no such sum in their hands, that all the late Captain's assets did not amount to a hundred pounds, and that the five hundred pounds in question must be a separate sum, of which Major Dobbin knew the particulars. More than ever convinced that there was some roguery, old Sedley pursued the Major. As his daughter's nearest friend, he demanded with a high hand, a statement of the late Captain's accounts. Dobbin's stammering, blushing, and awkwardness added to the other's convictions that he had a rogue to deal with; and in a majestic tone he told that officer a piece of his mind, as he called it, simply stating his belief that the Major was unlawfully detaining his late son-in-law's money.

Dobbin at this lost all patience, and if his accuser had not been so old and so broken, a quarrel might have ensued between them at the Slaughters' Coffee-house, in a box of which place of entertainment the gentlemen had their colloquy. "Come upstairs, sir," lisped out the Major. "I insist on your coming up the stairs, and I will show which is the injured party, poor George or I;" and, dragging the old gentleman up to his bed-room, he produced from his desk Osborne's accounts, and a bundle of I O U's which the latter had given, who, to do him justice, was always ready to give an I O U. "He paid his bills in England," Dobbin added, "but he had not a hundred pounds in the world when he fell. I and one or two of his brother-officers made up the little sum, which was all that we could spare, and you dare tell us that we are trying to cheat the widow and the orphan." Sedley was very contrite and humbled, though the fact is, that William Dobbin had told a great falsehood to the old gentleman; having himself given every shilling of the money, having buried his friend, and paid all the fees and charges incident upon the calamity and removal of poor Amelia.

About these expenses old Osborne had never given himself any trouble to think, nor any other relative of Amelia, nor Amelia herself, indeed. She trusted to Major Dobbin as an accountant, took his somewhat confused calculations for granted: and never once suspected how much she was in his debt.

Twice or thrice in the year, according to her promise, she wrote him letters to Madras, letters all about little Georgy. How he treasured these papers! Whenever Amelia wrote he answered, and not until then. But he sent over endless remembrances of himself to his godson and to her. He ordered and sent a box of scarfs, and a grand ivory set of chess-men from China. The pawns were little green and white men, with real swords and shields! the knights were on horseback, the castles were on the backs of elephants. "Mrs. Mango's own set at the Pineries was not so fine," Mr. Pestler remarked. These chess-men were the delight of Georgy's life, who printed his first letter in acknowledgment of this gift of his godpapa. He sent over preserves and pickles, which latter the young gentleman tried surreptitiously in the sideboard, and half-killed himself with eating. He thought it was a judgment upon him for stealing, they were so hot. Emmy wrote a comical little account of this mishap to the major: it pleased him to think that her spirits were rallying, and that she could be merry sometimes now. He sent over a pair of shawls, a white one for her, and a black one with palm-leaves for her mother, and a pair of red scarfs, as winter wrappers, for old Mr. Sedley and George. The shawls were worth fifty guineas a piece at the very least, as Mrs. Sedley knew. She wore hers in state at church at Brompton, and was congratulated by her female friends upon the splendid acquisition. Emmy's, too, became prettily her modest black gown. "What a pity it is she won't think of him!" Mrs. Sedley remarked to Mrs. Clapp, and to all her friends of Brompton. "Jos never sent us such presents, I am sure, and grudges us everything. It is evident that the Major is over head and ears in love with her: and yet, whenever I so much as hint it, she turns red and begins to cry, and goes and sits upstairs with her miniature. I'm sick of that miniature. I wish we had never seen those odious purse-proud Osbornes."

Amidst such humble scenes and associates George's early youth was passed, and the boy grew up delicate, sensitive, imperious, woman-bred—domineering the gentle mother whom he loved with passionate affection. He ruled all the rest of the little world round about him. As he grew, the elders were amazed at his haughty manner and his constant likeness to his father. He asked questions about everything, as inquiring youth will do. The profundity of his remarks and interrogatories astonished his old grandfather, who perfectly bored the club at the tavern with stories about the little lad's learning and genius. He suffered his grandmother with a good-humoured indifference. The small circle round about him believed that the equal of the boy did not exist upon the earth. Georgy inherited his father's pride, and perhaps thought they were not wrong.

When he grew to be about six years old, Dobbin began to write to him very much. The Major wanted to hear that Georgy was going to school, and hoped he would acquit himself with credit there: or would he have a good tutor at home? it was time that he should begin to learn; and his godfather and guardian hinted that he hoped to be allowed to defray the charges of the boy's education, which would fall heavily upon his mother's straitened income. The Major, in a word, was always thinking about Amelia and her little boy, and by orders to his agents kept the latter provided with picture-books, paint-boxes, desks, and all conceivable implements of amusement and instruction. Three days before George's sixth birth-day a gentleman in a gig, accompanied by a servant, drove up to Mr. Sedley's house, and asked to see Master George Osborne: it was Mr. Woolsey, military tailor, of Conduit Street, who came at the Major's order to measure the young gentleman for a suit of clothes. He had had the honour of making for the Captain, the young gentleman's father.

Sometimes, too, and by the Major's desire no doubt, his sisters, the Misses Dobbin, would call in the family carriage to take Amelia and the little boy for a drive if they were so inclined. The patronage and kindness of these ladies was very uncomfortable to Amelia, but she bore it meekly enough, for her nature was to yield; and, besides, the carriage and its splendours gave little Georgy immense pleasure. The ladies begged occasionally that the child might pass a day with them, and he was always glad to go to that fine garden-house at Denmark Hill, where they lived, and where there were such fine grapes in the hot-houses and peaches on the walls.

One day they kindly came over to Amelia with news which they were *sure* would delight her—something *very* interesting about their dear William.

"What was it: was he coming home?" she asked with pleasure beaming in her eyes.

"O, no—not the least—but they had very good reason to believe that dear William was about to be married—and to a relation of a very dear friend of Amelia's—to Miss Glorvina O'Dowd, Sir Michael O'Dowd's sister, who had gone out to join Lady O'Dowd at Madras—a very beautiful and accomplished girl, everybody said."

Amelia said "Oh!" Amelia was very *very* happy indeed. But she supposed Glorvina could not be like her old acquaintance, who was most kind—but—but she was very happy indeed. And by some impulse of which I cannot explain the meaning, she took George in her arms and kissed him with an extraordinary tenderness. Her eyes were quite moist when she put the child down; and she scarcely spoke a word during the whole of the drive—though she was so very happy indeed.

CHAPTER IV

A Cynical Chapter

OUR duty now takes us back for a brief space to some old Hampshire acquaintances of ours, whose hopes respecting the disposal of their rich kinswoman's property were so wofully disappointed. After counting upon thirty thousand pounds from his sister, it was a heavy blow to Bute Crawley to receive but five; out of which sum, when he had paid his own debts and those of Jim, his son at college, a very small fragment remained to portion off his four plain daughters. Mrs. Bute never knew, or at least never acknowledged, how far her own tyrannous behaviour had tended to ruin her husband. All that woman could do, she vowed and protested she had done. Was it her fault if she did not possess those sycophantic arts which her hypocritical nephew, Pitt Crawley, practised? She wished him all the happiness which he merited out of his ill-gotten gains. "At least the money will remain in the family," she said, charitably. "Pitt will never spend it, my dear, that is quite certain; for a greater miser does not exist in England, and he is as odious, though in a different way, as his spendthrift brother, the abandoned Rawdon."

So Mrs. Bute, after the first shock of rage and disappointment, began to accommodate herself as best she could to her altered fortunes, and to save and retrench with all her might. She instructed her daughters how to bear poverty cheerfully, and invented a thousand notable methods to conceal or evade it. She took them about to balls and public places in the neighbourhood, with praiseworthy energy: nay, she entertained her friends in a hospitable comfortable manner at the Rectory, and much more frequently than before dear Miss Crawley's legacy had fallen in. From her outward bearing nobody would have supposed that the family had been disappointed in their expectations: or have guessed from her frequent appearance in public how she pinched

and starved at home. Her girls had more milliners' furniture than they had ever enjoyed before. They appeared
perseveringly at the Winchester and Southampton assemblies; they penetrated to Cowes for the race-balls and re-
gatta-gaieties there; and their carriage, with the horses
taken from the plough, was at work perpetually, until it
began almost to be believed that the four sisters had had
fortunes left them by their aunt, whose name the family
never mentioned in public but with the most tender gratitude and regard. I know no sort of lying which is more
frequent in Vanity Fair than this; and it may be remarked
how people who practise it take credit to themselves for
their hypocrisy, and fancy that they are exceedingly virtuous and praiseworthy, because they are able to deceive
the world with regard to the extent of their means.

Mrs. Bute certainly thought herself one of the most
virtuous women in England, and the sight of her happy
family was an edifying one to strangers. They were so
cheerful, so loving, so well-educated, so simple! Martha
painted flowers exquisitely, and furnished half the charity-
bazaars in the county. Emma was a regular County Bulbul,
and her verses in the "Hampshire Telegraph" were the glory
of its Poet's Corner. Fanny and Matilda sang duets together, mamma playing the piano, and the other two sisters
sitting with their arms round each other's waists, and listening affectionately. Nobody saw the poor girls drumming at
the duets in private. No one saw mamma drilling them
rigidly hour after hour. In a word, Mrs. Bute put a good
face against fortune, and kept up appearances in the most
virtuous manner.

Everything that a good and respectable mother could do
Mrs. Bute did. She got over yachting men from Southampton, parsons from the Cathedral Close at Winchester,
and officers from the barracks there. She tried to inveigle
the young barristers at assizes, and encouraged Jim to bring
home friends with whom he went out hunting with the H.
H. What will not a mother do for the benefit of her beloved
ones?

Between such a woman and her brother-in-law, the odious
Baronet at the Hall, it is manifest that there could be very

little in common. The rupture between Bute and his brother
Sir Pitt was complete; indeed, between Sir Pitt and the
whole county, to which the old man was a scandal. His
dislike for respectable society increased with age, and the
lodge-gates had not opened to a gentleman's carriage-wheels
since Pitt and Lady Jane came to pay their visit of duty
after their marriage.

That was an awful and unfortunate visit, never to be
thought of by the family without horror. Pitt begged his
wife, with a ghastly countenance, never to speak of it; and
it was only through Mrs. Bute herself, who still knew everything which took place at the Hall, that the circumstances of
Sir Pitt's reception of his son and daughter-in-law were
ever known at all.

As they drove up the avenue of the park in their neat and
well-appointed carriage, Pitt remarked with dismay and
wrath great gaps among the trees—his trees,—which the old
Baronet was felling entirely without license. The park wore
an aspect of utter dreariness and ruin. The drives were
ill-kept, and the neat carriage splashed and floundered in
muddy pools along the road. The great sweep in front of the
terrace and entrance stair was black and covered with
mosses; the once trim flower-beds rank and weedy. Shutters
were up along almost the whole line of the house; the great
hall-door was unbarred after much ringing of the bell; an
individual in ribbons was seen flitting up the black oak
stair, as Horrocks at length admitted the heir of Queen's
Crawley and his bride into the halls of their fathers. He
led the way into Sir Pitt's "Library," as it was called, the
fumes of tobacco growing stronger as Pitt and Lady Jane
approached that apartment. "Sir Pitt ain't very well," Horrocks remarked apologetically, and hinted that his master
was afflicted with lumbago.

The library looked out on the front walk and park. Sir
Pitt had opened one of the windows, and was bawling out
thence to the postilion and Pitt's servant, who seemed to
be about to take the baggage down.

"Don't move none of them trunks," he cried, pointing
with a pipe which he held in his hand. "It's only a morning
visit, Tucker, you fool. Lor, what cracks that off hoss has

in his heels! Ain't there no one at the King's Head to rub
'em a little? How do, Pitt? How do, my dear? Come to
see the old man, hay? 'Gad—you've a pretty face, too. You
ain't like that old horse-godmother, your mother. Come and
give old Pitt a kiss, like a good little gal."

The embrace disconcerted the daughter-in-law somewhat,
as the caresses of the old gentleman, unshorn and perfumed
with tobacco, might well do. But she remembered that her
brother Southdown had mustachios, and smoked cigars, and
submitted to the Baronet with a tolerable grace.

"Pitt has got vat," said the Baronet, after this mark of
affection. "Does he read ee very long sermons, my dear?
Hundredth Psalm, Evening Hymn, hay Pitt? Go and get
a glass of Malmsey and a cake for my Lady Jane, Horrocks,
you great big booby, and don't stand stearing there like a
fat pig. I won't ask you to stop, my dear; you'll find it too
stoopid, and so should I too along a Pitt. I'm an old man
now, and like my own ways, and my pipe and backgammon
of a night."

"I can play at backgammon, sir," said Lady Jane, laughing. "I used to play with Papa and Miss Crawley, didn't I,
Mr. Crawley?"

"Lady Jane can play, sir, at the game to which you state
that you are so partial," Pitt said, haughtily.

"But she wawn't stop for all that. Naw, naw, goo back
to Mudbury and give Mrs. Rincer a benefit: or drive down
to the Rectory, and ask Buty for a dinner. He'll be charmed
to see you, you know; he's so much obliged to you for gettin'
the old woman's money. Ha, ha! Some of it will do to
patch up the Hall when I'm gone."

"I perceive, sir," said Pitt, with a heightened voice, "that
your people will cut down the timber."

"Yees, yees, very fine weather, and seasonable for the time
of year," Sir Pitt answered, who had suddenly grown deaf.
"But I'm gittin' old, Pitt, now. Law bless you, you ain't far
from fifty yourself. But he wears well, my pretty Lady
Jane, don't he? It's all godliness, sobriety, and a moral life.
Look at me, I'm not very fur from fowr-score—he, he;" and
he laughed, and took snuff, and leered at her and pinched her
hand.

Pitt once more brought the conversation back to the timber; but the Baronet was deaf again in an instant.

"I'm gittin' very old, and have been cruel bad this year with the lumbago. I shan't be here now for long; but I'm glad ee've come, daughter-in-law. I like your face, Lady Jane: it's got none of the damned high-boned Binkie look in it; and I'll give ee something pretty, my dear, to go to Court in." And he shuffled across the room to a cupboard, from which he took a little old case containing jewels of some value. "Take that," said he, "my dear; it belonged to my mother, and afterwards to the first Lady Crawley. Pretty pearls—never gave 'em the ironmonger's daughter. No, no. Take 'em and put 'em up quick," said he, thrusting the case into his daughter's hands, and clapping the door of the cabinet to, as Horrocks entered with a salver and refreshments.

"What have you a been and given Pitt's wife?" said the individual in ribbons, when Pitt and Lady Jane had taken leave of the old gentleman. It was Miss Horrocks, the butler's daughter—the cause of the scandal throughout the county,—the lady who reigned now almost supreme at Queen's Crawley.

The rise and progress of those Ribbons had been marked with dismay by the county and family. The Ribbons opened an account at the Mudbury Branch Savings Bank; the Ribbons drove to church, monopolising the pony-chaise, which was for the use of the servants at the Hall. The domestics were dismissed at her pleasure. The Scotch gardener, who still lingered on the premises, taking a pride in his walls and hot-houses, and indeed making a pretty good livelihood by the garden, which he farmed, and of which he sold the produce at Southampton, found the Ribbons eating peaches on a sunshiny morning at the south-wall, and had his ears boxed when he remonstrated about this attack on his property. He and his Scotch wife and his Scotch children, the only respectable inhabitants of Queen's Crawley, were forced to migrate, with their goods and their chattels, and left the stately comfortable gardens to go to waste, and the flower-beds to run to seed. Poor Lady Crawley's rose-garden became the dreariest wilderness.

Only two or three domestics shuddered in the bleak old servants' hall. The stables and offices were vacant, and shut up, and half ruined. Sir Pitt lived in private, and boozed nightly with Horrocks, his butler or house-steward (as he now began to be called), and the abandoned Ribbons. The times were very much changed since the period when she drove to Mudbury in the spring-cart, and called the small tradesmen "Sir." It may have been shame, or it may have been dislike of his neighbours, but the old Cynic of Queen's Crawley hardly issued from his park-gates at all now. He quarrelled with his agents, and screwed his tenants by letter. His days were passed in conducting his own correspondence; the lawyers and farm-bailiffs who had to do business with him, could not reach him but through the Ribbons, who received them at the door of the housekeeper's room, which commanded the back entrance by which they were admitted; and so the Baronet's daily perplexities increased, and his embarrassments multiplied round him.

The horror of Pitt Crawley may be imagined, as these reports of his father's dotage reached the most exemplary and correct of gentlemen. He trembled daily lest he should hear that the Ribbons was proclaimed his second legal mother-in-law. After that first and last visit, his father's name was never mentioned in Pitt's polite and genteel establishment. It was the skeleton in his house, and all the family walked by it in terror and silence. The Countess Southdown kept on dropping per coach at the lodge-gate the most exciting tracts, tracts which ought to frighten the hair off your head. Mrs. Bute at the parsonage nightly looked out to see if the sky was red over the elms behind which the Hall stood, and the mansion was on fire. Sir G. Wapshot and Sir H. Fuddle-stone, old friends of the house, wouldn't sit on the bench with Sir Pitt at Quarter Sessions, and cut him dead in the High-street of Southampton, where the reprobate stood offering his dirty old hands to them. Nothing had any effect upon him; he put his hands into his pockets, and burst out laughing, as he scrambled into his carriage and four; he used to burst out laughing at Lady Southdown's tracts; and he laughed at his sons, and at the world, and at the Ribbons when she was angry, which was not seldom.

Miss Horrocks was installed as housekeeper at Queen's Crawley, and ruled all the domestics there with great majesty and rigour. All the servants were instructed to address her as "Mum," or "Madam"—and there was one little maid, on her promotion, who persisted in calling her "My Lady," without any rebuke on the part of the housekeeper. "There has been better ladies, and there has been worser, Hester," was Miss Horrocks' reply to this compliment of her inferior: so she ruled, having supreme power over all except her father, whom, however, she treated with considerable haughtiness, warning him not to be too familiar in his behaviour to one "as was to be a Baronet's lady."

Indeed, she rehearsed that exalted part in life with great satisfaction to herself, and to the amusement of old Sir Pitt, who chuckled at her airs and graces, and would laugh by the hour together at her assumptions of dignity and imitations of genteel life. He swore it was as good as a play to see her in the character of a fine dame, and he made her put on one of the first Lady Crawley's court dresses, swearing (entirely to Miss Horrocks' own concurrence,) that the dress became her prodigiously, and threatening to drive her off that very instant to Court in a coach-and-four. She had the ransacking of the wardrobes of the two defunct ladies, and cut and hacked their posthumous finery so as to suit her own tastes and figure. And she would have liked to take possession of their jewels and trinkets too; but the old Baronet had locked them away in his private cabinet, nor could she coax or wheedle him out of the keys. And it is a fact, that some time after she left Queen's Crawley a copy-book belonging to this lady was discovered, which showed that she had taken great pains in private to learn the art of writing in general, and especially of writing her own name as Lady Crawley, Lady Betsy Horrocks, Lady Elizabeth Crawley, &c.

Though the good people of the Parsonage never went to the Hall, and shunned the horrid old dotard its owner, yet they kept a strict knowledge of all that happened there, and were looking out every day for the catastrophe for which Miss Horrocks was also eager. But fate intervened enviously, and prevented her from receiving the reward due to such immaculate love and virtue.

One day the Baronet surprised "her ladyship," as he jocularly called her, seated at that old and tuneless piano in the drawing-room, which had scarcely been touched since Becky Sharp played quadrilles upon it—seated at the piano with the utmost gravity, and squalling to the best of her power in imitation of the music which she had sometimes heard. The little kitchen-maid on her promotion was standing at her mistress's side, quite delighted during the operation, and wagging her head up and down, and crying, "Lor, Mum, 'tis bittiful,"—just like a genteel sycophant in a real drawing-room.

This incident made the old Baronet roar with laughter, as usual. He narrated the circumstance a dozen times to Horrocks in the course of the evening, and greatly to the discomfiture of Miss Horrocks. He thrummed on the table as if it had been a musical instrument, and squalled in imitation of her manner of singing. He vowed that such a beautiful voice ought to be cultivated, and declared she ought to have singing-masters, in which proposals she saw nothing ridiculous. He was in great spirits that night; and drank with his friend and butler an extraordinary quantity of rum-and-water—at a very late hour the faithful friend and domestic conducted his master to his bedroom.

Half an hour afterwards there was a great hurry and bustle in the house. Lights went about from window to window in the lonely desolate old Hall, whereof but two or three rooms were ordinarily occupied by its owner. Presently, a boy on a pony went galloping off to Mudbury, to the Doctor's house there. And in another hour (by which fact we ascertain how carefully the excellent Mrs. Bute Crawley had always kept up an understanding with the great house), that lady in her clogs and calash, the Reverend Bute Crawley, and James Crawley, her son, had walked over from the Rectory through the park, and had entered the mansion by the open hall-door.

They passed through the hall and the small oak parlour, on the table of which stood the three tumblers and the empty rum-bottle which had served for Sir Pitt's carouse, and through that apartment into Sir Pitt's study, where they found Miss Horrocks, of the guilty ribbons, with a wild air, trying at the presses and escritoires with a bunch of keys. She dropped them with a scream of terror, as little Mrs. Bute's eyes flashed out at her from under her black calash.

"Look at that, James and Mr. Crawley," cried Mrs. Bute, pointing at the scared figure of the black-eyed, guilty wench.

"He gave 'em me; he gave 'em me!" she cried.

"Gave them you, you abandoned creature!" screamed Mrs. Bute. "Bear witness, Mr. Crawley, we found this good-for-nothing woman in the act of stealing your brother's property; and she will be hanged, as I always said she would."

Betsy Horrocks, quite daunted, flung herself down on her knees, bursting into tears. But those who know a really good woman are aware that she is not in a hurry to forgive, and that the humiliation of an enemy is a triumph to her soul.

"Ring the bell, James," Mrs. Bute said. "Go on ringing it till the people come." The three or four domestics resident in the deserted old house came presently at that jangling and continued summons.

"Put that woman in the strong-room," she said. "We caught her in the act of robbing Sir Pitt. Mr. Crawley, you'll make out her committal—and, Beddoes, you'll drive her over in the spring-cart, in the morning, to Southampton Gaol."

"My dear," interposed the Magistrate and Rector—"she's only—"

"Are there no handcuffs?" Mrs. Bute continued, stamping in her clogs. "There used to be handcuffs. Where's the creature's abominable father?"

"He *did* give 'em me," still cried poor Betsy; "didn't he, Hester? You saw Sir Pitt—you know you did—give 'em me, ever so long ago—the day after Mudbury fair: not that I want 'em. Take 'em if you think they ain't mine." And here the unhappy wretch pulled out from her pocket a large pair of paste shoe-buckles which had excited her admiration, and which she had just appropriated out of one of the bookcases in the study, where they had lain.

"Law, Betsy, how could you go for to tell such a wicked story!" said Hester, the little kitchen-maid late on her promotion—"and to Madame Crawley, so good and kind, and his Rev'rince (with a curtsey), and you may search all *my* boxes, Mum, I'm sure, and here's my keys as I'm an honest girl though of pore parents and workhouse bred—and if you find so much as a beggarly bit of lace or a silk stocking out of all the gownds as *you've* had the picking of may I never go to church agin."

"Give up your keys, you hardened hussy," hissed out the virtuous little lady in the calash.

"And here's a candle, Mum, and if you please, Mum, I can show you her room, Mum, and the press in the housekeeper's room, Mum, where she keeps heaps and heaps of things, Mum," cried out the eager little Hester with a profusion of curtseys.

"Hold your tongue, if you please. I know the room which the creature occupies perfectly well. Mrs. Brown, have the goodness to come with me, and Beddoes don't you lose sight of that woman," said Mrs. Bute, seizing the candle.—"Mr. Crawley, you had better go upstairs, and see that they are not murdering your unfortunate brother" —and the calash, escorted by Mrs. Brown, walked away to the apartment which, as she said truly, she knew perfectly well.

Bute went upstairs, and found the Doctor from Mudbury, with the frightened Horrocks over his master in a chair. They were trying to bleed Sir Pitt Crawley.

With the early morning an express was sent off to Mr. Pitt Crawley by the Rector's lady, who assumed the command of everything, and had watched the old Baronet through the night. He had been brought back to a sort of life; he could not speak, but seemed to recognise people. Mrs. Bute kept resolutely by his bed-side. She never seemed to want to sleep, that little woman, and did not close her fiery black eyes once, though the Doctor snored in the arm-

chair.   Horrocks made some wild efforts to assert his
authority and assist his master; but Mrs. Bute called him a
tipsy old wretch, and bade him never show his face again
in that house, or he should be transported like his abominable
daughter.

Terrified by her manner, he slunk down to the oak parlour
where Mr. James was, who, having tried the bottle standing there and found no liquor in it, ordered Mr. Horrocks
to get another bottle of rum, which he fetched, with clean
glasses, and to which the Rector and his son sat down:
ordering Horrocks to put down the keys at that instant and
never to show his face again.

Cowed by this behaviour, Horrocks gave up the keys; and
he and his daughter slunk off silently through the night,
and gave up possession of the house of Queen's Crawley.

CHAPTER V

In Which Becky Is Recognised by the Family

THE heir of Crawley arrived at home, in due time, after this catastrophe, and henceforth may be said to have reigned in Queen's Crawley. For though the old Baronet survived many months, he never recovered the use of his intellect or his speech completely, and the government of the estate devolved upon his elder son. In a strange condition Pitt found it. Sir Pitt was always buying and mortgaging; he had twenty men of business, and quarrels with each; quarrels with all his tenants, and lawsuits with them; lawsuits with the lawyers; lawsuits with the Mining and Dock Companies in which he was proprietor; and with every person with whom he had business. To unravel these difficulties, and to set the estate clear, was a task worthy of the orderly and persevering diplomatist of Pumpernickel: and he set himself to work with prodigious assiduity. His whole family, of course, was transported to Queen's Crawley, whither Lady Southdown, of course, came too; and she set about converting the parish under the Rector's nose, and brought down her irregular clergy to the dismay of the angry Mrs. Bute. Sir Pitt had concluded no bargain for the sale of the living of Queen's Crawley; when it should drop, her Ladyship proposed to take the patronage into her own hands, and present a young protégé to the Rectory; on which subject the diplomatic Pitt said nothing.

Mrs. Bute's intentions with regard to Miss Betsy Horrocks were not carried into effect: and she paid no visit to Southampton Gaol. She and her father left the Hall, when the latter took possession of the Crawley Arms in the village, of which he had got a lease from Sir Pitt. The ex-butler had obtained a small freehold there likewise, which gave him a vote for the borough. The Rector had another of these votes, and these and four others formed

the representative body which returned the two members
for Queen's Crawley.

There was a show of courtesy kept up between the Rectory
and the Hall ladies, between the younger ones at least,
for Mrs. Bute and Lady Southdown never could meet
without battles, and gradually ceased seeing each other.
Her Ladyship kept her room when the ladies from the
Rectory visited their cousins at the Hall. Perhaps Mr.
Pitt was not very much displeased at these occasional
absences of his mamma-in-law. He believed the Binkie
family to be the greatest and wisest, and most interesting
in the world, and her Ladyship and his aunt had long held
ascendency over him; but sometimes he felt that she commanded him too much. To be considered young was complimentary doubtless; but at six-and-forty to be treated as
a boy was sometimes mortifying. Lady Jane yielded up
everything, however, to her mother. She was only fond
of her children in private; and it was lucky that Lady
Southdown's multifarious business, her conferences with
ministers, and her correspondence with all the missionaries
of Africa, Asia, and Australasia, &c., occupied the venerable
Countess a great deal, so that she had but little time to
devote to her granddaughter, the little Matilda, and her
grandson, Master Pitt Crawley. The latter was a feeble
child: and it was only by prodigious quantities of calomel that Lady Southdown was able to keep him in life
at all.

As for Sir Pitt he retired into those very apartments
where Lady Crawley had been previously extinguished, and
here was tended by Miss Hester, the girl upon her promotion, with constant care and assiduity. What love, what
fidelity, what constancy is there equal to that of a nurse
with good wages? They smooth pillows: and make arrow-
root: they get up at nights: they bear complaints and
querulousness: they see the sun shining out of doors and
don't want to go abroad: they sleep on armchairs, and eat
their meals in solitude: they pass long long evenings doing
nothing, watching the embers, and the patient's drink
simmering in the jug: they read the weekly paper the whole
week through; and Law's Serious Call or the Whole Duty

of Man suffices them for literature for the year—and we quarrel with them because, when their relations come to see them once a week, a little gin is smuggled in in their linen basket. Ladies, what man's love is there that would stand a year's nursing of the object of his affection? Whereas a nurse will stand by you for ten pounds a quarter, and we think her too highly paid. At least Mr. Crawley grumbled a good deal about paying half as much to Miss Hester for her constant attendance upon the Baronet his father.

Of sunshiny days this old gentleman was taken out in a chair on the terrace—the very chair which Miss Crawley had had at Brighton, and which had been transported thence with a number of Lady Southdown's effects to Queen's Crawley. Lady Jane always walked by the old man; and was an evident favourite with him. He used to nod many times to her and smile when she came in, and utter inarticulate deprecatory moans when she was going away. When the door shut upon her he would cry and sob—whereupon Hester's face and manner, which was always exceedingly bland and gentle while her lady was present, would change at once, and she would make faces at him and clench her fist, and scream out "Hold your tongue, you stoopid old fool," and twirl away his chair from the fire which he loved to look at—at which he would cry more. For this was all that was left after more than seventy years of cunning and struggling, and drinking, and scheming, and sin and selfishness—a whimpering old idiot put in and out of bed and cleaned and fed like a baby.

At last a day came when the nurse's occupation was over. Early one morning, as Pitt Crawley was at his steward's and bailiff's books in the study, a knock came to the door, and Hester presented herself dropping a curtsey, and said,

"If you please, Sir Pitt, Sir Pitt died this morning, Sir Pitt. I was a-making of his toast, Sir Pitt, for his gruel, Sir Pitt, which he took every morning regular at six, Sir Pitt, and—I thought I heard a moan-like, Sir Pitt—and—and—and—." She dropped another curtsey.

What was it that made Pitt's pale face flush quite red? Was it because he was Sir Pitt at last, with a seat in Parliament, and perhaps future honours in prospect? "I'll clear the estate now with the ready money," he thought, and rapidly calculated its incumbrances and the improvements which he would make. He would not use his aunt's money previously lest Sir Pitt should recover, and his outlay be in vain.

All the blinds were pulled down at the Hall and Rectory: the church bell was tolled, and the chancel hung in black; and Bute Crawley didn't go to a coursing meeting, but went and dined quietly at Fuddleston, where they talked about his deceased brother and young Sir Pitt over their port. Miss Betsy, who was by this time married to a saddler at Mudbury, cried a good deal. The family surgeon rode over and paid his respectful compliments, and inquiries for the health of their ladyships. The death was talked about at Mudbury and at the Crawley Arms; the landlord whereof had become reconciled with the Rector of late, who was occasionally known to step into the parlour and taste Mr. Horrocks' mild beer.

"Shall I write to your brother—or will you?" asked Lady Jane of her husband, Sir Pitt.

"I will write, of course," Sir Pitt said, "and invite him to the funeral; it will be but becoming."

"And—and—Mrs. Rawdon," said Lady Jane, timidly.

"Jane!" said Lady Southdown, "how can you think of such a thing?"

"Mrs. Rawdon must of course be asked," said Sir Pitt, resolutely.

"Not whilst *I* am in the house!" said Lady Southdown.

"Your Ladyship will be pleased to recollect that I am the head of this family," Sir Pitt replied. "If you please, Lady Jane, you will write a letter to Mrs. Rawdon Crawley, requesting her presence upon this melancholy occasion."

"Jane, I forbid you to put pen to paper!" cried the Countess.

"I believe I am the head of this family," Sir Pitt repeated; "and however much I may regret any circumstance which may lead to your Ladyship quitting this house, must, if you please, continue to govern it as I see fit."

Lady Southdown rose up as magnificent as Mrs. Siddons in Lady Macbeth, and ordered that horses might be put to

her carriage. If her son and daughter turned her out of
their house, she would hide her sorrows somewhere in loneliness, and pray for their conversion to better thoughts.

"We don't turn you out of our house, Mamma," said
the timid Lady Jane imploringly.

"You invite such company to it as no Christian lady
should meet, and I will have my horses to-morrow morning."

"Have the goodness to write, Jane, under my dictation,"
said Sir Pitt, rising, and throwing himself into an attitude
of command, like the portrait of a Gentleman in the Exhibition, "and begin. 'Queen's Crawley, September 14, 1822.—
My dear brother—' "

Hearing these decisive and terrible words, Lady Macbeth,
who had been waiting for a sign of weakness or vacillation
on the part of her son-in-law, rose, and with a scared look,
left the library. Lady Jane looked up to her husband as
if she would fain follow and soothe her mamma: but Pitt
forbade his wife to move.

"She won't go away," he said. "She has let her house
at Brighton, and has spent her last half-year's dividends.
A Countess living at an inn is a ruined woman. I have
been waiting long for an opportunity to take this—this
decisive step, my love; for, as you must perceive, it is impossible that there should be two chiefs in a family: and
now, if you please, we will resume the dictation. 'My
dear brother, the melancholy intelligence which it is my
duty to convey to my family must have been long antici-
pated by,' " &c.

In a word, Pitt having come to his kingdom, and having
by good luck, or desert rather, as he considered, assumed
almost all the fortune which his other relatives had expected, was determined to treat his family kindly and
respectably, and make a house of Queen's Crawley once
more. It pleased him to think that he should be its chief.
He proposed to use the vast influence that his commanding
talents and position must speedily acquire for him in the
county to get his brother placed and his cousins decently
provided for, and perhaps had a little sting of repentance
as he thought that he was the proprietor of all that they
had hoped for. In the course of three or four days' reign

his bearing was changed, and his plans quite fixed: he determined to rule justly and honestly, to depose Lady Southdown, and to be on the friendliest possible terms with all the relations of his blood.

So he dictated a letter to his brother Rawdon—a solemn and elaborate letter, containing the profoundest observations, couched in the longest words, and filling with wonder the simple little secretary, who wrote under her husband's order. "What an orator this will be," thought she, "when he enters the House of Commons" (on which point, and on the tyranny of Lady Southdown, Pitt had sometimes dropped hints to his wife in bed); "how wise and good, and what a genius my husband is! I fancied him a little cold; but how good, and what a genius!"

The fact is, Pitt Crawley had got every word of the letter by heart and had studied it, with diplomatic secrecy, deeply and perfectly, long before he thought fit to communicate it to his astonished wife.

This letter, with a huge black border and seal, was accordingly despatched by Sir Pitt Crawley to his brother the Colonel, in London. Rawdon Crawley was but half-pleased at the receipt of it. "What's the use of going down to that stupid place?" thought he. "I can't stand being alone with Pitt after dinner, and horses there and back will cost us twenty pound."

He carried the letter, as he did all difficulties, to Becky, upstairs in her bed-room—with her chocolate, which he always made and took to her of a morning.

He put the tray with the breakfast and the letter on the dressing-table, before which Becky sate combing her yellow hair. She took up the black-edged missive, and having read it, she jumped up from the chair, crying "Hurray!" and waving the note round her head.

"Hurray?" said Rawdon, wondering at the little figure capering about in a streaming flannel dressing-gown, with tawny locks dishevelled. "He's not left us anything, Becky. I had my share when I came of age."

"You'll never be of age, you silly old man," Becky replied. "Run out now to Madam Brunoy's, for I must have some mourning: and get a crape on your hat, and a black waistcoat—I don't think you've got one; order it to be brought home to-morrow, so that we may be able to start on Thursday."

"You don't mean to go?" Rawdon interposed.

"Of course I mean to go. I mean that Lady Jane shall present me at Court next year. I mean that your brother shall give you a seat in Parliament, you stupid old creature. I mean that Lord Steyne shall have your vote and his, my dear, old silly man; and that you shall be an Irish Secretary, or a West Indian Governor: or a Treasurer, or a Consul, or some such thing."

"Posting will cost a dooce of a lot of money," grumbled Rawdon.

"We might take Southdown's carriage, which ought to be present at the funeral, as he is a relation of the family: but, no—I intend that we shall go by the coach. They'll like it better. It seems more humble——"

"Rawdy goes of course?" the Colonel asked.

"No such thing; why pay an extra place? He's too big to travel bodkin between you and me. Let him stay here in the nursery, and Briggs can make him a black frock. Go you: and do as I bid you. And you had best tell Sparks, your man, that old Sir Pitt is dead, and that you will come in for something considerable when the affairs are arranged. He'll tell this to Raggles, who has been pressing for money, and it will console poor Raggles." And so Becky began sipping her chocolate.

When the faithful Lord Steyne arrived in the evening, he found Becky and her companion, who was no other than our friend Briggs, busy cutting, ripping, snipping, and tearing all sorts of black stuffs available for the melancholy occasion.

"Miss Briggs and I are plunged in grief and despondency for the death of our Papa," Rebecca said. "Sir Pitt Crawley is dead, my lord. We have been tearing our hair all the morning, and now we are tearing up our old clothes."

"Oh, Rebecca, how can you—"was all that Briggs could say as she turned up her eyes.

"Oh, Rebecca, how can you—" echoed my Lord. "So that old scoundrel's dead, is he? He might have been a

Peer if he had played his cards better. Mr. Pitt had very
nearly made him; but he ratted always at the wrong time.
What an old Silenus it was!"

"I might have been Silenus's widow," said Rebecca.
"Don't you remember, Miss Briggs, how you peeped in at
the door, and saw old Sir Pitt on his knees to me?" Miss
Briggs, our old friend, blushed very much at the remi-
niscence; and was glad when Lord Steyne ordered her to
go downstairs and make him a cup of tea.

Briggs was the house-dog whom Rebecca had provided
as guardian of her innocence and reputation. Miss Crawley
had left her a little annuity. She would have been content
to remain in the Crawley family with Lady Jane, who was
good to her and to everybody; but Lady Southdown dismissed poor Briggs as quickly as decency permitted; and
Mr. Pitt (who thought himself much injured by the un-
called-for generosity of his deceased relative towards a
lady who had only been Miss Crawley's faithful retainer a
score of years) made no objection to that exercise of the
dowager's authority. Bowls and Firkin likewise received
their legacies, and their dismissals; and married and set up
a lodging-house, according to the custom of their kind.

Briggs tried to live with her relations in the country, but
found that attempt was vain after the better society to
which she had been accustomed. Briggs's friends, small
tradesmen, in a country town, quarrelled over Miss Briggs's
forty pounds a-year, as eagerly and more openly than Miss
Crawley's kinsfolk had for that lady's inheritance. Briggs's
brother, a radical hatter and grocer, called his sister a
purse-proud aristocrat, because she would not advance a
part of her capital to stock his shop: and she would have
done so most likely, but that their sister, a dissenting shoemaker's lady, at variance with the hatter and grocer, who
went to another chapel, showed how their brother was on
the verge of bankruptcy, and took possession of Briggs for
a while. The dissenting shoemaker wanted Miss Briggs to
send his son to college, and make a gentleman of him. Between them the two families got a great portion of her
private savings out of her: and finally she fled to London

followed by the anathemas of both, and determined to seek for servitude again as infinitely less onerous than liberty. And advertising in the papers that a "Gentlewoman of agreeable manners, and accustomed to the best society, was anxious to," &c., she took up her residence with Mr. Bowls in Half Moon Street, and waited the result of the advertisement.

So it was that she fell in with Rebecca. Mrs. Rawdon's dashing little carriage and ponies was whirling down the street one day, just as Miss Briggs, fatigued, had reached Mr. Bowls's door, after a weary walk to the *Times* Office in the City, to insert her advertisement for the sixth time. Rebecca was driving, and at once recognized the gentle-woman with agreeable manners, and being a perfectly good-humoured woman, as we have seen, and having a regard for Briggs, she pulled up the ponies at the door-steps, gave the reins to the groom, and jumping out, had hold of both Briggs's hands, before she of the agreeable manners had recovered from the shock of seeing an old friend.

Briggs cried, and Becky laughed a great deal, and kissed the gentlewoman as soon as they got into the passage; and thence into Mrs. Bowls's front parlour, with the red moreen curtains, and the round looking-glass, with the chained eagle above, gazing upon the back of the ticket in the window which announced "Apartments to Let."

Briggs told all her history amidst those perfectly un-called-for sobs and ejaculations of wonder with which women of her soft nature salute an old acquaintance, or regard a rencontre in the street; for though people meet other people every day, yet some there are who insist upon discovering miracles; and women, even though they have disliked each other, begin to cry when they meet, deploring and remembering the time when they last quarrelled. So, in a word, Briggs told all her history, and Becky gave a narrative of her own life, with her usual artlessness and candour.

Mrs. Bowls, late Firkin, came and listened grimly in the passage to the hysterical sniffling and giggling which went on in the front parlour. Becky had never been a favourite of hers. Since the establishment of the married couple in London they had frequented their former friends of the house of Raggles, and did not like the latter's account of the Colonel's *ménage*. "*I* wouldn't trust him, Ragg, my boy," Bowls remarked: and his wife, when Mrs. Rawdon issued from the parlour, only saluted the lady with a very sour curtsey; and her fingers were like so many sausages, cold and lifeless, when she held them out in deference to Mrs. Rawdon, who persisted in shaking hands with the retired lady's maid. She whirled away into Piccadilly, nodding with the sweetest of smiles towards Miss Briggs, who hung nodding at the window close under the advertisement-card, and at the next moment was in the Park with a half dozen of dandies cantering after her carriage.

When she found how her friend was situated, and how having a snug legacy from Miss Crawley, salary was no object to our gentlewoman, Becky instantly formed some benevolent little domestic plans concerning her. This was just such a companion as would suit her establishment, and she invited Briggs to come to dinner with her that very evening, when she should see Becky's dear little darling Rawdon.

Mrs. Bowls cautioned her lodger against venturing into the lion's den, "wherein you will rue it, Miss B., mark my words, and as sure as my name is Bowls." And Briggs promised to be very cautious. The upshot of which caution was that she went to live with Mrs. Rawdon the next week, and had lent Rawdon Crawley six hundred pounds upon annuity before six months were over.

CHAPTER VI

IN WHICH BECKY REVISITS THE HALLS OF HER ANCESTORS

SO the mourning being ready, and Sir Pitt Crawley
warned of their arrival, Colonel Crawley and his wife
took a couple of places in the same old Highflyer coach,
by which Rebecca had travelled in the defunct Baronet's
company, on her first journey into the world some nine years
before. How well she remembered the Inn Yard, and the
ostler to whom she refused money, and the insinuating Cambridge lad who wrapped her in his coat on the journey!
Rawdon took his place outside, and would have liked to
drive, but his grief forbade him. He sat by the coachman,
and talked about horses and the road the whole way; and
who kept the inns, and who horsed the coach by which he
had travelled so many a time, when he and Pitt were boys
going to Eton. At Mudbury a carriage and a pair of horses
received them, with a coachman in black. "It's the old drag,
Rawdon," Rebecca said, as they got in. "The worms have
eaten the cloth a good deal—there's the stain which Sir Pitt
—ha! I see Dawson the Ironmonger has his shutters up—
which Sir Pitt made such a noise about. It was a bottle of
cherry brandy he broke which we went to fetch for your
aunt from Southampton. How time flies, to be sure! that
can't be Polly Talboys, that bouncing girl standing by her
mother at the cottage there. I remember her a mangy
little urchin picking weeds in the garden."

"Fine gal," said Rawdon, returning the salute which the
cottage gave him, by two fingers applied to his crape hat-
band. Becky bowed and saluted, and recognised people
here and there graciously. These recognitions were inexpressibly pleasant to her. It seemed as if she was not an
impostor any more, and was coming to the home of her
ancestors. Rawdon was rather abashed, and cast down on
the other hand. What recollections of boyhood and inno-

cence might have been flitting across his brain? What pangs
of dim remorse and doubt and shame?

"Your sisters must be young women now," Rebecca said,
thinking of those girls for the first time perhaps since she
had left them.

"Don't know, I'm shaw," replied the Colonel. "Hullo!
here's old Mother Lock. How-dy-do, Mrs. Lock? Remember me, don't you? Master Rawdon, hey? Dammy how
those old women last; she was a hundred when I was a boy."

They were going through the lodge-gates kept by old
Mrs. Lock, whose hand Rebecca insisted upon shaking, as
she flung open the creaking old iron gate, and the carriage
passed between the two moss-grown pillars surmounted by
the dove and serpent.

"The governor has cut into the timber," Rawdon said,
looking about, and then was silent—so was Becky. Both of
them were rather agitated, and thinking of old times. He
about Eton, and his mother, whom he remembered, a frigid
demure woman, and a sister who died, of whom he had been
passionately fond; and how he used to thrash Pitt; and
about little Rawdy at home. And Rebecca thought about her
own youth, and the dark secrets of those early tainted days;
and of her entrance into life by yonder gates; and of Miss
Pinkerton, and Joe, and Amelia.

The gravel walk and terrace had been scraped quite clean.
A grand painted hatchment was already over the great
entrance, and two very solemn and tall personages in black
flung open each a leaf of the door as the carriage pulled
up at the familiar steps. Rawdon turned red, and Becky
somewhat pale, as they passed through the old hall, arm in
arm. She pinched her husband's arm as they entered the
oak parlour, where Sir Pitt and his wife were ready to
receive them. Sir Pitt in black, Lady Jane in black, and my
Lady Southdown with a large black head piece of bugles
and feathers, which waved on her Ladyship's head like an
undertaker's tray.

Sir Pitt had judged correctly, that she would not quit the
premises. She contented herself by preserving a solemn and
stony silence, when in company of Pitt and his rebellious
wife, and by frightening the children in the nursery by the

ghastly gloom of her demeanour. Only a very faint bending of the head-dress and plumes welcomed Rawdon and his wife, as those prodigals returned to their family.

To say the truth, they were not affected very much one way or other by this coolness. Her Ladyship was a person only of secondary consideration in their minds just then—they were intent upon the reception which the reigning brother and sister would afford them.

Pitt, with rather a heightened colour, went up and shook his brother by the hand; and saluted Rebecca with a hand-shake and a very low bow. But Lady Jane took both the hands of her sister-in-law and kissed her affectionately. The embrace somehow brought tears into the eyes of the little adventuress—which ornaments, as we know, she wore very seldom.

The artless mark of kindness and confidence touched and pleased her; and Rawdon, encouraged by this demonstration on his sister's part, twirled up his mustachios, and took leave to salute Lady Jane with a kiss, which caused her Ladyship to blush exceedingly.

"Dev'lish nice little woman, Lady Jane," was his verdict, when he and his wife were together again. "Pitt's got fat, too, and is doing the thing handsomely." "He can afford it," said Rebecca, and agreed in her husband's farther opinion, "that the mother-in-law was a tremendous old Guy—and that the sisters were rather well-looking young women."

They, too, had been summoned from school to attend the funeral ceremonies. It seemed Sir Pitt Crawley, for the dignity of the house and family, had thought right to have about the place as many persons in black as could possibly be assembled. All the men and maids of the house, the old women of the Alms House, whom the elder Sir Pitt had cheated out of a great portion of their due, the Parish Clerk's family, and the special retainers of both Hall and Rectory were habited in sable; added to these, the under-taker's men, at least a score, with crapes and hat-bands, and who made a goodly show when the great burying show took place—but these are mute personages in our drama; and having nothing to do or say, need occupy a very little space here.

With regard to her sisters-in-law Rebecca did not attempt
to forget her former position of Governess towards them,
but recalled it frankly and kindly, and asked them about their
studies with great gravity, and told them that she had
thought of them many and many a day, and longed to know
of their welfare. In fact you would have supposed that ever
since she had left them she had not ceased to keep them
uppermost in her thoughts, and to take the tenderest interest
in their welfare. So supposed Lady Crawley herself and her
young sisters.

"She's hardly changed since eight years," said Miss
Rosalind to Miss Violet, as they were preparing for dinner.

"Those red-haired women look wonderfully well," replied
the other.

"Hers is much darker than it was; I think she must dye
it," Miss Rosalind added. "She is stouter, too, and altogether
improved," continued Miss Rosalind, who was disposed to
be very fat.

"At least she gives herself no airs, and remembers that
she was our Governess once," Miss Violet said, intimating
that it befitted all governesses to keep their proper place,
and forgetting altogether that she was granddaughter not
only of Sir Walpole Crawley, but of Mr. Dawson Mudbury,
and so had a coal-scuttle in her scutcheon. There are other
very well-meaning people whom one meets every day in
Vanity Fair, who are surely equally oblivious.

"It can't be true what the girls at the Rectory said, that
her mother was an opera-dancer—"

"A person can't help their birth," Rosalind replied with
great liberality. "And I agree with our brother, that as she
is in the family, of course we are bound to notice her. I
am sure Aunt Bute need not talk: she wants to marry Kate
to young Hooper, the wine-merchant, and absolutely asked
him to come to the Rectory for orders."

"I wonder whether Lady Southdown will go away; she
looked very glum upon Mrs. Rawdon," the other said.

"I wish she would. _I_ won't read the 'Washerwoman of
Finchley Common,'" vowed Violet; and so saying, and
avoiding a passage at the end of which a certain coffin was
placed with a couple of watchers, and lights perpetually

burning in the closed room, these young women came down
to the family dinner, for which the bell rang as usual.

But before this, Lady Jane conducted Rebecca to the
apartments prepared for her, which, with the rest of the
house, had assumed a very much improved appearance of
order and comfort during Pitt's regency, and here beholding
that Mrs. Rawdon's modest little trunks had arrived, and
were placed in the bed-room and dressing-room adjoining,
helped her to take off her neat black bonnet and cloak, and
asked her sister-in-law in what more she could be useful.

"What I should like best," said Rebecca, "would be to
go to the nursery; and see your dear little children." On
which the two ladies looked very kindly at each other, and
went to that apartment hand in hand.

Becky admired little Matilda, who was not quite four
years old, as the most charming little love in the world; and
the boy, a little fellow of two years—pale, heavy-eyed, and
large-headed, she pronounced to be a perfect prodigy in
point of size, intelligence, and beauty.

"I wish Mamma would not insist on giving him so much
medicine," Lady Jane said, with a sigh. "I often think
we should all be better without it." And then Lady Jane
and her new-found friend had one of those confidential
medical conversations about the children, which all mothers,
and most women, as I am given to understand, delight in.
Fifty years ago, and when the present writer, being an
interesting little boy, was ordered out of the room with the
ladies after dinner, I remember quite well that their talk
was chiefly about their ailments; and putting this question
directly to two or three since, I have always got from them
the acknowledgment that times are not changed. Let my
fair readers remark for themselves this very evening when
they quit the dessert-table, and assemble to celebrate the
drawing-room mysteries. Well—in half-an-hour Becky and
Lady Jane were close and intimate friends—and in the course
of the evening her Ladyship informed Sir Pitt that she
thought her new sister-in-law was a kind, frank, unaffected,
and affectionate young woman.

And so having easily won the daughter's good-will, the
indefatigable little woman bent herself to conciliate the

august Lady Southdown. As soon as she found her Ladyship alone, Rebecca attacked her on the nursery question at once, and said that her own little boy was saved, actually saved, by calomel, freely administered, when all the physicians in Paris had given the dear child up. And then she mentioned how often she had heard of Lady Southdown from that excellent man the Reverend Lawrence Grills, Minister of the chapel in May Fair, which she frequented; and how her views were very much changed by circumstances and misfortunes; and how she hoped that a past life spent in worldliness and error might not incapacitate her from *more serious* thought for the future. She described how in former days she had been indebted to Mr. Crawley for religious instruction, touched upon the "Washerwoman of Finchley Common," which she had read with the greatest profit, and asked about Lady Emily, its gifted author, now Lady Emily Hornblower, at Cape Town, where her husband had strong hopes of becoming Bishop of Caffraria.

But she crowned all, and confirmed herself in Lady Southdown's favour, by feeling very much agitated and unwell after the funeral, and requesting her Ladyship's medical advice, which the Dowager not only gave, but, wrapped up in a bed-gown, and looking more like Lady Macbeth than ever, came privately in the night to Becky's room, with a parcel of favourite tracts, and a medicine of her own composition, which she insisted that Mrs. Rawdon should take.

Becky first accepted the tracts, and began to examine them with great interest, engaging the Dowager in a conversation concerning them and the welfare of her soul, by which means she hoped that her body might escape medication. But after the religious topics were exhausted, Lady Macbeth would not quit Becky's chamber until her cup of night-drink was emptied too; and poor Mrs. Rawdon was compelled actually to assume a look of gratitude, and to swallow the medicine under the unyielding old Dowager's nose, who left her victim finally with a benediction.

It did not much comfort Mrs. Rawdon; her countenance was very queer when Rawdon came in and heard what had happened; and his explosions of laughter were as loud as usual, when Becky, with a fun which she could not disguise, even though it was at her own expense, described the occurrence, and how she had been victimised by Lady Southdown. Lord Steyne, and her son in London, had many a laugh over the story, when Rawdon and his wife returned to their quarters in May Fair. Becky acted the whole scene for them. She put on a night-cap and gown. She preached a great sermon in the true serious manner; she lectured on the virtue of the medicine which she pretended to administer, with gravity of imitation so perfect, that you would have thought it was the Countess's own Roman nose through which she snuffled. "Give us Lady Southdown and the black dose," was a constant cry amongst the folks in Becky's little drawing-room in May Fair. And for the first time in her life the Dowager Countess of Southdown was made amusing.

Sir Pitt remembered the testimonies of respect and veneration which Rebecca had paid personally to himself in early days, and was tolerably well disposed towards her. The marriage, ill-advised as it was, had improved Rawdon very much—that was clear from the Colonel's altered habits and demeanour—and had it not been a lucky union as regarded Pitt himself? The cunning diplomatist smiled inwardly as he owned that he owed his fortune to it, and acknowledged that he at least ought not to cry out against it. His satisfaction was not removed by Rebecca's own statements, behaviour, and conversation.

She doubled the deference which before had charmed him, calling out his conversational powers in such a manner as quite to surprise Pitt himself, who, always inclined to respect his own talents, admired them the more when Rebecca pointed them out to him. With her sister-in-law, Rebecca was satisfactorily able to prove, that it was Mrs. Bute Crawley who brought about the marriage which she afterwards so caluminated: that it was Mrs. Bute's avarice —who hoped to gain all Miss Crawley's fortune, and deprive Rawdon of his aunt's favour—which caused and invented all the wicked reports against Rebecca. "She succeeded in making us poor," Rebecca said, with an air of angelical patience; "but how can I be angry with a woman

who has given me one of the best husbands in the world?
And has not her own avarice been sufficiently punished by
the ruin of her own hopes, and the loss of the property by
which she sat so much store? Poor!" she cried. "Dear
Lady Jane, what care we for poverty? I am used to it
from childhood, and I am often thankful that Miss Crawley's money has gone to restore the splendour of the noble
old family of which I am so proud to be a member. I am
sure Sir Pitt will make a much better use of it than Rawdon would."

All these speeches were reported to Sir Pitt by the most
faithful of wives, and increased the favourable impression
which Rebecca made; so much so, that when on the third
day after the funeral the family party were at dinner, Sir
Pitt Crawley, carving fowls at the head of the table, actually said to Mrs. Rawdon, "Ahem! *Rebecca*, may I give
you a wing?"—a speech which made the little woman's
eyes sparkle with pleasure.

While Rebecca was prosecuting the above schemes and
hopes, and Pitt Crawley arranging the funeral ceremonial
and other matters connected with his future progress and
dignity, and Lady Jane busy with her nursery, as far as
her mother would let her, and the sun rising and setting,
and the clock-tower bell of the Hall ringing to dinner and
to prayers as usual, the body of the late owner of Queen's
Crawley lay in the apartment which he had occupied, watched
unceasingly by the professional attendants who were engaged for that rite. A woman or two, and three or four
undertaker's men, the best whom Southampton could furnish, dressed in black, and of a proper stealthy and tragical
demeanour, had charge of the remains which they watched
turn about, having the housekeeper's room for their place
of rendezvous when off duty, where they played at cards
in privacy and drank their beer.

The members of the family and servants of the house
kept away from the gloomy spot, where the bones of the
descendant of an ancient line of knights and gentlemen
lay, awaiting their final consignment to the family crypt.
No regrets attended them, save those of the poor woman
who had hoped to be Sir Pitt's wife and widow, and who

had fled in disgrace from the Hall over which she had so nearly been a ruler. Beyond her and a favourite old pointer he had, and between whom and himself an attachment subsisted during the period of his imbecility, the old man had not a single friend to mourn him, having indeed, during the whole course of his life, never taken the least pains to secure one. Could the best and kindest of us who depart from the earth, have an opportunity of revisiting it, I suppose he or she (assuming that any Vanity Fair feelings subsist in the sphere whither we are bound) would have a pang of mortification at finding how soon our survivors were consoled. And so Sir Pitt was forgotten—like the kindest and best of us—only a few weeks sooner.

Those who will may follow his remains to the grave, whither they were borne on the appointed day, in the most becoming manner, the family in black coaches, with their handkerchiefs up to their noses, ready for the tears which did not come: the undertaker and his gentlemen in deep tribulation: the select tenantry mourning out of compliment to the new landlord: the neighbouring gentry's carriages at three miles an hour, empty, and in profound affliction: the parson speaking out the formula about "our dear brother departed." As long as we have a man's body, we play our Vanities upon it, surrounding it with humbug and ceremonies, laying it in state, and packing it up in gilt nails and velvet: and we finish our duty by placing over it a stone, written all over with lies. Bute's curate, a smart young fellow from Oxford, and Sir Pitt Crawley, composed between them an appropriate Latin epitaph for the late lamented Baronet: and the former preached a classical sermon, exhorting the survivors not to give way to grief, and informing them in the most respectful terms that they also would be one day called upon to pass that gloomy and mysterious portal which had just closed upon the remains of their lamented brother. Then the tenantry mounted on horseback again, or stayed and refreshed themselves at the Crawley Arms. Then, after a lunch in the servants' hall at Queen's Crawley, the gentry's carriages wheeled off to their different destinations: then the undertaker's men, taking the ropes, palls, velvets, ostrich feathers, and other mortuary properties, clambered up on the roof of the hearse, and rode off to Southampton. Their faces relapsed into a natural expression as the horses, clearing the lodge-gates, got into a brisker trot on the open road; and squads of them might have been seen, speckling with black the public-house entrances, with pewter-pots flashing in the sunshine. Sir Pitt's invalid-chair was wheeled away into a tool-house in the garden: the old pointer used to howl sometimes at first, but these were the only accents of grief which were heard in the Hall of which Sir Pitt Crawley, Baronet, had been master for some three-score years.

As the birds were pretty plentiful, and partridge-shoot-ing is as it were the duty of an English gentleman of states-manlike propensities, Sir Pitt Crawley, the first shock of grief over, went out a little and partook of that diversion in a white hat with crape around it. The sight of those fields of stubble and turnips, now his own, gave him many secret joys. Sometimes, and with an exquisite humility, he took no gun, but went out with a peaceful bamboo cane; Rawdon, his big brother, and the keepers blazing away at his side.

Pitt's money and acres had a great effect upon his brother. The penniless Colonel became quite obsequious and respectful to the head of his house, and despised the milk-sop Pitt no longer. Rawdon listened with sympathy to his senior's prospects of planting and draining: gave his advice about the stables and cattle, rode over to Mud-bury to look at a mare, which he thought would carry Lady Jane, and offered to break her, &c.: the rebellious dragoon was quite humbled and subdued, and became a most creditable younger brother. He had constant bul-letins from Miss Briggs in London respecting little Rawdon, who was left behind there: who sent messages of his own. "I am very well," he wrote. "I hope you are very well. I hope Mamma is very well. The pony is very well. Grey takes me to ride in the Park. I can canter. I met the little boy who rode before. He cried when he cantered. I do not cry." Rawdon read these letters to his brother, and Lady

Jane, who was delighted with them. The Baronet promised
to take charge of the lad at school; and his kind-hearted
wife gave Rebecca a bank-note, begging her to buy a present
with it for her little nephew.

One day followed another, and the ladies of the house
passed their life in those calm pursuits and amusements
which satisfy country ladies. Bells rang to meals, and to
prayers. The young ladies took exercise on the pianoforte
every morning after breakfast, Rebecca giving them the
benefit of her instruction. Then they put on thick shoes
and walked in the park or shrubberies, or beyond the pal-
ings into the village, descending upon the cottages, with
Lady Southdown's medicine and tracts for the sick people
there. Lady Southdown drove out in a pony-chaise, when
Rebecca would take her place by the Dowager's side, and
listen to her solemn talk with the utmost interest. She
sang Handel and Haydn to the family of evenings, and
engaged in a large piece of worsted work, as if she had
been born to the business, and as if this kind of life was to
continue with her until she should sink to the grave in a
polite old age, leaving regrets and a great quantity of
consols behind her—as if there were not cares and
duns, schemes, shifts, and poverty, waiting outside the park
gates to pounce upon her when she issued into the world
again.

"It isn't difficult to be a country gentleman's wife," Rebecca thought. "I think I could be a good woman if I had
five thousand a-year. I could dawdle about in the nursery,
and count the apricots on the wall. I could water plants in
a green-house, and pick off dead leaves from the geraniums.
I could ask old women about their rheumatisms, and order
half-a-crown's worth of soup for the poor. I shouldn't miss
it much, out of five thousand a-year. I could even drive out
ten miles to dine at a neighbour's, and dress in the fashions
of the year before last. I could go to church and keep awake
in the great family pew: or go to sleep behind the curtains,
with my veil down, if I only had practice. I could pay everybody, if I had but the money. This is what the conjurors
here pride themselves upon doing. They look down with pity
upon us miserable sinners who have none. They think

themselves generous if they give our children a five-pound note, and us contemptible if we are without one." And who knows but Rebecca was right in her speculations—and that it was only a question of money and fortune which made the difference between her and an honest woman? If you take temptations into account, who is to say that he is better than his neighbour? A comfortable career of prosperity, if it does not make people honest, at least keeps them so.

An alderman coming from a turtle feast will not step out of his carriage to steal a leg of mutton; but put him to starve, and see if he will not purloin a loaf. Becky consoled herself by so balancing the chances and equalising the distribution of good and evil in the world.

The old haunts, the old fields and woods, the copses, ponds, and gardens, the rooms of the old house where she had spent a couple of years seven years ago, were all carefully revisited by her. She had been young there, or comparatively so, for she forgot the time when she ever *was* young—but she remembered her thoughts and feelings seven years back, and contrasted them with those which she had at present, now that she had seen the world and lived with great people, and raised herself far beyond her original humble station.

"I have passed beyond it, because I have brains," Becky thought, "and almost all the rest of the world are fools. I could not go back, and consort with those people now, whom I used to meet in my father's studio. Lords come up to my door with stars and garters instead of poor artists with screws of tobacco in their pockets. I have a gentleman for my husband, and an Earl's daughter for my sister, in the very house where I was little better than a servant a few years ago. But am I much better to do now in the world than I was when I was the poor painter's daughter, and wheedled the grocer round the corner for sugar and tea? Suppose I had married Francis who was so fond of me—I couldn't have been much poorer than I am now. Heigho! I wish I could exchange my position in society, and all my relations for a snug sum in the Three per Cent. Consols;" for so it was that Becky felt the Vanity of human

affairs, and it was in those securities that she would have
liked to cast anchor.

It may, perhaps, have struck her that to have been honest
and humble, to have done her duty, and to have marched
straightforward on her way, would have brought her as near
happiness as that path by which she was striving to attain
it. But,—just as the children at Queen's Crawley went round
the room, where the body of their father lay;—if ever Becky
had these thoughts, she was accustomed to walk round them,
and not look in. She eluded them, and despised them—or at
least she was committed to the other path from which retreat
was now impossible. And for my part I believe that remorse is the least active of all a man's moral senses—
the very easiest to be deadened when wakened: and in
some never wakened at all. We grieve at being found
out, and at the idea of shame or punishment; but the mere
sense of wrong makes very few people unhappy in Vanity
Fair.

So Rebecca, during her stay at Queen's Crawley, made
as many friends of the Mammon of Unrighteousness as she
could possibly bring under control. Lady Jane and her husband bade her farewell with the warmest demonstrations of
good-will. They looked forward with pleasure to the time
when, the family-house in Gaunt Street being repaired and
beautified, they were to meet again in London. Lady Southdown made her up a packet of medicine, and sent a letter
by her to the Rev. Lawrence Grills, exhorting that gentleman to save the brand who "honoured" the letter from the
burning. Pitt accompanied them with four horses in the
carriage to Mudbury, having sent on their baggage in a cart
previously, accompanied with loads of game.

"How happy you will be to see your darling little
boy again!" Lady Crawley said, taking leave of her kinswoman.

"O so happy!" said Rebecca, throwing up the green eyes.
She was immensely happy to be free of the place, and yet
loth to go. Queen's Crawley was abominably stupid; and
yet the air there was somehow purer than that which she
had been accustomed to breathe. Everybody had been dull,
but had been kind in their way. "It is all the influence of a

long course of Three per Cents," Becky said to herself, and was right very likely.

However, the London lamps flashed joyfully as the stage rolled into Piccadilly, and Briggs had made a beautiful fire in Curzon Street, and little Rawdon was up to welcome back his papa and mamma.

CHAPTER VII

WHICH TREATS OF THE OSBORNE FAMILY

CONSIDERABLE time has elapsed since we have seen our respectable friend, old Mr. Osborne of Russell Square. He has not been the happiest of mortals since last we met him. Events have occurred which have not improved his temper, and in more instances than one he has not been allowed to have his own way. To be thwarted in this reasonable desire was always very injurious to the old gentleman; and resistance became doubly exasperating when gout, age, loneliness, and the force of many disappointments combined to weigh him down. His stiff black hair began to grow quite white soon after his son's death; his face grew redder; his hands trembled more and more as he poured out his glass of port wine. He led his clerks a dire life in the City: his family at home were not much happier. I doubt if Rebecca, whom we have seen piously praying for Consols, would have exchanged her poverty and the dare-devil excitement and chances of her life, for Osborne's money and the humdrum gloom which enveloped him. He had proposed for Miss Swartz, but had been rejected scornfully by the partizans of that lady, who married her to a young sprig of Scotch nobility.

He was a man to have married a woman out of low life, and bullied her dreadfully afterwards: but no person presented herself suitable to his taste; and, instead, he tyrannised over his unmarried daughter, at home. She had a fine carriage and fine horses, and sate at the head of a table loaded with the grandest plate. She had a cheque-book, a prize footman to follow her when she walked, unlimited credit, and bows and compliments from all the tradesmen, and all the appurtenances of an heiress: but she spent a woful time. The little charity-girls at the Foundling, the sweep-eress at the crossing, the poorest under-kitchen-maid in the servants' hall, was happy compared to that unfortunate and now middle-aged young lady.

Frederick Bullock, Esq., of the house of Bullock, Hulker, and Bullock, had married Maria Osborne, not without a great deal of difficulty and grumbling on Mr. Bullock's part. George being dead and cut out of his father's will, Frederick insisted that the half of the old gentleman's property should be settled upon his Maria, and indeed, for a long time, refused "to come to the scratch" (it was Mr. Frederick's own expression) on any other terms. Osborne said Fred had agreed to take his daughter with twenty thousand, and he should bind himself to no more. "Fred might take it, and welcome, or leave it, and go and be hanged." Fred, whose hopes had been raised when George had been disinherited, thought himself infamously swindled by the old merchant, and for some time made as if he would break off the match altogether. Osborne withdrew his account from Bullock and Hulker's, went on 'Change with a horsewhip which he swore he would lay across the back of a certain scoundrel that should be nameless, and demeaned himself in his usual violent manner. Jane Osborne condoled with her sister Maria during this family feud. "I always told you, Maria, that it was your money he loved, and not you," she said, soothingly.

'He selected *me* and my money at any rate: he didn't choose you and yours," replied Maria, tossing up her head.

The rupture was, however, only temporary. Fred's father and senior partners counselled him to take Maria, even with the twenty thousand settled, half down, and half at the death of Mr. Osborne, with the chances of the further division of the property. So he "knuckled down," again to use his own phrase; and sent old Hulker with peaceable overtures to Osborne. It was his father, he said, who would not hear of the match, and had made the difficulties; he was most anxious to keep the engagement. The excuse was sulkily accepted by Mr. Osborne. Hulker and Bullock were a high family of the City aristocracy, and connected with the "nobs" at the West End. It was something for the old man to be able to say, "My son, sir, of the house of Hulker, Bullock, and Co., sir; my daughter's cousin, Lady Mango, sir, daughter of the Right Hon. the Earl of Castlemouldy." In his imagination he saw his house peopled by the "nobs." So he forgave young Bullock, and consented that the marriage should take place.

It was a grand affair—the bridegroom's relatives giving the breakfast, their habitations being near St. George's, Hanover Square, where the business took place. The "nobs of the West End" were invited, and many of them signed the book. Mr. Mango and Lady Mary Mango were there, with the dear young Gwendoline and Guinever Mango as bridesmaids; Colonel Bludyer of the Dragoon Guards (eldest son of the house of Bludyer Brothers, Mincing Lane), another cousin of the bridegroom, and the Honourable Mrs. Bludyer; the Honourable George Boulter, Lord Levant's son, and his lady, Miss Mango that was; Lord Viscount Castletoddy; Honourable James McMull and Mrs. McMull (formerly Miss Swartz), and a host of fashionables, who have all married into Lombard Street, and done a great deal to ennoble Cornhill.

The young couple had a house near Berkeley Square, and a small villa at Roehampton, among the banking colony there. Fred was considered to have made rather a *mésalliance* by the ladies of his family, whose grandfather had been in a Charity School, and who were allied through the husbands with some of the best blood in England. And Maria was bound, by superior pride and great care in the composition of her visiting-book, to make up for the defects of birth; and felt it her duty to see her father and sister as little as possible.

That she should utterly break with the old man, who had still so many scores of thousand pounds to give away, is absurd to suppose. Fred Bullock would never allow her to do that. But she was still young and incapable of hiding her feelings: and by inviting her papa and sister to her third-rate parties, and behaving very coldly to them when they came, and by avoiding Russell Square, and indiscreetly begging her father to quit that odious vulgar place; she did more harm than all Frederick's diplomacy could repair, and perilled her chance of her inheritance like a giddy heedless creature as she was.

"So Russell Square is not good enough for Mrs. Maria, hay?" said the old gentleman, rattling up the carriage-windows as he and his daughter drove away one night from Mrs. Frederick Bullock's, after dinner. "So she invites her father and sister to a second day's dinner (if those sides, or *ontrys*, as she calls 'em, weren't served yesterday, I'm d—d), and to meet City folks and littery men, and keeps the Earls and the Ladies, and the Honourables to herself. Honourables? Damn Honourables. I am a plain British merchant I am: and could buy the beggarly hounds over and over. Lords, indeed!—why, at one of her *swarreys* I saw one of 'em speak to a damn fiddler—a fellar I despise. And they won't come to Russell Square, won't they? Why, I'll lay my life I've got a better glass of wine, and pay a better figure for it, and can show a handsomer service of silver, and can lay a better dinner on my mahogany, than ever they see on theirs—the cringing, sneaking, stuck-up fools. Drive on quick, James: I want to get back to Russell Square—ha, ha!" and he sank back into the corner with a furious laugh. With such reflections on his own superior merit, it was the custom of the old gentleman not unfrequently to console himself.

Jane Osborne could not but concur in these opinions respecting her sister's conduct; and when Mrs. Frederick's first-born, Frederick Augustus Howard Stanley Devereux Bullock, was born, old Osborne, who was invited to the christening and to be godfather, contented himself with sending the child a gold cup, with twenty guineas inside it for the nurse. "That's more than any of your Lords will give, *I'll* warrant," he said, and refused to attend at the ceremony.

The splendour of the gift, however, caused great satisfaction to the house of Bullock. Maria thought that her father was very much pleased with her, and Frederick augured the best for his little son and heir.

One can fancy the pangs with which Miss Osborne in her solitude in Russell Square read the *Morning Post,* where her sister's name occurred every now and then, in the articles headed "Fashionable Reunions," and where she had an opportunity of reading a description of Mrs. F. Bullock's costume, when presented at the Drawing-room by Lady Fred-

erica Bullock. Jane's own life, as we have said, admitted of
no such grandeur. It was an awful existence. She had to
get up of black winter's mornings to make breakfast for her
scowling old father, who would have turned the whole house
out of doors if his tea had not been ready at half-past eight.
She remained silent opposite to him, listening to the urn hissing, and sitting in tremor while the parent read his paper,
and consumed his accustomed portion of muffins and tea. At
half-past nine he rose and went to the City, and she was
almost free till dinner-time, to make visitations in the kitchen,
and to scold the servants: to drive abroad and descend upon
the tradesmen, who were prodigiously respectful: to leave
her cards and her papa's at the great glum respectable houses
of their City friends; or to sit alone in the large drawing-
room, expecting visitors; and working at a huge piece of
worsted by the fire, on the sofa, hard by the great Iphigenia
clock, which ticked and tolled with mournful loudness in the
dreary room. The great glass over the mantel-piece, faced
by the other great console glass at the opposite end of the
room, increased and multiplied between them the brown
Holland bag in which the chandelier hung; until you saw
these brown Holland bags fading away in endless perspec-
tives, and this apartment of Miss Osborne's seemed the centre
of a system of drawing-rooms. When she removed the
cordovan leather from the grand piano, and ventured to play
a few notes on it, it sounded with a mournful sadness, start-
ling the dismal echoes of the house. George's picture was
gone, and laid upstairs in a lumber-room in the garret; and
though there was a consciousness of him, and father and
daughter often instinctively knew that they were thinking of
him, no mention was ever made of the brave and once
darling son.

At five o'clock Mr. Osborne came back to his dinner,
which he and his daughter took in silence (seldom broken,
except when he swore and was savage, if the cooking was
not to his liking), or which they shared twice in a month
with a party of dismal friends of Osborne's rank and age.
Old Dr. Gulp and his lady from Bloomsbury Square: old
Mr. Frowser, the attorney, from Bedford Row, a very great
man, and from his business, hand-in-glove with the "nobs at

the West End;" old Colonel Livermore, of the Bombay Army, and Mrs. Livermore, from Upper Bedford Place: old Serjeant Toffy and Mrs. Toffy; and sometimes old Sir Thomas Coffin and Lady Coffin, from Bedford Square. Sir Thomas was celebrated as a hanging judge, and the particular tawny port was produced when he dined with Mr. Osborne.

These people and their like gave the pompous Russell Square merchant pompous dinners back again. They had solemn rubbers of whist, when they went upstairs after drinking, and their carriages were called at half-past ten. Many rich people, whom we poor devils are in the habit of envying, lead contentedly an existence like that above described. Jane Osborne scarcely ever met a man under sixty, and almost the only bachelor who appeared in their society was Mr. Smirk, the celebrated ladies' doctor.

I can't say that nothing had occurred to disturb the monotony of this awful existence: the fact is, there had been a secret in poor Jane's life which had made her father more savage and morose than even nature, pride, and over-feeding had made him. This secret was connected with Miss Wirt, who had a cousin an artist, Mr. Smee, very celebrated since as a portrait-painter and R.A., but who once was glad enough to give drawing-lessons to ladies of fashion. Mr. Smee has forgotten where Russell Square is now, but he was glad enough to visit it in the year 1818, when Miss Osborne had instruction from him.

Smee (formerly a pupil of Sharpe of Frith Street, a dissolute, irregular, and unsuccessful man, but a man with great knowledge of his art) being the cousin of Miss Wirt, we say, and introduced by her to Miss Osborne, whose hand and heart were still free after various incomplete love affairs, felt a great attachment for this lady, and it is believed inspired one in her bosom. Miss Wirt was the confidante of this intrigue. I know not whether she used to leave the room where the master and his pupil were painting, in order to give them an opportunity for exchanging those vows and sentiments which cannot be uttered advantageously in the presence of a third party: I know not whether she hoped that should her cousin succeed in carrying off the rich merchant's daughter, he would give Miss Wirt a portion of the wealth which she had enabled him to win—all that is certain is, that Mr. Osborne got some hint of the transaction, came back from the City abruptly, and entered the drawing-room with his bamboo cane; found the painter, the pupil, and the companion all looking exceedingly pale there; turned the former out of doors with menaces that he would break every bone in his skin, and half-an-hour afterwards dismissed Miss Wirt likewise, kicking her trunks down the stairs, trampling on her band-boxes, and shaking his fist at her hackney coach, as it bore her away.

Jane Osborne kept her bed-room for many days. She was not allowed to have a companion afterwards. Her father swore to her that she should not have a shilling of his money if she made any match without his concurrence; and as he wanted a woman to keep his house, he did not choose that she should marry: so that she was obliged to give up all projects with which Cupid had any share. During her papa's life, then, she resigned herself to the manner of existence here described, and was content to be an Old Maid. Her sister, meanwhile, was having children with finer names every year —and the intercourse between the two grew fainter continually. "Jane and I do not move in the same sphere of life," Mrs. Bullock said. "I regard her as a sister, of course"— which means—what does it mean when a lady says that she regards Jane as a sister?

It has been described how the Misses Dobbin lived with their father at a fine villa at Denmark Hill, where there were beautiful graperies and peach-trees which delighted little Georgy Osborne. The Misses Dobbin, who drove often to Brompton to see our dear Amelia, came sometimes to Russell Square too, to pay a visit to their old acquaintance Miss Osborne. I believe it was in consequence of the commands of their brother the Major in India (for whom their papa had a prodigious respect), that they paid attention to Mrs. George; for the Major, the godfather and guardian of Amelia's little boy, still hoped that the child's grandfather might be induced to relent towards him, and acknowledge him for the sake of his son. The Misses Dobbin kept Miss Osborne acquainted with the state of Amelia's affairs;

how she was living with her father and mother; how poor
they were; how they wondered what men, and such men as
their brother and dear Captain Osborne, could find in such an
insignificant little chit; how she was still, as heretofore, a
namby-pamby milk-and-water affected creature—but how
the boy was really the noblest little boy ever seen—for the
hearts of all women warm towards young children, and the
sourest spinster is kind to them.

One day, after great entreaties on the part of the Misses
Dobbin, Amelia allowed little George to go and pass a day
with them at Denmark Hill—a part of which day she spent
herself in writing to the Major in India. She congratulated
him on the happy news which his sisters had just conveyed
to her. She prayed for his prosperity, and that of the bride
he had chosen. She thanked him for a thousand thousand
kind offices and proofs of steadfast friendship to her in her
affliction. She told him the last news about little Georgy, and
how he was gone to spend that very day with his sisters in
the country. She underlined the letter a great deal, and
she signed herself affectionately his friend, Amelia Osborne.
She forgot to send any message of kindness to Lady O'Dowd,
as her wont was—and did not mention Glorvina by name,
and only in italics, as the Major's *bride,* for whom she begged
blessings. But the news of the marriage removed the re-
serve which she had kept up towards him. She was glad to
be able to own and feel how warmly and gratefully she
regarded him—and as for the idea of being jealous of Glorvina, (Glorvina, indeed!) Amelia would have scouted it, if
an angel from heaven had hinted it to her.

That night, when Georgy came back in the pony-carriage
in which he rejoiced, and in which he was driven by Sir Wm.
Dobbin's old coachman, he had round his neck a fine gold
chain and watch. He said an old lady, not pretty, had given
it him, who cried and kissed him a great deal. But he didn't
like her. He liked grapes very much. And he only liked his
mamma. Amelia shrank and started: the timid soul felt a
presentiment of terror when she heard that the relations of
the child's father had seen him.

Miss Osborne came back to give her father his dinner. He
had made a good speculation in the City, and was rather in a

good humour that day, and chanced to remark the agitation under which she laboured. "What's the matter, Miss Osborne?" he deigned to say.

The woman burst into tears. "O, sir," she said, "I've seen little George. He is as beautiful as an angel—and so like him!" The old man opposite to her did not say a word, but flushed up, and began to tremble in every limb.

CHAPTER VIII

In Which the Reader Has to Double the Cape

THE astonished reader must be called upon to transport himself ten thousand miles to the military station of Bundlegunge, in the Madras division of our Indian empire, where our gallant old friends of the —th regiment are quartered under the command of the brave Colonel, Sir Michael O'Dowd. Time has dealt kindly with that stout officer, as it does ordinarily with men who have good stomachs and good tempers, and are not perplexed over much by fatigue of the brain. The Colonel plays a good knife and fork at tiffin, and resumes those weapons with great success at dinner. He smokes his hookah after both meals, and puffs as quietly while his wife scolds him, as he did under the fire of the French at Waterloo. Age and heat have not diminished the activity or the eloquence of the descendant of the Malonys and the Molloys. Her Ladyship, our old acquaintance, is as much at home at Madras as at Brussels—in the cantonment as under the tents. On the march you saw her at the head of the regiment seated on a royal elephant, a noble sight. Mounted on that beast, she has been into action with tigers in the jungle: she has been received by native princes, who have welcomed her and Glorvina into the recesses of their zenanas and offered her shawls and jewels which it went to her heart to refuse. The sentries of all arms salute her wherever she makes her appearance: and she touches her hat gravely to their salutation. Lady O'Dowd is one of the greatest ladies in the Presidency of Madras—her quarrel with Lady Smith, wife of Sir Minos Smith the puisne judge, is still remembered by some at Madras when the Colonel's lady snapped her fingers in the Judge's lady's face, and said *she'd* never walk behind ever a beggarly civilian. Even now, though it is five-and-twenty years ago, people remember Lady O'Dowd perform-

90

ing a jig at Government House, where she danced down two
Aides-de-Camp, a Major of Madras cavalry, and two gentlemen of the Civil Service; and, persuaded by Major Dobbin,
C.B., second in command of the —th, to retire to the supper-
room, *lassata nondum satiata recessit*.

Peggy O'Dowd is indeed the same as ever: kind in act
and thought: impetuous in temper; eager to command: a
tyrant over her Michael: a dragon amongst all the ladies
of the regiment: a mother to all the young men, whom she
tends in their sickness, defends in all their scrapes, and with
whom Lady Peggy is immensely popular. But the Subalterns'
and Captains' ladies (the Major is unmarried) cabal against
her a good deal. They say that Glorvina gives herself airs,
and that Peggy herself is intolerably domineering. She in-
terfered with a little congregation which Mrs. Kirk had got
up, and laughed the young men away from her sermons,
stating that a soldier's wife had no business to be a parson:
that Mrs. Kirk would be much better mending her husband's
clothes: and, if the regiment wanted sermons, that she had
the finest in the world, those of her uncle, the Dean. She
abruptly put a termination to a flirtation which Lieutenant
Stubble of the regiment had commenced with the Surgeon's
wife, threatening to come down upon Stubble for the money
which he had borrowed from her (for the young fellow
was still of an extravagant turn) unless he broke off at once
and went to the Cape, on sick leave. On the other hand, she
housed and sheltered Mrs. Posky, who fled from her bun-
galow one night, pursued by her infuriate husband, wielding
his second brandy bottle, and actually carried Posky through
the delirium tremens, and broke him of the habit of drinking,
which had grown upon that officer, as all evil habits will
grow upon men. In a word, in adversity she was the best
of comforters, in good fortune the most troublesome of
friends; having a perfectly good opinion of herself always,
and an indomitable resolution to have her own way.

Among other points, she had made up her mind that
Glorvina should marry our old friend Dobbin. Mrs. O'Dowd
knew the Major's expectations and appreciated his good
qualities, and the high character which he enjoyed in his
profession. Glorvina, a very handsome, fresh-coloured,

black-haired, blue-eyed young lady, who could ride a horse, or play a sonata with any girl out of the County Cork, seemed to be the very person destined to insure Dobbin's happiness—much more than that poor good little weak-spur'ted Amelia, about whom he used to take on so.—"Look at Glorvina enter a room," Mrs. O'Dowd would say, "and compare her with that poor Mrs. Osborne, who couldn't say bo to a goose. She'd be worthy of you, Major—you're a quiet man yourself, and want some one to talk for ye. And though she does not come of such good blood as the Malonys or Molloys, let me tell ye, she's of an ancient family that any nobleman might be proud to marry into."

But before she had come to such a resolution, and determined to subjugate Major Dobbin by her endearments, it must be owned that Glorvina had practised them a good deal elsewhere. She had had a season in Dublin, and who knows how many in Cork, Killarney, and Mallow? She had flirted with all the marriageable officers whom the depôts of her country afforded, and all the bachelor squires who seemed eligible. She had been engaged to be married a half score times in Ireland, besides the clergyman at Bath who used her so ill. She had flirted all the way to Madras with the Captain and chief-mate of the Ramchunder East India-man, and had a season at the Presidency with her brother and Mrs. O'Dowd, who was staying there, while the Major of the regiment was in command at the station. Everybody admired her there: everybody danced with her: but no one proposed who was worth the marrying; one or two exceedingly young subalterns sighed after her, and a beardless civilian or two; but she rejected these as beneath her pretensions; and other and younger virgins than Glorvina were married before her. There are women, and handsome women too, who have this fortune in life. They fall in love with the utmost generosity; they ride and walk with half the Army-list, though they draw near to forty, and yet the Misses O'Grady are the Misses O'Grady still: Glorvina persisted that but for Lady O'Dowd's unlucky quarrel with the Judge's lady, she would have made a good match at Madras, where old Mr. Chutney, who was at the head of the civil service (and who afterwards married Miss Dolby, a young lady only

thirteen years of age, who had just arrived from school in
Europe), was just at the point of proposing to her.

Well, although Lady O'Dowd and Glorvina quarrelled a
great number of times every day, and upon almost every
conceivable subject—indeed, if Mick O'Dowd had not possessed the temper of an angel two such women constantly
about his ears would have driven him out of his senses—
yet they agreed between themselves on this point, that Glorvina should marry Major Dobbin, and were determined that
the Major should have no rest until the arrangement was
brought about. Undismayed by forty or fifty previous defeats,
Glorvina laid siege to him. She sang Irish Melodies at him
unceasingly. She asked him so frequently and pathetically,
Will ye come to the bower? that it is a wonder how any man
of feeling could have resisted the invitation. She was never
tired of inquiring, if Sorrow had his young days faded; and
was ready to listen and weep like Desdemona at the stories
of his dangers and his campaigns. It has been said that our
honest and dear old friend used to perform on the flute in
private: Glorvina insisted upon having duets with him, and
Lady O'Dowd would rise and artlessly quit the room, when
the young couple were so engaged. Glorvina forced the
Major to ride with her of mornings. The whole cantonment
saw them set out and return. She was constantly writing
notes over to him at his house, borrowing his books, and
scoring with her great pencil-marks such passages of sentiment or humour as awakened her sympathy. She borrowed
his horses, his servants, his spoons, and palankin;—no wonder that public rumour assigned her to him, and that the
Major's sisters in England should fancy they were about to
have a sister-in-law.

Dobbin, who was thus vigorously besieged, was in the
meanwhile in a state of the most odious tranquillity. He
used to laugh when the young fellows of the regiment joked
him about Glorvina's manifest attentions to him. "Bah!"
said he, "she is only keeping her hand in—she practises
upon me as she does upon Mrs. Tozer's piano, because it's
the most handy instrument in the station. I am much too
battered and old for such a fine young lady as Glorvina."
And so he went on riding with her, and copying music and

verses into her albums, and playing at chess with her very submissively; for it is with these simple amusements that some officers in India are accustomed to while away their leisure moments; while others of a less domestic turn hunt hogs, and shoot snipes, or gamble and smoke cheroots, and betake themselves to brandy-and-water. As for Sir Michael O'Dowd, though his lady and her sister both urged him to call upon the Major to explain himself, and not keep on torturing a poor innocent girl in that shameful way, the old soldier refused point-blank to have anything to do with the conspiracy. "Faith, the Major's big enough to choose for himself," Sir Michael said; "he'll ask ye when he wants ye;" —or else he would turn the matter off jocularly, declaring that "Dobbin was too young to keep house, and had written home to ask lave of his mamma." Nay, he went farther, and in private communications with his Major, would caution and rally him—crying, "Mind your oi, Dob, my boy, them girls is bent on mischief—me Lady has just got a box of gowns from Europe, and there's a pink satin for Glorvina, which will finish ye, Dob, if it's in the power of woman or satin to move ye."

But the truth is, neither beauty nor fashion could conquer him. Our honest friend had but one idea of a woman in his head, and that one did not in the least resemble Miss Glorvina O'Dowd in pink satin. A gentle little woman in black, with large eyes and brown hair, seldom speaking save when spoken to, and then in a voice not the least resembling Miss Glorvina's—a soft young mother tending an infant and beckoning the Major up with a smile to look at him—a rosy-cheeked lass coming singing into the room in Russell Square or hanging on George Osborne's arm, happy and loving—there was but this image that filled our honest Major's mind by day and by night, and reigned over it always. Very likely Amelia was not like the portrait the Major had formed of her: there was a figure in a book of fashions which his sisters had in England, and with which William had made away privately, pasting it into the lid of his desk, and fancying he saw some resemblance to Mrs. Osborne in the print, whereas I have seen it, and can vouch that it is but the picture of a high-waisted gown with an impossible doll's face simpering over it—and, perhaps, Mr. Dobbin's sentimental Amelia was no more like the real one than this absurd little print which he cherished. But what man in love, of us, is better informed?—or is he much happier when he sees and owns his delusion? Dobbin was under this spell. He did not bother his friends and the public much about his feelings, or indeed lose his natural rest or appetite on account of them. His head has grizzled since we saw him last; and a line or two of silver may be seen in the soft brown hair likewise. But his feelings are not in the least changed or oldened; and his love remains as fresh as a man's recollections of boyhood are.

We have said how the two Misses Dobbin and Amelia, the Major's corespondents in Europe, wrote him letters from England; Mrs. Osborne congratulating him with great candour and cordiality upon his approaching nuptials with Miss O'Dowd.

"Your sister has just kindly visited me," Amelia wrote in her letter, "and informed me of an *interesting event*. upon which I beg to offer my *most sincere congratulations*. I hope the young lady to whom I hear you are to be *united* will in every respect prove worthy of one who is himself all kindness and goodness. The poor widow has only her prayers to offer, and her cordial cordial wishes for *your prosperity!* Georgy sends his love to *his dear godpapa,* and hopes that you will not forget him. I tell him that you are about to form *other ties,* with one who I am sure merits *all your affection,* but that, although such ties must of course be the strongest and most sacred, and supersede *all others,* yet that I am sure the widow and the child whom you have ever protected and loved will always *have a corner in your heart.*" The letter, which has been before alluded to, went on in this strain, protesting throughout as to the extreme satisfaction of the writer.

This letter, which arrived by the very same ship which brought out Lady O'Dowd's box of millinery from London (and which you may be sure Dobbin opened before any one of the other packets which the mail brought him), put the receiver into such a state of mind that Glorvina, and her pink satin, and everything belonging to her, became per-

fectly odious to him. The Major cursed the talk of women;
and the sex in general. Everything annoyed him that day
—the parade was insufferably hot and wearisome. Good
heavens! was a man of intellect to waste his life, day after
day, inspecting cross-belts, and putting fools through their
manœuvres? The senseless chatter of the young men at
mess was more than ever jarring. What cared he, a man
on the high road to forty, to know how many snipes Lieutenant Smith had shot, or what were the performances of
Ensign Brown's mare? The jokes about the table filled him
with shame. He was too old to listen to the banter of the
assistant-surgeon and the slang of the youngsters, at which
old O'Dowd, with his bald head and red face, laughed quite
easily. The old man had listened to those jokes any time
these thirty years—Dobbin himself had been fifteen years
hearing them. And after the boisterous dulness of the mess-
table, the quarrels and scandal of the ladies of the regiment!
It was unbearable, shameful. "O Amelia, Amelia," he
thought, "you to whom I have been so faithful—you reproach
me! It is because you cannot feel for me, that I drag on
this wearisome life. And you reward me after years of devotion by giving me your blessing upon my marriage, forsooth with this flaunting Irish girl!" Sick and sorry felt
poor William: more than ever wretched and lonely. He
would like to have done with life and its vanity altogether—
so bootless and unsatisfactory the struggle, so cheerless and
dreary the prospect seemed to him. He lay all that night
sleepless, and yearning to go home. Amelia's letter had fallen
as a blank upon him. No fidelity, no constant truth and passion, could move her into warmth. She would not see that he
loved her. Tossing in his bed, he spoke out to her. "Good
God, Amelia!" he said, "don't you know that I only love
you in the world—you, who are a stone to me—you, whom
I tended through months and months of illness and grief,
and who bade me farewell with a smile on your face, and
forgot me before the door shut between us!" The native
servants lying outside his verandahs beheld with wonder
the Major, so cold and quiet ordinarily, at present so passionately moved and cast down. Would she have pitied him
had she seen him? He read over and over all the letters

which he ever had from her—letters of business relative to the little property which he had made her believe her husband had left to her—brief notes of invitation—every scrap of writing that she had ever sent to him—how cold, how kind, how hopeless, how selfish they were!

Had there been some kind gentle soul near at hand who could read and appreciate this silent generous heart, who knows but that the reign of Amelia might have been over, and that friend William's love might have flowed into a kinder channel? But there was only Glorvina of the jetty ringlets with whom his intercourse was familiar, and this dashing young woman was not bent upon loving the Major, but rather on making the Major admire *her*—a most vain and hopeless task, too, at least considering the means that the poor girl possessed to carry it out. She curled her hair and showed her shoulders at him, as much as to say, did ye ever see such jet ringlets and such a complexion? She grinned at him so that he might see that every tooth in her head was sound—and he never heeded all these charms. Very soon after the arrival of the box of millinery, and perhaps indeed in honour of it, Lady O'Dowd and the ladies of the King's Regiment gave a ball to the Company's Regiments and the civilians at the station. Glorvina sported the killing pink frock, and the Major, who attended the party and walked very ruefully up and down the rooms, never so much as perceived the pink garment. Glorvina danced past him in a fury with all the young subalterns of the station, and the Major was not in the least jealous of her performance, or angry because Captain Bangles of the Cavalry handed her to supper. It was not jealousy, or frocks or shoulders, that could move him, and Glorvina had nothing more.

So these two were each exemplifying the Vanity of this life, and each longing for what he or she could not get. Glorvina cried with rage at the failure. She had set her mind on the Major "more than on any of the others," she owned, sobbing. "He'll break my heart, he will, Peggy," she would whimper to her sister-in-law when they were good friends; "sure every one of me frocks must be taken in—it's such a skeleton I'm growing." Fat or thin, laughing or melancholy, on horseback or the music-stool, it was all the same to the Major. And the Colonel, puffing his pipe and listening to these complaints, would suggest that Glory should have some black frocks out in the next box from London, and told a mysterious story of a lady in Ireland who died of grief for the loss of her husband before she got ere a one.

While the Major was going on in this tantalizing way, not proposing, and declining to fall in love, there came another ship from Europe bringing letters on board, and amongst them some more for the heartless man. These were home letters bearing an earlier post-mark than that of the former packets, and as Major Dobbin recognised among his the handwriting of his sister, who always crossed and recrossed her letters to her brother,—gathered together all the possible bad news which she could collect, abused him and read him lectures with sisterly frankness, and always left him miserable for the day after "dearest William" had achieved the perusal of one of her epistles—the truth must be told that dearest William did not hurry himself to break the seal of Miss Dobbin's letter, but waited for a particularly favourable day and mood for doing so. A fortnight before, he had written to scold her for telling those absurd stories to Mrs. Osborne, and had despatched a letter in reply to that lady, undeceiving her with respect to the reports concerning him, and assuring her that "he had no sort of present intention of altering his condition."

Two or three nights after the arrival of the second package of letters, the Major had passed the evening pretty cheerfully at Lady O'Dowd's house, where Glorvina thought that he listened with rather more attention than usual to the Meeting of the Wathers, the Minsthrel Boy, and one or two other specimens of song with which she favoured him (the truth is, he was no more listening to Glorvina than to the howling of the jackals in the moonlight outside, and the delusion was hers as usual), and having played his game at chess with her, (cribbage with the surgeon was Lady O'Dowd's favourite evening pastime,) Major Dobbin took leave of the Colonel's family at his usual hour, and retired to his own house.

There on his table, his sister's letter lay reproaching him. He took it up, ashamed rather of his negligence regarding it, and prepared himself for a disagreeable hour's communing with that crabbed-handed absent relative. . . . It may have been an hour after the Major's departure from the Colonel's house—Sir Michael was sleeping the sleep of the just; Glorvina had arranged her black ringlets in the innumerable little bits of paper, in which it was her habit to confine them; Lady O'Dowd, too, had gone to her bed in the nuptial chamber, on the ground-floor, and had tucked her musquito curtains round her fair form, when the guard at the gates of the Commanding-officer's compound, beheld Major Dobbin, in the moonlight, rushing towards the house with a swift step and a very agitated countenance, and he passed the sentinel and went up to the windows of the Colonel's bed-chamber.

"O'Dowd—Colonel!" said Dobbin, and kept up a great shouting.

"Heavens, Meejor!" said Glorvina of the curl-papers, putting out her head too, from her window.

"What is it, Dob, me boy?" said the Colonel, expecting there was a fire in the station, or that the route had come from head-quarters.

"I—I must have leave of absence. I must go to England—on the most urgent private affairs," Dobbin said.

"Good heavens, what has happened!" thought Glorvina, trembling with all the papillotes.

"I want to be off—now—to-night," Dobbin continued; and the Colonel getting up, came out to parley with him.

In the postscript of Miss Dobbin's cross-letter, the Major had just come upon a paragraph, to the following effect:—
"I drove yesterday to see your old *acquaintance,* Mrs. Osborne. The wretched place they live at, since they were bankrupts, you know—Mr. S., to judge from a *brass plate* on the door of his hut (it is little better) is a coal merchant The little boy, your godson, is certainly a fine child, though forward, and inclined to be saucy and self-willed. But we have taken notice of him as you wish it, and have introduced him to his aunt, Miss O., who was rather pleased with him. Perhaps his grandpapa, not the bankrupt one, who is almost doting, but Mr. Osborne, of Russell Square, may be induced

to relent towards the child of your friend, *his erring and self-willed son*.   And Amelia will not be ill-disposed to give him up.   The widow is *consoled,* and is about to marry a reverend gentleman, the Rev. Mr. Binny, one of the curates of Brompton.   A poor match.   But Mrs. O. is getting old, and I saw a great deal of grey in her hair—she was in very good spirits: and your little godson overate himself at our house. Mamma sends her love with that of your affectionate, Ann Dobbin."

CHAPTER IX

A Roundabout Chapter Between London and Hampshire

OUR old friends the Crawleys' family house, in Great Gaunt Street, still bore over its front the hatchment which had been placed there as a token of mourning for Sir Pitt Crawley's demise, yet this heraldic emblem was in itself a very splendid and gaudy piece of furniture, and all the rest of the mansion became more brilliant than it had ever been during the late baronet's reign. The black outer-coating of the bricks was removed, and they appeared with a cheerful, blushing face streaked with white: the old bronze lions of the knocker were gilt handsomely, the railings painted, and the dismallest house in Great Gaunt Street became the smartest in the whole quarter, before the green leaves in Hampshire had replaced those yellowing ones which were on the trees in Queen's Crawley avenue when old Sir Pitt Crawley passed under them for the last time.

A little woman, with a carriage to correspond, was perpetually seen about this mansion; an elderly spinster, accompanied by a little boy, also might be remarked coming thither daily. It was Miss Briggs and little Rawdon, whose business it was to see to the inward renovation of Sir Pitt's house, to superintend the female band engaged in stitching the blinds and hangings, to poke and rummage in the drawers and cupboards crammed with the dirty relics and congregated trumperies of a couple of generations of Lady Crawleys, and to take inventories of the china, the glass, and other properties in the closets and store-rooms.

Mrs. Rawdon Crawley was general-in-chief over these arrangements, with full orders from Sir Pitt to sell, barter, confiscate, or purchase furniture; and she enjoyed herself not a little in an occupation which gave full scope to her taste and ingenuity. The renovation of the house was determined upon when Sir Pitt came to town in November

101

to see his lawyers, and when he passed nearly a week in Curzon Street, under the roof of his affectionate brother and sister.

He had put up at an hotel at first; but, Becky, as soon as she heard of the Baronet's arrival, went off alone to greet him, and returned in an hour to Curzon Street with Sir Pitt in the carriage by her side. It was impossible sometimes to resist this artless little creature's hospitalities, so kindly were they pressed, so frankly and amiably offered. Becky seized Pitt's hand in a transport of gratitude when he agreed to come. "Thank you," she said, squeezing it, and looking into the Baronet's eyes, who blushed a good deal; "how happy this will make Rawdon!" She bustled up to Pitt's bedroom, leading on the servants, who were carrying his trunks thither. She came in herself laughing, with a coal-scuttle out of her own room.

A fire was blazing already in Sir Pitt's apartment (it was Miss Briggs's room, by the way, who was sent upstairs to sleep with the maid). "I knew I should bring you," she said, with pleasure beaming in her glance. Indeed, she was really sincerely happy at having him for a guest.

Becky made Rawdon dine out once or twice on business, while Pitt stayed with them, and the Baronet passed the happy evening alone with her and Briggs. She went downstairs to the kitchen and actually cooked little dishes for him. "Isn't it a good salmi?" she said; "I made it for you. I can make you better dishes than that: and will when you come to see me."

"Everything you do, you do well," said the Baronet, gallantly. "The salmi is excellent indeed."

"A poor man's wife," Rebecca replied, gaily, "must make herself useful, you know:" on which her brother-in-law vowed that " she was fit to be the wife of an Emperor, and that to be skillful in domestic duties was surely one of the most charming of woman's qualities." And Sir Pitt thought, with something like mortification, of Lady Jane at home, and of a certain pie which she had insisted on making, and serving to him at dinner—a most abominable pie.

Besides the salmi, which was made of Lord Steyne's pheasants from his lordship's cottage of Stillbrook, Becky gave her brother-in-law a bottle of white wine, some that Rawdon had brought with him from France, and had picked up for nothing, the little story-teller said; whereas the liquor was, in truth, some White Hermitage from the Marquis of Steyne's famous cellars, which brought fire into the Baronet's pallid cheeks and a glow into his feeble frame.

Then when he had drunk up the bottle of *petit vin blanc,* she gave him her hand and took him up to the drawing-room, and made him snug on the sofa by the fire, and let him talk as she listened with the tenderest kindly interest, sitting by him, and hemming a shirt for her dear little boy. Whenever Mrs. Rawdon wished to be particularly humble and virtuous, this little shirt used to come out of her work-box. It had got to be too small for Rawdon long before it was finished.

Well, Rebecca listened to Pitt, she talked to him, she sang to him, she coaxed him, and cuddled him, so that he found himself more and more glad every day to get back from the lawyer's at Gray's Inn, to the blazing fire in Curzon Street—a gladness in which the men of law like-wise participated, for Pitt's harangues were of the longest —and so that when he went away he felt quite a pang at departing. How pretty she looked kissing her hand to him from the carriage and waving her handkerchief when he had taken his place in the mail! She put the handker-chief to her eyes once. He pulled his sealskin cap over his, as the coach drove away, and, sinking back, he thought to himself how she respected him and how he deserved it, and how Rawdon was a foolish dull fellow who didn't half appreciate his wife: and how mum and stupid his own wife was compared to that brilliant little Becky. Becky had hinted every one of these things herself, perhaps, but so delicately and gently, that you hardly knew when or where. And, before they parted, it was agreed that the house in London should be redecorated for the next season, and that the brothers' families should meet again in the country at Christmas.

"I wish you could have got a little money out of him," Rawdon said to his wife moodily when the Baronet was gone. "I should like to give something to old Raggles, hanged if I shouldn't. It ain't right, you know, that the old fellow should be kept out of all his money. It may be inconvenient, and he might let to somebody else besides us, you know."

"Tell him," said Becky, "that as soon as Sir Pitt's affairs are settled, everybody will be paid, and give him a little something on account. Here's a cheque that Pitt left for the boy," and she took from her bag and gave her husband a paper which his brother had handed over to her, on behalf of the little son and heir of the younger branch of the Crawleys.

The truth is, she had tried personally the ground on which her husband expressed a wish that she should venture—tried it ever so delicately, and found it unsafe. Even at a hint about embarrassments, Sir Pitt Crawley was off and alarmed. And he began a long speech, explaining how straitened he himself was in money matters; how the tenants would not pay; how his father's affairs, and the expenses attendant upon the demise of the old gentleman, had involved him; how he wanted to pay off incumbrances; and how the bankers and agents were overdrawn; and Pitt Crawley ended by making a compromise with his sister-in-law, and giving her a very small sum for the benefit of her little boy.

Pitt knew how poor his brother and his brother's family must be. It could not have escaped the notice of such a cool and experienced old diplomatist, that Rawdon's family had nothing to live upon, and that houses and carriages are not to be kept for nothing. He knew very well that he was the proprietor or appropriator of the money, which, according to all proper calculation, ought to have fallen to his younger brother, and he had, we may be sure, some secret pangs of remorse within him, which warned him that he ought to perform some act of justice, or, let us say, compensation, towards these disappointed relations. A just, decent man, not without brains, who said his prayers, and knew his catechism, and did his duty outwardly through life, he could not be otherwise than aware that something was due to his brother at his hands, and that morally he was Rawdon's debtor.

But, as one reads in the columns of the *Times* newspaper every now and then, queer announcements from the Chancellor of the Exchequer, acknowledging the receipt of £50 from A. B., or £10 from W. T., as conscience money, on account of taxes due by the said A. B. or W. T., which payments the penitents beg the Right Honourable gentleman to acknowledge through the medium of the public press;—so is the Chancellor no doubt, and the reader likewise, always perfectly sure that the above-named A. B. and W. T. are only paying a very small instalment of what they really owe, and that the man who sends up a twenty-pound note has very likely hundreds or thousands more for which he ought to account. Such, at least, are my feelings, when I see A. B. or W. T.'s insufficient acts of repentance. And I have no doubt that Pitt Crawley's contrition, or kindness if you will, towards his younger brother, by whom he had so much profited, was only a very small dividend upon the capital sum in which he was indebted to Rawdon. Not everybody is willing to pay even so much. To part with money is a sacrifice beyond almost all men endowed with a sense of order. There is scarcely any man alive who does not think himself meritorious for giving his neighbour five pounds. Thriftless gives, not from a beneficent pleasure in giving, but from a lazy delight in spending. He would not deny himself one enjoyment; not his opera-stall, not his horse, not his dinner, not even the pleasure of giving Lazarus the five pounds. Thrifty, who is good, wise, just, and owes no man a penny, turns from a beggar, haggles with a hackney-coachman, or denies a poor relation, and I doubt which is the most selfish of the two. Money has only a different value in the eyes of each.

So, in a word, Pitt Crawley thought he would do something for his brother, and then thought that he would think about it some other time.

And with regard to Becky, she was not a woman who expected too much from the generosity of her neighbours, and so was quite content with all that Pitt Crawley had done for her. She was acknowledged by the head of the family. If Pitt would not give her anything, he would get something for her some day. If she got no money from her brother-in-law, she got what was as good as money—credit. Raggles was made rather easy in his mind by the spectacle of the union between the brothers, by a small payment on the spot, and by the promise of a much larger sum speedily to be assigned to him. And Rebecca told Miss Briggs, whose Christmas dividend upon the little sum lent by her, Becky paid with an air of candid joy, and as if her exchequer was brimming over with gold—Rebecca, we say, told Miss Briggs, in strict confidence, that she had conferred with Sir Pitt, who was famous as a financier, on Briggs's special behalf, as to the most profitable investment of Miss B.'s remaining capital; that Sir Pitt, after much consideration, had thought of a most safe and advantageous way in which Briggs could lay out her money; that, being especially interested in her as an attached friend of the late Miss Crawley, and of the whole family, and that long before he left town, he had recommended that she should be ready with the money at a moment's notice, so as to purchase at the most favourable opportunity the shares which Sir Pitt had in his eye. Poor Miss Briggs was very grateful for this mark of Sir Pitt's attention—it came so unsolicited, she said, for she never should have thought of removing the money from the funds—and the delicacy enhanced the kindness of the office; and she promised to see her man of business immediately, and be ready with her little cash at the proper hour.

And this worthy woman was so grateful for the kindness of Rebecca in the matter, and for that of her generous benefactor, the Colonel, that she went out and spent a great part of her year's dividend in the purchase of a black velvet coat for little Rawdon, who, by the way, was grown almost too big for black velvet now, and was of a size and age befitting him for the assumption of the virile jacket and pantaloons.

He was a fine open-faced boy, with blue eyes and waving flaxen hair, sturdy in limb, but generous and soft in heart: fondly attaching himself to all who were good to him—to the pony— to Lord Southdown, who gave him the horse—(he used to blush and glow all over when he saw that kind young nobleman)—to the groom who had charge of the

pony—to Molly, the cook, who crammed him with ghost
stories at night, and with good things from the dinner—to
Briggs, whom he plagued and laughed at—and to his
father especially, whose attachment towards the lad was
curious too to witness. Here, as he grew to be about eight
years old, his attachments may be said to have ended. The
beautiful mother-vision had faded away after a while.
During near two years she had scarcely spoken to the child.
She disliked him. He had the measles and the hooping-
cough. He bored her. One day when he was standing at
the landing-place, having crept down from the upper regions,
attracted by the sound of his mother's voice, who was singing to Lord Steyne, the drawing-room door opening suddenly,
discovered the little spy, who but a moment before had been
rapt in delight, and listening to the music.

His mother came out and struck him violently a couple
of boxes on the ear. He heard a laugh from the Marquis
in the inner room (who was amused by this free and artless
exhibition of Becky's temper), and fled down below to his
friends of the kitchen, bursting in an agony of grief.

"It is not because it hurts me," little Rawdon gasped
out—"only—only"—sobs and tears wound up the sentence
in a storm. It was the little boy's heart that was bleeding.
"Why mayn't I hear her singing? Why don't she ever
sing to me—as she does to that bald-headed man with the
large teeth?" He gasped out at various intervals these
exclamations of rage and grief. The cook looked at the
housemaid: the housemaid looked knowingly at the footman—the awful kitchen inquisition which sits in judgment
in every house, and knows everything,—sate on Rebecca at
that moment.

After this incident, the mother's dislike increased to
hatred: the consciousness that the child was in the house
was a reproach and a pain to her. His very sight annoyed
her. Fear, doubt, and resistance sprang up, too, in the
boy's own bosom. They were separated from that day of
the boxes on the ear.

Lord Steyne also heartily disliked the boy. When they
met by mischance, he made sarcastic bows or remarks to
the child, or glared at him with savage-looking eyes. Raw-

don used to stare him in the face, and double his little fists in return. He knew his enemy; and this gentleman, of all who came to the house, was the one who angered him most. One day the footman found him squaring his fists at Lord Steyne's hat in the hall. The footman told the circumstance as a good joke to Lord Steyne's coachman; that officer imparted it to Lord Steyne's gentleman, and to the servants' hall in general. And very soon afterwards, when Mrs. Rawdon Crawley made her appearance at Gaunt House, the porter who unbarred the gates, the servants of all uniforms in the hall, the functionaries in white waistcoats, who bawled out from landing to landing the names of Colonel and Mrs. Rawdon Crawley, knew about her, or fancied they did. The man who brought her refreshment and stood behind her chair, had talked her character over with the large gentleman in motley-coloured clothes at his side. Bon Dieu! it is awful, that servants' inquisition! You see a woman in a great party in a splendid saloon, surrounded by faithful admirers, distributing sparkling glances, dressed to perfection, curled, rouged, smiling and happy:—Discovery walks respectfully up to her, in the shape of a huge powdered man with large calves and a tray of ices—with Calumny (which is as fatal as truth)—behind him, in the shape of the hulking fellow carrying the wafer-biscuits. Madam, your secret will be talked over by those men at their club at the public-house to-night. Jeames will tell Chawles his notions about you over their pipes and pewter beer-pots. Some people ought to have mutes for servants in Vanity Fair—mutes who could not write. If you are guilty, tremble. That fellow behind your chair may be a Janissary with a bow-string in his plush breeches pocket. If you are not guilty, have a care of appearances: which are as ruinous as guilt.

"Was Rebecca guilty or not?" the Vehmgericht of the servants' hall had pronounced against her.

And, I shame to say, she would not have got credit had they not believed her to be guilty. It was the sight of the Marquis of Steyne's carriage-lamps at her door, contemplated by Raggles, burning in the blackness of midnight, "that kep him up," as he afterwards said; that even more than Rebecca's arts and coaxings.

And so—guiltless very likely—she was writhing and pushing onward towards what they call "a position in society," and the servants were pointing at her as lost and ruined. So you see Molly, the housemaid, of a morning, watching a spider in the door-post lay his thread and laboriously crawl up it, until, tired of the sport, she raises her broom and sweeps away the thread and the artificer.

A day or two before Christmas, Becky, her husband and her son, made ready and went to pass the holidays at the seat of their ancestors at Queen's Crawley. Becky would have liked to leave the little brat behind, and would have done so but for Lady Jane's urgent invitations to the youngster; and the symptoms of revolt and discontent which Rawdon manifested at her neglect of her son. "He's the finest boy in England," the father said, in a tone of reproach to her, "and you don't seem to care for him, Becky, as much as you do for your spaniel. He shan't bother you much: at home he will be away from you in the nursery, and he shall go outside on the coach with me."

"Where you go yourself because you want to smoke those filthy cigars," replied Mrs. Rawdon.

"I remember when you liked 'em though," answered the husband.

Becky laughed: she was almost always good-humoured. "That was when I was on my promotion, Goosey," she said. "Take Rawdon outside with you, and give him a cigar too if you like."

Rawdon did not warm his little son for the winter's journey in this way, but he and Briggs wrapped up the child in shawls and comforters, and he was hoisted respectfully on to the roof of the coach in the dark morning, under the lamps of the White Horse Cellar: and with no small delight he watched the dawn rise, and made his first journey to the place which his father still called home. It was a journey of infinite pleasure to the boy, to whom the incidents of the road afforded endless interest: his father answering to him all questions connected with it, and telling him who lived in the great white house to the right, and whom the park belonged to. His mother, inside the vehicle, with her maid and her furs, her wrappers, and her scent bottles, made such a to-do that you would have thought she never had been in a stage-coach before—much less, that she had been turned out of this very one to make room for a paying passenger on a certain journey performed some half-score years ago.

It was dark again when little Rawdon was wakened up to enter his uncle's carriage at Mudbury, and he sate and looked out of it wondering as the great iron gates flew open, and at the white trunks of the limes as they swept by, until they stopped, at length, before the light windows of the Hall, which were blazing and comfortable with Christmas welcome. The hall-door was flung open—a big fire was burning in the great old fire-place—a carpet was down over the chequered black flags—"It's the old Turkey one that used to be in the Ladies' Gallery," thought Rebecca, and the next instant was kissing Lady Jane."

She and Sir Pitt performed the same salute with great gravity: but Rawdon having been smoking, hung back rather from his sister-in-law, whose two children came up to their cousin: and, while Matilda held out her hand and kissed him, Pitt Binkie Southdown, the son and heir, stood aloof rather, and examined him as a little dog does a big dog.

Then the kind hostess conducted her guests to the snug apartments blazing with cheerful fires. Then the young ladies came and knocked at Mrs. Rawdon's door, under the pretence that they were desirous to be useful, but in reality to have the pleasure of inspecting the contents of her band and bonnet-boxes, and her dresses which, though black, were of the newest London fashion. And they told her how much the Hall was changed for the better, and how old Lady Southdown was gone, and how Pitt was taking his station in the county, as became a Crawley in fact. Then the great dinner-bell having rung, the family assembled at dinner, at which meal Rawdon Junior was placed by his aunt, the good-natured lady of the house: Sir Pitt being uncommonly attentive to his sister-in-law at his own right hand.

Little Rawdon exhibited a fine appetite, and showed a gentleman-like behaviour.

"I like to dine here," he said to his aunt when he had completed his meal, at the conclusion of which, and after a decent grace by Sir Pitt, the youngest son and heir was introduced, and was perched on a high chair by the Baronet's side, while the daughter took possession of the place and the little wine-glass prepared for her near her mother. "I like to dine here," said Rawdon Minor, looking up at his relation's kind face.

"Why?" said the good Lady Jane.

"I dine in the kitchen when I am at home," replied Rawdon Minor, "or else with Briggs." But Becky was so engaged with the Baronet, her host, pouring out a flood of compliments and delights and raptures, and admiring young Pitt Binkie, whom she declared to be the most beautiful, intelligent, noble-looking little creature, and so like his father, that she did not hear the remarks of her own flesh and blood at the other end of the broad shining table.

As a guest, and it being the first night of his arrival, Rawdon the Second was allowed to sit up until the hour when tea being over, and a great gilt book being laid on the table before Sir Pitt, all the domestics of the family streamed in, and Sir Pitt read prayers. It was the first time the poor little boy had ever witnessed or heard of such a ceremonial.

The house had been much improved even since the Baronet's brief reign, and was pronounced by Becky to be perfect, charming, delightful, when she surveyed it in his company. As for little Rawdon, who examined it with the children for his guides, it seemed to him a perfect palace of enchantment and wonder. There were long galleries, and ancient state bed-rooms, there were pictures and old China, and armour. There were the rooms in which grandpapa died, and by which the children walked with terrified looks.

"Who was grandpapa?" he asked; and they told him how he used to be very old, and used to be wheeled about in a garden-chair, and they showed him the garden-chair one day rotting in the out-house in which it had lain since the old gentleman had been wheeled away yonder to the church, of which the spire was glittering over the park elms.

The brothers had good occupation for several mornings in examining the improvements which had been effected by Sir Pitt's genius and economy. And as they walked or rode, and looked at them, they could talk without too much boring each other. And Pitt took care to tell Rawdon what a heavy outlay of money these improvements had occasioned; and that a man of landed and funded property was often very hard pressed for twenty pounds. "There is that new lodge gate," said Pitt, pointing to it humbly with the bamboo cane, "I can no more pay for it before the dividends in January than I can fly."

"I can lend you, Pitt, till then," Rawdon answered rather ruefully; and they went in and looked at the restored lodge, where the family arms were just new scraped in stone; and where old Mrs. Lock, for the first time these many long years, had tight doors, sound roofs, and whole windows.

CHAPTER X

SIR PITT CRAWLEY had done more than repair fences and restore dilapidated lodges on the Queen's Crawley estate. Like a wise man he had set to work to rebuild the injured popularity of his house, and stop up the gaps and ruins in which his name had been left by his disreputable and thriftless old predecessor. He was elected for the borough speedily after his father's demise; a magistrate, a member of parliament, a county magnate and representative of an ancient family, he made it his duty to show himself before the Hampshire public, subscribed handsomely to the county charities, called assiduously upon all the county folk, and laid himself out in a word to take that position in Hampshire, and in the Empire afterwards, to which he thought his prodigious talents justly entitled him. Lady Jane was instructed to be friendly with the Fuddlestones, and the Wapshots, and the other famous baronets, their neighbours. Their carriages might frequently be seen in the Queen's Crawley avenue now; they dined pretty frequently at the Hall (where the cookery was so good, that it was clear Lady Jane very seldom had a hand in it), and in return Pitt and his wife most energetically dined out in all sorts of weather, and at all sorts of distances. For though Pitt did not care for joviality, being a frigid man of poor health and appetite, yet he considered that to be hospitable and condescending was quite incumbent on his station, and every time that he got a headache from too long and after-dinner sitting, he felt that he was a martyr to duty. He talked about crops, corn-laws, politics, with the best country gentlemen. He (who had been formerly inclined to be a sad freethinker on these points) entered into poaching and game preserving with ardour. He didn't hunt: he wasn't a hunting man; he was a man of books and peaceful

113

habits: but he thought that the breed of horses must be kept up in the country, and that the breed of foxes must therefore be looked to, and for his part, if his friend, Sir Huddlestone Fuddlestone, liked to draw his country, and meet as of old the F. hounds used to do at Queen's Crawley, he should be happy to see him there, and the gentlemen of the Fuddlestone hunt. And to Lady Southdown's dismay too he became more orthodox in his tendencies every day: gave up preaching in public and attending meeting-houses; went stoutly to Church; called on the Bishop, and all the Clergy at Winchester: and made no objection when the Venerable Archdeacon Trumper asked for a game of whist. What pangs must have been those of Lady Southdown, and what an utter cast-away she must have thought her son-in-law for permitting such a godless diversion! and when, on the return of the family from an oratorio at Winchester, the Baronet announced to the young ladies that he should next year very probably take them to the "county balls," they worshipped him for his kindness. Lady Jane was only too obedient, and perhaps glad herself to go. The Dowager wrote off the direst descriptions of her daughter's worldly behaviour to the authoress of the "Washerwoman of Finchley Common" at the Cape; and her house in Brighton being about this time unoccupied, returned to that watering-place, her absence being not very much deplored by her children. We may suppose, too, that Rebecca, on paying a second visit to Queen's Crawley, did not feel particularly grieved at the absence of the lady of the medicine chest; though she wrote a Christmas letter to her Ladyship, in which she respectfully recalled herself to Lady Southdown's recollection, spoke with gratitude of the delight which her Ladyship's conversation had given her on the former visit, dilated on the kindness with which her Ladyship had treated her in sickness, and declared that everything at Queen's Crawley reminded her of her absent friend.

A great part of the altered demeanour and popularity of Sir Pitt Crawley might have been traced to the counsels of that astute little lady of Curzon Street. "*You* remain a baronet—you consent to be a mere country gentleman," she said to him, while he had been her guest in London. "No,

Sir Pitt Crawley, I know you better. I know your talents
and your ambition. You fancy you hide them both: but
you can conceal neither from me. I showed Lord Steyne
your pamphlet on malt. He was familiar with it: and said
it was in the opinion of the whole Cabinet the most masterly
thing that had appeared on the subject. The Ministry has
its eye upon you, and I know what you want. You want to
distinguish yourself in Parliament; every one says you are
the finest speaker in England (for your speeches at Oxford
are still remembered). You want to be Member for the
County, where, with your own vote and your borough at
your back, you can command anything. And you want to
be Baron Crawley of Queen's Crawley, and will be before
you die. I saw it all. I could read your heart, Sir Pitt.
If I had a husband who possessed your intellect as he does
your name, I sometimes think I should not be unworthy of
him—but—but I am your kinswoman now," she added with
a laugh. "Poor little penniless I have got a little interest—
and who knows, perhaps the mouse may be able to aid the
lion."

Pitt Crawley was amazed and enraptured with her speech.
"How that woman comprehends me!" he said. "I never
could get Jane to read three pages of the malt-pamphlet.
She has no idea that I have commanding talents or secret
ambition. So they remember my speaking at Oxford, do
they? The rascals! now that I represent my borough and
may sit for the county, they begin to recollect me! Why,
Lord Steyne cut me at the levee last year: they are beginning to find out that Pitt Crawley is some one at last. Yes,
the man was always the same whom these people neglected:
it was only the opportunity that was wanting, and I will
show them now that I can speak and act as well as write.
Achilles did not declare himself until they gave him the
sword. I hold it now, and the world shall yet hear of Pitt
Crawley."

Therefore it was that this roguish diplomatist had grown
so hospitable; that he was so civil to oratorios and hospitals;
so kind to Deans and Chapters; so generous in giving and
accepting dinners; so uncommonly gracious to farmers on
market-days; and so much interested about county business;

and that the Christmas at the Hall was the gayest which
had been known there for many a long day.

On Christmas Day a great family gathering took place.
All the Crawleys from the Rectory came to dine. Rebecca
was as frank and fond of Mrs. Bute, as if the other had
never been her enemy; she was affectionately interested in
the dear girls, and surprised at the progress which they had
made in music since her time: and insisted upon encoring
one of the duets out of the great song-books which Jim,
grumbling, had been forced to bring under his arm from
the Rectory. Mrs. Bute, perforce, was obliged to adopt a
decent demeanour towards the little adventuress—of course
being free to discourse with her daughters afterwards about
the absurd respect with which Sir Pitt treated his sister-in-
law. But Jim, who had sate next to her at dinner, declared she was a trump: and one and all of the Rector's
family agreed that the little Rawdon was a fine boy.
They respected a possible baronet in the boy, between
whom and the title there was only the little sickly pale Pitt
Binkie.

The children were very good friends. Pitt Binkie was too
little a dog for such a big dog as Rawdon to play with: and
Matilda being only a girl, of course not fit companion for a
young gentleman who was near eight years old, and going
into jackets very soon. He took the command of this small
party at once—the little girl and the little boy following
him about with great reverence at such times as he condescended to sport with them. His happiness and pleasure
in the country were extreme. The kitchen garden pleased
him hugely, the flowers moderately, but the pigeons and the
poultry, and the stables when he was allowed to visit them,
were delightful objects to him. He resisted being kissed by
the Misses Crawley: but he allowed Lady Jane sometimes to
embrace him: and it was by her side that he liked to sit
when, the signal to retire to the drawing-room being given,
the ladies left the gentlemen to their claret—by her side
rather than by his mother. For Rebecca seeing that tenderness was the fashion, called Rawdon to her one evening, and
stooped down and kissed him in the presence of all the
ladies.

He looked her full in the face after the operation, trembling and turning very red, as his wont was when moved. "You never kiss me at home, Mamma," he said; at which there was a general silence and consternation, and a by no means pleasant look in Becky's eyes.

Rawdon was fond of his sister-in-law, for her regard for his son. Lady Jane and Becky did not get on *quite* so well at this visit as on occasion of the former one, when the Colonel's wife was bent upon pleasing. Those two speeches of the child struck rather a chill. Perhaps Sir Pitt was rather too attentive to her.

But Rawdon, as became his age and size, was fonder of the society of the men than of the women; and never wearied of accompanying his sire to the stables, whither the Colonel retired to smoke his cigar—Jim, the Rector's son, sometimes joining his cousin in that and other amusements. He and the Baronet's keeper were very close friends, their mutual taste for "dawgs" bringing them much together. On one day, Mr. James, the Colonel, and Horn, the keeper, went and shot pheasants, taking little Rawdon with them. On another most blissful morning, these four gentlemen partook of the amusement of rat-hunting in a barn, than which sport Rawdon as yet had never seen anything more noble.

They stopped up the ends of certain drains in the barn, into the other openings of which ferrets were inserted; and then stood silently aloof, with uplifted stakes in their hands, and an anxious little terrier (Mr. James's celebrated "dawg" Forceps, indeed,) scarcely breathing from excitement, listening motionless on three legs, to the faint squeaking of the rats below. Desperately bold at last, the persecuted animals bolted above-ground: the terrier accounted for one, the keeper for another; Rawdon, from flurry and excitement, missed his rat, but on the other hand he half-murdered a ferret.

But the greatest day of all was that on which Sir Huddlestone Fuddlestone's hounds met upon the lawn at Queen's Crawley.

That was a famous sight for little Rawdon. At half-past ten, Tom Moody, Sir Huddlestone Fuddlestone's huntsman,

was seen trotting up the avenue, followed by the noble pack
of hounds in a compact body—the rear being brought up
by the two whips clad in stained scarlet frocks—light hard-
featured lads on well-bred lean horses, possessing marvellous
dexterity in casting the points of their long heavy whips at
the thinnest part of any dog's skin who dares to straggle
from the main body, or to take the slightest notice, or even
so much as wink, at the hares and rabbits starting under
their noses.

Next comes boy Jack, Tom Moody's son, who weighs five
stone, measures eight-and-forty inches, and will never be any
bigger. He is perched on a large raw-boned hunter, half-
covered by a capacious saddle. This animal is Sir Huddlestone Fuddlestone's favourite horse—the Nob. Other
horses, ridden by other small boys, arrive from time to
time, awaiting their masters, who will come cantering on
anon.

Tom Moody rides up to the door of the Hall, where he
is welcomed by the butler, who offers him drink, which he
declines. He and his pack then draw off into a sheltered
corner of the lawn, where the dogs roll on the grass, and
play or growl angrily at one another, ever and anon breaking out into furious fight speedily to be quelled by Tom's
voice, unmatched at rating, or the snaky thongs of the
whips.

Many young gentlemen canter up on thoroughbred hacks,
spatter-dashed to the knee, and enter the house to drink
cherry-brandy and pay their respects to the ladies, or, more
modest and sportsman-like, divest themselves of their mud-
boots, exchange their hacks for their hunters, and warm
their blood by a preliminary gallop round the lawn. Then
they collect round the pack in the corner, and talk with
Tom Moody of past sport, and the merits of Sniveller and
Diamond, and of the state of the country and of the wretched
breed of foxes.

Sir Huddlestone presently appears mounted on a clever
cob, and rides up to the Hall, where he enters and does the
civil thing by the ladies, after which, being a man of few
words, he proceeds to business. The hounds are drawn up
to the hall-door and little Rawdon descends amongst them,

excited yet half alarmed by the caresses which they bestow
upon him, at the thumps he receives from their waving
tails, and at their canine bickerings, scarcely restrained by
Tom Moody's tongue and lash.

Meanwhile, Sir Huddlestone has hoisted himself un-
wieldily on the Nob: "Let's try Sowster's Spinney, Tom,"
says the Baronet, "Farmer Mangle tells me there are two
foxes in it." Tom blows his horn and trots off, followed
by the pack, by the whips, by the young gents from
Winchester, by the farmers of the neighborhood, by the
labourers of the parish on foot, with whom the day is a
great holiday; Sir Huddlestone bringing up the rear with
Colonel Crawley, and the whole *cortége* disappears down
the avenue.

The Reverend Bute Crawley (who has been too modest
to appear at the public meet before his nephew's windows),
and whom Tom Moody remembers forty years back a slender
divine riding the wildest horses, jumping the widest brooks,
and larking over the newest gates in the country,—his
Reverence, we say, happens to trot out from the Rectory
Lane on his powerful black horse, just as Sir Huddlestone
passes; he joins the worthy baronet. Hounds and horsemen
disappear, and little Rawdon remains on the door-steps,
wondering and happy.

During the progress of this memorable holiday, little
Rawdon, if he had got no special liking for his uncle, always
awful and cold, and locked up in his study, plunged in
justice-business and surrounded by bailiffs and farmers—has
gained the good graces of his married and maiden aunts,
of the two little folks of the Hall, and of Jim of the Rectory,
whom Sir Pitt is encouraging to pay his addresses to one of
the young ladies, with an understanding doubtless that he
shall be presented to the living when it shall be vacated by
his fox-hunting old sire. Jim has given up that sport
himself, and confines himself to a little harmless duck or
snipe-shooting, or a little quiet trifling with the rats during
the Christmas holidays, after which he will return to the
University, and try and not be plucked, once more. He has
already eschewed green coats, red neckcloths, and other
worldly ornaments, and is preparing himself for a change

in his condition. In this cheap and thrifty way Sir Pitt tries to pay off his debt to his family.

Also before this merry Christmas was over, the Baronet had screwed up courage enough to give his brother another draft on his bankers, and for no less a sum than a hundred pounds, an act which caused Sir Pitt cruel pangs at first, but which made him glow afterwards to think himself one of the most generous of men. Rawdon and his son went away with the utmost heaviness of heart. Becky and the ladies parted with some alacrity, however: and our friend returned to London to commence those avocations with which we find her occupied when this chapter begins. Under her care the Crawley House in Great Gaunt Street was quite rejuvenescent, and ready for the reception of Sir Pitt and his family, when the Baronet came to London to attend his duties in Parliament, and to assume that position in the country for which his vast genius fitted him.

For the first session, this profound dissembler hid his projects and never opened his lips but to present a petition from Mudbury. But he attended assiduously in his place, and learned thoroughly the routine and business of the House. At home he gave himself up to the perusal of Blue Books, to the alarm and wonder of Lady Jane, who thought he was killing himself by late hours and intense application. And he made acquaintance with the ministers, and the chiefs of his party, determining to rank as one of them before many years were over.

Lady Jane's sweetness and kindness had inspired Rebecca with such a contempt for her ladyship as the little woman found no small difficulty in concealing. That sort of goodness and simplicity which Lady Jane possessed, annoyed our friend Becky, and it was impossible for her at times not to show, or to let the other divine her scorn. Her presence, too, rendered Lady Jane uneasy. Her husband talked constantly with Becky. Signs of intelligence seemed to pass between them: and Pitt spoke with her on subjects on which he never thought of discoursing with Lady Jane. The latter did not understand them to be sure, but it was mortifying to remain silent; still more mortifying to know that you had nothing to say, and hear that little audacious Mrs. Rawdon dashing on from subject to subject, with a word for every man, and a joke always pat; and to sit in one's own house alone, by the fireside, and watching all the men round your rival.

In the country, when Lady Jane was telling stories to the children, who clustered about her knees (little Rawdon into the bargain, who was very fond of her)—and Becky came into the room, sneering with green scornful eyes, poor Lady Jane grew silent under those baleful glances. Her simple little fancies shrank away tremulously, as fairies in the story-books, before a superior bad angel. She could not go on, although Rebecca, with the smallest inflection of sarcasm in her voice, besought her to continue that charming story. And on her side gentle thoughts and simple pleasures were odious to Mrs. Becky; they discorded with her; she hated people for liking them; she spurned children and children-lovers. "I have no taste for bread and butter," she would say, when caricaturing Lady Jane and her ways to my Lord Steyne.

"No more has a certain person for holy water," his lordship replied with a bow and a grin, and a great jarring laugh afterwards.

So these two ladies did not see much of each other except upon those occasions, when the younger brother's wife, having an object to gain from the other, frequented her. They my-loved and my-deared each other assiduously, but kept apart generally: whereas Sir Pitt, in the midst of his multiplied avocations, found daily time to see his sister-in-law.

On the occasion of his first Speaker's dinner, Sir Pitt took the opportunity of appearing before his sister-in-law in his uniform—that old diplomatic suit which he had worn when attaché to the Pumpernickel legation.

Becky complimented him upon that dress, and admired him almost as much as his own wife and children, to whom he displayed himself before he set out. She said that it was only the thoroughbred gentleman who could wear the Court suit with advantage: it was only your men of ancient race whom the *culotte courte* became. Pitt looked down with complacency at his legs, which had not, in truth, much more symmetry or swell than the lean Court sword which dangled by his side: looked down at his legs, and thought in his heart that he was killing.

When he was gone, Mrs. Becky made a caricature of his figure, which she showed to Lord Steyne when he arrived. His lordship carried off the sketch, delighted with the accuracy of the resemblance. He had done Sir Pitt Crawley the honour to meet him at Mrs. Becky's house, and had been most gracious to the new Baronet and member. Pitt was struck too by the deference with which the great Peer treated his sister-in-law, by her ease and sprightliness in the conversation, and by the delight with which the other men of the party listened to her talk. Lord Steyne made no doubt but that the Baronet had only commenced his career in public life, and expected rather anxiously to hear him as an orator; as they were neighbours (for Great Gaunt Street leads into Gaunt Square, whereof Gaunt House, as everybody knows, forms one side) my lord hoped that as soon as Lady Steyne arrived in London she would have the honour of making the acquaintance of Lady Crawley. He left a card upon his neighbour in the course of a day or two; having never thought fit to notice his predecessor, though they had lived near each other for near a century past.

In the midst of these intrigues and fine parties and wise and brilliant personages Rawdon felt himself more and more isolated every day. He was allowed to go to the club more: to dine abroad with bachelor friends: to come and go when he liked, without any questions being asked. And he and Rawdon the younger many a time would walk to Gaunt Street, and sit with the lady and the children there while Sir Pitt was closeted with Rebecca, on his way to the House, or on his return from it.

The ex-Colonel would sit for hours in his brother's house very silent, and thinking and doing as little as possible. He was glad to be employed of an errand: to go and make inquiries about a horse or a servant: or to carve the roast mutton for the dinner of the children. He was beat and cowed into laziness and submission. Delilah had imprisoned him and cut his hair off, too. The bold and reckless young blood of ten years back was subjugated, and was turned into a torpid, submissive, middle-aged, stout gentleman.

And poor Lady Jane was aware that Rebecca had captivated her husband: although she and Mrs. Rawdon my-deared and my-loved each other every day they met.

CHAPTER XI

Struggles and Trials

OUR friends at Brompton were meanwhile passing their Christmas after their fashion, and in a manner by no means too cheerful.

Out of the hundred pounds a year, which was about the amount of her income, the widow Osborne had been in the habit of giving up nearly three-fourths to her father and mother, for the expenses of herself and her little boy. With £120 more, supplied by Jos, this family of four people, attended by a single Irish servant who also did for Clapp and his wife, might manage to live in decent comfort through the year, and hold up their heads yet, and be able to give a friend a dish of tea still, after the storms and disappointments of their early life. Sedley still maintained his ascendency over the family of Mr. Clapp, his ex-clerk. Clapp remembered the time when, sitting on the edge of the chair, he tossed off a bumper to the health of "Mrs. S——, Miss Emmy, and Mr. Joseph in India," at the merchant's rich table in Russell Square. Time magnified the splendour of those recollections in the honest clerk's bosom. Whenever he came up from the kitchen-parlour to the drawing-room, and partook of tea or gin-and-water with Mr. Sedley, he would say, "This was not what you was accustomed to once, sir," and as gravely and reverentially drink the health of the ladies as he had done in the days of their utmost prosperity. He thought Miss 'Melia's playing the divinest music ever performed, and her the finest lady. He never would sit down before Sedley at the club even, nor would he have that gentleman's character abused by any member of the society. He had seen the first men in London shaking hands with Mr. S——; he said, "He'd known him in times when Rothschild might be seen on 'Change with him any day, and he owed him personally everythink."

Clapp, with the best of characters and handwritings, had been able very soon after his master's disaster to find other employment for himself. "Such a little fish as me can swim in any bucket," he used to remark, and a member of the house from which old Sedley had seceded was very glad to make use of Mr. Clapp's services, and to reward them with a comfortable salary. In fine, all Sedley's wealthy friends had dropped off one by one, and this poor ex-dependent still remained faithfully attached to him.

Out of the small residue of her income, which Amelia kept back for herself, the widow had need of all the thrift and care possible in order to enable her to keep her darling boy dressed in such a manner as became George Osborne's son, and to defray the expenses of the little school to which, after much misgiving and reluctance, and many secret pangs and fears on her own part, she had been induced to send the lad. She had sate up of nights conning lessons and spelling over crabbed grammars and geography books in order to teach them to Georgy. She had worked even at the Latin accidence, fondly hoping that she might be capable of instructing him in that language. To part with him all day: to send him out to the mercy of a schoolmaster's cane and his schoolfellows' roughness, was almost like weaning him over again, to that weak mother, so tremulous and full of sensibility. He, for his part, rushed off to school with the utmost happiness. He was longing for the change. That childish gladness wounded his mother, who was herself so grieved to part with him. She would rather have had him more sorry, she thought: and then was deeply repentant within herself, for daring to be so selfish as to wish her own son to be unhappy.

Georgy made great progress in the school, which was kept by a friend of his mother's constant admirer, the Rev. Mr. Binny. He brought home numberless prizes and testimonials of ability. He told his mother countless stories every night about his school-companions: and what a fine fellow Lyons was, and what a sneak Sniffin was; and how Steel's father actually supplied the meat for the establishment, whereas Golding's mother came in a carriage to fetch him every Saturday: and how Neat had straps to his trow-

sers—might he have straps?—and how Bull Major was so
strong (though only in Eutropius) that it was believed he
could lick the Usher, Mr. Ward, himself. So Amelia
learned to know every one of the boys in that school as
well as Georgy himself: and of nights she used to help
him in his exercises and puzzle her little head over his
lessons as eagerly as if she was herself going in the morning into the presence of the master. Once, after a certain
combat with Master Smith, George came home to his
mother with a black eye, and bragged prodigiously to his
parent and his delighted old grandfather about his valour
in the fight, in which, if the truth was known, he did not
behave with particular heroism, and in which he decidedly
had the worst. But Amelia has never forgiven that Smith
to this day, though he is now a peaceful apothecary near
Leicester Square.

In these quiet labours and harmless cares the gentle
widow's life was passing away, a silver hair or two marking the progress of time on her head, and a line deepening
ever so little on her fair forehead. She used to smile at
these marks of time. "What matters it," she asked, "for
an old woman like me?" All she hoped for was to live to
see her son great, famous, and glorious, as he deserved to
be. She kept his copybooks, his drawings, and compositions, and showed them about in her little circle, as if they
were miracles of genius. She confided some of these specimens to Miss Dobbin; to show them to Miss Osborne,
George's aunt, to show them to Mr. Osborne himself—to
make that old man repent of his cruelty and ill-feeling
towards him who was gone. All her husband's faults and
foibles she had buried in the grave with him: she only remembered the lover, who had married her at all sacrifices;
the noble husband so brave and beautiful, in whose arms
she had hung on the morning when he had gone away to
fight, and die gloriously for his king. From heaven the
hero must be smiling down upon that paragon of a boy
whom he had left to comfort and console her.

We have seen how one of George's grandfathers (Mr.
Osborne), in his easy-chair in Russell Square, daily grew
more violent and moody, and how his daughter, with her

fine carriage, and her fine horses, and her name on half the
public charity-lists of the town, was a lonely, miserable,
persecuted old maid. She thought again and again of the
beautiful little boy, her brother's son, whom she had seen.
She longed to be allowed to drive in the fine carriage to the
house in which he lived; and she used to look out day after
day as she took her solitary drive in the Park, in hopes that
she might see him. Her sister, the banker's lady, occasionally condescended to pay her old home and companion
a visit in Russell Square. She brought a couple of sickly
children attended by a prim nurse, and in a faint genteel
giggling tone cackled to her sister about her fine acquaintance, and how her little Frederick was the image of Lord
Claud Lollypop, and her sweet Maria had been noticed by
the Baroness as they were driving in their donkey-chaise
at Roehampton. She urged her to make her papa do something for the darlings. Frederick she had determined
should go into the Guards; and if they made an elder son
of him (and Mr. Bullock was positively ruining and pinch-
ing himself to death to buy land) how was the darling girl
to be provided for? "I expect *you*, dear," Mrs. Bullock
would say, "for of course my share of our Papa's property
must go to the head of the house, you know. Dear Rhoda
McMull will disengage the whole of the Castletoddy property as soon as poor dear Lord Castletoddy dies, who is
quite epileptic; and little Macduff McMull will be Viscount
Castletoddy. Both the Mr. Bludyers of Mincing Lane have
settled their fortunes on Fanny Bludyer's little boy. My
darling Frederick must positively be an eldest son; and—
and do ask Papa to bring us back his account in Lombard
Street, will you, dear? It doesn't look well, his going to
Stumpy and Rowdy's." After which kind of speeches, in
which fashion and the main chance were blended together,
and after a kiss, which was like the contact of an oyster—
Mrs. Frederick Bullock would gather her starched nurslings,
and simper back into her carriage.

Every visit which this leader of *ton* paid to her family
was more unlucky for her. Her father paid more money
into Stumpy and Rowdy's. Her patronage became more
and more insufferable. The poor widow in the little cot-

tage at Brompton, guarding her treasure there, little knew how eagerly some people coveted it.

On that night when Jane Osborne had told her father that she had seen his grandson, the old man had made her no reply: but he had shown no anger—and had bade her good-night on going himself to his room in rather a kindly voice. And he must have meditated on what she said, and have made some inquiries of the Dobbin family regarding her visit; for a fortnight after it took place, he asked her where was her little French watch and chain she used to wear?

"I bought it with my money, sir," she said in a great fright.

"Go and order another like it, or a better if you can get it," said the old gentleman, and lapsed again into silence.

Of late the Misses Dobbin more than once repeated their entreaties to Amelia, to allow George to visit them. His aunt had shown her inclination; perhaps his grandfather himself, they hinted, might be disposed to be reconciled to him. Surely, Amelia could not refuse such advantageous chances for the boy. Nor could she: but she acceded to their overtures with a very heavy and suspicious heart, was always uneasy during the child's absence from her, and welcomed him back as if he was rescued out of some danger. He brought back money and toys, at which the widow looked with alarm and jealousy: she asked him always if he had seen any gentleman—"Only old Sir William, who drove him about in the four-wheeled chaise, and Mr. Dobbin, who arrived on the beautiful bay horse in the afternoon— in the green coat and pink neck-cloth, with the gold-headed whip, who promised to show him the Tower of London, and take him out with the Surrey hounds." At last, he said "There *was* an old gentleman, with thick eye-brows and a broad hat, and large chain and seals." He came one day as the coachman was lunging Georgy round the lawn on the gray pony. "He looked at me very much. He shook very much. I said 'My name is Norval' after dinner. My aunt began to cry. She is always crying." Such was George's report on that night.

Then Amelia knew that the boy had seen his grand-father: and looked out feverishly for a proposal which she was sure would follow, and which came, in fact, in a few days afterwards. Mr. Osborne formally offered to take the boy, and make him heir to the fortune which he had intended that his father should inherit. He would make Mrs. George Osborne an allowance, such as to assure her a decent competency. If Mrs. George Osborne proposed to marry again, as Mr. O. heard was her intention, he would not withdraw that allowance. But it must be understood, that the child would live entirely with his grandfather in Russell Square, or at whatever other place Mr. O. should select; and that he would be occasionally permitted to see Mrs. George Osborne at her own residence. This message was brought or read in a letter one day, when her mother was from home, and her father absent as usual in the City.

She was never seen angry but twice or thrice in her life, and it was in one of these moods that Mr. Osborne's attorney had the fortune to behold her. She rose up trembling and flushing very much as soon as, after reading the letter, Mr. Poe handed it to her, and she tore the paper into a hundred fragments, which she trod on. "I marry again!— I take money to part from my child! Who dares insult me by proposing such a thing? Tell Mr. Osborne it is a cowardly letter, sir—a cowardly letter—I will not answer it. I wish you good morning, sir—and she bowed me out of the room like a tragedy Queen," said the lawyer who told the story.

Her parents never remarked her agitation on that day, and she never told them of the interview. They had their own affairs to interest them, affairs which deeply interested this innocent and unconscious lady. The old gentleman, her father, was always dabbling in speculation. We have seen how the Wine Company and the Coal Company had failed him. But, prowling about the City always eagerly and restlessly still, he lighted upon some other scheme, of which he thought so well that he embarked in it in spite of the remonstrances of Mr. Clapp, to whom indeed he never dared to tell how far he had engaged himself in it. And as it was always Mr. Sedley's maxim not to talk about

money matters before women, they had no inkling of the
misfortunes that were in store for them until the unhappy
old gentleman was forced to make gradual confessions.

The bills of the little household, which had been settled
weekly, first fell into arrear. The remittances had not arrived from India, Mr. Sedley told his wife with a disturbed
face. As she had paid her bills very regularly hitherto,
one or two of the tradesmen to whom the poor lady was
obliged to go round asking for time were very angry
at a delay to which they were perfectly used from more
irregular customers. Emmy's contribution, paid over cheerfully without any questions, kept the little company in
half rations however. And the first six months passed
away pretty easily: old Sedley still keeping up with the
notion that his shares must rise and that all would be
well.

No sixty pounds, however, came to help the household
at the end of the half year; and it fell deeper and deeper
into trouble—Mrs. Sedley, who was growing infirm and
was much shaken, remained silent or wept a great deal
with Mrs. Clapp in the kitchen. The butcher was particularly surly: the grocer insolent: once or twice little Georgy
had grumbled about the dinners: and Amelia, who still
would have been satisfied with a slice of bread for her own
dinner, could not but perceive that her son was neglected,
and purchased little things out of her private purse to keep
the boy in health.

At last they told her, or told her such a garbled story
as people in difficulties tell. One day, her own money
having been received, and Amelia about to pay it over:
she who had kept an account of the moneys expended by
her, proposed to keep a certain portion back out of her
dividend, having contracted engagements for a new suit
for Georgy.

Then it came out that Jos's remittances were not paid;
that the house was in difficulties, which Amelia ought to
have seen before, her mother said, but she cared for nothing or nobody except Georgy. At this she passed all her
money across the table, without a word, to her mother, and
returned to her room to cry her eyes out. She had a great

access of sensibility too that day, when obliged to go and
countermand the clothes, the darling clothes on which she
had set her heart for Christmas Day, and the cut and fashion
of which she had arranged in many conversations with a
small milliner, her friend.

Hardest of all, she had to break the matter to Georgy,
who made a loud outcry. Everybody had new clothes at
Christmas. The others would laugh at him. He *would*
have new clothes. She had promised them to him. The
poor widow had only kisses to give him. She darned the
old suit in tears. She cast about among her little ornaments to see if she could sell anything to procure the desired
novelties. There was her India shawl that Dobbin had
sent her. She remembered in former days going with her
mother to a fine India shop on Ludgate Hill, where the
ladies had all sorts of dealings and bargains in these articles.
Her cheeks flushed and her eyes shone with pleasure as
she thought of this resource, and she kissed away George
to school in the morning, smiling brightly after him. The
boy felt that there was good news in her look.

Packing up her shawl in a handkerchief (another of the
gifts of the good Major), she hid them under her cloak, and
walked flushed and eager all the way to Ludgate Hill,
tripping along by the Park wall, and running over the
crossing, so that many a man turned as she hurried by him,
and looked after her rosy pretty face. She calculated how
she should spend the proceeds of her shawl: how, besides
the clothes, she would buy the books that he longed for,
and pay his half-year's schooling; and how she would buy
a cloak for her father instead of that old great-coat which
he wore. She was not mistaken as to the value of the
Major's gift. It was a very fine and beautiful web: and
the merchant made a very good bargain when he gave her
twenty guineas for her shawl.

She ran on amazed and flurried with her riches to Dar-
ton's shop in St. Paul's Churchyard, and there purchased
the "Parents' Assistant," and the "Sandford and Merton"
Georgy longed for, and got into the coach there with her
parcel, and went home exulting. And she pleased herself
by writing in the fly-leaf in her neatest little hand, "George

Osborne, A Christmas gift from his affectionate mother."
The books are extant to this day, with the fair delicate
superscription.

She was going from her own room with the books in her
hand to place them on George's table, where he might find
them on his return from school; when in the passage, she
and her mother met. The gilt bindings of the seven handsome little volumes caught the old lady's eye.

"What are those?" she said.

"Some books for Georgy," Amelia replied—"I—I promised
them to him at Christmas."

"Books!" cried the elder lady, indignantly. "Books, when
the whole house wants bread! Books, when to keep you
and your son in luxury, and your dear father out of gaol,
I've sold every trinket I had, the India shawl from my back—
even down to the very spoons, that our tradesmen mightn't
insult us, and that Mr. Clapp, which indeed he is justly
entitled, being not a hard landlord, and a civil man, and a
father, might have his rent. O Amelia! you break my
heart with your books and that boy of yours, whom you
are ruining, though part with him you will not. O Amelia,
may God send you a more dutiful child than I have had!
There's Jos deserts his father in his old age: and there's
George, who might be provided for, and who might be rich,
going to school like a lord, with a gold watch and chain
round his neck—while my dear, dear old man is without a
sh—shilling." Hysteric sobs and cries ended Mrs. Sedley's
speech—it echoed through every room in the small house,
whereof the other female inmates heard every word of the
colloquy.

"O mother, mother!" cried poor Amelia in reply. "You
told me nothing—I—I promised him the books. I—I only
sold my shawl this morning. Take the money—take everything"—and with quivering hands she took out her silver,
and her sovereigns—her precious golden sovereigns, which
she thrust into the hands of her mother, whence they overflowed and tumbled, rolling down the stairs.

And then she went into her room, and sank down in
despair and utter misery. She saw it all now. Her selfishness was sacrificing the boy. But for her he might have

wealth, station, education, and his father's place, which the
elder George had forfeited for her sake.   She had but to
speak the words, and her father was restored to competency:
and the boy raised to fortune.   O what a conviction it was
to that tender and stricken heart!

CHAPTER XII

GAUNT HOUSE

ALL the world knows that Lord Steyne's town palace stands in Gaunt Square, out of which Great Gaunt Street leads, whither we first conducted Rebecca, in the time of the departed Sir Pitt Crawley. Peering over the railings and through the black trees into the garden of the Square, you see a few miserable governesses with wan-faced pupils wandering round and round it, and round the dreary grass-plot in the centre of which rises the statue of Lord Gaunt, who fought at Minden, in a three-tailed wig, and otherwise habited like a Roman Emperor. Gaunt House occupies nearly a side of the Square. The remaining three sides are composed of mansions that have passed away into dowagerism;—tall, dark houses, with window-frames of stone, or picked out of a lighter red. Little light seems to be behind those lean, comfortless casements now: and hospitality to have passed away from those doors as much as the laced lacqueys and link-boys of old times, who used to put out their torches in the blank iron extinguishers that still flank the lamps over the steps. Brass plates have penetrated into the square —Doctors, the Diddlesex Bank Western Branch—the English and European Reunion, &c.—it has a dreary look— nor is my Lord Steyne's palace less dreary. All I have ever seen of it is the vast wall in front, with the rustic columns at the great gate, through which an old porter peers sometimes with a fat and gloomy red face— and over the wall the garret and bed-room windows, and the chimneys, out of which there seldom comes any smoke now. For the present Lord Steyne lives at Naples, preferring the view of the Bay and Capri and Vesuvius, to the dreary aspect of the wall in Gaunt Square.

A few score yards down New Gaunt Street, and leading
into Gaunt Mews indeed, is a little modest back door, which
you would not remark from that of any of the other stables.
But many a little close carriage has stopped at that door,
as my informant (little Tom Eaves, who knows everything,
and who showed me the place) told me. "The Prince and
Perdita have been in and out of that door, sir," he has
often told me; "Marianne Clarke has entered it with the
Duke of ——. It conducts to the famous *petits apparte-
ments* of Lord Steyne—one, sir, fitted up all in ivory and
white satin, another in ebony and black velvet; there is a
little banqueting-room taken from Sallust's house at Pom-
peii, and painted by Cosway—a little private kitchen, in
which every saucepan was silver and all the spits were
gold. It was there that Egalité Orleans roasted partridges
on the night when he and the Marquis of Steyne won a
hundred thousand from a great personage at ombre. Half
of the money went to the French Revolution, half to purchase Lord Gaunt's Marquisate and Garter—and the remainder—" but it forms no part of our scheme to tell what
became of the remainder, for every shilling of which, and
a great deal more, little Tom Eaves, who knows everybody's affairs, is ready to account.

Besides his town palace, the Marquis had castles and
palaces in various quarters of the three kingdoms, whereof
the descriptions may be found in the road-books—Castle
Strongbow, with its woods, on the Shannon shore; Gaunt
Castle, in Carmarthenshire, where Richard II. was taken
prisoner—Gauntly Hall in Yorkshire, where I have been
informed there were two hundred silver teapots for the
breakfasts of the guests of the house, with everything to
correspond in splendour; and Stillbrook in Hampshire,
which was my lord's farm, an humble place of residence,
of which we all remember the wonderful furniture which
was sold at my lord's demise by a late celebrated auc-
tioneer.

The Marchioness of Steyne was of the renowned and
ancient family of the Caerlyons, Marquises of Camelot, who
have preserved the old faith ever since the conversion of
the venerable Druid, their first ancestor, and whose pedi-

gree goes far beyond the date of the arrival of King Brute
in these islands. Pendragon is the title of the eldest son
of the house. The sons have been called Arthurs, Uthers,
and Caradocs, from immemorial time. Their heads have
fallen in many a local conspiracy. Elizabeth chopped off
the head of the Arthur of her day, who had been Chamberlain to Philip and Mary, and carried letters between the
Queen of Scots and her uncles the Guises. A cadet of the
house was an officer of the great Duke, and distinguished
in the famous Saint Bartholomew conspiracy. During the
whole of Mary's confinement, the house of Camelot con-
spired in her behalf. It was as much injured by its charges
in fitting out an armament against the Spaniards, during the
time of the Armada, as by the fines and confiscations levied
on it by Elizabeth for harbouring of priests, obstinate re-
cusancy, and Popish misdoings. A recreant of James's time
was momentarily perverted from his religion by the argu-
ments of that great theologian, and the fortunes of the
family somewhat restored by his timely weakness. But
the Earl of Camelot, of the reign of Charles, returned to
the old creed of his family, and they continued to fight for
it, and ruin themselves for it, as long as there was a Stuart
left to head or to instigate a rebellion.

Lady Mary Caerlyon was brought up at a Parisian convent; the Dauphiness Marie Antoinette was her godmother.
In the pride of her beauty she had been married—sold, it
was said—to Lord Gaunt, then at Paris, who won vast
sums from the lady's brother at some of Philip of Orleans's
banquets. The Earl of Gaunt's famous duel with the
Count de la Marche, of the Grey Musqueteers, was attrib-
uted by common report to the pretensions of that officer
(who had been a page, and remained a favourite of the
Queen) to the hand of the beautiful Lady Mary Caerlyon.
She was married to Lord Gaunt while the Count lay ill of
his wound, and came to dwell at Gaunt House, and to figure for a short time in the splendid Court of the Prince of
Wales. Fox had toasted her. Morris and Sheridan had
written songs about her. Malmesbury had made her his
best bow; Walpole had pronounced her charming; Devonshire had been almost jealous of her; but she was scared

by the wild pleasures and gaieties of the society into which
she was flung, and after she had borne a couple of sons,
shrank away into a life of devout seclusion. No wonder
that my Lord Steyne, who liked pleasure and cheerfulness,
was not often seen after their marriage, by the side of this
trembling, silent, superstitious, unhappy lady.

The before-mentioned Tom Eaves (who has no part in
this history, except that he knew all the great folks in
London and the stories and mysteries of each family), had
further information regarding my Lady Steyne, which may
or may not be true. "The humiliations," Tom used to
say, "which that woman has been made to undergo, in her
own house, have been frightful; Lord Steyne has made her
sit down to table with women with whom I would rather
die than allow Mrs. Eaves to associate—with Lady Crackenbury, with Mrs. Chippenham, with Madame de la Cruchecassée, the French secretary's wife," (from every one of
which ladies Tom Eaves—who would have sacrificed his
wife for knowing them—was too glad to get a bow or a
dinner), "with the *reigning favourite,* in a word. And do
you suppose that that woman, of that family, who are as
proud as the Bourbons, and to whom the Steynes are but
lacqueys and mushrooms of yesterday (for after all, they are
not of the Old Gaunts, but of a minor and doubtful branch
of the house); do you suppose, I say" (the reader must
bear in mind that it is always Tom Eaves who speaks),
"that the Marchioness of Steyne, the haughtiest woman in
England, would bend down to her husband so submissively, if there were not some cause? Pooh! I tell you
there are *secret reasons.* I tell you, that in the emigration,
the Abbé de la Marche who was here and was employed in
the Quiberoon business with Puisaye and Tinteniac, was
the same Colonel of Mosquetaires Gris with whom Steyne
fought in the year '86—that he and the Marchioness met
again: that it was after the Reverend Colonel was shot in
Brittany, that Lady Steyne took to those extreme practices
of devotion which she carries on now; for she is closeted
with her director every day—she is at service at Spanish
Place, every morning, I've watched her there—that is, I've
happened to be passing there—and depend on it there's a

mystery in her case. People are not so unhappy unless they have something to repent of," added Tom Eaves with a knowing wag of his head; "and depend on it, that woman would not be so submissive as she is, if the Marquis had not some sword to hold over her."

So, if Mr. Eaves's information be correct, it is very likely that this lady, in her high station, had to submit to many a private indignity, and to hide many secret griefs under a calm face. And let us, my brethren who have not our names in the Red Book, console ourselves by thinking comfortably how miserable our betters may be, and that Damocles, who sits on satin cushions, and is served on gold plate, has an awful sword hanging over his head in the shape of a bailiff, or an hereditary disease, or a family secret, which peeps out every now and then from the embroidered arras in a ghastly manner, and will be sure to drop one day or the other in the right place.

In comparing, too, the poor man's situation with that of the great, there is (always according to Mr. Eaves) another source of comfort for the former. You who have little or no patrimony to bequeath or to inherit, may be on good terms with your father or your son, whereas the heir of a great prince, such as my Lord Steyne, must naturally be angry at being kept out of his kingdom, and eye the occupant of it with no very agreeable glances. "Take it as a rule," this sardonic old Eaves would say, "the fathers and elder sons of all great families hate each other. The Crown Prince is always in opposition to the crown or hankering after it. Shakspeare knew the world, my good sir, and when he describes Prince Hal (from whose family the Gaunts pretend to be descended, though they are no more related to John of Gaunt than you are), trying on his father's coronet, he gives you a natural description of all heirs-apparent. If you were heir to a dukedom and a thousand pounds a day, do you mean to say you would not wish for possession? Pooh! And it stands to reason that every great man, having experienced this feeling towards his father, must be aware that his son entertains it towards himself; and so they can't but be suspicious and hostile.

"Then again, as to the feeling of elder towards younger sons. My dear sir, you ought to know that every elder brother looks upon the cadets of the house as his natural enemies, who deprive him of so much ready money which ought to be his by right. I have often heard George Mac Turk, Lord Bajazet's eldest son, say that if he had his will when he came to the title, he would do what the sultans do, and clear the estate by chopping off all his younger brothers' heads at once; and so the case is, more or less, with them all. I tell you they are all Turks in their hearts. Pooh! sir, they know the world." And here, haply, a great man coming up, Tom Eaves's hat would drop off his head, and he would rush forward with a bow and a grin, which showed that he knew the world too—in the Tom-eavesian way, that is. And having laid out every shilling of his fortune on an annuity, Tom could afford to bear no malice to his nephews and nieces, and to have no other feeling with regard to his betters, but a constant and generous desire to dine with them.

Between the Marchioness and the natural and tender regard of mother for children, there was that cruel barrier placed of difference of faith. The very love which she might feel for her sons, only served to render the timid and pious lady more fearful and unhappy. The gulf which separated them was fatal and impassable. She could not stretch her weak arms across it, or draw her children over to that side away from which her belief told her there was no safety. During the youth of his sons, Lord Steyne, who was a good scholar and amateur casuist, had no better sport in the evening after dinner in the country than in setting the boys' tutor, the Reverend Mr. Trail (now my Lord Bishop of Ealing), on her ladyship's director, Father Mole, over their wine and in pitting Oxford against St. Acheul. He cried "Bravo, Latimer! Well said Loyola!" alternately; he promised Mole a bishopric if he would come over; and vowed he would use all his influence to get Trail a cardinal's hat if he would secede. Neither divine allowed himself to be conquered; and though the fond mother hoped that her youngest and favourite son would be reconciled to her church—his mother church—a sad and awful disappointment awaited the devout lady—a disappointment which seemed to be a judgment upon her for the sin of her marriage.

My Lord Gaunt married, as every person who frequents the Peerage knows, the Lady Blanche Thistlewood, a daughter of the noble house of Bareacres, before mentioned in this veracious history. A wing of Gaunt House was assigned to this couple; for the head of the family chose to govern it, and while he reigned to reign supreme: his son and heir, however, living little at home, disagreeing with his wife, and borrowing upon post-obits such moneys as he required beyond the very moderate sums which his father was disposed to allow him. The Marquis knew every shilling of his son's debts. At his lamented demise, he was found himself to be possessor of many of his heir's bonds, purchased for their benefit, and devised by his Lordship to the children of his younger son.

As, to my Lord Gaunt's dismay, and the chuckling delight of his natural enemy and father, the Lady Gaunt had no children—the Lord George Gaunt was desired to return from Vienna, where he was engaged in waltzing and diplomacy, and to contract a matrimonial alliance with the Honourable Joan, only daughter of John Johnes, First Baron Helvellyn, and head of the firm of Jones, Brown, and Robinson, of Threadneedle Street, Bankers; from which union sprang several sons and daughters, whose doings do not appertain to this story.

The marriage at first was a happy and prosperous one. My Lord George Gaunt could not only read, but write pretty correctly. He spoke French with considerable fluency; and was one of the finest waltzers in Europe. With these talents, and his interest at home, there was little doubt that his lordship would rise to the highest dignities in his profession. The lady, his wife, felt that courts were her sphere; and her wealth enabled her to receive splendidly in those continental towns whither her husband's diplomatic duties led him. There was talk of appointing him minister, and bets were laid at the Travellers' that he would be ambassador ere long, when of a sudden, rumours arrived of the secretary's extraordinary behaviour.

At a grand diplomatic dinner given by his chief, he had started up, and declared that a *pâté de foie gras* was poisoned. He went to a ball at the hotel of the Bavarian envoy, the Count de Springbock-Hohenlaufen, with his head shaved, and dressed as a Capuchin friar. It was not a masked ball, as some folks wanted to persuade you. It was something queer, people whispered. His grandfather was so. It was in the family.

His wife and family returned to this country, and took up their abode at Gaunt House. Lord George gave up his post on the European continent, and was gazetted to Brazil. But people knew better; he never returned from that Brazil expedition—never died there—never lived there—never was there at all. He was nowhere: he was gone out altogether. "Brazil," said one gossip to another, with a grin—"Brazil is St. John's Wood. Rio Janeiro is a cottage surrounded by four walls; and George Gaunt is accredited to a keeper, who has invested him with the order of the Strait-Waistcoat." These are the kinds of epitaphs which men pass over one another in Vanity Fair.

Twice or thrice in a week, in the earliest morning, the poor mother went for her sins and saw the poor invalid. Sometimes he laughed at her (and his laughter was more pitiful than to hear him cry); sometimes she found the brilliant dandy diplomatist of the Congress of Vienna dragging about a child's toy, or nursing the keeper's baby's doll. Sometimes he knew her and Father Mole, her director and companion: oftener he forgot her, as he had done wife, children, love, ambition, vanity. But he remembered his dinner-hour, and used to cry if his wine-and-water was not strong enough.

It was the mysterious taint of the blood: the poor mother had brought it from her own ancient race. The evil had broken out once or twice in the father's family, long before Lady Steyne's sins had begun, or her fasts and tears and penances had been offered in their expiation. The pride of the race was struck down as the firstborn of Pharaoh. The dark mark of fate and doom was on the threshold,— the tall old threshold surmounted by coronets and carved heraldry.

The absent lord's children meanwhile prattled and grew on quite unconscious that the doom was over them too. First they talked of their father, and devised plans against his return. Then the name of the living dead man was less frequently in their mouth—then not mentioned at all. But the stricken old grandmother trembled to think that these too were the inheritors of their father's shame as well as of his honours: and watched sickening for the day when the awful ancestral curse should come down on them.

This dark presentiment also haunted Lord Steyne. He tried to lay the horrid bed-side ghost in Red Seas of wine and jollity, and lost sight of it sometimes in the crowd and rout of his pleasures. But it always came back to him when alone, and seemed to grow more threatening with years. "I have taken your son," it said, "why not you? I may shut you up in a prison some day like your son George. I may tap you on the head to-morrow, and away go pleasure and honours, feasts and beauty, friends, flatterers, French cooks, fine horses and houses—in exchange for a prison, a keeper, and a straw mattress like George Gaunt's." And then my lord would defy the ghost which threatened him: for he knew of a remedy by which he could baulk his enemy.

So there was splendour and wealth, but no great happiness perchance, behind the tall carved portals of Gaunt House with its smoky coronets and ciphers. The feasts there were of the grandest in London, but there was not over-much content therewith, except among the guests who sate at my lord's table. Had he not been so great a Prince very few possibly would have visited him: but in Vanity Fair the sins of very great personages are looked at indulgently. *"Nous regardons à deux fois"* (as the French lady said) before we condemn a person of my lord's undoubted quality. Some notorious carpers and squeamish moralists might be sulky with Lord Steyne, but they were glad enough to come when he asked them.

"Lord Steyne is really too bad," Lady Slingstone said, "but everybody goes, and of course I shall see that my girls come to no harm." "His lordship is a man to whom I owe much, everything in life," said the Right Reverend

Doctor Trail, thinking that the Archbishop was rather
shaky; and Mrs. Trail and the young ladies would as soon
have missed going to church as to one of his lordship's
parties. "His morals are bad," said little Lord Southdown
to his sister, who meekly expostulated, having heard ter-
rific legends from her mamma with respect to the doings at
Gaunt House; "but hang it, he's got the best dry Sillery
in Europe!" And as for Sir Pitt Crawley, Bart.—Sir Pitt
that pattern of decorum, Sir Pitt who had led off at missionary meetings,—he never for one moment thought of not
going too. "Where you see such persons as the Bishop of
Ealing and the Countess of Slingstone, you may be pretty
sure, Jane," the Baronet would say, "that *we* cannot be
wrong. The great rank and station of Lord Steyne put
him in a position to command people in our station in life.
The Lord Lieutenant of a County, my dear, is a respectable
man. Besides George Gaunt and I were intimate in early
life: he was my junior when we were attachés at Pumpernickel together."

In a word everybody went to wait upon this great man
—everybody who was asked: as you the reader (do not say
nay) or I the writer hereof would go if we had an invitation.

CHAPTER XIII

In Which the Reader Is Introduced to the Very Best of Company

AT last Becky's kindness and attention to the chief of her husband's family were destined to meet with an exceeding great reward; a reward which, though certainly somewhat unsubstantial, the little woman coveted with greater eagerness than more positive benefits. If she did not wish to lead a virtuous life, at least she desired to enjoy a character for virtue, and we know that no lady in the genteel world can possess this desideratum, until she has put on a train and feathers, and has been presented to her Sovereign at Court. From that august interview they come out stamped as honest women. The Lord Chamberlain gives them a certificate of virtue. And as dubious goods or letters are passed through an oven at quarantine, sprinkled with aromatic vinegar, and then pronounced clean—many a lady whose reputation would be doubtful otherwise and liable to give infection, passes through the wholesome ordeal of the Royal presence, and issues from it free from all taint.

It might be very well for my Lady Bareacres, my Lady Tufto, Mrs. Bute Crawley in the country, and other ladies who had come into contact with Mrs. Rawdon Crawley, to cry fie at the idea of the odious little adventuress making her curtsey before the Sovereign, and to declare that, if dear good Queen Charlotte had been alive, *she* never would have admitted such an extremely ill-regulated personage into her chaste drawing-room. But when we consider, that it was the First Gentleman in Europe in whose high presence Mrs. Rawdon passed her examination, and as it were, took her degree in reputation, it surely must be flat disloyalty to doubt any more about her virtue. I, for my part, look back with love and awe to that Great Character in history. Ah, what a high and noble appreciation of Gentlewomanhood there must have been in Vanity Fair, when that revered and august being was invested, by the universal acclaim of the refined and educated portion of this empire, with the title of Premier Gentilhomme of his Kingdom. Do you remember, dear M——, oh friend of my youth, how one blissful night five-and-twenty years since, the "Hypocrite" being acted, Elliston being manager, Dowton and Liston performers, two boys had leave from their loyal masters to go out from Slaughter House School where they were educated, and to appear on Drury Lane stage, amongst a crowd which assembled there to greet the king. THE KING? There he was. Beef-eaters were before the august box: the Marquis of Steyne (Lord of the Powder Closet) and other great officers of state were behind the chair on which he sate, *He* sate—florid of face, portly of person, covered with orders, and in a rich curling head of hair—How we sang God save him! How the house rocked and shouted with that magnificent music. How they cheered, and cried, and waved handkerchiefs. Ladies wept: mothers clasped their children: some fainted with emotion. People were suffocated in the pit, shrieks and groans rising up amidst the writhing and shouting mass there of his people who were, and indeed showed themselves almost to be, ready to die for him. Yes, we saw him. Fate cannot deprive us of *that*. Others have seen Napoleon. Some few still exist who have beheld Frederick the Great, Doctor Johnson, Marie Antoinette, &c.—be it our reasonable boast to our children, that we saw George the Good, the Magnificent, the Great.

Well, there came a happy day in Mrs. Rawdon Crawley's existence when this angel was admitted into the paradise of a Court which she coveted; her sister-in-law acting as her godmother. On the appointed day, Sir Pitt and his lady, in their great family carriage (just newly built, and ready for the Baronet's assumption of the office of High Sheriff of his county), drove up to the little house in Curzon Street, to the edification of Raggles, who was watching from his green-grocer's shop, and saw fine plumes within, and enormous bunches of flowers in the breasts of the new livery-coats of the footmen.

Sir Pitt, in a glittering uniform, descended and went into Curzon Street, his sword between his legs. Little Rawdon stood with his face against the parlour window-panes, smiling and nodding with all his might to his aunt in the carriage within; and presently Sir Pitt issued forth from the house again, leading forth a lady with grand feathers, covered in a white shawl, and holding up daintily a train of magnificent brocade. She stepped into the vehicle as if she were a princess and accustomed all her life to go to Court, smiling graciously on the footman at the door, and on Sir Pitt, who followed her into the carriage.

Then Rawdon followed in his old Guards' uniform, which had grown wofully shabby, and was much too tight. He was to have followed the procession, and waited upon his sovereign in a cab; but that his good-natured sister-in-law insisted that they should be a family party. The coach was large, the ladies not very big, they would hold their trains in their laps—finally, the four went fraternally together; and their carriage presently joined the line of royal equipages which was making its way down Piccadilly and St. James's Street, towards the old brick palace where the Star of Brunswick was in waiting to receive his nobles and gentlefolks.

Becky felt as if she could bless the people out of the carriage windows, so elated was she in spirit, and so strong a sense had she of the dignified position which she had at last attained in life. Even our Becky had her weaknesses, and as one often sees how men pride themselves upon excellences which others are slow to perceive: how, for instance, Comus firmly believes that he is the greatest tragic actor in England; how Brown, the famous novelist, longs to be considered, not a man of genius, but a man of fashion; while Robinson, the great lawyer, does not in the least care about his reputation in Westminster Hall, but believes himself incomparable across country, and at a five-barred gate—so to be, and to be thought, a respectable woman was Becky's aim in life, and she got up the genteel with amazing assiduity, readiness, and success. We have said, there were times when she believed herself to be a fine lady, and forgot that there was no money in the chest at

home—duns round the gate, tradesmen to coax and wheedle—no ground to walk upon, in a word. And as she
went to Court in the carriage, the family carriage, she
adopted a demeanour so grand, self-satisfied, deliberate,
and imposing, that it made even Lady Jane laugh. She
walked into the royal apartments with a toss of the head
which would have befitted an empress, and I have no doubt
had she been one, she would have become the character
perfectly.

We are authorised to state that Mrs. Rawdon Crawley's
costume de cour on the occasion of her presentation to the
Sovereign was of the most elegant and brilliant description.
Some ladies we may have seen—we who wear stars and
cordons, and attend the St. James's assemblies, or we, who,
in muddy boots, dawdle up and down Pall Mall, and peep
into the coaches as they drive up with the great folks in
their feathers—some ladies of fashion, I say, we may have
seen, about two o'clock of the forenoon of a levee day, as
the laced-jacketed band of the Life Guards are blowing
triumphal marches seated on those prancing music-stools,
their cream-coloured chargers—who are by no means lovely
and enticing objects at that early period of noon. A stout
countess of sixty *décolletée,* painted, wrinkled, with rouge up
to her drooping eyelids, and diamonds twinkling in her wig,
is a wholesome and edifying, but not a pleasant sight. She
has the faded look of a St. James's Street illumination, as it
may be seen of an early morning, when half the lamps are
out, and the others are blinking wanly, as if they were about
to vanish like ghosts before the dawn. Such charms as
those of which we catch glimpses while her ladyship's carriage passes should appear abroad at night alone. If even
Cynthia looks haggard of an afternoon, as we may see her
sometimes in the present winter season, with Phœbus staring
her out of countenance from the opposite side of the heavens,
how much more can old Lady Castlemouldy keep her head up
when the sun is shining full upon it through the chariot
windows, and showing all the chinks and crannies with which
time has marked her face! No. Drawing-rooms should be
announced for November, or the first foggy day: or the
elderly sultanas of our Vanity Fair should drive up in closed

litters, descend in a covered way, and make their curtsey
to the Sovereign under the protection of lamplight.

Our beloved Rebecca had no need, however, of any such
a friendly halo to set off her beauty. Her complexion could
bear any sunshine as yet; and her dress, though if you were
to see it now, any present lady of Vanity Fair would pro-
nounce it to be the most foolish and preposterous attire ever
worn, was as handsome in her eyes and those of the public,
some five-and-twenty years since, as the most brilliant costume of the most famous beauty of the present season. A
score of years hence that too, that milliner's wonder, will
have passed into the domain of the absurd, along with all
previous vanities. But we are wandering too much. Mrs.
Rawdon's dress was pronounced to be charmante on the
eventful day of her presentation. Even good little Lady Jane
was forced to acknowledge this effect, as she looked at her
kinswoman; and owned sorrowfully to herself that she was
quite inferior in taste to Mrs. Becky.

She did not know how much care, thought, and genius
Mrs. Rawdon had bestowed upon that garment. Rebecca
had as good taste as any milliner in Europe, and such a
clever way of doing things as Lady Jane little understood.
The latter quickly spied out the magnificence of the brocade
of Becky's train, and the splendour of the lace on her dress.

The brocade was an old remnant, Becky said; and as for
the lace, it was a great bargain. She had had it these hundred years.

"My dear Mrs. Crawley, it must have cost a little fortune," Lady Jane said, looking down at her own lace, which
was not nearly so good; and then examining the quality of
the ancient brocade which formed the material of Mrs.
Rawdon's Court dress, she felt inclined to say that she could
not afford such fine clothing, but checked that speech, with
an effort, as one uncharitable to her kinswoman.

And yet, if Lady Jane had known all, I think even her
kindly temper would have failed her. The fact is, when
she was putting Sir Pitt's house in order, Mrs. Rawdon had
found the lace and the brocade in old wardrobes, the property of the former ladies of the house, and had quietly carried the goods home, and had suited them to her own little

person. Briggs saw her take them, asked no questions, told
no stories; but I believe quite sympathised with her on this
matter, and so would many another honest woman.

And the diamonds—"Where the doose did you get the
diamonds, Becky?" said her husband, admiring some jewels
which he had never seen before, and which sparkled in her
ears and on her neck with brilliance and profusion.

Becky blushed a little, and looked at him hard for a moment. Pitt Crawley blushed a little too, and looked out of
window. The fact is, he had given her a very small portion
of the brilliants; a pretty diamond clasp, which confined a
pearl necklace which she wore; and the Baronet had omitted
to mention the circumstances to his lady.

Becky looked at her husband, and then at Sir Pitt, with
an air of saucy triumph—as much as to say, "Shall I be-
tray you?"

"Guess!" she said to her husband. "Why, you silly man,"
she continued, "where do you suppose I got them?—all except
the little clasp, which a dear friend of mine gave me long
ago. I hired them, to be sure. I hired them at Mr. Polonius's, in Coventry Street. You don't suppose that all the
diamonds which go to Court belong to the wearers; like those
beautiful stones which Lady Jane has, and which are much
handsomer than any which I have, I am certain."

"They are family jewels," said Sir Pitt, again looking
uneasy. And in this family conversation the carriage rolled
down the street, until its cargo was finally discharged at
the gates of the palace where the Sovereign was sitting in
state.

The diamonds, which had created Rawdon's admiration,
never went back to Mr. Polonius, of Coventry Street, and
that gentleman never applied for their restoration; but they
retired into a little private repository, in an old desk, which
Amelia Sedley had given her years and years ago, and in
which Becky kept a number of useful and, perhaps, valuable things, about which her husband knew nothing. To
know nothing, or little, is in the nature of some husbands.
To hide, in the nature of how many women? O ladies!
how many of you have surreptitious milliners' bills? How
many of you have gowns and bracelets, which you daren't

show, or which you wear trembling?—trembling, and coaxing with smiles the husband by your side, who does not know the new velvet gown from the old one, or the new bracelet from last year's, or has any notion that the ragged-looking yellow lace scarf cost forty guineas, and that Madame Bobinot is writing dunning letters every week for the money!

Thus Rawdon knew nothing about the brilliant diamond ear-rings, or the superb brilliant ornament which decorated the fair bosom of his lady; but Lord Steyne, who was in his place at Court, as Lord of the Powder Closet, and one of the great dignitaries and illustrious defences of the throne of England, and came up with all his stars, garters, collars, and cordons, and paid particular attention to the little woman, knew whence the jewels came, and who paid for them.

As he bowed over her he smiled, and quoted the hackneyed and beautiful lines, from the "Rape of the Lock," about Belinda's diamonds, "which Jews might kiss and infidels adore."

"But I hope your lordship is orthodox," said the little lady, with a toss of her head. And many ladies round about whispered and talked, and many gentlemen nodded and whispered, as they saw what marked attention the great nobleman was paying to the little adventuress.

What were the circumstances of the interview between Rebecca Crawley, née Sharp, and her Imperial Master, it does not become such a feeble and inexperienced pen as mine to attempt to relate. The dazzled eyes close before that Magnificent Idea. Loyal respect and decency tell even the imagination not to look too keenly and audaciously about the sacred audience-chamber, but to back away rapidly, silently, and respectfully, making profound bows out of the August Presence.

This may be said, that in all London there was no more loyal heart than Becky's after this interview. The name of her king was always on her lips, and he was proclaimed by her to be the most charming of men. She went to Colnaghi's and ordered the finest portrait of him that art had produced, and credit could supply. She chose that famous one in which the best of monarchs is represented in a frock-coat with a fur collar, and breeches and silk stockings, simpering on a sofa from under his curly brown wig. She had him painted in a brooch and wore it—indeed she amused and somewhat pestered her acquaintance with her perpetual talk about his urbanity and beauty. Who knows? Perhaps the little woman thought she might play the part of a Maintenon or a Pompadour.

But the finest sport of all after her presentation was to hear her talk virtuously. She had a few female acquaint-ances, not, it must be owned, of the very highest reputation in Vanity Fair. But being made an honest woman of, so to speak, Becky would not consort any longer with these dubious ones, and cut Lady Crackenbury when the latter nodded to her from her opera-box; and gave Mrs. Washington White the go-by in the Ring. "One must, my dear, show one is somebody," she said. "One mustn't be seen with doubtful people. I pity Lady Crackenbury from my heart; and Mrs. Washington White may be a very good-natured person. *You* may go and dine with them, as you like your rubber. But *I* mustn't, and won't; and you will have the goodness to tell Smith to say I am not at home when either of them calls."

The particulars of Becky's costume were in the news-papers—feathers, lappets, superb diamonds, and all the rest. Lady Crackenbury read the paragraph in bitterness of spirit, and discoursed to her followers about the airs which that woman was giving herself. Mrs. Bute Crawley and her young ladies in the country had a copy of the *Morning Post* from town; and gave a vent to their honest indigna-tion. "If you had been sandy-haired, green-eyed, and a French rope-dancer's daughter," Mrs. Bute said to her eldest girl (who, on the contrary, was a very swarthy, short, and snub-nosed young lady), "you might have had superb diamonds forsooth, and have been presented at Court by your cousin, the Lady Jane. But you're only a gentlewoman, my poor dear child. You have only some of the best blood in England in your veins, and good principles and piety for your portion. I, myself, the wife of a Baronet's younger brother, too, never thought of such a

thing as going to Court—nor would other people, if good
Queen Charlotte had been alive." In this way the worthy
Rectoress consoled herself: and her daughters sighed, and
sate over the Peerage all night.

A few days after the famous presentation, another great
and exceeding honour was vouchsafed to the virtuous
Becky. Lady Steyne's carriage drove up to Mr. Rawdon
Crawley's door, and the footman, instead of driving down
the front of the house, as by his tremendous knocking he
appeared to be inclined to do, relented, and only delivered
in a couple of cards, on which were engraven the names
of the Marchioness of Steyne and the Countess of Gaunt.
If these bits of pasteboard had been beautiful pictures, or
had had a hundred yards of Malines lace rolled round them,
worth twice the number of guineas, Becky could not have
regarded them with more pleasure. You may be sure they
occupied a conspicuous place in the china bowl on the drawing-room table, where Becky kept the cards of her visitors.
Lord! lord! how poor Mrs. Washington White's card and
Lady Crackenbury's card, which our little friend had been
glad enough to get a few months back, and of which the
silly little creature was rather proud once—Lord! lord! I
say, how soon at the appearance of these grand court cards,
did those poor little neglected deuces sink down to the
bottom of the pack. Steyne! Bareacres, Johnes of
Helvellyn! and Caerlyon of Camelot! we may be sure that
Becky and Briggs looked out those august names in the
Peerage, and followed the noble races up through all the
ramifications of the family tree.

My Lord Steyne coming to call a couple of hours afterwards, and looking about him, and observing everything as
was his wont, found his ladies' cards already ranged as the
trumps of Becky's hand, and grinned, as this old cynic
always did at any naïve display of human weakness. Becky
came down to him presently: whenever the dear girl expected his lordship, her toilette was prepared, her hair in
perfect order, her mouchoirs, aprons, scarfs, little morocco
slippers, and other female gimcracks arranged, and she
seated in some artless and agreeable posture ready to re-

ceive him—whenever she was surprised, of course she had to fly to her apartment to take a rapid survey of matters in the glass, and to trip down again to wait upon the great peer.

She found him grinning over the bowl. She was discovered, and she blushed a little. "Thank you, Monseigneur," she said. "You see your ladies have been here. How good of you! I couldn't come before—I was in the kitchen making a pudding."

"I know you were, I saw you through the area-railings as I drove up," replied the old gentleman.

"You see everything," she replied.

"A few things, but not that, my pretty lady," he said good-naturedly. "You silly little fibster! I heard you in the room overhead, where I have no doubt you were putting a little rouge on; you must give some of yours to my Lady Gaunt, whose complexion is quite preposterous; and I heard the bed-room door open, and then you came downstairs."

"Is it a crime to try and look my best when *you* come here?" answered Mrs. Rawdon plaintively, and she rubbed her cheek with her handkerchief as if to show there was no rouge at all, only genuine blushes and modesty in her case. About this who can tell? I know there is some rouge that won't come off on a pocket-handkerchief; and some so good that even tears will not disturb it.

"Well," said the old gentleman, twiddling round his wife's card, "you are bent on becoming a fine lady. You pester my poor old life out to get you into the world. You won't be able to hold your own there, you silly little fool. You've got no money."

"You will get us a place," interposed Becky, "as quick as possible."

"You've got no money, and you want to compete with those who have. You poor little earthenware pipkin, you want to swim down the stream along with the great copper kettles. All women are alike. Everybody is striving for what is not worth the having! Gad! I dined with the King yesterday, and we had neck of mutton and turnips. A dinner of herbs is better than a stalled ox very often.

You will go to Gaunt House. You give an old fellow no rest until you get there. It's not half so nice as here. You'll be bored there. I am. My wife is as gay as Lady Macbeth, and my daughters as cheerful as Regan and Goneril. I daren't sleep in what they call my bed-room. The bed is like the baldaquin of St. Peter's, and the pictures frighten me. I have a little brass bed in a dressing-room: and a little hair mattress like an anchorite. I am an anchorite. Ho! ho! You'll be asked to dinner next week. And *gare aux femmes,* look out and hold your own! How the women will bully you!" This was a very long speech for a man of few words like my Lord Steyne; nor was it the first which he uttered for Becky's benefit on that day.

Briggs looked up from the work-table at which she was seated in the farther room, and gave a deep sigh as she heard the great Marquis speak so lightly of her sex.

"If you don't turn off that abominable sheep-dog," said Lord Steyne, with a savage look over his shoulder at her, "I will have her poisoned."

"I always give my dog dinner from my own plate," said Rebecca, laughing mischievously; and having enjoyed for some time the discomfiture of my lord, who hated poor Briggs for interrupting his tête-à-tête with the fair Colonel's wife, Mrs. Rawdon at length had pity upon her admirer, and calling to Briggs, praised the fineness of the weather to her, and bade her to take out the child for a walk.

"I can't send her away," Becky said presently, after a pause, and in a very sad voice. Her eyes filled with tears as she spoke, and she turned away her head.

"You owe her her wages, I suppose?" said the Peer.

"Worse than that," said Becky, still casting down her eyes; "I have ruined her."

"Ruined her?—then why don't you turn her out?" the gentleman asked.

"Men do that," Becky answered bitterly. "Women are not so bad as you. Last year when we were reduced to our last guinea, she gave us everything. She shall never leave me, until we are ruined utterly ourselves, which does not seem far off, or until I can pay her the utmost farthing."

"—— it, how much is it?" said the Peer, with an oath.
And Becky, reflecting on the largeness of his means, men-
tioned not only the sum which she had borrowed from Miss
Briggs, but one of nearly double the amount.

This caused the Lord Steyne to break out in another brief
and energetic expression of anger, at which Rebecca held
down her head the more, and cried bitterly. "I could not
help it. It was my only chance. I dare not tell my husband. He would kill me if I told him what I have done.
I have kept it a secret from everybody but you—and you
forced it from me. Ah, what shall I do, Lord Steyne?
for I am very, very unhappy!"

Lord Steyne made no reply except by beating the devil's
tattoo, and biting his nails. At last he clapped his hat on
his head, and flung out of the room. Rebecca did not rise
from her attitude of misery until the door slammed upon
him, and his carriage whirled away. Then she rose up
with the queerest expression of victorious mischief glittering in her green eyes. She burst out laughing once or twice
to herself, as she sate at work: and sitting down to the
piano, she rattled away a triumphant voluntary on the keys,
which made the people pause under her window to listen to
her brilliant music.

That night, there came two notes from Gaunt House for
the little woman, the one containing a card of invitation
from Lord and Lady Steyne to a dinner at Gaunt House
next Friday: while the other enclosed a slip of gray paper
bearing Lord Steyne's signature and the address of Messrs.
Jones, Brown, and Robinson, Lombard Street.

Rawdon heard Becky laughing in the night once or twice.
It was only her delight at going to Gaunt House and facing
the ladies there, she said, which amused her so. But the
truth was, that she was occupied with a great number of
other thoughts. Should she pay off old Briggs and give
her her *congé?* Should she astonish Raggles by settling
his account? She turned over all these thoughts on her
pillow, and on the next day, when Rawdon went out to
pay his morning visit to the Club, Mrs. Crawley (in a
modest dress with a veil on) whipped off in a hackney-coach
to the City: and being landed at Messrs. Jones and Robin-

son's bank, presented a document there to the authority at the desk, who, in reply, asked her "How she would take it?"

She gently said "she would take a hundred and fifty pounds in small notes and the remainder in one note:" and passing through St. Paul's Churchyard stopped there and bought the handsomest black silk gown for Briggs which money could buy; and which, with a kiss and the kindest speeches, she presented to the simple old spinster.

Then she walked to Mr. Raggles, inquired about his children affectionately, and gave him fifty pounds on account. Then she went to the livery-man from whom she jobbed her carriages and gratified him with a similar sum. "And I hope this will be a lesson to you, Spavin," she said, "and that on the next Drawing-room day my brother, Sir Pitt, will not be inconvenienced by being obliged to take four of us in his carriage to wait upon His Majesty, because my *own* carriage is not forthcoming." It appears there had been a difference on the last Drawing-room day. Hence the degradation which the Colonel had almost suffered, of being obliged to enter the presence of his Sovereign in a hack cab.

These arrangements concluded, Becky paid a visit up-stairs to the before-mentioned desk, which Amelia Sedley had given her years and years ago, and which contained a number of useful and valuable little things: in which private museum she placed the one note which Messrs. Jones and Robinson's cashier had given her.

CHAPTER XIV

In Which We Enjoy Three Courses and a Dessert

WHEN the ladies of Gaunt House were at breakfast that morning, Lord Steyne (who took his chocolate in private, and seldom disturbed the females of his household, or saw them except upon public days, or when they crossed each other in the hall, or when from his pit-box at the Opera he surveyed them in their box on the grand tier)—his lordship, we say, appeared among the ladies and the children who were assembled over the tea and toast, and a battle royal ensued apropos of Rebecca.

"My Lady Steyne," he said, "I want to see the list for your dinner on Friday; and I want you, if you please, to write a card for Colonel and Mrs. Crawley."

"Blanche writes them," Lady Steyne said in a flutter. "Lady Gaunt writes them."

"I will not write to that person," Lady Gaunt said, a tall and stately lady, who looked up for an instant and then down again after she had spoken. It was not good to meet Lord Steyne's eyes for those who had offended him.

"Send the children out of the room. Go!" said he, pulling at the bell-rope. The urchins, always frightened before him, retired: their mother would have followed too. "Not you," he said. "You stop."

"My Lady Steyne," he said, "once more will you have the goodness to go to the desk, and write that card for your dinner on Friday?"

"My Lord, I will not be present at it," Lady Gaunt said; "I will go home."

"I wish you would, and stay there. You will find the bailiffs at Bareacres very pleasant company, and I shall be freed from lending money to your relations, and from your own damned tragedy airs. Who are you to give orders here? You have no money. You've got no brains. You

158 WILLIAM MAKEPEACE THACKERAY

were here to have children, and you have not had any.
Gaunt's tired of you; and George's wife is the only person
in the family who doesn't wish you were dead. Gaunt
would marry again if you were."

"I wish I were," her Ladyship answered, with tears and
rage in her eyes.

"You, forsooth, must give yourself airs of virtue; while
my wife, who is an immaculate saint, as everybody knows,
and never did wrong in her life, has no objection to meet
my young friend Mrs. Crawley. My Lady Steyne knows
that appearances are sometimes against the best of women;
that lies are often told about the most innocent of them.
Pray, Madam, shall I tell you some little anecdotes about
my Lady Bareacres, your mamma?"

"You may strike me if you like, sir, or hit any cruel
blow," Lady Gaunt said. To see his wife and daughter
suffering always put his Lordship into a good humour.

"My sweet Blanche," he said, "I am a gentleman, and
never lay my hand upon a woman, save in the way of kindness. I only wish to correct little faults in your character.
You women are too proud, and sadly lack humility, as
Father Mole, I'm sure, would tell my Lady Steyne if he
were here. You mustn't give yourselves airs: you must
be meek and humble, my blessings. For all Lady Steyne
knows, this calumniated, simple, good-humoured Mrs.
Crawley is quite innocent—even more innocent than herself.
Her husband's character is not good, but it is as good as
Bareacres', who has played a little and not paid a great
deal, who cheated you out of the only legacy you ever had,
and left you a pauper on my hands. And Mrs. Crawley is
not very well born; but she is not worse than Fanny's
illustrious ancestor, the first de la Jones."

"The money which I brought into the family, sir," Lady
George cried out—

"You purchased a contingent reversion with it," the
Marquis said, darkly. "If Gaunt dies, your husband may
come to his honours; your little boys may inherit them,
and who knows what besides? In the meanwhile, ladies,
be as proud and virtuous as you like abroad, but don't give
me any airs. As for Mrs. Crawley's character, I shan't

demean myself or that most spotless and perfectly irre-
proachable lady, by even hinting that it requires a defence.
You will be pleased to receive her with the utmost cordiality,
as you will receive all persons whom I present in this
house. This house?" He broke out with a laugh. "Who
is the master of it? and what is it? This Temple of Virtue
belongs to me. And if I invite all Newgate or all Bedlam
here, by —— they shall be welcome."

After this vigorous allocution, to one of which sort Lord
Steyne treated his "Hareem" whenever symptoms of in-
subordination appeared in his household, the crest-fallen
women had nothing for it but to obey. Lady Gaunt wrote
the invitation which his Lordship required, and she and her
mother-in-law drove in person, and with bitter and humiliated hearts, to leave the cards on Mrs. Rawdon, the
reception of which caused that innocent woman so much
pleasure.

There were families in London who would have sacrificed
a year's income to receive such an honour at the hands of
those great ladies. Mrs. Frederick Bullock, for instance,
would have gone on her knees from May Fair to Lombard
Street, if Lady Steyne and Lady Gaunt had been waiting
in the City to raise her up, and say, "Come to us next
Friday,"—not to one of the great crushes and grand balls
of Gaunt House, whither everybody went, but to the sacred,
unapproachable, mysterious, delicious entertainments, to be
admitted to one of which was a privilege, and an honour,
and a blessing indeed.

Severe, spotless, and beautiful, Lady Gaunt held the very
highest rank in Vanity Fair. The distinguished courtesy
with which Lord Steyne treated her, charmed everybody who
witnessed his behaviour, caused the severest critics to admit
how perfect a gentleman he was, and to own that his Lordship's heart at least was in the right place.

The ladies of Gaunt House called Lady Bareacres in to
their aid, in order to repulse the common enemy. One of
Lady Gaunt's carriages went to Hill Street for her Ladyship's mother, all whose equipages were in the hands of
the bailiffs, whose very jewels and wardrobe, it was said,
had been seized by those inexorable Israelites. Bareacres

Castle was theirs, too, with all its costly pictures, furniture, and articles of vertu—the magnificent Vandykes; the noble Reynolds pictures; the Lawrence portraits, tawdry and beautiful, and, thirty years ago, deemed as precious as works of real genius; the matchless Dancing Nymph of Canova, for which Lady Bareacres had sate in her youth— Lady Bareacres splendid then, and radiant in wealth, rank, and beauty—a toothless, bald, old woman now—a mere rag of a former robe of state. Her lord, painted at the same time by Lawrence, as waving his sabre in front of Bareacres Castle, and clothed in his uniform as Colonel of the Thistlewood Yeomanry, was a withered, old, lean man in a greatcoat and a Brutus wig: slinking about Gray's Inn of mornings chiefly, and dining alone at clubs. He did not like to dine with Steyne now. They had run races of pleasure together in youth when Bareacres was the winner. But Steyne had more bottom than he, and had lasted him out. The Marquis was ten times a greater man now than the young Lord Gaunt of '85; and Bareacres nowhere in the race—old, beaten, bankrupt, and broken down. He had borrowed too much money of Steyne to find it pleasant to meet his old comrade often. The latter, whenever he wished to be merry, used jeeringly to ask Lady Gaunt, why her father had not come to see her? "He has not been here for four months," Lord Steyne would say. "I can always tell by my cheque-book afterwards, when I get a visit from Bareacres. What a comfort it is, my ladies, I bank with one of my sons' fathers-in-law, and the other banks with me!"

Of the other illustrious persons whom Becky had the honour to encounter on this her first presentation to the grand world, it does not become the present historian to say much. There was his Excellency the Prince of Peterwaradin, with his Princess; a nobleman tightly girthed, with a large military chest, on which the *plaque* of his order shone magnificently, and wearing the red collar of the Golden Fleece round his neck. He was the owner of countless flocks. "Look at his face. I think he must be descended from a sheep," Becky whispered to Lord Steyne. Indeed, his Excellency's countenance, long, solemn, and

white, with the ornament round his neck, bore some resemblance to that of a venerable bell-wether.

There was Mr. John Paul Jefferson Jones, titularly attached to the American Embassy, and correspondent of the
New York Demagogue; who, by way of making himself
agreeable to the company, asked Lady Steyne, during a
pause in the conversation at dinner, how his dear friend,
George Gaunt, liked the Brazils?—He and George had been
most intimate at Naples, and had gone up Vesuvius together.
Mr. Jones wrote a full and particular account of the dinner,
which appeared duly in the *Demagogue*. He mentioned the
names and titles of all the guests, giving biographical
sketches of the principal people. He described the persons
of the ladies with great eloquence; the service of the table;
the size and costume of the servants; enumerated the dishes
and wines served; the ornaments of the sideboard, and the
probable value of the plate. Such a dinner he calculated
could not be dished up under fifteen or eighteen dollars per
head. And he was in the habit, until very lately, of sending
over *protégés*, with letters of recommendation to the present
Marquis of Steyne, encouraged to do so by the intimate
terms on which he had lived with his dear friend, the late
lord. He was most indignant that a young and insignificant
aristocrat, the Earl of Southdown, should have taken the
pas of him in their procession to the dining-room. "Just
as I was stepping up to offer my hand to a very pleasing
and witty fashionable, the brilliant and exclusive Mrs.
Rawdon Crawley,"—he wrote, "the young patrician interposed between me and the lady, and whisked my Helen off
without a word of apology. I was fain to bring up the rear
with the Colonel, the lady's husband, a stout red-faced warrior who distinguished himself at Waterloo, where he had
better luck than befell some of his brother red-coats at
New Orleans."

The Colonel's countenance on coming into this polite
society wore as many blushes as the face of a boy of sixteen
assumes when he is confronted with his sister's schoolfellows. It has been told before that honest Rawdon had
not been much used at any period of his life to ladies' com-

pany. With the men at the Club or the Mess-room, he was well enough; and could ride, bet, smoke, or play at billiards with the boldest of them. He had had his time for female friendships too: but that was twenty years ago, and the ladies were of the rank of those with whom Young Marlow in the comedy is represented as having been familiar before he became abashed in the presence of Miss Hard-castle. The times are such that one scarcely dares to allude to that kind of company which thousands of our young men in Vanity Fair are frequenting every day, which nightly fills casinos and dancing-rooms, which is known to exist as well as the Ring in Hyde Park or the Congregation at St. James's—but which the most squeamish if not the most moral of societies is determined to ignore. In a word, although Colonel Crawley was now five-and-forty years of age, it had not been his lot in life to meet with a half-dozen good women, besides his paragon of a wife. All except her and his kind sister Lady Jane, whose gentle nature had tamed and won him, scared the worthy Colonel; and on occasion of his first dinner at Gaunt House he was not heard to make a single remark except to state that the weather was very hot. Indeed Becky would have left him at home, but that virtue ordained that her husband should be by her side to protect the timid and flut-tering little creature on her first appearance in polite society.

On her first appearance Lord Steyne stepped forward, taking her hand, and greeting her with great courtesy, and presenting her to Lady Steyne, and their ladyships, her daughters. Their ladyships made three stately curtsies, and the elder lady to be sure gave her hand to the new comer, but it was as cold and lifeless as marble.

Becky took it, however, with grateful humility; and performing a reverence which would have done credit to the best dancing-master, put herself at Lady Steyne's feet, as it were, by saying that his Lordship had been her father's earliest friend and patron, and that she, Becky, had learned to honour and respect the Steyne family from the days of her childhood. The fact is, that Lord Steyne had once purchased a couple of pictures of the late Sharp, and the affectionate orphan could never forget her gratitude for that favour.

The Lady Bareacres then came under Becky's cognizance —to whom the Colonel's lady made also a most respectful obeisance: it was returned with severe dignity by the exalted person in question.

"I had the pleasure of making your Ladyship's acquaintance at Brussels, ten years ago," Becky said, in the most winning manner. "I had the good fortune to meet Lady Bareacres, at the Duchess of Richmond's ball, the night before the battle of Waterloo. And I recollect your Ladyship, and my Lady Blanche, your daughter, sitting in the carriage in the porte-cochère at the Inn, waiting for horses. I hope your Ladyship's diamonds are safe."

Everybody's eyes looked into their neighbour's. The famous diamonds had undergone a famous seizure, it appears, about which Becky, of course, knew nothing. Rawdon Crawley retreated with Lord Southdown into a window, where the latter was heard to laugh immoderately, as Rawdon told him the story of Lady Bareacres wanting horses, and "knuckling down by Jove," to Mrs. Crawley. "I think I needn't be afraid of *that* woman," Becky thought. Indeed, Lady Bareacres exchanged terrified and angry looks with her daughter, and retreated to a table, where she began to look at pictures with great energy.

When the Potentate from the Danube made his appearance, the conversation was carried on in the French language, and the Lady Bareacres and the younger ladies found, to their farther mortification, that Mrs. Crawley was much better acquainted with that tongue, and spoke it with a much better accent than they. Becky had met other Hungarian magnates with the army in France in 1816-17. She asked after her friends with great interest. The foreign personages thought that she was a lady of great distinction; and the Prince and the Princess asked severally of Lord Steyne and the Marchioness, whom they conducted to dinner, who was that petite dame who spoke so well?

Finally, the procession being formed in the order described by the American diplomatist, they marched into the apartment where the banquet was served: and which, as I have promised the reader he shall enjoy it, he shall have the liberty of ordering himself so as to suit his fancy.

But it was when the ladies were alone that Becky knew the tug of war would come. And then indeed the little woman found herself in such a situation, as made her acknowledge the correctness of Lord Steyne's caution to her to beware of the society of ladies above her own sphere. As they say the persons who hate Irishmen most are Irishmen; so, assuredly, the greatest tyrants over women are women. When poor little Becky, alone with the ladies, went up to the fire-place whither the great ladies had repaired, the great ladies marched away and took possession of a table of drawings. When Becky followed them to the table of drawings, they dropped off one by one to the fire again. She tried to speak to one of the children (of whom she was commonly fond in public places), but Master George Gaunt was called away by his mamma; and the stranger was treated with such cruelty finally, that even Lady Steyne herself pitied her, and went up to speak to the friendless little woman.

"Lord Steyne," said her Ladyship, as her wan cheeks glowed with a blush, "says you sing and play very beautifully, Mrs. Crawley—I wish you would do me the kindness to sing to me."

"I will do anything that may give pleasure to my Lord Steyne or to you," said Rebecca, sincerely grateful, and seating herself at the piano, began to sing.

She sang religious songs of Mozart, which had been early favourites of Lady Steyne, and with such sweetness and tenderness that the lady, lingering round the piano, sate down by its side, and listened until the tears rolled down her eyes. It is true that the opposition ladies at the other end of the room kept up a loud and ceaseless buzzing and talking: but the Lady Steyne did not hear those rumours. She was a child again—and had wandered back through a forty years' wilderness to her Convent Garden. The chapel organ had pealed the same tones, the organist, the sister whom she loved best of the community, had taught them to her in those early happy days. She was a girl once more, and the brief period of her happiness bloomed out again for an hour—she started when the jarring doors were flung open, and with a loud laugh from Lord Steyne, the men of the party entered full of gaiety.

He saw at a glance what had happened in his absence: and was grateful to his wife for once. He went and spoke to her, and called her by her Christian name, so as again to bring blushes to her pale face—"My wife says you have been singing like an angel," he said to Becky. Now there are angels of two kinds, and both sorts, it is said, are charming in their way.

Whatever the previous portion of the evening had been, the rest of that night was a great triumph for Becky. She sang her very best, and it was so good that every one of the men came and crowded round the piano. The women, her enemies, were left quite alone. And Mr. Paul Jefferson Jones thought he had made a conquest of Lady Gaunt by going up to her Ladyship, and praising her delightful friend's first-rate singing.

CHAPTER XV

Contains a Vulgar Incident

THE MUSE, whoever she be, who presides over this Comic History, must now descend from the genteel heights in which she has been soaring, and have the goodness to drop down upon the lowly roof of John Sedley at Brompton, and describe what events are taking place there. Here, too, in this humble tenement, live care, and distrust, and dismay. Mrs. Clapp in the kitchen is grumbling in secret to her husband about the rent, and urging the good fellow to rebel against his old friend and patron and his present lodger. Mrs. Sedley has ceased to visit her landlady in the lower regions now, and indeed is in a position to patronise Mrs. Clapp no longer. How can one be condescending to a lady to whom one owes a matter of forty pounds, and who is perpetually throwing out hints for the money? The Irish maidservant has not altered in the least in her kind and respectful behaviour; but Mrs. Sedley fancies that she is growing insolent and ungrateful, and, as the guilty thief who fears each bush an officer, sees threatening innuendoes and hints of capture in all the girl's speeches and answers. Miss Clapp, grown quite a young woman now, is declared by the soured old lady to be an unbearable and impudent little minx. Why Amelia can be so fond of her, or have her in her room so much, or walk out with her so constantly, Mrs. Sedley cannot conceive. The bitterness of poverty has poisoned the life of the once cheerful and kindly woman. She is thankless for Amelia's constant and gentle bearing towards her; carps at her for her efforts at kindness or service: rails at her for her silly pride in her child, and her neglect of her parents. Georgy's house is not a very lively one since uncle Jos's annuity has been withdrawn, and the little family are almost upon famine diet.

Amelia thinks, and thinks, and racks her brain, to find

some means of increasing the small pittance upon which the household is starving. Can she give lessons in anything? paint card-racks? do fine work? She finds that women are working hard, and better than she can, for twopence a-day. She buys a couple of begilt Bristol boards at the Fancy Stationer's, and paints her very best upon them—a shepherd with a red waistcoat on one, and a pink face smiling in the midst of a pencil landscape—a shepherdess on the other, crossing a little bridge, with a little dog, nicely shaded. The man of the Fancy Repository and Brompton Emporium of Fine Arts (of whom she bought the screens, vainly hoping that he would re-purchase them when ornamented by her hand), can hardly hide the sneer with which he examines these feeble works of art. He looks askance at the lady who waits in the shop, and ties up the cards again in their envelope of whitey-brown paper, and hands them to the poor widow and Miss Clapp, who had never seen such beautiful things in her life, and had been quite confident that the man must give at least two guineas for the screens. They try at other shops in the interior of London, with faint sickening hopes. "Don't want 'em," says one. "Be off," says another fiercely. Three-and-sixpence has been spent in vain—the screens retire to Miss Clapp's bed-room, who persists in thinking them lovely.

She writes out a little card in her neatest hand, and after long thought and labour of composition; in which the public is informed that "A Lady who has some time at her disposal, wishes to undertake the education of some little girls, whom she would instruct in English, in French, in Geography, in History, and in Music—address A. O., at Mr. Brown's;" and she confides the card to the gentleman of the Fine Art Repository, who consents to allow it to lie upon the counter, where it grows dingy and flyblown. Amelia passes the door wistfully many a time, in hopes that Mr. Brown will have some news to give her; but he never beckons her in. When she goes to make little purchases, there is no news for her. Poor simple lady, tender and weak—how are you to battle with the struggling violent world?

She grows daily more care-worn and sad: fixing upon her child alarmed eyes, whereof the little boy cannot interpret the expression. She starts up of a night and peeps into his room stealthily, to see that he is sleeping and not stolen away. She sleeps but little now. A constant thought and terror is haunting her. How she weeps and prays in the long silent nights—how she tries to hide from herself the thought which will return to her, that she ought to part with the boy, that she is the only barrier between him and prosperity. She can't, she can't. Not now, at least. Some other day. Oh! it is too hard to think of and to bear.

A thought comes over her which makes her blush and turn from herself,—her parents might keep the annuity—the curate would marry her and give a home to her and the boy. But George's picture and dearest memory are there to rebuke her. Shame and love say no to the sacrifice. She shrinks from it as from something unholy; and such thoughts never found a resting-place in that pure and gentle bosom.

The combat, which we describe in a sentence or two, lasted for many weeks in poor Amelia's heart: during which she had no confidante; indeed, she could never have one: as she would not allow to herself the possibility of yielding: though she was giving way daily before the enemy with whom she had to battle. One truth after another was marshalling itself silently against her, and keeping its ground. Poverty and misery for all, want and degradation for her parents, injustice to the boy—one by one the outworks of the little citadel were taken, in which the poor soul passionately guarded her only love and treasure.

At the beginning of the struggle, she had written off a letter of tender supplication to her brother at Calcutta, imploring him not to withdraw the support which he had granted to their parents, and painting in terms of artless pathos their lonely and hapless condition. She did not know the truth of the matter. The payment of Jos's annuity was still regular: but it was a money-lender in the City who was receiving it: old Sedley had sold it for a sum of money wherewith to prosecute his bootless schemes. Emmy was calculating eagerly the time that would elapse before the letter would arrive and be answered. She had written down the date in her pocket-book of the day when she dispatched it. To her son's guardian, the good Major at Madras, she had not communicated any of her griefs and perplexities. She had not written to him since she wrote to congratulate him on his approaching marriage. She thought with sickening despondency, that that friend,—the only one, the one who had felt such a regard for her,—was fallen away.

One day, when things had come to a very bad pass—when the creditors were pressing, the mother in hysteric grief, the father in more than usual gloom, the inmates of the family avoiding each other, each secretly oppressed with his private unhappiness and notion of wrong—the father and daughter happened to be left alone together; and Amelia thought to comfort her father, by telling him what she had done. She had written to Joseph—an answer must come in three or four months. He was always generous, though careless. He could not refuse, when he knew how straitened were the circumstances of his parents.

Then the poor old gentleman revealed the whole truth to her—that his son was still paying the annuity, which his own imprudence had flung away. He had not dared to tell it sooner. He thought Amelia's ghastly and terrified look, when, with a trembling, miserable voice he made the confession, conveyed reproaches to him for his concealment. "Ah!" said he, with quivering lips and turning away, "you despise your old father now!"

"O papa! it is not that," Amelia cried out, falling on his neck, and kissing him many times. "You are always good and kind. You did it for the best. It is not for the money —it is—O my God! my God! have mercy upon me, and give me strength to bear this trial;" and she kissed him again wildly, and went away.

Still the father did not know what that explanation meant, and the burst of anguish with which the poor girl left him. It was that she was conquered. The sentence was passed. The child must go from her—to others—to forget her. Her heart and her treasure—her joy, hope, love, worship—her God, almost! She must give him up; and then—and then she would go to George: and they would watch over the child, and wait for him until he came to them in Heaven.

She put on her bonnet, scarcely knowing what she did, and went out to walk in the lanes by which George used to come back from school, and where she was in the habit of going on his return to meet the boy. It was May, a half-holiday. The leaves were all coming out, the weather was brilliant: the boy came running to her flushed with health, singing, his bundle of school-books hanging by a thong. There he was. Both her arms were round him. No, it was impossible. They could not be going to part. "What is the matter, mother?" said he; "you look very pale."

"Nothing, my child," she said, and stooped down and kissed him.

That night Amelia made the boy read the story of Samuel to her, and how Hannah, his mother, having weaned him, brought him to Eli the High Priest to minister before the Lord. And he read the song of gratitude which Hannah sang: and which says, who it is who maketh poor and maketh rich, and bringeth low and exalteth—how the poor shall be raised up out of the dust, and how, in his own might, no man shall be strong. Then he read how Samuel's mother made him a little coat, and brought it to him from year to year when she came up to offer the yearly sacrifice. And then, in her sweet simple way, George's mother made commentaries to the boy upon this affecting story. How Hannah, though she loved her son so much, yet gave him up because of her vow. And how she must always have thought of him as she sat at home, far away, making the little coat; and Samuel, she was sure, never forgot his mother: and how happy she must have been as the time came (and the years pass away very quick) when she should see her boy, and how good and wise he had grown. This little sermon she spoke with a gentle solemn voice, and dry eyes, until she came to the account of their meeting—then the discourse broke off suddenly, the tender heart overflowed, and taking the boy to her breast, she rocked him in her arms, and wept silently over him in a sainted agony of tears.

Her mind being made up, the widow began to take such measures as seemed right to her for advancing the end which she proposed. One day, Miss Osborne, in Russell Square (Amelia had not written the name or number of the house for ten years—her youth, her early story came back

to her as she wrote the superscription)—one day Miss
Osborne got a letter from Amelia which made her blush
very much and look towards her father, sitting glooming
in his place at the other end of the table.

In simple terms, Amelia told her reasons which had
induced her to change her mind respecting her boy. Her
father had met with fresh misfortunes which had entirely
ruined him. Her own pittance was so small that it would
barely enable her to support her parents, and would not
suffice to give George the advantages which were his due.
Great as her sufferings would be at parting with him she
would, by God's help, endure them for the boy's sake. She
knew that those to whom he was going would do all in their
power to make him happy. She described his disposition,
such as she fancied it; quick and impatient of control
or harshness; easily to be moved by love and kindness.
In a postscript, she stipulated that she should have a
written agreement, that she should see the child as often
as she wished,—she could not part with him under any other
terms.

"What? Mrs. Pride has come down, has she?" old
Osborne said, when with a tremulous eager voice Miss
Osborne read him the letter—"Reg'lar starved out, hey?
ha, ha! I knew she would." He tried to keep his dignity
and to read his paper as usual—but he could not follow it.
He chuckled and swore to himself behind the sheet.

At last he flung it down: and scowling at his daughter,
as his wont was, went out of the room into his study adjoining, from whence he presently returned with a key. He
flung it to Miss Osborne.

"Get the room over mine—his room that was—ready," he
said. "Yes, sir," his daughter replied in a tremble. It was
George's room. It had not been opened for more than ten
years. Some of his clothes, papers, handkerchiefs, whips
and caps, fishing-rods and sporting gear, were still there.
An army list of 1814, with his name written on the cover;
a little dictionary he was wont to use in writing; and the
Bible his mother had given him, were on the mantel-piece;
with a pair of spurs, and a dried inkstand covered with the
dust of ten years. Ah! since that ink was wet, what days

and people had passed away! The writing-book still on the table, was blotted with his hand.

Miss Osborne was much affected when she first entered this room with the servants under her. She sank quite pale on the little bed. "This is blessed news, mam—indeed, mam," the housekeeper said; "and the good old times is returning, mam. The dear little feller, to be sure, mam; how happy he will be! But some folks in May Fair, mam, will owe him a grudge, mam;" and she clicked back the bolt which held the window-sash, and let the air into the chamber.

"You had better send that woman some money," Mr. Osborne said, before he went out. "She shan't want for nothing. Send her a hundred pound."

"And I'll go and see her to-morrow?" Miss Osborne asked.

"That's your look out. She don't come in here, mind. No, by—, not for all the money in London. But she mustn't want now. So look out, and get things right." With which brief speeches Mr. Osborne took leave of his daughter, and went on his accustomed way into the City.

"Here, Papa, is some money," Amelia said that night, kissing the old man, her father, and putting a bill for a hundred pounds into his hands. "And—and—Mamma, don't be harsh with Georgy. He—he is not going to stop with us long." She could say nothing more, and walked away silently to her room. Let us close it upon her prayers and her sorrow. I think we had best speak little about so much love and grief.

Miss Osborne came the next day, according to the promise contained in her note, and saw Amelia. The meeting between them was friendly. A look and a few words from Miss Osborne showed the poor widow that, with regard to this woman at least, there need be no fear lest she should take the first place in her son's affections. She was cold, sensible, not unkind. The mother had not been so well pleased, perhaps, had the rival been better looking, younger, more affectionate, warmer-hearted. Miss Osborne, on the other hand, thought of old times and memories, and could not but be touched with the poor mother's pitiful situation. She was conquered, and laying down her arms, as it were, she humbly submitted. That day they arranged together the preliminaries of the treaty of capitulation.

George was kept from school the next day, and saw his aunt. Amelia left them alone together, and went to her room. She was trying the separation:—as that poor gentle Lady Jane Grey felt the edge of the axe that was to come down and sever her slender life. Days were passed in parleys, visits, preparations. The widow broke the matter to Georgy with great caution; she looked to see him very much affected by the intelligence. He was rather elated than otherwise, and the poor woman turned sadly away. He bragged about the news that day to the boys at school; told them how he was going to live with his grandpapa, his father's father, not the one who comes here sometimes; and that he would be very rich, and have a carriage, and a pony, and go to a much finer school, and when he was rich he would buy Leader's pencil-case, and pay the tart-woman. The boy was the image of his father, as his fond mother thought.

Indeed I have no heart, on account of our dear Amelia's sake, to go through the story of George's last days at home.

At last the day came, the carriage drove up, the little humble packets containing tokens of love and remembrance were ready and disposed in the hall long since—George was in his new suit, for which the tailor had come previously to measure him. He had sprung up with the sun and put on the new clothes; his mother hearing him from the room close by, in which she had been lying, in speechless grief and watching. Days before she had been making preparations for the end; purchasing little stores for the boy's use; marking his books and linen; talking with him and preparing him for the change—fondly fancying that he needed preparation.

So that he had change, what cared he? He was longing for it. By a thousand eager declarations as to what he would do, when he went to live with his grandfather, he had shown the poor widow how little the idea of parting had cast him down. "He would come and see his mamma often on the pony," he said: "he would come and fetch her in the carriage; they would drive in the Park, and she should have everything she wanted." The poor mother was fain to content herself with these selfish demonstrations of attachment, and tried to convince herself how sincerely her son loved her. He must love her. All children were so: a little anxious for novelty, and—no, not selfish, but self-willed. Her child must have his enjoyments and ambition in the world. She herself, by her own selfishness and imprudent love for him, had denied him his just rights and pleasures hitherto.

I know few things more affecting than that timorous debasement and self-humiliation of a woman. How she owns that it is she and not the man who is guilty: how she takes all the faults on her side: how she courts in a manner punishment for the wrongs which she has not committed, and persists in shielding the real culprit! It is those who injure women who get the most kindness from them—they are born timid and tyrants, and maltreat those who are humblest before them.

So poor Amelia had been getting ready in silent misery for her son's departure, and had passed many and many a long solitary hour in making preparations for the end. George stood by his mother, watching her arrangements without the least concern. Tears had fallen into his boxes; passages had been scored in his favourite books; old toys, relics, treasures had been hoarded away for him, and packed with strange neatness and care,—and of all these things the boy took no note. The child goes away smiling as the mother breaks her heart. By heavens it is pitiful, the bootless love of women for children in Vanity Fair.

A few days are past: and the great event of Amelia's life is consummated. No angel has intervened. The child is sacrificed and offered up to fate; and the widow is quite alone.

The boy comes to see her often, to be sure. He rides on a pony with a coachman behind him, to the delight of his old grandfather, Sedley, who walks proudly down the lane by his side. She sees him, but he is not her boy any more. Why, he rides to see the boys at the little school, too, and to show off before them his new wealth and splendour. In two days he has adopted a slightly imperious air and patronising manner. He was born to command, his mother thinks, as his father was before him.

It is fine weather now. Of evenings on the days when he does not come, she takes a long walk into London,—yes, as far as Russell Square, and rests on the stone by the railing of the garden opposite Mr. Osborne's house. It is so pleasant and cool. She can look up and see the drawing-room windows illuminated, and, at about nine o'clock, the chamber in the upper story where Georgy sleeps. She knows—He has told her. She prays there as the light goes out, prays with an humble humble heart, and walks home shrinking and silent. She is very tired when she comes home. Perhaps she will sleep the better for that long weary walk; and she may dream about Georgy.

One Sunday she happened to be walking in Russell Square, at some distance from Mr. Osborne's house (she could see it from a distance though) when all the bells of Sabbath were ringing, and George and his aunt came out to go to church; a little sweep asked for charity, and the footman, who carried the books, tried to drive him away; but Georgy stopped and gave him money. May God's blessing be on the boy! Emmy ran round the square, and coming up to the sweep, gave him her mite too. All the bells of Sabbath were ringing, and she followed them until she came to the Foundling Church, into which she went. There she sat in a place whence she could see the head of the boy under his father's tombstone. Many hundred fresh children's voices rose up there and sang hymns to the Father Beneficent; and little George's soul thrilled with delight at the burst of glorious psalmody. His mother could not see him for awhile, through the mist that dimmed her eyes.

CHAPTER XVI

In Which a Charade Is Acted Which May or May Not Puzzle the Reader

AFTER Becky's appearance at my Lord Steyne's private and select parties, the claims of that estimable woman as regards fashion were settled; and some of the very greatest and tallest doors in the metropolis were speedily opened to her—doors so great and tall that the beloved reader and writer hereof may hope in vain to enter at them. Dear brethren, let us tremble before those august portals. I fancy them guarded by grooms of the chamber with flaming silver forks with which they prong all those who have not the right of the entrée. They say the honest newspaper-fellow who sits in the hall, and takes down the names of the great ones who are admitted to the feasts, dies after a little time. He can't survive the glare of fashion long. It scorches him up, as the presence of Jupiter in full dress wasted that poor imprudent Semele—a giddy moth of a creature who ruined herself by venturing out of her natural atmosphere. Her myth ought to be taken to heart amongst the Tyburnians, the Belgravians,—her story, and perhaps Becky's too. Ah, ladies!—ask the Reverend Mr. Thurifer if Belgravia is not a sounding brass, and Tyburnia a tinkling cymbal. These are vanities. Even these will pass away. And some day or other (but it will be after our time, thank goodness), Hyde Park Gardens will be no better known than the celebrated horticultural outskirts of Babylon; and Belgrave Square will be as desolate as Baker Street, or Tadmor in the wilderness.

Ladies, are you aware that the great Pitt lived in Baker Street? What would not your grandmothers have given to be asked to Lady Hester's parties in that now decayed mansion? I have dined in it—*moi qui vous parle.* I peopled the chamber with ghosts of the mighty dead. As we sate soberly

176

drinking claret there with men of to-day, the spirits of the departed came in and took their places round the darksome board. The pilot who weathered the storm tossed off great bumpers of spiritual port: the shade of Dundas did not leave the ghost of a heeltap.—Addington sate bowing and smirking in a ghastly manner, and would not be behindhand when the noiseless bottle went round; Scott, from under bushy eyebrows, winked at the apparition of a beeswing; Wilberforce's eyes went up to the ceiling, so that he did not seem to know how his glass went up full to his mouth and came down empty;—up to the ceiling which was above us only yesterday, and which the great of the past days have all looked at. They let the house as a furnished lodging now. Yes, Lady Hester once lived in Baker Street, and lies asleep in the wilderness. Eothen saw her there—not in Baker Street: but in the other solitude.

It is all vanity to be sure: but who will not own to liking a little of it? I should like to know what well-constituted mind, merely because it is transitory, dislikes roast beef? That is a vanity; but may every man who reads this, have a wholesome portion of it through life, I beg: aye, though my readers were five hundred thousand. Sit down, gentlemen, and fall to, with a good hearty appetite; the fat, the lean, the gravy, the horse-radish as you like it—don't spare it. Another glass of wine, Jones, my boy—a little bit of the Sunday side. Yes, let us eat our fill of the vain thing, and be thankful therefor. And let us make the best of Becky's aristocratic pleasures likewise—for these too, like all other mortal delights, were but transitory.

The upshot of her visit to Lord Steyne was, that His Highness the Prince of Peterwaradin took occasion to renew his acquaintance with Colonel Crawley, when they met on the next day at the Club, and to compliment Mrs. Crawley in the Ring of Hyde Park with a profound salute of the hat. She and her husband were invited immediately to one of the Prince's small parties at Levant House, then occupied by His Highness during the temporary absence from England of its noble proprietor. She sank after dinner to a very little *comité*. The Marquis of Steyne was present, paternally superintending the progress of his pupil.

At Levant House Becky met one of the finest gentlemen and greatest ministers that Europe has produced—the Duc de la Jabotière, then Ambassador from the Most Christian King, and subsequently Minister to that monarch. I declare I swell with pride as these august names are transcribed by my pen; and I think in what brilliant company my dear Becky is moving. She became a constant guest at the French Embassy, where no party was considered to be complete without the presence of the charming Madame Rawdonn Cravley.

Messieurs de Truffigny (of the Périgord family) and Champignac, both attachés of the Embassy, were straightway smitten by the charms of the fair Colonel's wife: and both declared, according to the wont of their nation, (for who ever yet met a Frenchman, come out of England, that has not left half a dozen families miserable, and brought away as many hearts in his pocket-book?) both, I say, declared that they were *au mieux* with the charming Madame Rawdonn.

But I doubt the correctness of the assertion. Champignac was very fond of écarté, and made many *parties* with the Colonel of evenings, while Becky was singing to Lord Steyne in the other room; and as for Truffigny, it is a well-known fact that he dared not go to the Travellers', where he owed money to the waiters, and if he had not had the Embassy as a dining-place, the worthy young gentleman must have starved. I doubt, I say, that Becky would have selected either of these young men as a person on whom she would bestow her special regard. They ran of her messages, purchased her gloves and flowers, went in debt for opera-boxes for her, and made themselves amiable in a thousand ways. And they talked English with adorable simplicity, and to the constant amusement of Becky and my Lord Steyne, she would mimic one or other to his face, and compliment him on his advance in the English language with a gravity which never failed to tickle the Marquis, her sardonic old patron. Truffigny gave Briggs a shawl by way of winning over Becky's confidante, and

asked her to take charge of a letter which the simple
spinster handed over in public to the person to whom it was
addressed; and the composition of which amused everybody who read it greatly. Lord Steyne read it: everybody
but honest Rawdon; to whom it was not necessary to tell
everything that passed in the little house in May Fair.

Here, before long, Becky received not only "the best"
foreigners (as the phrase is in our noble and admirable
society slang), but some of the best English people too.
I don't mean the most virtuous, or indeed the least virtuous, or the cleverest, or the stupidest, or the richest, or
the best born, but "the best,"—in a word, people about
whom there is no question—such as the great Lady Fitz-
Willis, that Patron Saint of Almack's, the great Lady
Slowbore, the great Lady Grizzel Macbeth (she was Lady
G. Glowry, daughter of Lord Grey of Glowry), and the
like. When the Countess of Fitz-Willis (her ladyship is
of the Kingstreet family, see Debrett and Burke) takes up
a person, he or she is safe. There is no question about them
any more. Not that my Lady Fitz-Willis is any better
than anybody else, being, on the contrary, a faded person,
fifty-seven years of age, and neither handsome, nor wealthy,
nor entertaining; but it is agreed on all sides that she is of
the "best people." Those who go to her are of the best:
and from an old grudge probably to Lady Steyne (for whose
coronet her ladyship, then the youthful Georgina Frederica,
daughter of the Prince of Wales's favourite, the Earl of
Portansherry, had once tried), this great and famous leader
of the fashion chose to acknowledge Mrs. Rawdon Crawley:
made her a most marked curtsey at the assembly over which
she presided: and not only encouraged her son, St. Kitts
(his lordship got his place through Lord Steyne's interest),
to frequent Mrs. Crawley's house, but asked her to her own
mansion, and spoke to her twice in the most public and
condescending manner during dinner. The important fact
was known all over London that night. People who had
been crying fie about Mrs. Crawley were silent. Wenham,
the wit and lawyer, Lord Steyne's right-hand man, went
about everywhere praising her: some who had hesitated,
came forward at once and welcomed her; little Tom Toady,

who had warned Southdown about visiting such an abandoned woman, now besought to be introduced to her. In a word, she was admitted to be among the "best" people. Ah, my beloved readers and brethren, do not envy poor Becky prematurely—glory like this is said to be fugitive. It is currently reported that even in the very inmost circles, they are no happier than the poor wanderers outside the zone; and Becky, who penetrated into the very centre of fashion, and saw the great George IV. face to face, has owned since that there too was Vanity.

We must be brief in descanting upon this part of her career. As I cannot describe the mysteries of freemasonry, although I have a shrewd idea that it is a humbug: so an uninitiated man cannot take upon himself to pourtray the great world accurately, and had best keep his opinions to himself whatever they are.

Becky has often spoken in subsequent years of this season of her life, when she moved among the very greatest circles of the London fashion. Her success excited, elated, and then bored her. At first no occupation was more pleasant than to invent and procure (the latter a work of no small trouble and ingenuity, by the way, in a person of Mrs. Rawdon Crawley's very narrow means)—to procure, we say, the prettiest new dresses and ornaments; to drive to fine dinner parties, where she was welcomed by great people; and from the fine dinner parties to fine assemblies, whither the same people came with whom she had been dining, whom she had met the night before, and would see on the morrow—the young men faultlessly appointed, handsomely cravatted, with the neatest glossy boots and white gloves—the elders portly, brass-buttoned, noble-looking, polite, and prosy—the young ladies blonde, timid, and in pink—the mothers grand, beautiful, sumptuous, solemn, and in diamonds. They talked in English, not in bad French, as they do in the novels. They talked about each others' houses, and characters, and families: just as the Joneses do about the Smiths. Becky's former acquaintances hated and envied her: the poor woman herself was yawning in spirit. "I wish I were out of it," she said to herself. "I would rather be a parson's wife, and teach a

Sunday School than this; or a sergeant's lady and ride in
the regimental waggon; or, O how much gayer it would be
to wear spangles and trowsers, and dance before a booth at
a fair."

"You would do it very well," said Lord Steyne, laughing. She used to tell the great man her *ennuis* and perplexities in her artless way—they amused him.

"Rawdon would make a very good Ecuyer—Master of
the Ceremonies—what do you call him—the man in the
large boots and the uniform, who goes round the ring
cracking the whip? He is large, heavy, and of a military
figure. I recollect," Becky continued, pensively, "my father
took me to see a show at Brookgreen Fair when I was a
child; and when we came home I made myself a pair of
stilts, and danced in the studio to the wonder of all the pupils."

"I should have liked to see it," said Lord Steyne.

"I should like to do it now," Becky continued. "How
Lady Blinkey would open her eyes, and Lady Grizzel Macbeth would stare! Hush! silence! there is Pasta beginning to sing." Becky always made a point of being con-
spicuously polite to the professional ladies and gentlemen
who attended at these aristocratic parties—of following
them into the corners where they sat in silence, and shaking hands with them, and smiling in the view of all persons. She was an artist herself, as she said very truly:
there was a frankness and humility in the manner in which
she acknowledged her origin, which provoked, or disarmed,
or amused lookers-on, as the case might be. "How cool
that woman is," said one; "what airs of independence she
assumes, where she ought to sit still and be thankful if
anybody speaks to her!" "What an honest and good-natured soul she is!" said another. "What an artful little
minx!" said a third. They were all right very likely; but
Becky went her own way, and so fascinated the professional
personages, that they would leave off their sore throats in
order to sing at her parties, and give her lessons for nothing.

Yes, she gave parties in the little house in Curzon Street.
Many scores of carriages, with blazing lamps, blocked up
the street, to the disgust of No. 100, who could not rest
for the thunder of the knocking, and of 102, who could not

sleep for envy. The gigantic footmen who accompanied
the vehicles were too big to be contained in Becky's little
hall, and were billeted off in the neighbouring public-
houses, whence, when they were wanted, call-boys summoned them from their beer. Scores of the great dandies
of London squeezed and trod on each other on the little
stairs, laughing to find themselves there; and many spotless and severe ladies of *ton* were seated in the little drawing-room, listening to the professional singers, who were
singing according to their wont, and as if they wished to
blow the windows down. And the day after, there appeared among the fashionable *réunions* in the *Morning Post*
a paragraph to the following effect:

"Yesterday, Colonel and Mrs. Crawley entertained a
select party at dinner at their house in May Fair. Their
Excellencies the Prince and Princess of Peterwaradin, H.
E. Papoosh Pasha, the Turkish Ambassador (attended by
Kibob Bey, dragoman of the mission), the Marquess of
Steyne, Earl of Southdown, Sir Pitt and Lady Jane Crawley, Mr. Wagg, &c. After dinner Mrs. Crawley had an
assembly which was attended by the Duchess (Dowager) of
Stilton, Duc de la Gruyère, Marchioness of Cheshire, Mar-
chese Alessandro Strachino, Comte de Brie, Baron Schap-
zuger, Chevalier Tosti, Countess of Slingstone, and Lady
F. Macadam, Major-General and Lady G. Macbeth, and
(2) Miss Macbeths; Viscount Paddington, Sir Horace Fogey, Hon. Bedwin Sands, Bobbachy Bahawder," and an
&c., which the reader may fill at his pleasure through a
dozen close lines of small type.

And in her commerce with the great our dear friend
showed the same frankness which distinguished her transactions with the lowly in station. On one occasion, when
out at a very fine house, Rebecca was (perhaps rather
ostentatiously) holding a conversation in the French language with a celebrated tenor singer of that nation, while
the Lady Grizzel Macbeth looked over her shoulder scowling at the pair.

"How very well you speak French," Lady Grizzel said,
who herself spoke the tongue in an Edinburgh accent most
remarkable to hear.

"I ought to know it," Becky modestly said, casting down her eyes. "I taught it in a school, and my mother was a Frenchwoman."

Lady Grizzel was won by her humility, and was mollified towards the little woman. She deplored the fatal levelling tendencies of the age, which admitted persons of all classes into the society of their superiors; but her ladyship owned, that this one at least was well behaved and never forgot her place in life. She was a very good woman: good to the poor: stupid, blameless, unsuspicious. —It is not her ladyship's fault that she fancies herself better than you and me. The skirts of her ancestors' garments have been kissed for centuries: it is a thousand years, they say, since the tartans of the head of the family were embraced by the defunct Duncan's lords and councillors, when the great ancestor of the House became King of Scotland.

Lady Steyne, after the music scene, succumbed before Becky, and perhaps was not disinclined to her. The younger ladies of the house of Gaunt were also compelled into submission. Once or twice they set people at her, but they failed. The brilliant Lady Stunnington tried a passage of arms with her, but was routed with great slaughter by the intrepid little Becky. When attacked sometimes, Becky had a knack of adopting a demure *ingénue* air, under which she was most dangerous. She said the wickedest things with the most simple unaffected air when in this mood, and would take care artlessly to apologise for her blunders, so that all the world should know that she had made them.

Mr. Wagg, the celebrated wit, and a led captain and trencher-man of my Lord Steyne, was caused by the ladies to charge her; and the worthy fellow, leering at his patronesses, and giving them a wink, as much as to say, "Now look out for sport,"—one evening began an assault upon Becky, who was unsuspiciously eating her dinner. The little woman, attacked on a sudden, but never without arms, lighted up in an instant, parried and riposted with a home-thrust, which made Wagg's face tingle with shame; then she returned to her soup with the most perfect calm and a quiet smile on her face. Wagg's great patron, who gave him dinners and lent him a little money sometimes, and whose election, newspaper, and other jobs Wagg did, gave the luckless fellow such a savage glance with the eyes as almost made him sink under the table and burst into tears. He looked piteously at my lord, who never spoke to him during dinner, and at the ladies, who disowned him. At last Becky herself took compassion upon him, and tried to engage him in talk. He was not asked to dinner again for six weeks; and Fiche, my lord's confidential man, to whom Wagg naturally paid a good deal of court, was instructed to tell him that if he ever dared to say a rude thing to Mrs. Crawley again, or make her the butt of his stupid jokes, Milor would put every one of his notes of hand into his lawyer's hands, and sell him up without mercy. Wagg wept before Fiche, and implored his dear friend to intercede for him. He wrote a poem in favour of Mrs. R. C., which appeared in the very next number of the "Harumscarum Magazine," which he conducted. He implored her good will at parties where he met her. He cringed and coaxed Rawdon at the club. He was allowed to come back to Gaunt House after a while. Becky was always good to him, always amused, never angry.

His lordship's vizier and chief confidential servant (with a seat in parliament and at the dinner table), Mr. Wenham, was much more prudent in his behaviour and opinions than Mr. Wagg. However much he might be disposed to hate all parvenus (Mr. Wenham himself was a staunch old True Blue Tory, and his father a small coal-merchant in the north of England), this aide-de-camp of the Marquis never showed any sort of hostility to the new favourite: but pursued her with stealthy kindnesses, and a sly and deferential politeness, which somehow made Becky more uneasy than other people's overt hostilities.

How the Crawleys got the money which was spent upon the entertainments with which they treated the polite world, was a mystery which gave rise to some conversation at the time, and probably added zest to these little festivities. Some persons averred that Sir Pitt Crawley gave his

brother a handsome allowance: if he did, Becky's power
over the Baronet must have been extraordinary indeed, and
his character greatly changed in his advanced age. Other
parties hinted that it was Becky's habit to levy contributions on all her husband's friends: going to this one in
tears with an account that there was an execution in the
house; falling on her knees to that one, and declaring that
the whole family must go to gaol or commit suicide unless
such and such a bill could be paid. Lord Southdown, it
was said, had been induced to give many hundreds through
these pathetic representations. Young Feltham, of the —th
Dragoons (and son of the firm of Tiler and Feltham, hat-
ters and army accoutrement makers), and whom the Crawleys introduced into fashionable life, was also cited as
one of Becky's victims in the pecuniary way. People
declared that she got money from various simply disposed
persons under pretence of getting them confidential appointments under Government. Who knows what stories
were or were not told of our dear and innocent friend?
Certain it is, that if she had had all the money which she
was said to have begged or borrowed or stolen, she might
have capitalised and been honest for life, whereas,—but
this is advancing matters.

The truth is, that by economy and good management—
by a sparing use of ready money and by paying scarcely
anybody,—people can manage, for a time at least, to make
a great show with very little means: and it is our belief
that Becky's much-talked-of parties, which were not, after
all was said, very numerous, cost this lady very little more
than the wax candles which lighted the walls. Stillbrook
and Queen's Crawley supplied her with game and fruit in
abundance. Lord Steyne's cellars were at her disposal, and
that excellent nobleman's famous cooks presided over her
little kitchen, or sent by my lord's order the rarest delicacies
from their own. I protest it is quite shameful in the world
to abuse a simple creature, as people of her time abuse
Becky, and I warn the public against believing one-tenth of
the stories against her. If every person is to be banished
from society who runs into debt and cannot pay—if we are
to be peering into everybody's private life, speculating upon

their income, and cutting them if we don't approve of their expenditure—why, what a howling wilderness and intolerable dwelling Vanity Fair would be! Every man's hand would be against his neighbour in this case, my dear sir, and the benefits of civilisation would be done away with. We should be quarrelling, abusing, avoiding one another. Our houses would become caverns: and we should go in rags because we cared for nobody. Rents would go down. Parties wouldn't be given any more. All the tradesmen of the town would be bankrupt. Wine, wax-lights, comestibles, rouge, crinoline-petticoats, diamonds, wigs, Louis-Quatorze gim-cracks, and old china, park hacks, and splendid high-stepping carriage horses—all the delights of life, I say,—would go to the deuce, if people did but act upon their silly principles, and avoid those whom they dislike and abuse. Whereas, by a little charity and mutual forbearance, things are made to go on pleasantly enough: we may abuse a man as much as we like, and call him the greatest rascal unhanged—but do we wish to hang him therefore? No. We shake hands when we meet. If his cook is good we forgive him, and go and dine with him; and we expect he will do the same by us. Thus trade flourishes—civilisation advances: peace is kept; new dresses are wanted for new assemblies every week; and the last year's vintage of Lafitte will remunerate the honest proprietor who reared it.

At the time whereof we are writing, though the Great George was on the throne and ladies wore *gigots* and large combs like tortoise-shell shovels in their hair, instead of the simple sleeves and lovely wreaths which are actually in fashion, the manners of the very polite world were not, I take it, essentially different from those of the present day: and their amusements pretty similar. To us, from the outside, gazing over the policeman's shoulders at the bewildering beauties as they pass into Court or ball, they may seem beings of unearthly splendour, and in the enjoy-ment of an exquisite happiness by us unattainable. It is to console some of these dissatisfied beings, that we are narrating our dear Becky's struggles, and triumphs, and disappointments, of all of which, indeed, as is the case with all persons of merit, she had her share.

At this time the amiable amusement of acting charades had come among us from France: and was considerably in vogue in this country, enabling the many ladies amongst us who had beauty to display their charms, and the fewer number who had cleverness, to exhibit their wit. My Lord Steyne was incited by Becky, who perhaps believed herself endowed with both the above qualifications, to give an entertainment at Gaunt House, which should include some of these little dramas—and we must take leave to introduce the reader to this brilliant *réunion,* and, with a melancholy welcome too, for it will be among the very last of the fashionable entertainments to which it will be our fortune to conduct him.

A portion of that splendid room, the picture gallery of Gaunt House, was arranged as the charade theatre. It had been so used when George III. was king; and a picture of the Marquis of Gaunt is still extant, with his hair in powder and a pink ribbon, in a Roman shape, as it was called, enacting the part of Cato in Mr. Addison's tragedy of that name, performed before their Royal Highnesses the Prince of Wales, the Bishop of Osnaburgh, and Prince William Henry, then children like the actor. One or two of the old properties were drawn out of the garrets, where they had lain ever since, and furbished up anew for the present festivities.

Young Bedwin Sands, then an elegant dandy and Eastern traveller, was manager of the revels. An Eastern traveller was somebody in those days, and the adventurous Bedwin, who had published his quarto, and passed some months under the tents in the desert, was a personage of no small importance.—In his volume there were several pictures of Sands in various oriental costumes; and he travelled about with a black attendant of most unprepossessing appearance, just like another Brian de Bois Guilbert. Bedwin, his costumes, and black man, were hailed at Gaunt House as very valuable acquisitions.

He led off the first charade. A Turkish officer with an immense plume of feathers (the Janizaries were supposed to be still in existence, and the tarboosh had not as yet displaced the ancient and majestic head-dress of the true believers), was seen couched on a divan, and making believe to puff at a narghile, in which, however, for the sake of the ladies, only a fragrant pastille was allowed to smoke. The Turkish dignitary yawns and expresses signs of weariness and idleness. He claps his hands and Mesrour the Nubian appears, with bare arms, bangles, yataghans, and every Eastern ornament—gaunt, tall, and hideous. He makes a salaam before my lord the Aga.

A thrill of terror and delight runs through the assembly. The ladies whisper to one another. The black slave was given to Bedwin Sands by an Egyptian Pasha in exchange for three dozen of Maraschino. He has sewn up ever so many odalisques in sacks and tilted them into the Nile.

"Bid the slave-merchant enter," says the Turkish voluptuary with a wave of his hand. Mesrour conducts the slave-merchant into my lord's presence: he brings a veiled female with him. He removes the veil. A thrill of applause bursts through the house. It is Mrs. Winkworth (she was a Miss Absolom) with the beautiful eyes and hair. She is in a gorgeous oriental costume; the black braided locks are twined with innumerable jewels; her dress is covered over with gold piastres. The odious Mahometan expresses himself charmed by her beauty. She falls down on her knees, and entreats him to restore her to the mountains where she was born, and where her Circassian lover is still deploring the absence of his Zuleikah. No entreaties will move the obdurate Hassan. He laughs at the notion of the Circassian bridegroom. Zuleikah covers her face with her hands, and drops down in an attitude of the most beautiful despair. There seems to be no hope for her, when—when the Kislar Aga appears.

The Kislar Aga brings a letter from the Sultan. Hassan receives and places on his head the dread firman. A ghastly terror seizes him, while on the negro's face (it is Mesrour again in another costume) appears a ghastly joy. "Mercy! mercy!" cries the Pasha: while the Kislar Aga, grinning horribly, pulls out—a *bow-string*.

The curtain draws just as he is going to use that awful weapon. Hassan from within bawls out, "First two syllables"—and Mrs. Rawdon Crawley, who is going to act in the charade, comes forward and compliments Mrs. Winkworth on the admirable taste and beauty of her costume.

The second part of the charade takes place. It is still an Eastern scene. Hassan, in another dress, is in an attitude by Zuleikah, who is perfectly reconciled to him. The Kislar Aga has become a peaceful black slave. It is sunrise on the desert, and the Turks turn their heads eastwards and bow to the sand. As there are no dromedaries at hand, the band facetiously plays "The Camels are coming." An enormous Egyptian head figures in the scene. It is a musical one,— and, to the surprise of the oriental travellers, sings a comic song, composed by Mr. Wagg. The Eastern voyagers go off dancing, like Papageno and the Moorish King, in the "Magic Flute." "Last two syllables" roars the head.

The last act opens. It is a Grecian tent this time. A tall and stalwart man reposes on a couch there. Above him hang his helmet and shield. There is no need for them now. Ilium is down. Iphigenia is slain. Cassandra is a prisoner in his outer halls. The king of men (it is Colonel Crawley, who, indeed, has no notion about the sack of Ilium or the conquest of Cassandra), the anax andrôn is asleep in his chamber at Argos. A lamp casts the broad shadow of the sleeping warrior flickering on the wall—the sword and shield of Troy glitter in its light. The band plays the awful music of "Don Juan," before the statue enters.

Ægisthus steals in pale and on tiptoe. What is that ghastly face looking out balefully after him from behind the arras? He raises his dagger to strike the sleeper, who turns in his bed, and opens his broad chest as if for the blow. He cannot strike the noble slumbering chieftain. Clytemnestra glides swiftly into the room like an apparition —her arms are bare and white,—her tawny hair floats down her shoulders,—her face is deadly pale,—and her eyes are lighted up with a smile so ghastly, that people quake as they look at her.

A tremor ran through the room. "Good God!" somebody said, "it's Mrs. Rawdon Crawley."

Scornfully she snatches the dagger out of Ægisthus's hand, and advances to the bed. You see it shining over her head in the glimmer of the lamp, and—and the lamp goes out, with a groan, and all is dark.

The darkness and the scene frightened people. Rebecca performed her part so well, and with such ghastly truth, that the spectators were all dumb, until, with a burst, all the lamps of the hall blazed out again, when everybody began to shout applause. "Brava! brava!" old Steyne's strident voice was heard roaring over all the rest. "By —, she'd do it too," he said between his teeth. The performers were called by the whole house, which sounded with cries of "Manager! Clytemnestra!" AGAMEMNON could not be got to show in his classical tunic, but stood in the background with Ægisthus and others of the performers of the little play. Mr. Bedwin Sands led on Zuleikah and Clytemnestra. A great personage insisted on being presented to the charming Clytemnestra. "Heigh ha? Run him through the body. Marry somebody else, hay?" was the apposite remark made by His Royal Highness.

"Mrs. Rawdon Crawley was quite killing in the part," said Lord Steyne. Becky laughed; gay, and saucy looking, and swept the prettiest little curtsey ever seen.

Servants brought in salvers covered with numerous cool dainties, and the performers disappeared to get ready for the second charade-tableau.

The three syllables of this charade were to be depicted in pantomime, and the performance took place in the following wise :—

First syllable. Colonel Rawdon Crawley, C.B., with a slouched hat and a staff, a great coat, and a lantern borrowed from the stables, passed across the stage bawling out, as if warning the inhabitants of the hour. In the lower window are seen two bagmen playing apparently at the game of cribbage, over which they yawn much. To them enters one looking like Boots, (the Honourable G. Ringwood) which character the young gentleman performed to perfection, and divests them of their lower coverings; and presently Chambermaid (the Right Honourable Lord Southdown) with two candlesticks, and a warming-pan. She ascends to the upper apartment, and warms the bed. She uses the

warming-pan as a weapon wherewith she wards off the
attention of the bagmen. She exits. They put on their
night-caps, and pull down the blinds. Boots comes out and
closes the shutters of the ground-floor chamber. You hear
him bolting and chaining the door within. All the lights go
out. The music plays *Dormez, dormez, chers Amours.* A
voice from behind the curtain says, "First syllable."

Second syllable. The lamps are lighted up all of a sudden.
The music plays the old air from John of Paris, *Ah quel
plaisir d'être en voyage.* It is the same scene. Between the
first and second floors of the house represented, you behold
a sign on which the Steyne arms are painted. All the bells
are ringing all over the house. In the lower apartment you
see a man with a long slip of paper presenting it to another,
who shakes his fists, threatens and vows that it is monstrous.
"Ostler, bring round my gig," cries another at the door. He
chucks Chambermaid (the Right Honourable Lord Southdown) under the chin; she seems to deplore his absence, as
Calypso did that of that other eminent traveller Ulysses.
Boots (the Honourable G. Ringwood) passes with a wooden
box, containing silver flagons, and cries "Pots" with such
exquisite humour and naturalness, that the whole house rings
with applause, and a bouquet is thrown to him. Crack,
crack, crack, go the whips. Landlord, chambermaid, waiter
rush to the door; but just as some distinguished guest is
arriving, the curtains close, and the invisible theatrical manager cries out "Second syllable."

"I think it must be 'Hotel'," says Captain Grigg of the
Life Guards; there is a general laugh at the Captain's cleverness. He is not very far from the mark.

While the third syllable is in preparation, the band begins a nautical medley—"All in the Downs," "Cease Rude
Boreas," "Rule Britannia," "In the Bay of Biscay O!"—
some maritime event is about to take place. A bell is heard
ringing as the curtain draws aside. "Now, gents, for the
shore!" a voice exclaims. People take leave of each other.
They point anxiously as if towards the clouds, which are
represented by a dark curtain, and they nod their heads in
fear. Lady Squeams (the Right Honourable Lord Southdown), her lap-dog, her bags, reticules, and husband sit

down, and cling hold of some ropes. It is evidently a ship.

The Captain (Colonel Crawley, C.B.), with a cocked hat and a telescope, comes in, holding his hat on his head, and looks out; his coat tails fly about as if in the wind. When he leaves go of his hat to use his telescope, his hat flies off, with immense applause. It is blowing fresh. The music rises and whistles louder and louder; the mariners go across the stage staggering, as if the ship was in severe motion. The Steward (the Honourable G. Ringwood) passes reeling by, holding six basins. He puts one rapidly by Lord Squeams —Lady Squeams, giving a pinch to her dog, which begins to howl piteously, puts her pocket-handkerchief to her face, and rushes away as for the cabin. The music rises up to the wildest pitch of stormy excitement, and the third syllable is concluded.

There was a little ballet, "Le Rossignol," in which Montessu and Noblet used to be famous in those days, and which Mr. Wagg transferred to the English stage as an opera, putting his verse, of which he was a skilful writer, to the pretty airs of the ballet. It was dressed in old French costume, and little Lord Southdown now appeared admirably attired in the disguise of an old woman hobbling about the stage with a faultless crooked stick.

Trills of melody were heard behind the scenes, and gurgling from a sweet pasteboard cottage covered with roses and trellis work. "Philomèle, Philomèle," cries the old woman, and Philomèle comes out.

More applause—it is Mrs. Rawdon Crawley in powder and patches, the most *ravissante* little Marquise in the world.

She comes in laughing, humming, and frisks about the stage with all the innocence of theatrical youth—she makes a curtsey. Mamma says "Why, child, you are always laughing and singing," and away she goes, with—

THE ROSE UPON MY BALCONY

The rose upon my balcony the morning air perfuming,
Was leafless all the winter time and pining for the spring;
You ask me why her breath is sweet and why her cheek is blooming,
It is because the sun is out and birds begin to sing,

The nightingale, whose melody is through the greenwood ringing,
Was silent when the boughs were bare and winds were blowing keen:
And if, Mamma, you ask of me the reason of his singing,
It is because the sun is out and all the leaves are green.

Thus each performs his part, Mamma, the birds have found their
        voices,
The blowing rose a flush, Mamma, her bonny cheek to dye;
And there's sunshine in my heart, Mamma, which wakens and
        rejoices,
And so I sing and blush, Mamma, and that's the reason why.

During the intervals of the stanzas of this ditty, the
good-natured personage addressed as mamma by the singer,
and whose large whiskers appeared under her cap, seemed
very anxious to exhibit her maternal affection by embracing
the innocent creature who performed the daughter's part.
Every caress was received with loud acclamations of
laughter by the sympathising audience. At its conclusion
(while the music was performing a symphony as if ever so
many birds were warbling) the whole house was unanimous
for an *encore:* and applause and bouquets without end were
showered upon the NIGHTINGALE of the evening. Lord
Steyne's voice of applause was loudest of all. Becky, the
nightingale, took the flowers which he threw to her, and
pressed them to her heart with the air of a consummate
comedian. Lord Steyne was frantic with delight. His
guests' enthusiasm harmonised with his own. Where was
the beautiful black-eyed Houri whose appearance in the
first charade had caused such delight? She was twice as
handsome as Becky, but the brilliancy of the latter had
quite eclipsed her. All voices were for her. Stephens,
Caradori, Ronzi de Begnis, people compared her to one or
the other, and agreed with good reason, very likely, that
had she been an actress none on the stage could have sur-
passed her. She had reached her culmination: her voice
rose trilling and bright over the storm of applause: and
soared as high and joyful as her triumph. There was a
ball after the dramatic entertainments, and everybody
pressed round Becky as the great point of attraction of the
evening. The Royal Personage declared with an oath, that
she was perfection, and engaged her again and again in
conversation. Little Becky's soul swelled with pride and

delight at these honours; she saw fortune, fame, fashion before her. Lord Steyne was her slave; followed her everywhere, and scarcely spoke to any one in the room beside; and paid her the most marked compliments and attention. She still appeared in her Marquise costume, and danced a minuet with Monsieur de Truffigny, Monsieur Le Duc de la Jabotière's attaché; and the Duke, who had all the traditions of the ancient court, pronounced that Madame Crawley was worthy to have been a pupil of Vestris, or to have figured at Versailles. Only a feeling of dignity, the gout, and the strongest sense of duty and personal sacrifice, prevented his Excellency from dancing with her himself; and he declared in public, that a lady who could talk and dance like Mrs. Rawdon, was fit to be ambassadress at any court in Europe. He was only consoled when he heard that she was half a French woman by birth. "None but a compatriot," his Excellency declared, "could have performed that majestic dance in such a way."

Then she figured in a waltz with Monsieur de Klingenspohr, the Prince of Peterwaradin's cousin and attaché. The delighted Prince, having less *retenue* than his French diplomatic colleague, insisted upon taking a turn with the charming creature, and twirled round the ball-room with her, scattering the diamonds out of his boot-tassels and hussar jacket until his highness was fairly out of breath. Papoosh Pasha himself would have liked to dance with her if that amusement had been the custom of his country. The company made a circle round her, and applauded as wildly as if she had been a Noblet or a Taglioni. Everybody was in ecstasy; and Becky too, you may be sure. She passed by Lady Stunnington with a look of scorn. She patronised Lady Gaunt and her astonished and mortified sister-in-law—she *écrased* all rival charmers. As for poor Mrs. Winkworth, and her long hair and great eyes, which had made such an effect at the commencement of the evening; where was she now? Nowhere in the race. She might tear her long hair and cry her great eyes out; but there was not a person to heed or to deplore the discomfiture.

The greatest triumph of all was at supper time. She was placed at the grand exclusive table with his Royal

Highness the exalted personage before mentioned, and the rest of the great guests. She was served on gold plate. She might have had pearls melted into her champagne if she liked—another Cleopatra; and the potentate of Peter-waradin would have given half the brilliants off his jacket for a kind glance from those dazzling eyes. Jabotière wrote home about her to his government. The ladies at the other tables, who supped off mere silver, and marked Lord Steyne's constant attention to her, vowed it was a monstrous infatuation, a gross insult to ladies of rank. If sarcasm could have killed, Lady Stunnington would have slain her on the spot.

Rawdon Crawley was scared at these triumphs. They seemed to separate his wife farther than ever from him somehow. He thought with a feeling very like pain how immeasurably she was his superior.

When the hour of departure came, a crowd of young men followed her to her carriage, for which the people without bawled, the cry being caught up by the link-men who were stationed outside the tall gates of Gaunt House, congratu-lating each person who issued from the gate and hoping his Lordship had enjoyed this noble party.

Mrs. Rawdon Crawley's carriage, coming up to the gate after due shouting, rattled into the illuminated court-yard, and drove up to the covered way. Rawdon put his wife into the carriage, which drove off. Mr. Wenham had pro-posed to him to walk home, and offered the Colonel the refreshment of a cigar.

They lighted their cigars by the lamp of one of the many link-boys outside, and Rawdon walked on with his friend Wenham. Two persons separated from the crowd and followed the two gentlemen; and when they had walked down Gaunt Square a few score of paces, one of the men came up, and touching Rawdon on the shoulder, said, "Beg your pardon, Colonel, I vish to speak to you most particular." This gentleman's acquaintance gave a loud whistle as the latter spoke, at which signal a cab came clattering up from those stationed at the gate of Gaunt House—and the aide-de-camp ran round and placed himself in front of Colonel Crawley.

That gallant officer at once knew what had befallen him. He was in the hands of the bailiffs. He started back, falling against the man who had first touched him.

"We're three on us—it's no use bolting," the man behind said.

"It's you, Moss, is it?" said the Colonel, who appeared to know his interlocutor. "How much is it?"

"Only a small thing," whispered Mr. Moss, of Cursitor Street, Chancery Lane, and assistant officer to the Sheriff of Middlesex—"One hundred and sixty-six, six and eight-pence, at the suit of Mr. Nathan."

"Lend me a hundred, Wenham, for God's sake," poor Rawdon said—"I've got seventy at home."

"I've not got ten pounds in the world," said poor Mr. Wenham—"Good night, my dear fellow."

"Good night," said Rawdon ruefully. And Wenham walked away—and Rawdon Crawley finished his cigar as the cab drove under Temple Bar.

CHAPTER XVII

In Which Lord Steyne Shows Himself in a Most Amiable Light

WHEN Lord Steyne was benevolently disposed, he did nothing by halves, and his kindness towards the Crawley family did the greatest honour to his benevolent discrimination. His lordship extended his good-will to little Rawdon: he pointed out to the boy's parents the necessity of sending him to a public school; that he was of an age now when emulation, the first principles of the Latin language, pugilistic exercises, and the society of his fellow-boys would be of the greatest benefit to the boy. His father objected that he was not rich enough to send the child to a good public school; his mother, that Briggs was a capital mistress for him, and had brought him on (as indeed was the fact) famously in English, the Latin rudiments, and in general learning: but all these objections disappeared before the generous perseverance of the Marquis of Steyne. His lordship was one of the governors of that famous old collegiate institution called the Whitefriars. It had been a Cistercian Convent in old days, when the Smithfield, which is contiguous to it, was a tournament ground. Obstinate heretics used to be brought thither convenient for burning hard by. Henry VIII., the Defender of the Faith, seized upon the monastery and its possessions, and hanged and tortured some of the monks who could not accommodate themselves to the pace of his reform. Finally, a great merchant bought the house and land adjoining, in which, and with the help of other wealthy endowments of land and money, he established a famous foundation hospital for old men and children. An extern school grew round the old almost monastic foundation, which subsists still with its middle-age costume and usages: and all Cistercians pray that it may long flourish.

197

Of this famous house, some of the greatest noblemen, prelates, and dignitaries in England are governors: and as the boys are very comfortably lodged, fed, and educated, and subsequently inducted to good scholarships at the University and livings in the Church, many little gentlemen are devoted to the ecclesiastical profession from their tenderest years, and there is considerable emulation to procure nominations for the foundation. It was originally intended for the sons of poor and deserving clerics and laics; but many of the noble governors of the Institution, with an enlarged and rather capricious benevolence, selected all sorts of objects for their bounty. To get an education for nothing, and a future livelihood and profession assured, was so excellent a scheme that some of the richest people did not disdain it; and not only great men's relations, but great men themselves, sent their sons to profit by the chance—Right Rev. Prelates sent their own kinsmen or the sons of their clergy, while, on the other hand, some great noblemen did not disdain to patronise the children of their confidential servants,—so that a lad entering this establishment had every variety of youthful society wherewith to mingle.

Rawdon Crawley, though the only book which he studied was the Racing Calendar, and though his chief recollections of polite learning were connected with the floggings which he received at Eton in his early youth, had that decent and honest reverence for classical learning which all English gentlemen feel, and was glad to think that his son was to have a provision for life, perhaps, and a certain opportunity of becoming a scholar. And although his boy was his chief solace and companion, and endeared to him by a thousand small ties, about which he did not care to speak to his wife, who had all along shown the utmost indifference to their son, yet Rawdon agreed at once to part with him, and to give up his own greatest comfort and benefit for the sake of the welfare of the little lad. He did not know how fond he was of the child until it became necessary to let him go away. When he was gone, he felt more sad and downcast than he cared to own—far sadder than the boy himself, who was happy enough to enter a new career.

and find companions of his own age. Becky burst out laughing once or twice, when the Colonel, in his clumsy, incoherent way, tried to express his sentimental sorrows at the boy's departure. The poor fellow felt that his dearest pleasure and closest friend was taken from him. He looked often and wistfully at the little vacant bed in his dressing-room, where the child used to sleep. He missed him sadly of mornings, and tried in vain to walk in the Park without him. He did not know how solitary he was until little Rawdon was gone. He liked the people who were fond of him; and would go and sit for long hours with his good-natured sister Lady Jane, and talk to her about the virtues, and good looks, and hundred good qualities of the child.

Young Rawdon's aunt, we have said, was very fond of him, as was her little girl, who wept copiously when the time for her cousin's departure came. The elder Rawdon was thankful for the fondness of mother and daughter. The very best and honestest feelings of the man came out in these artless outpourings of paternal feeling in which he indulged in their presence, and encouraged by their sympathy. He secured not only Lady Jane's kindness, but her sincere regard, by the feelings which he manifested, and which he could not show to his own wife. The two kins-women met as seldom as possible. Becky laughed bitterly at Jane's feelings and softness; the other's kindly and gentle nature could not but revolt at her sister's callous behaviour.

It estranged Rawdon from his wife more than he knew or acknowledged to himself. She did not care for the estrangement. Indeed, she did not miss him or anybody. She looked upon him as her errand-man and humble slave. He might be ever so depressed or sulky, and she did not mark his demeanour, or only treated it with a sneer. She was busy thinking about her position, or her pleasures, or her advancement in society; she ought to have held a great place in it, that is certain.

It was honest Briggs who made up the little kit for the boy which he was to take to school. Molly, the house-maid, blubbered in the passage when he went away—Molly kind and faithful in spite of a long arrear of unpaid wages. Mrs. Becky could not let her husband have the carriage to take

the boy to school.   Take the horses into the City!—such a
thing was never heard of.   Let a cab be brought.   She did
not offer to kiss him when he went: nor did the child propose
to embrace her; but gave a kiss to old Briggs (whom, in general, he was very shy of caressing), and consoled her by
pointing out that he was to come home on Saturdays, when
she would have the benefit of seeing him.   As the cab rolled
towards the City, Becky's carriage rattled off to the Park.
She was chattering and laughing with a score of young dandies by the Serpentine, as the father and son entered at the
old gates of the school—where Rawdon left the child, and
came away with a sadder, purer feeling in his heart than perhaps that poor battered fellow had ever known since he himself came out of the nursery.

He walked all the way home very dismally, and dined
alone with Briggs.   He was very kind to her, and grateful
for her love and watchfulness over the boy.   His conscience
smote him that he had borrowed Briggs's money and aided in
deceiving her.   They talked about little Rawdon a long time,
for Becky only came home to dress and go out to dinner—
and then he went off uneasily to drink tea with Lady Jane,
and tell her of what had happened, and how little Rawdon
went off like a trump, and how he was to wear a gown and
little knee-breeches, and how young Blackball, Jack Blackball's son, of the old regiment, had taken him in charge and
promised to be kind to him.

In the course of a week, young Blackball had constituted
little Rawdon his fag, shoe-black, and breakfast toaster;
initiated him into the mysteries of the Latin Grammar,
and thrashed him three or four times; but not severely.
The little chap's good-natured honest face won his way for
him.   He only got that degree of beating which was, no
doubt, good for him; and as for blacking shoes, toasting
bread, and fagging in general, were these offices not deemed
to be necessary parts of every young English gentleman's
education?

Our business does not lie with the second generation and
Master Rawdon's life at school, otherwise the present tale
might be carried to any indefinite length.   The Colonel
went to see his son a short time afterwards, and found the

lad sufficiently well and happy, grinning and laughing in his little black gown and little breeches.

His father sagaciously tipped Blackball, his master, a sovereign, and secured that young gentleman's good will towards his fag. As a *protégé* of the great Lord Steyne, the nephew of a County member, and son of a Colonel and C.B., whose name appeared in some of the most fashionable parties in the *Morning Post,* perhaps the school authorities were disposed not to look unkindly on the child. He had plenty of pocket-money, which he spent in treating his comrades royally to raspberry tarts, and he was often allowed to come home on Saturdays to his father, who always made a jubilee of that day. When free, Rawdon would take him to the play, or send him thither with the footman; and on Sundays he went to church with Briggs and Lady Jane and his cousins. Rawdon marvelled over his stories about school, and fights, and fagging. Before long, he knew the names of all the masters and the principal boys as well as little Rawdon himself. He invited little Rawdon's crony from school, and made both the children sick with pastry, and oysters, and porter after the play. He tried to look knowing over the Latin grammar when little Rawdon showed him what part of that work he was "in." "Stick to it, my boy," he said to him with much gravity, "there's nothing like a good classical education! nothing!"

Becky's contempt for her husband grew greater every day. "Do what you like,—dine where you please,—go and have ginger-beer and sawdust at Astley's, or psalm-singing with Lady Jane,—only don't expect *me* to busy myself with the boy. I have your interests to attend to, as you can't attend to them yourself. I should like to know where you would have been now, and in what sort of a position in society, if I had not looked after you?" Indeed, nobody wanted poor old Rawdon at the parties whither Becky used to go. She was often asked without him now. She talked about great people as if she had the fee-simple of May Fair; and when the Court went into mourning, she always wore black.

Little Rawdon being disposed of Lord Steyne, who took such a parental interest in the affairs of this amiable poor family, thought that their expenses might be very advantageously curtailed by the departure of Miss Briggs; and that Becky was quite clever enough to take the management of her own house. It has been narrated in a former chapter, how the benevolent nobleman had given his _protégé_ money to pay off her little debt to Miss Briggs, who however still remained behind with her friends; whence my lord came to the painful conclusion that Mrs. Crawley had made some other use of the money confided to her than that for which her generous patron had given the loan. However, Lord Steyne was not so rude as to impart his suspicions upon this head to Mrs. Becky, whose feelings might be hurt by any controversy on the money question, and who might have a thousand painful reasons for disposing otherwise of his lordship's generous loan. But he determined to satisfy himself of the real state of the case: and instituted the necessary inquiries in a most cautious and delicate manner.

In the first place he took an early opportunity of pumping Miss Briggs. That was not a difficult operation. A very little encouragement would set that worthy woman to talk volubly, and pour out all within her. And one day when Mrs. Rawdon had gone out to drive (as Mr. Fiche, his lordship's confidential servant, easily learned at the livery stables where the Crawleys kept their carriage and horses, or rather, where the livery-man kept a carriage and horses for Mr. and Mrs. Crawley)—my lord dropped in upon the Curzon Street house—asked Briggs for a cup of coffee—told her that he had good accounts of the little boy at school—and in five minutes found out from her that Mrs. Rawdon had given her nothing except a black silk gown, for which Miss Briggs was immensely grateful.

He laughed within himself at this artless story. For the truth is, our dear friend Rebecca had given him a most circumstantial narration of Briggs's delight at receiving her money—eleven hundred and twenty-five pounds—and in what securities she had invested it; and what a pang Becky herself felt in being obliged to pay away such a delightful sum of money. "Who knows," the dear woman may have thought within herself, "perhaps he may give me a little

more?" **My lord,** however, made no such proposal to the
little schemer—very likely thinking that he had been sufficiently generous already.

He had the curiosity, then, to ask Miss Briggs about the
state of her private affairs—and she told his lordship can-
didly what her position was—how Miss Crawley had left
her a legacy—how her relatives had had part of it—how
Colonel Crawley had put out another portion, for which she
had the best security and interest—and how Mr. and Mrs.
Rawdon had kindly busied themselves with Sir Pitt, who
was to dispose of the remainder most advantageously for
her, when he had time. My lord asked how much the
Colonel had already invested for her, and Miss Briggs at
once and truly told him that the sum was six hundred and
odd pounds.

But as soon as she had told her story, the voluble Briggs
repented of her frankness, and besought my lord not to tell
Mr. Crawley of the confessions which she had made. "The
Colonel was so kind—Mr. Crawley might be offended and
pay back the money, for which she could get no such good
interest anywhere else." Lord Steyne, laughing, promised
he never would divulge their conversation, and when he and
Miss Briggs parted he laughed still more.

"What an accomplished little devil it is!" thought he.
"What a splendid actress and manager! She had almost
got a second supply out of me the other day, with her coaxing ways. She beats all the women I have ever seen in the
course of all my well-spent life. They are babies compared
to her. I am a greenhorn myself, and a fool in her hands
—an old fool. She is unsurpassable in lies." His lordship's
admiration for Becky rose immeasurably at this proof of
her cleverness. Getting the money was nothing—but getting
double the sum she wanted, and paying nobody—it was a
magnificent stroke. And Crawley, my lord thought—Crawley
is not such a fool as he looks and seems. He has managed
the matter cleverly enough on his side. Nobody would ever
have supposed from his face and demeanour that he knew
anything about this money business; and yet he put her up
to it, and has spent the money, no doubt. In this opinion my
lord, we know, was mistaken; but it influenced a good deal his

behaviour towards Colonel Crawley, whom he began to treat with even less **than** the semblance of respect which he had formerly shown towards that gentleman. It never entered into the head of Mrs. Crawley's patron that the little lady might be making a purse for herself; and, perhaps, if the truth must be told, he judged of Colonel Crawley by his experience of other husbands, whom he had known in the course of the long and well-spent life which had made him acquainted with a great deal of the weakness of mankind. My lord had bought so many men during his life, that he was surely to be pardoned for supposing that he had found the price of this one.

He taxed Becky upon the point on the very first occasion when he met her alone, and he complimented her, good-humouredly, on her cleverness in getting more than the money which she required. Becky was only a little taken aback. It was not the habit of this dear creature to tell falsehoods, except when necessity compelled, but in these great emergencies it was her practise to lie very freely; and in an instant she was ready with another neat plausible circumstantial story which she administered to her patron. The previous statement which she had made to him was a falsehood—a wicked falsehood; she owned it; but who had made her tell it? "Ah, my Lord," she said, "you don't know all I have to suffer and bear in silence: you see me gay and happy before you—you little know what I have to endure when there is no protector near me. It was my husband, by threats and the most savage treatment, forced me to ask for that sum about which I deceived you. It was he, who, foreseeing that questions might be asked regarding the disposal of the money, forced me to account for it as I did. He took the money. He told me he had paid Miss Briggs; I did not want, I did not dare to doubt him. Pardon the wrong which a desperate man is forced to commit, and pity a miserable, miserable woman." She burst into tears as she spoke. Persecuted virtue never looked more bewitchingly wretched.

They had a long conversation, driving round and round the Regent's Park in Mrs. Crawley's carriage together, a conversation of which it is not necessary to repeat the details: but the upshot of it was, that, when Becky came home, she flew to her dear Briggs with a smiling face, and announced that she had some very good news for her. Lord Steyne had acted in the noblest and most generous manner. He was always thinking how and when he could do good. Now that little Rawdon was gone to school, a dear companion and friend was no longer necessary to her. She was grieved beyond measure to part with Briggs; but her means required that she should practise every retrenchment, and her sorrow was mitigated by the idea that her dear Briggs would be far better provided for by her generous patron than in her humble home. Mrs. Pilkington, the housekeeper at Gauntly Hall, was growing exceedingly old, feeble, and rheumatic: she was not equal to the work of superintending that vast mansion, and must be on the look-out for a successor. It was a splendid position. The family did not go to Gauntly once in two years. At other times the housekeeper was the mistress of the magnificent mansion—had four covers daily for her table; was visited by the clergy and the most respectable people of the county—was the lady of Gauntly, in fact; and the two last housekeepers before Mrs. Pilkington had married rectors of Gauntly: but Mrs. P. could not, being the aunt of the present Rector. The place was not to be hers yet; but she might go down on a visit to Mrs. Pilkington, and see whether she would like to succeed her.

What words can paint the ecstatic gratitude of Briggs! All she stipulated for was that little Rawdon should be allowed to come down and see her at the Hall. Becky promised this—anything. She ran up to her husband when he came home, and told him the joyful news. Rawdon was glad, deuced glad; the weight was off his conscience about poor Briggs's money. She was provided for, at any rate; but—but his mind was disquiet. He did not seem to be all right somehow. He told little Southdown what Lord Steyne had done, and the young man eyed Crawley with an air which surprised the latter.

He told Lady Jane of this second proof of Steyne's bounty, and she, too, looked odd and alarmed; so did Sir Pitt. "She is too clever and—and gay to be allowed to go from party to party without a companion," both said. "You must go with her, Rawdon, wherever she goes, and you *must* have somebody with her—one of the girls from Queen's Crawley, perhaps, though they were rather giddy guardians for her."

Somebody Becky should have. But in the meantime it was clear that honest Briggs must not lose her chance of settlement for life; and so she and her bags were packed, and she set off on her journey. And so two of Rawdon's out-sentinels were in the hands of the enemy.

Sir Pitt went and expostulated with his sister-in-law upon the subject of the dismissal of Briggs, and other matters of delicate family interest. In vain she pointed out to him how necessary was the protection of Lord Steyne for her poor husband; how cruel it would be on their part to deprive Briggs of the position offered to her. Cajolements, coaxings, smiles, tears could not satisfy Sir Pitt, and he had something very like a quarrel with his once admired Becky. He spoke of the honour of the family: the unsullied reputation of the Crawleys; expressed himself in indignant tones about her receiving those young Frenchmen—those wild young men of fashion, my Lord Steyne himself, whose carriage was always at her door, who passed hours daily in her company, and whose constant presence made the world talk about her. As the head of the house he implored her to be more prudent. Society was already speaking lightly of her. Lord Steyne, though a nobleman of the greatest station and talents, was a man whose attentions would compromise any woman; he besought, he implored, he commanded his sister-in-law to be watchful in her intercourse with that nobleman.

Becky promised anything and everything Pitt wanted; but Lord Steyne came to her house as often as ever, and Sir Pitt's anger increased. I wonder was Lady Jane angry or pleased that her husband at last found fault with his favourite Rebecca? Lord Steyne's visits continuing, his own ceased; and his wife was for refusing all further intercourse with that nobleman, and declining the invitation to the Charade-night which the Marchioness sent to her; but Sir Pitt thought it was necessary to accept it, as his Royal Highness would be there.

Although he went to the party in question, Sir Pitt quitted it very early, and his wife, too, was very glad to come away. Becky hardly so much as spoke to him or noticed her sister-in-law. Pitt Crawley declared her behaviour was monstrously indecorous, reprobated in strong terms the habit of play-acting and fancy dressing, as highly unbecoming a British female; and after the charades were over, took his brother Rawdon severely to task for appearing himself, and allowing his wife to join in such improper exhibitions.

Rawdon said she should not join in any more such amusements: but indeed, and perhaps from hints from his elder brother and sister, he had already become a very watchful and exemplary domestic character. He left off his clubs and billiards. He never left home. He took Becky out to drive: he went laboriously with her to all her parties. Whenever my Lord Steyne called, he was sure to find the Colonel. And when Becky proposed to go out without her husband, or received invitations for herself, he peremptorily ordered her to refuse them; and there was that in the gentleman's manner which enforced obedience. Little Becky, to do her justice, was charmed with Rawdon's gallantry. If he was surly, she never was. Whether friends were present or absent, she had always a kind smile for him, and was attentive to his pleasure and comfort. It was the early days of their marriage over again: the same good humour, *prévenances,* merriment, and artless confidence and regard. "How much pleasanter it is," she would say, "to have you by my side in the carriage than that foolish old Briggs! Let us always go on so, dear Rawdon. How nice it would be, and how happy we should always be, if we had but the money!" He fell asleep after dinner in his chair; he did not see the face opposite to him, haggard, weary, and terrible; it lighted up with fresh candid smiles when he woke. It kissed him gaily. He wondered that he had ever had suspicions. No, he never had suspicions; all those dumb doubts and surly misgivings which had been gathering on his mind, were mere idle jealousies. She was fond of him; she always had been. As for her shining in society, it was no fault of her; she was formed to shine there. Was there any woman who could talk, or sing, or do anything like

her? If she would but like the boy! Rawdon thought.
But the mother and son never could be brought together.

And it was while Rawdon's mind was agitated with these
doubts and perplexities that the incident occurred which
was mentioned in the last chapter; and the unfortunate
Colonel found himself a prisoner away from home.

CHAPTER XVIII

A Rescue and a Catastrophe

FRIEND RAWDON drove on then to Mr. Moss's mansion in Cursitor Street, and was duly inducted into that dismal place of hospitality. Morning was breaking over the cheerful housetops of Chancery Lane as the rattling cab woke up the echoes there. A little pink-eyed Jew-boy, with a head as ruddy as the rising morn, let the party into the house, and Rawdon was welcomed to the ground-floor apartments by Mr. Moss, his travelling companion and host, who cheerfully asked him if he would like a glass of something warm after his drive.

The Colonel was not so depressed as some mortals would be, who, quitting a palace and a *placens uxor*, find themselves barred into a spunging-house; for, if the truth must be told, he had been a lodger at Mr. Moss's establishment once or twice before.

We have not thought it necessary in the previous course of this narrative to mention these trivial little domestic incidents: but the reader may be assured that they can't unfrequently occur in the life of a man who lives on nothing a-year.

Upon his first visit to Mr. Moss, the Colonel, then a bachelor, had been liberated by the generosity of his Aunt; on the second mishap, little Becky, with the greatest spirit and kindness, had borrowed a sum of money from Lord Southdown, and had coaxed her husband's creditor (who was her shawl, velvet-gown, lace pocket handkerchief, trinket, and gim-crack purveyor, indeed) to take a portion of the sum claimed, and Rawdon's promissory note for the remainder: so on both these occasions the capture and release had been conducted with the utmost gallantry on all sides, and Moss and the Colonel were therefore on the very best of terms.

"You'll find your old bed, Colonel, and everything comfortable," that gentleman said, "as I may honestly say, You may be pretty sure it's kep aired, and by the best of company, too. It was slep in the night afore last by the Honorable Capting Famish, of the Fiftieth Dragoons, whose Mar took him out, after a fortnight, jest to punish him, she said. But, Law bless you, I promise you, he punished my champagne, and had a party ere every night—reglar tip-top swells, down from the clubs and the West End—Capting Ragg, the Honorable Deuceace, who lives in the Temple, and some fellers as knows a good glass of wine, I warrant you. I've got a Doctor of Diwinity upstairs, five gents in the Coffee-room, and Mrs. Moss has a tably-dy-hoty at half-past five, and a little cards or music afterwards, when we shall be most happy to see you."

"I'll ring when I want anything," said Rawdon, and went quietly to his bed-room. He was an old soldier, we have said, and not to be disturbed by any little shocks of fate. A weaker man would have sent off a letter to his wife on the instant of his capture. "But what is the use of disturbing her night's rest?" thought Rawdon. "She won't know whether I am in my room or not. It will be time enough to write to her when she has had her sleep out, and I have had mine. It's only a hundred-and-seventy, and the deuce is in it if we can't raise that." And so, thinking about little Rawdon (whom he would not have know that he was in such a queer place), the Colonel turned into the bed lately occupied by Captain Famish, and fell asleep. It was ten o'clock when he woke up, and the ruddy-headed youth brought him, with conscious pride, a fine silver dressing-case, wherewith he might perform the operation of shaving. Indeed Mr. Moss's house, though somewhat dirty, was splendid throughout. There were dirty trays, and wine-coolers, *en permanence* on the sideboard, huge dirty gilt cornices, with dingy yellow satin hangings to the barred windows which looked into Cursitor Street—vast and dirty gilt picture-frames surrounding pieces sporting and sacred, all of which works were by the greatest masters; and fetched the greatest prices, too, in the bill transactions, in the course of which they were sold and bought over and over again. The Colonel's breakfast was served to him in the same dingy and gorgeous plated ware. Miss Moss, a dark-eyed maid in curl papers, appeared with the teapot, and, smiling, asked the Colonel how he had slep? and she brought him in the *Morning Post,* with the names of all the great people who had figured at Lord Steyne's entertainment the night before. It contained a brilliant account of the festivities, and of the beautiful and accomplished Mrs. Rawdon Crawley's admirable personifications.

After a lively chat with this lady (who sat on the edge of the breakfast table in an easy attitude displaying the drapery of her stocking and an ex-white satin shoe, which was down at heel), Colonel Crawley called for pens and ink, and paper; and being asked how many sheets, chose one which was brought to him between Miss Moss's own finger and thumb. Many a sheet had that dark-eyed damsel brought in; many a poor fellow had scrawled and blotted hurried lines of entreaty, and paced up and down that awful room until his messenger brought back the reply. Poor men always use messengers instead of the post. Who has not had their letters, with the wafers wet, and the announcement that a person is waiting in the hall?

Now on the score of his application, Rawdon had not many misgivings.

"DEAR BECKY, (Rawdon wrote),

"*I hope you slept well.* Don't be *frightened* if I don't bring you in your *coffy.* Last night as I was coming home smoaking, I met with an *accadent.* I was *nabbed* by Moss of Cursitor Street—from whose *gilt and splendid parler* I write this—the same that had me this time two years. Miss Moss brought in my tea—she is grown very *fat,* and, as usual, had *her stockens down at heal.*

"It's Nathan's business—a hundred-and-fifty—with costs, hundred-and-seventy. Please send me my desk and some *cloths*—I'm in pumps and a white tye (something like Miss M.'s stockings)—I've seventy in it. And as soon as you get this, Drive to Nathan's—offer him seventy-five down, and ask *him to renew*—say I'll take wine—we may as well have some dinner sherry; but not *picturs,* they're too dear.

"If he won't stand it. Take my ticker and such of your things as you can *spare,* and send them to Balls—we must, of coarse, have the sum to-night. It won't do to let it stand over, as to-morrow's Sunday; the beds here are not very *clean,* and there may be other things out against me—I'm glad it an't Rawdon's Saturday for coming home. God bless you.   Yours in haste,   R. C.

"P.S.   Make haste and come."

This letter, sealed with a wafer, was dispatched by one of the messengers who are always hanging about Mr. Moss's establishment; and Rawdon, having seen him depart, went out in the court-yard, and smoked his cigar with a tolerably easy mind—in spite of the bars overhead; for Mr. Moss's court-yard is railed in like a cage, lest the gentlemen who are boarding with him should take a fancy to escape from his hospitality.

Three hours, he calculated, would be the utmost time required, before Becky should arrive and open his prison doors: and he passed these pretty cheerfully in smoking, in reading the paper, and in the coffee-room with an acquaintance, Captain Walker, who happened to be there, and with whom he cut for sixpences for some hours, with pretty equal luck on either side.

But the day passed away and no messenger returned— no Becky.   Mr. Moss's tably-dy-hoty was served at the appointed hour of half-past five, when such of the gentlemen lodging in the house as could afford to pay for the banquet, came and partook of it in the splendid front parlour before described, and with which Mr. Crawley's temporary lodging communicated, when Miss M. (Miss Hem, as her papa called her), appeared without the curl papers of the morning, and Mrs. Hem did the honours of a prime boiled leg of mutton and turnips, of which the Colonel ate with a very faint appetite.   Asked whether he would "stand" a bottle of champagne for the company, he consented, and the ladies drank to his 'ealth, and Mr. Moss, in the most polite manner, "looked towards him."

In the midst of this repast, however, the door-bell was heard,—young Moss of the ruddy hair, rose up with the keys and answered the summons, and coming back, told the Colonel that the messenger had returned with a bag, a desk and a letter, which he gave him.   "No ceremony, Colonel, I beg," said Mrs. Moss with a wave of her hand, and he opened the letter rather tremulously.—It was a beautiful letter, highly scented, on a pink paper, and with a light green seal.

"MON PAUVRE CHER PETIT, (Mrs. Crawley wrote),

"I could not sleep *one wink* for thinking of what had become of *my odious old monstre:* and only got to rest in the morning after sending for Mr. Blench (for I was in a fever), who gave me a composing draught and left orders with Finette that I should be disturbed *on no account.* So that my poor old man's messenger, who had *bien mauvaise mine* Finette says, and *sentoit le Genièvre,* remained in the hall for some hours waiting my bell. You may fancy my state when I read your poor dear old ill-spelt letter.

"Ill as I was, I instantly called for the carriage, and as soon as I was dressed (though I couldn't drink a drop of chocolate—I assure you I couldn't without my *monstre* to bring it to me), I drove *ventre à terre* to Nathan's. I saw him—I wept—I cried—I fell at his odious knees. Nothing would mollify the horrid man. He would have all the money, he said, or keep my poor monstre in prison. I drove home with the intention of paying that *triste visite chez mon oncle* (when every trinket I have should be at your disposal though they would not fetch a hundred pounds, for some, you know, are with *ce cher oncle* already), and found Milor there with the Bulgarian old sheep-faced monster, who had come to compliment me upon last night's performances. Paddington came in, too, drawling and lisping and twiddling his hair; so did Champignac, and his chef—everybody with *foison* of compliments and pretty speeches—plaguing poor me, who longed to be rid of them, and was thinking *every moment of the time* of *mon pauvre prisonnier.*

"When they were gone, I went down on my knees to Milor; told him we were going to pawn everything, and begged and prayed him to give me two hundred pounds. He pish'd and psha'd in a fury —told me not to be such a fool as to pawn—and said he would see whether he could lend me the money. At last he went away, promising that he would send it me in the morning: when I will bring it to my poor old monster with a kiss from his affectionate

"BECKY.

"I am writing in bed. Oh I have such a headache and such a heartache !"

When Rawdon read over this letter, he turned so red and looked so savage, that the company at the table d'hôte easily perceived that bad news had reached him. All his suspicions, which he had been trying to banish, returned upon him. She could not even go out and sell her trinkets to free him. She could laugh and talk about compliments paid to her, whilst he was in prison. Who had put him there? Wenham had walked with him. Was there . . . .

He could hardly bear to think of what he suspected. Leaving the room hurriedly, he ran into his own—opened his desk, wrote two hurried lines, which he directed to Sir Pitt or Lady Crawley, and bade the messenger carry them at once to Gaunt Street, bidding him to take a cab, and promising him a guinea if he was back in an hour.

In the note he besought his dear brother and sister, for the sake of God; for the sake of his dear child and his honour; to come to him and relieve him from his difficulty. He was in prison: he wanted a hundred pounds to set him free—he entreated them to come to him.

He went back to the dining-room after dispatching his messenger, and called for more wine. He laughed and talked with a strange boisterousness, as the people thought. Sometimes he laughed madly at his own fears, and went on drinking for an hour; listening all the while for the carriage which was to bring his fate back.

At the expiration of that time, wheels were heard whirling up to the gate—the young Janitor went out with his gate-keys. It was a lady whom he let in at the bailiff's door.

"Colonel Crawley," she said, trembling very much. He, with a knowing look, locked the outer door upon her—then unlocked and opened the inner one, and calling out, "Colonel, you're wanted," led her into the back parlour, which he occupied.

Rawdon came in from the dining-parlour where all those people were carousing, into his back room; a flare of coarse light following him into the apartment where the lady stood, still very nervous.

"It is I, Rawdon," she said, in a timid voice, which she strove to render cheerful. "It is Jane." Rawdon was quite overcome by that kind voice and presence. He ran up to her—caught her in his arms—gasped out some inarticulate words of thanks, and fairly sobbed on her shoulder. She did not know the cause of his emotion.

The bills of Mr. Moss were quickly settled, perhaps to the disappointment of that gentleman, who had counted on having the Colonel as his guest over Sunday at least; and Jane, with beaming smiles and happiness in her eyes, carried away Rawdon from the bailiff's house, and they went homewards in the cab in which she had hastened to his release. "Pitt was gone to a parliamentary dinner," she said, "when Rawdon's note came, and so, dear Rawdon, I—I came myself;" and she put her kind hand in his. Perhaps it was well for Rawdon Crawley that Pitt was away at that dinner. Rawdon thanked his sister a hundred times, and with an ardour of gratitude which touched and almost alarmed that soft-hearted woman. "Oh," said he, in his rude, artless way, "you—you don't know how I'm changed since I've known you, and—and little Rawdy. I—I'd like to change somehow. You see I want—I want —to be—"—He did not finish the sentence, but she could interpret it. And that night after he left her, and as she sate by her own little boy's bed, she prayed humbly for that poor wayworn sinner.

Rawdon left her and walked home rapidly. It was nine o'clock at night. He ran across the streets, and the great squares of Vanity Fair, and at length came up breathless opposite his own house. He started back and fell against the railings, trembling as he looked up. The drawing-room windows were blazing with light. She had said that she was in bed and ill. He stood there for some time, the light from the rooms on his pale face.

He took out his door-key and let himself into the house. He could hear laughter in the upper rooms. He was in the ball-dress in which he had been captured the night before. He went silently up the stairs; leaning against the banisters at the stair-head.—Nobody was stirring in the house besides—all the servants had been sent away. Rawdon heard laughter within—laughter and singing. Becky was singing a snatch of the song of the night before; a hoarse voice shouted "Bravo! Bravo!"—it was Lord Steyne's.

Rawdon opened the door and went in. A little table with a dinner was laid out—and wine and plate. Steyne was hanging over the sofa on which Becky sate. The wretched woman was in a brilliant full toilette, her arms and all her fingers sparkling with bracelets and rings; and the brilliants on her breast which Steyne had given her. He had her hand in his, and was bowing over it to kiss it.

when Becky started up with a faint scream as she caught sight of Rawdon's white face. At the next instant she tried a smile, a horrid smile, as if to welcome her husband: and Steyne rose up, grinding his teeth, pale, and with fury in his looks.

He, too, attempted a laugh—and came forward holding out his hand. "What, come back! How d'ye do, Crawley?" he said, the nerves of his mouth twitching as he tried to grin at the intruder.

There was that in Rawdon's face which caused Becky to fling herself before him. "I am innocent, Rawdon," she said; "before God, I am innocent." She clung hold of his coat, of his hands; her own were all covered with serpents, and rings, and baubles. "I am innocent.—Say I am innocent," she said to Lord Steyne.

He thought a trap had been laid for him, and was as furious with the wife as with the husband. "You innocent! Damn you," he screamed out. "You innocent! Why every trinket you have on your body is paid for by me. I have given you thousands of pounds which this fellow has spent, and for which he has sold you. Innocent, by —— ! You're as innocent as your mother, the ballet-girl, and your husband the bully. Don't think to frighten me as you have done others. Make way, sir, and let me pass;" and Lord Steyne seized up his hat, and, with flame in his eyes, and looking his enemy fiercely in the face, marched upon him, never for a moment doubting that the other would give way.

But Rawdon Crawley springing out, seized him by the neckcloth, until Steyne, almost strangled, writhed, and bent under his arm. "You lie, you dog!" said Rawdon. "You lie, you coward and villain!" And he struck the Peer twice over the face with his open hand, and flung him bleeding to the ground. It was all done before Rebecca could interpose. She stood there trembling before him. She admired her husband, strong, brave, and victorious.

"Come here," he said.—She came up at once.

"Take off those things."—She began, trembling, pulling the jewels from her arms, and the rings from her shaking fingers, and held them all in a heap, quivering and looking up at him. "Throw them down," he said, and she dropped them. He tore the diamond ornament out of her breast and flung it at Lord Steyne. It cut him on his bald forehead. Steyne wore the scar to his dying day.

"Come upstairs," Rawdon said to his wife. "Don't kill me, Rawdon," she said. He laughed savagely.—"I want to see .if that man lies about the money as he has about me. Has he given you any?"

"No," said Rebecca, "that is——"

"Give me your keys," Rawdon answered, and they went out together.

Rebecca gave him all the keys but one: and she was in hopes that he would not have remarked the absence of that. It belonged to the little desk which Amelia had given her in early days, and which she kept in a secret place. But Rawdon flung open boxes and wardrobes, throwing the multifarious trumpery of their contents here and there, and at last he found the desk. The woman was forced to open it. It contained papers, love-letters many years old—all sorts of small trinkets and woman's memoranda. And it contained a pocket-book with bank-notes. Some of these were dated ten years back, too, and one was quite a fresh one—a note for a thousand pounds which Lord Steyne had given her.

"Did he give you this?" Rawdon said.

"Yes," Rebecca answered.

"I'll send it to him to-day," Rawdon said (for day had dawned again, and many hours had passed in this search), "and I will pay Briggs, who was kind to the boy, and some of the debts. You will let me know where I shall send the rest to you. You might have spared me a hundred pounds, Becky, out of all this—I have always shared with you."

"I am innocent," said Becky. And he left her without another word.

What were her thoughts when he left her? She remained for hours after he was gone, the sunshine pouring into the room, and Rebecca sitting alone on the bed's edge. The drawers were all opened and their contents scattered about, —dresses and feathers, scarfs and trinkets, a heap of tumbled vanities lying in a wreck. Her hair was falling

over her shoulders; her gown was torn where Rawdon had
wrenched the brilliants out of it. She heard him go downstairs a few minutes after he left her, and the door slamming
and closing on him. She knew he would never come back.
He was gone for ever. Would he kill himself?—she thought
—not until after he had met Lord Steyne. She thought of
her long past life, and all the dismal incidents of it. Ah,
how dreary it seemed, how miserable, lonely and profitless!
Should she take laudanum, and end it, too—have done with
all hopes, schemes, debts, and triumphs? The French maid
found her in this position—sitting in the midst of her miserable ruins with clasped hands and dry eyes. The woman was
her accomplice and in Steyne's pay. "Mon Dieu, Madame,
what has happened?" she asked.

What *had* happened? Was she guilty or not? She said
not; but who could tell what was truth which came from
those lips; or if that corrupt heart was in this case pure?
All her lies and her schemes, all her selfishness and her
wiles, all her wit and genius had come to this bankruptcy.
The woman closed the curtains, and with some entreaty and
show of kindness, persuaded her mistress to lie down on the
bed. Then she went below and gathered up the trinkets
which had been lying on the floor since Rebecca dropped
them there at her husband's orders, and Lord Steyne went
away.

CHAPTER XIX

THE mansion of Sir Pitt Crawley, in Great Gaunt Street, was just beginning to dress itself for the day, as Rawdon, in his evening costume, which he had now worn two days, passed by the scared female who was scouring the steps, and entered into his brother's study. Lady Jane, in her morning-gown, was up and above stairs in the nursery superintending the toilettes of her children, and listening to the morning prayers which the little creatures performed at her knee. Every morning she and they performed this duty privately, and before the public ceremonial at which Sir Pitt presided, and at which all the people of the household were expected to assemble. Rawdon sate down in the study before the Baronet's table, set out with the orderly blue books and the letters, the neatly docketed bills and symmetrical pamphlets; the locked account-books, desks, and dispatch boxes, the Bible, the *Quarterly Review,* and the *Court Guide,* which all stood as if on parade awaiting the inspection of their chief.

A book of family sermons, one of which Sir Pitt was in the habit of administering to his family on Sunday mornings, lay ready on the study table, and awaiting his judicious selection. And by the sermon-book was the *Observer* newspaper, damp and neatly folded, and for Sir Pitt's own private use. His gentleman alone took the opportunity of perusing the newspaper before he laid it by his master's desk. Before he had brought it into the study that morning, he had read in the journal a flaming account of "Festivities at Gaunt House," with the names of all the distinguished personages invited by the Marquis of Steyne to meet his Royal Highness. Having made comments upon this entertainment to the housekeeper and her niece as they were taking early tea and hot buttered toast in the former

219

lady's apartment, and wondered how the Rawding Crawleys could git on, the valet had damped and folded the paper once more, so that it looked quite fresh and innocent against the arrival of the master of the house.

Poor Rawdon took up the paper and began to try and read it until his brother should arrive. But the print fell blank upon his eyes; and he did not know in the least what he was reading. The Government news and appointments (which Sir Pitt as a public man was bound to peruse, otherwise he would by no means permit the introduction of Sunday papers into his household), the theatrical criticisms, the fight for a hundred pounds a-side between the Barking Butcher and the Tutbury Pet, the Gaunt House chronicle itself, which contained a most complimentary though guarded account of the famous charades of which Mrs. Becky had been the heroine—all these passed as in a haze before Rawdon, as he sate waiting the arrival of the chief of the family.

Punctually, as the shrill-toned bell of the black marble study clock began to chime nine, Sir Pitt made his appearance, fresh, neat, smugly shaved, with a waxy clean face, and stiff shirt collar, his scanty hair combed and oiled, trimming his nails as he descended the stairs majestically, in a starched cravat and a grey flannel dressing-gown,—a real old English gentleman, in a word,—a model of neatness and every propriety. He started when he saw poor Rawdon in his study in tumbled clothes, with blood-shot eyes, and his hair over his face. He thought his brother was not sober, and had been out all night on some orgy. "Good gracious, Rawdon," he said, with a blank face, "what brings you here at this time of the morning? Why ain't you at home?"

"Home," said Rawdon, with a wild laugh. "Don't be frightened, Pitt. I'm not drunk. Shut the door; I want to speak to you."

Pitt closed the door and came up to the table, where he sate down in the other arm-chair.—that one placed for the reception of the steward, agent, or confidential visitor who came to transact business with the Baronet,—and trimmed his nails more vehemently than ever.

"Pitt, it's all over with me," the Colonel said, after a pause. "I'm done."

"I always said it would come to this," the Baronet cried, peevishly, and beating a tune with his clean-trimmed nails. "I warned you a thousand times. I can't help you any more. Every shilling of my money is tied up. Even the hundred pounds that Jane took you last night were promised to my lawyer to-morrow morning; and the want of it will put me to great inconvenience. I don't mean to say that I won't assist you ultimately. But as for paying your creditors in full, I might as well hope to pay the National Debt. It is madness, sheer madness, to think of such a thing. You must come to a compromise. It's a painful thing for the family; but everybody does it. There was George Kitely, Lord Ragland's son, went through the Court last week, and was what they call white-washed, I believe. Lord Ragland would not pay a shilling for him, and——"

"It's not money I want," Rawdon broke in. "I'm not come to you about myself. Never mind what happens to me——"

"What is the matter, then?" said Pitt, somewhat relieved.

"It's the boy," said Rawdon, in a husky voice. "I want you to promise me that you will take charge of him when I'm gone. That dear good wife of yours has always been good to him; and he's fonder of her than he is of his . . . —Damn it. Look here, Pitt—you know that I was to have had Miss Crawley's money. I wasn't brought up like a younger brother: but was always encouraged to be extravagant and kep idle. But for this I might have been quite a different man. I didn't do my duty with the regiment so bad. You know how I was thrown over about the money, and who got it."

"After the sacrifices I have made, and the manner in which I have stood by you, I think this sort of reproach is useless," Sir Pitt said. "Your marriage was your own doing, not mine."

"That's over now," said Rawdon.—"That's over now." And the words were wrenched from him with a groan, which made his brother start.

"Good God! is she dead?" Sir Pitt said, with a voice of genuine alarm and commiseration.

"I wish *I* was," Rawdon replied. "If it wasn't for little

Rawdon I'd have cut my throat this morning—and that damned villain's too."

Sir Pitt instantly guessed the truth, and surmised that Lord Steyne was the person whose life Rawdon wished to take. The Colonel told his senior briefly, and in broken accents, the circumstances of the case. "It was a regular plan between that scoundrel and her," he said. "The bailiffs were put upon me: I was taken as I was going out of his house: when I wrote to her for money, she said she was ill in bed, and put me off to another day. And when I got home I found her in diamonds and sitting with that villain alone."

He then went on to describe hurriedly the personal conflict with Lord Steyne. To an affair of that nature, of course, he said, there was but one issue; and after his conference with his brother, he was going away to make the necessary arrangements for the meeting which must ensue. "And as it may end fatally with me," Rawdon said with a broken voice, "and as the boy has no mother, I must leave him to you and Jane, Pitt—only it will be a comfort to me if you will promise me to be his friend."

The elder brother was much affected, and shook Rawdon's hand with a cordiality seldom exhibited by him. Rawdon passed his hand over his shaggy eyebrows. "Thank you, brother," said he. "I know I can trust your word."

"I will, upon my honour," the Baronet said. And thus, and almost mutely, this bargain was struck between them.

Then Rawdon took out of his pocket the little pocket-book which he had discovered in Becky's desk: and from which he drew a bundle of notes which it contained. "Here's six hundred," he said—"you didn't know I was so rich. I want you to give the money to Briggs, who lent it to us—and who was kind to the boy—and I've always felt ashamed of having taken the poor old woman's money. And here's some more—I've only kept back a few pounds—which Becky may as well have, to get on with." As he spoke he took hold of the other notes to give to his brother, but his hands shook, and he was so agitated that the pocket-book fell from him, and out of it the thousand-pound note which had been the last of the unlucky Becky's winnings.

Pitt stooped and picked them up, amazed at so much wealth. "Not that," Rawdon said—"I hoped to put a bullet into the man whom that belongs to." He had thought to himself, it would be a fine revenge to wrap a ball in the note, and kill Steyne with it.

After this colloquy the brothers once more shook hands and parted. Lady Jane had heard of the Colonel's arrival and was waiting for her husband in the adjoining dining-room, with female instinct, auguring evil. The door of the dining-room happened to be left open, and the lady of course was issuing from it as the two brothers passed out of the study. She held out her hand to Rawdon, and said she was glad he was come to breakfast; though she could perceive, by his haggard unshorn face, and the dark looks of her husband, that there was very little question of breakfast between them. Rawdon muttered some excuses about an engagement, squeezing hard the timid little hand which his sister-in-law reached out to him. Her imploring eyes could read nothing but calamity in his face; but he went away without another word. Nor did Sir Pitt vouchsafe her any explanation. The children came up to salute him, and he kissed them in his usual frigid manner. The mother took both of them close to herself, and held a hand of each of them as they knelt down to prayers, which Sir Pitt read to them, and to the servants in their Sunday suits or liveries, ranged upon chairs on the other side of the hissing tea-urn. Breakfast was so late that day, in consequence of the delays which had occurred, that the church-bells began to ring whilst they were sitting over their meal: and Lady Jane was too ill, she said, to go church, though her thoughts had been entirely astray during the period of family devotion.

Rawdon Crawley meanwhile hurried on from Great Gaunt Street, and knocking at the great bronze Medusa's head which stands on the portal of Gaunt House, brought out the purple Silenus in a red and silver waistcoat, who acts as porter of that palace. The man was scared also by the Colonel's dishevelled appearance, and barred the way as if afraid that the other was going to force it. But Colonel Crawley only took out a card and enjoined him particularly to send it in to Lord Steyne, and to mark the address written on it, and say that Colonel Crawley would be all day after one o'clock at the Regent Club in St. James's Street—not at home. The fat red-faced man looked after him with astonishment as he strode away; so did the people in their Sunday clothes who were out so early; the charity boys with shining faces, the greengrocer lolling at his door, and the publican shutting his shutters in the sunshine, against service commenced. The people joked at the cab-stand about his appearance, as he took a carriage there, and told the driver to drive him to Knightsbridge Barracks.

All the bells were jangling and tolling as he reached that place. He might have seen his old acquaintance Amelia on her way from Brompton to Russell Square had he been looking out. Troops of schools were on their march to church, the shiny pavement and outsides of coaches in the suburbs were thronged with people out upon their Sunday pleasure; but the Colonel was much too busy to take any heed of these phenomena, and, arriving at Knightsbridge, speedily made his way up to the room of his old friend and comrade Captain Macmurdo, who Crawley found, to his satisfaction, was in barracks.

Captain Macmurdo, a veteran officer and Waterloo man, greatly liked by his regiment, in which want of money alone prevented him from attaining the highest ranks, was enjoying the forenoon calmly in bed. He had been at a fast supper-party, given the night before by Captain the Honourable George Cinqbars, at his house in Brompton Square, to several young men of the regiment, and a number of ladies of the corps de ballet, and old Mac, who was at home with people of all ages and ranks, and consorted with generals, dog-fanciers, opera-dancers, bruisers, and every kind of person, in a word, was resting himself after the night's labours, and, not being on duty, was in bed.

His room was hung round with boxing, sporting, and dancing pictures, presented to him by comrades as they retired from the regiment, and married and settled into quiet life. And as he was now nearly fifty years of age, twenty-four of which he had passed in the corps, he had a singular museum. He was one of the best shots in England, and, for a heavy man, one of the best riders; indeed, he and

Crawley had been rivals when the latter was in the army. To be brief, Mr. Macmurdo was lying in bed, reading in *Bell's Life* an account of that very fight between the Tutbury Pet and the Barking Butcher, which has been before mentioned—a venerable bristly warrior, with a little close-shaved grey head, with a silk nightcap, a red face and nose, and a great dyed moustache.

When Rawdon told the Captain he wanted a friend, the latter knew perfectly well on what duty of friendship he was called to act, and indeed had conducted scores of affairs for his acquaintances with the greatest prudence and skill. His Royal Highness the late lamented Commander-in-Chief had had the greatest regard for Macmurdo on this account; and he was the common refuge of gentlemen in trouble.

"What's the row about, Crawley, my boy?" said the old warrior. "No more gambling business, hay, like that when we shot Captain Marker?"

"It's about—about my wife," Crawley answered, casting down his eyes and turning very red.

The other gave a whistle. "I always said she'd throw you over," he began:—indeed there were bets in the regiment and at the clubs regarding the probable fate of Colonel Crawley, so lightly was his wife's character esteemed by his comrades and the world; but seeing the savage look with which Rawdon answered the expression of this opinion, Macmurdo did not think fit to enlarge upon it further.

"Is there no way out of it, old boy?" the Captain continued in a grave tone. "Is it only suspicion, you know, or—or what is it? Any letters? Can't you keep it quiet? Best not make any noise about a thing of that sort if you can help it." "Think of his only finding her out now," the Captain thought to himself, and remembered a hundred particular conversations at the mess-table, in which Mrs. Crawley's reputation had been torn to shreds.

"There's no way but one out of it," Rawdon replied—"and there's only a way out of it for one of us, Mac—do you understand? I was put out of the way: arrested: I found 'em alone together. I told him he was a liar and a coward, and knocked him down and thrashed him."

"Serve him right," Macmurdo said. "Who is it?"

Rawdon answered it was Lord Steyne.

"The deuce! a Marquis! they said he—that is, they said you——"

"What the devil do you mean?" roared out Rawdon; "do you mean that you ever heard a fellow doubt about my wife, and didn't tell me, Mac?"

"The world's very censorious, old boy," the other replied. "What the deuce was the good of my telling you what any tom-fools talked about?"

"It was damned unfriendly, Mac," said Rawdon, quite overcome; and, covering his face with his hands, he gave way to an emotion, the sight of which caused the tough old campaigner opposite him to wince with sympathy. "Hold up, old boy," he said; "great man or not, we'll put a bullet in him, damn him. As for women, they're all so."

"You don't know how fond I was of that one," Rawdon said, half inarticulately. "Damme, I followed her like a footman. I gave up everything I had to her. I'm a beggar because I would marry her. By Jove, Sir, I've pawned my own watch in order to get her anything she fancied: and she —she's been making a purse for herself all the time, and grudged me a hundred pound to get me out of quod." He then fiercely and incoherently, and with an agitation under which his counsellor had never before seen him labour, told Macmurdo the circumstances of the story. His adviser caught at some stray hints in it.

"She may be innocent, after all," he said. "She says so. Steyne has been a hundred times alone with her in the house before."

"It may be so," Rawdon answered sadly; "but this don't look very innocent;" and he showed the Captain the thousand-pound note which he had found in Becky's pocket-book. "This is what he gave her, Mac: and she kep it unknown to me: and with this money in the house, she refused to stand by me when I was locked up." The Captain could not but own that the secreting of the money had a very ugly look.

Whilst they were engaged in their conference, Rawdon dispatched Captain Macmurdo's servant to Curzon Street, with an order to the domestic there to give up a bag of clothes of which the Colonel had great need. And during the man's absence, and with great labour and a Johnson's Dictionary, which stood them in much stead, Rawdon and his second composed a letter, which the latter was to send to Lord Steyne. Captain Macmurdo had the honour of waiting upon the Marquis of Steyne, on the part of Colonel Rawdon Crawley, and begged to intimate that he was empowered by the Colonel to make any arrangements for the meeting which, he had no doubt, it was his Lordship's intention to demand, and which the circumstances of the morning had rendered inevitable. Captain Macmurdo begged Lord Steyne, in the most polite manner, to appoint a friend, with whom he (Captain M'M.) might communicate, and desired that the meeting might take place with as little delay as possible.

In a postscript the Captain stated that he had in his possession a bank-note for a large amount, which Colonel Crawley had reason to suppose was the property of the Marquis of Steyne. And he was anxious, on the Colonel's behalf, to give up the note to its owner.

By the time this note was composed, the Captain's servant returned from his mission to Colonel Crawley's house in Curzon Street, but without the carpet-bag and portmanteau, for which he had been sent: and with a very puzzled and odd face.

"They won't give 'em up," said the man; "there's a regular shinty in the house; and everything at sixes and sevens. The landlord's come in and took possession. The servants was a drinkin' up in the drawing-room. They said—they said you had gone off with the plate, Colonel" —the man added after a pause:—"One of the servants is off already. And Simpson, the man as was very noisy and drunk indeed, says nothing shall go out of the house until his wages is paid up."

The account of this little revolution in May Fair astonished and gave a little gaiety to an otherwise very *triste* conversation. The two officers laughed at Rawdon's discomfiture.

"I'm glad the little 'un isn't at home," Rawdon said, biting his nails. "You remember him, Mac, don't you, in the Riding School? How he sat the kicker to be sure! didn't he?"

"That he did, old boy," said the good-natured Captain. "Little Rawdon was then sitting, one of fifty gown boys, in the Chapel of Whitefriars School: thinking, not about the sermon, but about going home next Saturday, when his father would certainly tip him, and perhaps would take him to the play."

"He's a regular trump, that boy," the father went on, still musing about his son. "I say, Mac, if anything goes wrong —if I drop—I should like you to—to go and see him, you know: and say that I was very fond of him, and that. And —dash it—old chap, give him these gold sleeve-buttons: it's all I've got." He covered his face with his black hands: over which the tears rolled and made furrows of white. Mr. Macmurdo had also occasion to take off his silk nightcap and rub it across his eyes.

"Go down and order some breakfast," he said to his man in a loud cheerful voice—"What'll you have, Crawley? Some devilled kidneys and a herring—let's say—And, Clay, lay out some dressing things for the Colonel: we were always pretty much of a size, Rawdon, my boy, and neither of us ride so light as we did when we first entered the corps." With which, and leaving the Colonel to dress himself, Macmurdo turned round towards the wall, and resumed the perusal of *Bell's Life,* until such time as his friend's toilette was complete, and he was at liberty to commence his own.

This, as he was about to meet a lord, Captain Macmurdo performed with particular care. He waxed his mustachios into a state of brilliant polish, and put on a tight cravat and a trim buff waistcoat; so that all the young officers in the mess-room, whither Crawley had preceded his friend, complimented Mac on his appearance at breakfast, and asked if he was going to be married that Sunday?

CHAPTER XX

In Which the Same Subject Is Pursued

BECKY did not rally from the state of stupor and confusion in which the events of the previous night had plunged her intrepid spirit, until the bells of the Curzon Street Chapels were ringing for afternoon service, and rising from her bed she began to ply her own bell, in order to summon the French maid who had left her some hours before.

Mrs. Rawdon Crawley rang many times in vain; and though, on the last occasion, she rang with such vehemence as to pull down the bell-rope, Mademoiselle Fifine did not make her appearance,—no, not though her mistress, in a great pet, and with the bell-rope in her hand, came out to the landing-place with her hair over her shoulders, and screamed out repeatedly for her attendant.

The truth is, she had quitted the premises for many hours, and upon that permission which is called French leave among us. After picking up the trinkets in the drawing-room, Mademoiselle had ascended to her own apartments, packed and corded her own boxes there, tripped out and called a cab for herself, brought down her trunks with her own hand, and without ever so much as asking the aid of any of the other servants, who would probably have refused it, as they hated her cordially, and without wishing any one of them good-bye, had made her exit from Curzon Street.

The game, in her opinion, was over in that little domestic establishment. Fifine went off in a cab, as we have known more exalted persons of her nation to do under similar circumstances: but, more provident or lucky than these, she secured not only her own property, but some of her mistress's (if indeed that lady could be said to have any property at all)—and not only carried off the trinkets before alluded to, and some favourite dresses on which she had long kept her eye, but four richly gilt Louis Quatorze candlesticks, six gilt Albums, Keepsakes, and Books of Beauty, a gold enamelled snuff-box which had once belonged to Madame du Barry, and the sweetest little inkstand and mother-of-pearl blotting book, which Becky used when she composed her charming little pink notes, had vanished from the premises in Curzon Street together with Mademoiselle Fifine, and all the silver laid on the table for the little *festin* which Rawdon interrupted. The plated ware Mademoiselle left behind her 'was too cumbrous, probably for which reason, no doubt, she also left the fire irons, the chimney-glasses, and the rosewood cottage piano.

A lady very like her subsequently kept a milliner's shop in the Rue du Helder at Paris, where she lived with great credit and enjoyed the patronage of my Lord Steyne. This person always spoke of England as of the most treacherous country in the world, and stated to her young pupils that she had been *affreusement volé* by natives of that island. It was no doubt compassion for her misfortunes which induced the Marquis of Steyne to be so kind to Madame de Saint-Amaranthe. May she flourish as she deserves,—she appears no more in our quarter of Vanity Fair.

Hearing a buzz and a stir below, and indignant at the impudence of those servants who would not answer her summons, Mrs. Crawley flung her morning robe round her, and descended majestically to the drawing-room, whence the noise proceeded.

The cook was there with blackened face, seated on the beautiful chintz sofa by the side of Mrs. Raggles, to whom she was administering Maraschino. The page with the sugar-loaf buttons, who carried about Becky's pink notes, and jumped about her little carriage with such alacrity, was now engaged putting his fingers into a cream dish; the footman was talking to Raggles, who had a face full of perplexity and woe—and yet, though the door was open, and Becky had been screaming a half dozen of times a few feet off, not one of her attendants had obeyed her call. "Have a little drop, do'ee now, Mrs. Raggles," the cook was saying as Becky entered, the white cashmere dressing-gown flouncing around her.

"Simpson! Trotter!" the mistress of the house cried in great wrath. "How dare you stay here when you heard me call? How dare you sit down in my presence? Where's my maid?" The page withdrew his fingers from his mouth with a momentary terror: but the cook took off a glass of Maraschino, of which Mrs. Raggles had had enough, staring at Becky over the little gilt glass as she drained its contents. The liquor appeared to give the odious rebel courage.

"*Your* sofy, indeed!" Mrs. Cook said. "I'm a settin' on Mrs. Raggles's sofy. Don't you stir, Mrs. Raggles, Mum. I'm a settin' on Mr. and Mrs. Raggles's sofy, which they bought with honest money, and very dear it cost 'em, too. And I'm thinkin' if I set here until I'm paid my wages, I shall set a precious long time, Mrs. Raggles; and set I will, too—ha! ha!" and with this she filled herself another glass of the liquor, and drank it with a more hideously satirical air.

"Trotter! Simpson! turn that drunken wretch out," screamed Mrs. Crawley.

"I shawn't," said Trotter the footman; "turn out yourself. Pay our selleries, and turn me out too. *We'll* go fast enough."

"Are you all here to insult me?" cried Becky in a fury; "when Colonel Crawley comes home I'll—"

At this the servants burst into a hoarse haw-haw, in which, however, Raggles, who still kept a most melancholy countenance, did not join. "He ain't a comin' back," Mr. Trotter resumed. "He sent for his things, and I wouldn't let 'em go, although Mr. Raggles would: and I don't b'lieve he's no more a Colonel than I am. He's hoff: and I suppose you're a goin' after him. You're no better than swindlers, both on you. Don't be a bullyin' *me*. I won't stand it. Pay us our selleries, I say. Pay us our selleries."

It was evident, from Mr. Trotter's flushed countenance and defective intonation, that he, too, had had recourse to vinous stimulus.

"Mr. Raggles," said Becky, in a passion of vexation, "you will not surely let me be insulted by that drunken man?" "Hold your noise, Trotter; do now," said Simpson the page. He was affected by his mistress's deplorable situation, and succeeded in preventing an outrageous denial of the epithet "drunken" on the footman's part.

"O Mam," said Raggles, "I never thought to live to see this year day. I've known the Crawley family ever since I was born. I lived butler with Miss Crawley for thirty years; and I little thought one of that family was a goin' to ruin me—yes, ruin me"—said the poor fellow with tears in his eyes. "Har you a goin' to pay me? You've lived in this 'ouse four year. You've 'ad my substance: my plate and linning. You ho me a milk and butter bill of two 'undred pound, you must 'ave noo laid hegs for your homlets, and cream for your spanil dog."

"She didn't care what her own flesh and blood had," interposed the cook. "Many's the time, he'd have starved but for me."

"He's a charity boy now, Cooky," said Mr. Trotter, with a drunken "ha! ha!"—and honest Raggles continued, in a lamentable tone, an enumeration of his griefs. All he said was true. Becky and her husband had ruined him. He had bills coming due next week and no means to meet them. He would be sold up and turned out of his shop and his house, because he had trusted to the Crawley family. His tears and lamentations made Becky more peevish than ever.

"You all seem to be against me,'" she said, bitterly. "What do you want? I can't pay you on Sunday. Come back to-morrow and I'll pay you everything. I thought Colonel Crawley had settled with you. He will to-morrow. I declare to you upon my honour that he left home this morning with fifteen hundred pounds in his pocket-book. He has left me nothing. Apply to him. Give me a bonnet and shawl and let me go out and find him. There was a difference between us this morning. You all seem to know it. I promise you upon my word that you shall all be paid. He has got a good appointment. Let me go out and find him."

This audacious statement caused Raggles and the other personages present to look at one another with a wild surprise, and with it Rebecca left them. She went upstairs and dressed herself this time without the aid of her French maid. She went into Rawdon's room, and there saw that a trunk and bag were packed ready for removal, with a pencil direction that they should be given when called for; then she went into the Frenchwoman's garret; everything was clean, and all the drawers emptied there. She bethought herself of the trinkets which had been left on the ground, and felt certain that the woman had fled. "Good Heavens! was ever such ill luck as mine?" she said; "to be so near, and to lose all. Is it all too late?" No; there was one chance more.

She dressed herself, and went away unmolested this time, but alone. It was four o'clock. She went swiftly down the streets (she had no money to pay for a carriage), and never stopped until she came to Sir Pitt Crawley's door, in Great Gaunt Street. Where was Lady Jane Crawley? She was at church. Becky was not sorry. Sir Pitt was in his study, and had given orders not to be disturbed—she must see him—she slipped by the sentinel in livery at once, and was in Sir Pitt's room before the astonished Baronet had even laid down the paper.

He turned red and started back from her with a look of great alarm and horror.

"Do not look so," she said. "I am not guilty, Pitt, dear Pitt; you were my friend once. Before God, I am not guilty. I seem so. Everything is against me. And O! at such a moment! just when all my hopes were about to be realized: just when happiness was in store for us."

"Is this true, what I see in the paper then?" Sir Pitt said—a paragraph in which had greatly surprised him.

"It was true. Lord Steyne told me on Friday night, the night of that fatal ball. He has been promised an appointment any time these six months. Mr. Martyr, the Colonial Secretary, told him yesterday that it was made out. That unlucky arrest ensued; that horrible meeting. I was only guilty of too much devotedness to Rawdon's service. I have received Lord Steyne alone a hundred times before. I confess I had money of which Rawdon knew nothing. Don't you know how careless he is of it, and could I dare to confide it to him?" And so she went on with a perfectly connected story, which she poured into the ears of her perplexed kinsman.

It was to the following effect. Becky owned, and with perfect frankness, but deep contrition, that having remarked Lord Steyne's partiality for her (at the mention of which Pitt blushed), and being secure of her own virtue, she had determined to turn the great peer's attachment to the advantage of herself and her family. "I looked for a peerage for you, Pitt," she said (the brother-in-law again turned red). "We have talked about it. Your genius and Lord Steyne's interest made it more than probable, had not this dreadful calamity come to put an end to all our hopes. But, first, I own that it was my object to rescue my dear husband,—him whom I love in spite of all his ill usage and suspicions of me,—to remove him from the poverty and ruin which was impending over us. I saw Lord Steyne's partiality for me," she said, casting down her eyes. "I own that I did everything in my power to make myself pleasing to him, and as far as an honest woman may, to secure his—his esteem. It was only on Friday morning that the news arrived of the death of the Governor of Coventry Island, and my Lord instantly secured the appointment for my dear husband. It was intended as a surprise for him,—he was to see it in the papers to-day. Even after that horrid arrest took place (the expenses of which Lord Steyne generously said he would settle, so that I was in a manner prevented from coming to my husband's assistance), my Lord was laughing with me, and saying that my dearest Rawdon would be consoled when he read of his appointment in the paper, in that shocking spun—bailiff's house. And then—then he came home. His suspicions were excited,—the dreadful scene took place between my Lord and my cruel, cruel Rawdon—and, O my God, what will happen next? Pitt, dear Pitt! pity me, and reconcile us!" And as she spoke she flung herself down on her knees, and bursting into tears, seized hold of Pitt's hand, which she kissed passionately.

It was in this very attitude that Lady Jane, who, returning from church, ran to her husband's room directly she heard Mrs. Rawdon Crawley was closeted there, found the Baronet and his sister-in-law.

"I am surprised that woman has the audacity to enter this house," Lady Jane said, trembling in every limb, and turning quite pale. (Her ladyship had sent out her maid directly after breakfast, who had communicated with Raggles and Rawdon Crawley's household, who had told her all, and a great deal more than they knew, of that story, and many others besides.) "How dare Mrs. Crawley to enter the house of—of an honest family?"

Sir Pitt started back, amazed at his wife's display of vigour. Becky still kept her kneeling posture, and clung to Sir Pitt's hand.

"Tell her that she does not know all. Tell her that I am innocent, dear Pitt," she whimpered out.

"Upon my word, my love, I think you do Mrs. Crawley injustice," Sir Pitt said; at which speech Rebecca was vastly relieved. "Indeed I believe her to be——"

"To be what?" cried out Lady Jane, her clear voice thrilling, and her heart beating violently as she spoke. "To be a wicked woman—a heartless mother, a false wife? She never loved her dear little boy, who used to fly here and tell me of her cruelty to him. She never came into a family but she strove to bring misery with her, and to weaken the most sacred affections with her wicked flattery and falsehood. She has deceived her husband, as she has deceived everybody; her soul is black with vanity, worldliness, and all sorts of crime. I tremble when I touch her. I keep my children out of her sight. I——"

"Lady Jane!" cried Sir Pitt, starting up. "This is really language——"

"I have been a true and faithful wife to you, Sir Pitt," Lady Jane continued, intrepidly; "I have kept my marriage vow as I made it to God, and have been obedient and gentle as a wife should. But righteous obedience has its limits, and I declare that I will not bear that—that woman again under my roof: if she enters it, I and my children will leave it. She is not worthy to sit down with Christian people. You—you must choose, sir, between her and me;" and with this my Lady swept out of the room, fluttering with her own audacity, and leaving Rebecca and Sir Pitt not a little astonished at it.

As for Becky, she was not hurt; nay, she was pleased. "It was the diamond-clasp you gave me," she said to Sir Pitt, reaching him out her hand; and before she left him (for which event you may be sure my Lady Jane was looking out from her dressing-room window in the upper story) the Baronet had promised to go and seek out his brother, and endeavour to bring about a reconciliation.

Rawdon found some of the young fellows of the regiment seated in the mess-room at breakfast, and was induced without much difficulty to partake of that meal, and of the devilled legs of fowls and soda-water with which these young gentlemen fortified themselves. Then they had a conversation befitting the day and their time of life: about the next pigeon-match at Battersea, with relative bets upon Ross and Osbaldiston: about Mademoiselle Ariane of the French Opera, and who had left her, and how she was consoled by Panther Carr; and about the fight between the Butcher and the Pet, and the probabilities that it was a cross. Young Tandyman, a hero of seventeen, laboriously endeavouring to get up a pair of mustachios, had seen the fight, and spoke in the most scientific manner about the battle, and the conditions of the men. It was he who had driven the Butcher on to the ground in his drag, and passed the whole of the previous night with him. Had there not been foul play he must have won it. All the old files of the Ring were in it: and Tandyman wouldn't pay; no, dammy, he wouldn't pay.—It was but a year since the young Cornet, now so knowing a hand in Cribb's parlour, had a still lingering liking for toffy, and used to be birched at Eton.

So they went on talking about dancers, fights, drinking, demireps, until Macmurdo came down and joined the boys and the conversation. He did not appear to think that any especial reverence was due to their boyhood; the old fellow cut in with stories, to the full as choice as any the

youngest rake present had to tell;—nor did his own grey
hairs nor their smooth faces detain them. Old Mac was
famous for his good stories. He was not exactly a lady's
man; that is, men asked him to dine rather at the houses
of their mistresses than of their mothers. There can
scarcely be a life lower, perhaps, than his; but he was
quite contented with it, such as it was, and led it in perfect
good nature, simplicity, and modesty of demeanour.

By the time Mac had finished a copious breakfast, most
of the others had concluded their meal. Young Lord
Varinas was smoking an immense Meerschaum pipe, while
Captain Hugues was employed with a cigar: that violent
little devil Tandyman, with his little bull-terrier between
his legs, was tossing for shillings with all his might (that
fellow was always at some game or other) against Captain
Deuceace; and Mac and Rawdon walked off to the Club,
neither, of course, having given any hint of the business
which was occupying their minds. Both, on the other
hand, had joined pretty gaily in the conversation; for why
should they interrupt it? Feasting, drinking, ribaldry,
laughter, go on alongside of all sorts of other occupations
in Vanity Fair,—the crowds were pouring out of church as
Rawdon and his friend passed down St. James's Street
and entered into their Club.

The old bucks and habitués, who ordinarily stand gaping
and grinning out of the great front window of the Club,
had not arrived at their posts as yet,—the newspaper-room
was almost empty. One man was present whom Rawdon
did not know; another to whom he owed a little score for
whist, and whom, in consequence, he did not care to meet;
a third was reading the *Royalist* (a periodical famous for
its scandal and its attachment to Church and King) Sunday
paper at the table, and, looking up at Crawley with some
interest, said, "Crawley, I congratulate you."

"What do you mean?" said the Colonel.

"It's in the *Observer* and the *Royalist* too," said Mr.
Smith.

"What?" Rawdon cried, turning very red. He thought
that the affair with Lord Steyne was already in the public
prints. Smith looked up wonderingly and smiling at the

agitation which the Colonel exhibited as he took up the paper, and trembling, began to read.

Mr. Smith and Mr. Brown (the gentleman with whom Rawdon had the outstanding whist account) had been talking about the Colonel just before he came in.

"It is come just in the nick of time," said Smith. "I suppose Crawley had not a shilling in the world."

"It's a wind that blows everybody good," Mr. Brown said. "He can't go away without paying me a pony he owes me."

"What's the salary?" asked Smith.

"Two or three thousand," answered the other. "But the climate's so infernal, they don't enjoy it long. Liverseege died after eighteen months of it: and the man before went off in six weeks, I hear."

"Some people say his brother is a very clever man. I always found him a d—— bore," Smith ejaculated. "He must have good interest, though. He must have got the Colonel the place."

"*He!*" said Brown, with a sneer—"Pooh.—It was Lord Steyne got it."

"How do you mean?"

"A virtuous woman is a crown to her husband," answered the other, enigmatically, and went to read his papers.

Rawdon, for his part, read in the *Royalist* the following astonishing paragraph:—

"GOVERNORSHIP OF COVENTRY ISLAND.—H.M.S. Yellowjack, Commander Jaunders, has brought letters and papers from Coventry Island. H. E. Sir Thomas Liverseege had fallen a victim to the prevailing fever at Swampton. His loss is deeply felt in the flourishing colony. We hear that the Governorship has been offered to Colonel Rawdon Crawley, C.B., a distinguished Waterloo officer. We need not only men of acknowledged bravery, but men of administrative talents to superintend the affairs of our colonies; and we have no doubt that the gentleman selected by the Colonial Office to fill the lamented vacancy which has occurred at Coventry Island is admirably calculated for the post which he is about to occupy."

"Coventry Island! where was it? who had appointed him to the government? You must take me out as your secretary, old boy," Captain Macmurdo said laughing; and as Crawley and his friend sat wondering and perplexed

over the announcement, the Club waiter brought in to the
Colonel a card, on which the name of Mr. Wenham was
engraved, who begged to see Colonel Crawley.

The Colonel and his aide-de-camp went out to meet the
gentleman, rightly conjecturing that he was an emissary of
Lord Steyne. "How d'ye do, Crawley? I am glad to
see you," said Mr. Wenham, with a bland smile, and grasp-
ing Crawley's hand with great cordiality.

"You come, I suppose, from——"

"Exactly," said Mr. Wenham.

"Then this is my friend Captain Macmurdo, of the Life
Guards Green."

"Delighted to know Captain Macmurdo, I'm sure," Mr.
Wenham said, and tendered another smile and shake of
the hand to the second, as he had done to the principal.
Mac put out one finger, armed with a buckskin glove, and
made a very frigid bow to Mr. Wenham over his tight
cravat. He was, perhaps, discontented at being put in
communication with a *pékin,* and thought that Lord Steyne
should have sent him a Colonel at the very least.

"As Macmurdo acts for me, and knows what I mean,"
Crawley said; "I had better retire and leave you together."

"Of course," said Macmurdo.

"By no means, my dear Colonel," Mr. Wenham said;
"the interview which I had the honour of requesting was
with you personally, though the company of Captain Macmurdo cannot fail to be also most pleasing. In fact, Captain, I hope that our conversation will lead to none but the
most agreeable results, very different from those which my
friend Colonel Crawley appears to anticipate."

"Humph!" said Captain Macmurdo.—Be hanged to
these civilians, he thought to himself, they are always for
arranging and speechifying. Mr. Wenham took a chair
which was not offered to him—took a paper from his
pocket, and resumed—

"You have seen this gratifying announcement in the
papers this morning, Colonel? Government has secured a
most valuable servant, and you, if you accept office, as I
presume you will, an excellent appointment. Three thousand a year, delightful climate, excellent government-

house, all your own way in the Colony, and a certain promotion. I congratulate you with all my heart. I presume
you know, gentlemen, to whom my friend is indebted for
this piece of patronage?"

"Hanged if I know," the Captain said: his principal
turned very red.

"To one of the most generous and kindest men in the
world, as he is one of the greatest—to my excellent friend,
the Marquis of Steyne."

"I'll see him d—— before I take his place," growled
out Rawdon.

"You are irritated against my noble friend," Mr. Wenham calmly resumed: "and now, in the name of common
sense and justice, tell me why?"

"*Why?*" cried Rawdon in surprise.

"Why? Dammy!" said the Captain, ringing his stick
on the ground.

"Dammy, indeed," said Mr. Wenham, with the most
agreeable smile; "still, look at the matter as a man of the
world—as an honest man, and see if you have not been in
the wrong. You come home from a journey, and find—
what?—my Lord Steyne supping at your house in Curzon
Street with Mrs. Crawley. Is the circumstance strange or
novel? Has he not been a hundred times before in the
same position? Upon my honour and word as a gentleman," (Mr. Wenham here put his hand on his waistcoat
with a parliamentary air,) "I declare I think that your
suspicions are monstrous and utterly unfounded, and that
they injure an honourable gentleman who has proved his
good will toward you by a thousand benefactions—and a
most spotless and innocent lady."

"You don't mean to say that—that Crawley's mistaken?"
said Mr. Macmurdo.

"I believe that Mrs. Crawley is an innocent as my wife,
Mrs. Wenham," Mr. Wenham said, with great energy.
"I believe that, misled by an infernal jealousy, my friend
here strikes a blow against not only an infirm and old man
of high station, his constant friend and benefactor, but
against his wife, his own dearest honour, his son's future
reputation, and his own prospects in life."

"I will tell you what happened," Mr. Wenham continued with great solemnity; "I was sent for this morning by my Lord Steyne, and found him in a pitiable state, as, I need hardly inform Colonel Crawley, any man of age and infirmity would be after a personal conflict with a man of your strength. I say to your face; it was a cruel advantage you took of that strength, Colonel Crawley. It was not only the body of my noble and excellent friend which was wounded—his heart, sir, was bleeding. A man whom he had loaded with benefits and regarded with affection, had subjected him to the foulest indignity. What was this very appointment, which appears in the journals of to-day, but a proof of his kindness to you? When I saw his Lordship this morning I found him in a state pitiable indeed to see: and as anxious as you are to revenge the outrage committed upon him, by blood. You know he has given his proofs, I presume, Colonel Crawley?"

"He has plenty of pluck," said the Colonel. "Nobody ever said he hadn't."

"His first order to me was to write a letter of challenge, and to carry it to Colonel Crawley. One or other of us," he said, "must not survive the outrage of last night."

Crawley nodded. "You're coming to the point, Wenham," he said.

"I tried my utmost to calm Lord Steyne. Good God! sir," I said, "how I regret that Mrs. Wenham and myself had not accepted Mrs. Crawley's invitation to sup with her!"

"She asked you to sup with her?" Captain Macmurdo said.

"After the Opera. Here's the note of invitation—stop —no, this is another paper—I thought I had it, but it's of no consequence, and I pledge you my word to the fact. If we had come—and it was only one of Mrs. Wenham's headaches which prevented us—she suffers under them a good deal, especially in the spring—if we had come, and you had returned home, there would have been no quarrel, no insult, no suspicion—and so it is positively because my poor wife has a headache that you are to bring death down upon two men of honour, and plunge two of the most excellent and ancient families in the kingdom into disgrace and sorrow."

Mr. Macmurdo looked at his principal with the air of a man profoundly puzzled: and Rawdon felt with a kind of rage that his prey was escaping him. He did not believe a word of the story, and yet, how discredit or disprove it?

Mr. Wenham continued with the same fluent oratory, which in his place in parliament he had so often practised— "I sate for an hour or more by Lord Steyne's bedside, beseeching, imploring Lord Steyne to forego his intention of demanding a meeting. I pointed out to him that the circumstances were after all suspicious—they were suspicious. I acknowledge it,—any man in your position might have been taken in—I said that a man furious with jealousy is to all intents and purposes a madman, and should be as such regarded—that a duel between you must lead to the disgrace of all parties concerned—that a man of his Lordship's exalted station had no right in these days, when the most atrocious revolutionary principles, and the most dangerous levelling doctrines are preached among the vulgar, to create a public scandal; and that, however innocent, the common people would insist that he was guilty. In fine, I implored him not to send the challenge."

"I don't believe one word of the whole story," said Rawdon, grinding his teeth. "I believe it a d—— lie, and that you're in it, Mr. Wenham. If the challenge don't come from him, by Jove it shall come from me."

Mr. Wenham turned deadly pale at this savage interruption of the Colonel, and looked towards the door.

But he found a champion in Captain Macmurdo. That gentleman rose up with an oath, and rebuked Rawdon for his language. "You put the affair into my hands, and you shall act as I think fit, by Jove, and not as you do. You have no right to insult Mr. Wenham with this sort of language; and dammy, Mr. Wenham, you deserve an apology. And as for a challenge to Lord Steyne, you may get somebody else to carry it, I won't. If my lord, after being thrashed, chooses to sit still, dammy let him. And as for the affair with—with Mrs. Crawley, my belief is, there's nothing proved at all: that your wife's innocent, as inno-

cent as Mr. Wenham says she is: and at any rate, that you
would be a d— fool not to take the place and hold your
tongue."

"Captain Macmurdo, you speak like a man of sense,"
Mr. Wenham cried out, immensely relieved—"I forget any
words that Colonel Crawley has used in the irritation of
the moment."

"I thought you would," Rawdon said, with a sneer.

"Shut your mouth, you old stoopid," the Captain said,
good-naturedly. "Mr. Wenham ain't a fighting man; and
quite right, too."

"This matter, in my belief," the Steyne emissary cried,
"ought to be buried in the most profound oblivion. A
word concerning it should never pass these doors. I speak
in the interest of my friend, as well as of Colonel Crawley,
who persists in considering me his enemy."

"I suppose Lord Steyne won't talk about it very much,"
said Captain Macmurdo; "and I don't see why our side
should. The affair ain't a very pretty one, any way you
take it; and the less said about it the better. It's you are
thrashed, and not us; and if you are satisfied, why, I
think, we should be."

Mr. Wenham took his hat, upon this, and Captain Macmurdo following him to the door, shut it upon himself and
Lord Steyne's agent, leaving Rawdon chafing within.
When the two were on the other side, Macmurdo looked
hard at the other ambassador, and with an expression of
anything but respect on his round jolly face.

"You don't stick at a trifle, Mr. Wenham," he said.

"You flatter me, Captain Macmurdo," answered the
other, with a smile. "Upon my honour and conscience
now, Mrs. Crawley did ask us to sup after the Opera."

"Of course; and Mrs. Wenham had one of her head-
aches. I say, I've got a thousand-pound note here, which
I will give you if you will give me a receipt, please; and
I will put the note up in an envelope for Lord Steyne.
My man shan't fight him. But we had rather not take his
money."

"It was all a mistake,—all a mistake, my dear sir," the
other said, with the utmost innocence of manner; and was

bowed down the Club steps by Captain Macmurdo, just as Sir Pitt Crawley ascended them. There was a slight acquaintance between these two gentlemen; and the Captain, going back with the Baronet to the room where the latter's brother was, told Sir Pitt, in confidence, that he had made the affair all right between Lord Steyne and the Colonel.

Sir Pitt was well pleased, of course, at this intelligence; and congratulated his brother warmly upon the peaceful issue of the affair, making appropriate moral remarks upon the evils of duelling, and the unsatisfactory nature of that sort of settlement of disputes.

And after this preface, he tried with all his eloquence to effect a reconciliation between Rawdon and his wife. He recapitulated the statements which Becky had made, pointed out the probabilities of their truth, and asserted his own firm belief in her innocence.

But Rawdon would not hear of it. "She has kep money concealed from me these ten years," he said. "She swore, last night only, she had none from Steyne. She knew it was all up, directly I found it. If she's not guilty, Pitt, she's as bad as guilty; and I'll never see her again,—never." His head sank down on his chest as he spoke the words; and he looked quite broken and sad.

"Poor old boy," Macmurdo said, shaking his head.

Rawdon Crawley resisted for some time the idea of taking the place which had been procured for him by so odious a patron: and was also for removing the boy from the school where Lord Steyne's interest had placed him. He was induced, however, to acquiesce in these benefits by the entreaties of his brother and Macmurdo: but mainly by the latter pointing out to him what a fury Steyne would be in, to think that his enemy's fortune was made through his means.

When the Marquis of Steyne came abroad after his accident, the Colonial Secretary bowed up to him and congratulated himself and the Service upon having made so excellent an appointment. These congratulations were received with a degree of gratitude which may be imagined on the part of Lord Steyne.

The secret of the *rencontre* between him and Colonel
Crawley was buried in the profoundest oblivion, as Wenham said; that is by the seconds and the principals. But
before that evening was over it was talked of at fifty din-
ner-tables in Vanity Fair. Little Cackleby himself went
to seven evening parties, and told the story with comments
and emendations at each place. How Mrs. Washington
White revelled in it! The Bishopess of Ealing was shocked
beyond expression: the Bishop went and wrote his name
down in the visiting-book at Gaunt House that very day.
Little Southdown was sorry: so you may be sure was his
sister Lady Jane, very sorry. Lady Southdown wrote it
off to her other daughter at the Cape of Good Hope. It
was town-talk for at least three days, and was only kept
out of the newspapers by the exertions of Mr. Wagg, acting upon a hint from Mr. Wenham.

The bailiffs and brokers seized upon poor Raggles in
Curzon Street, and the late fair tenant of that poor little
mansion was in the meanwhile—where? Who cared?
Who asked after a day or two? Was she guilty or not?
We all know how charitable the world is, and how the
verdict of Vanity Fair goes when there is a doubt. Some
people said she had gone to Naples in pursuit of Lord
Steyne; whilst others averred that his Lordship quitted
that city, and fled to Palermo on hearing of Becky's arrival;
some said she was living in Bierstadt, and had become a
dame d'honneur to the Queen of Bulgaria; some that she
was at Boulogne; and others, at a boarding-house at
Cheltenham.

Rawdon made her a tolerable annuity; and we may be
sure that she was a woman who could make a little money
go a great way, as the saying is. He would have paid his
debts on leaving England, could he have got any Insurance
Office to take his life: but the climate of Coventry Island
was so bad that he could borrow no money on the strength
of his salary. He remitted, however, to his brother punctually, and wrote to his little boy regularly every mail.
He kept Macmurdo in cigars; and sent over quantities of
shells, cayenne pepper, hot pickles, guava jelly, and colonial
produce to Lady Jane. He sent his brother home the

Swamp Town Gazette, in which the new Governor was praised with immense enthusiasm; whereas the *Swamp Town Sentinel,* whose wife was not asked to Government House, declared that his Excellency was a tyrant, compared to whom Nero was an enlightened philanthropist. Little Rawdon used to like to get the papers and read about his Excellency.

His mother never made any movement to see the child. He went home to his aunt for Sundays and holidays; he soon knew every bird's nest about Queen's Crawley, and rode out with Sir Huddlestone's hounds, which he admired so on his first well-remembered visit to Hampshire.

CHAPTER XXI

Georgy Is Made a Gentleman

GEORGY OSBORNE was now fairly established in his grandfather's mansion in Russell Square: occupant of his father's room in the house, and heir-apparent of all the splendours there. The good looks, gallant bearing, and gentlemanlike appearance of the boy won the grandsire's heart for him. Mr. Osborne was as proud of him as ever he had been of the elder George.

The child had many more luxuries and indulgences than had been awarded to his father. Osborne's commerce had prospered greatly of late years. His wealth and importance in the City had very much increased. He had been glad enough in former days to put the elder George to a good private school; and a commission in the army for his son had been a source of no small pride to him: for little George and his future prospects the old man looked much higher.

He would make a gentleman of the little chap, was Mr. Osborne's constant saying regarding little Georgy. He saw him in his mind's eye, a collegian, a parliament-man,—a Baronet, perhaps. The old man thought he would die contented if he could see his grandson in a fair way to such honours. He would have none but a tip-top college man to educate him,—none of your quacks and pretenders —no, no. A few years before, he used to be savage, and inveigh against all parsons, scholars, and the like,—declaring that they were a pack of humbugs, and quacks, that weren't fit to get their living but by grinding Latin and Greek, and a set of supercilious dogs, that pretended to look down upon British merchants and gentlemen, who could buy up half a hundred of 'em. He would mourn now, in a very solemn manner, that his own education had been neglected, and repeatedly point out, in pompous orations to Georgy, the necessity and excellence of classical acquirements.

When they met at dinner the grandsire used to ask the lad what he had been reading during the day, and was greatly interested at the report the boy gave of his own studies; pretending to understand little George when he spoke regarding them. He made a hundred blunders, and showed his ignorance many a time. It did not increase the respect which the child had for his senior. A quick brain and a better education elsewhere showed the boy very soon that his grandsire was a dullard; and he began accordingly to command him and to look down upon him; for his previous education, humble and contracted as it had been, had made a much better gentleman of Georgy than any plans of his grandfather could make him. He had been brought up by a kind, weak, and tender woman, who had no pride about anything, but about him, and whose heart was so pure and whose bearing was so meek and humble, that she could not but needs to be a true lady. She busied herself in gentle offices and quiet duties; if she never said brilliant things, she never spoke or thought unkind ones; guileless and artless, loving and pure, indeed how could our poor little Amelia be other than a real gentlewoman!

Young Georgy lorded over this soft and yielding nature: and the contrast of its simplicity and delicacy with the coarse pomposity of the dull old man with whom he next came in contact, made him lord over the latter too. If he had been a Prince Royal he could not have been better brought up to think well of himself.

Whilst his mother was yearning after him at home, and I do believe every hour of the day, and during most hours of the sad lonely nights, thinking of him, this young gentleman had a number of pleasures and consolations administered to him, which made him for his part bear the separation from Amelia very easily. Little boys who cry when they are going to school—cry because they are going to a very uncomfortable place. It is only a very few who weep from sheer affection. When you think that the eyes of your childhood dried at the sight of a piece of gingerbread, and that a plum-cake was a compensation for the agony of parting with your mamma and sisters; O my friend and brother, you need not be too confident of your own fine feelings.

Well, then, Master George Osborne had every comfort and luxury that a wealthy and lavish old grandfather thought fit to provide. The coachman was instructed to purchase for him the handsomest pony which could be bought for money; and on this George was taught to ride, first at a riding-school, whence, after having performed satisfactorily without stirrups, and over the leaping-bar, he was conducted through the New Road to Regent's Park, and then to Hyde Park, where he rode in state with Martin the coachman behind him. Old Osborne, who took matters more easily in the City now, where he left his affairs to his junior partners, would often ride out with Miss O. in the same fashionable direction. As little Georgy came cantering up with his dandyfied air, and his heels down, his grandfather would nudge the lad's aunt, and say, "Look, Miss O." And he would laugh, and his face would grow red with pleasure, as he nodded out of the window to the boy, as the groom saluted the carriage, and the footman saluted Master George. Here too his aunt, Mrs. Frederick Bullock (whose chariot might daily be seen in the Ring, with bullocks or emblazoned on the panels and harness, and three pasty-faced little Bullocks, covered with cockades and feathers, staring from the windows),—Mrs. Frederick Bullock, I say, flung glances of the bitterest hatred at the little upstart as he rode by with his hand on his side and his hat on one ear, as proud as a lord.

Though he was scarcely eleven years of age, Master George wore straps, and the most beautiful little boots like a man. He had gilt spurs, and a gold-headed whip, and a fine pin in his handkerchief; and the neatest little kid gloves which Lamb's Conduit Street could furnish. His mother had given him a couple of neckcloths, and carefully hemmed and made some little shirts for him; but when her Samuel came to see the widow, they were replaced by much finer linen. He had little jewelled buttons in the lawn shirt fronts. Her humble presents had been put aside—I believe Miss Osborne had given them to the coachman's boy. Amelia tried to think she was pleased at the change. Indeed, she was happy and charmed to see the boy looking so beautiful.

She had had a little black profile of him done for a shilling; and this was hung up by the side of another portrait over her bed. One day the boy came on his accustomed visit, galloping down the little street at Brompton, and bringing, as usual, all the inhabitants to the windows to admire his splendour, and with great eagerness, and a look of triumph in his face, he pulled a case out of his great-coat—(it was a natty white great-coat, with a cape and a velvet collar)—pulled out a red morocco case, which he gave her.

"I bought it with my own money, Mamma," he said. "I thought you'd like it."

Amelia opened the case, and giving a little cry of delighted affection, seized the boy and embraced him a hundred times. It was a miniature of himself, very prettily done (though not half handsome enough, we may be sure, the widow thought). His grandfather had wished to have a picture of him by an artist whose works, exhibited in a shop-window, in Southampton Row, had caught the old gentleman's eyes; and George, who had plenty of money, bethought him of asking the painter how much a copy of the little portrait would cost, saying that he would pay for it out of his own money, and that he wanted to give it to his mother.

The pleased painter executed it for a small price; and old Osborne himself, when he heard of the incident, growled out his satisfaction, and gave the boy twice as many sovereigns as he paid for the miniature.

But what was the grandfather's pleasure compared to Amelia's ecstasy? That proof of the boy's affection charmed her so, that she thought no child in the world was like hers for goodness. For long weeks after, the thought of his love made her happy. She slept better with the picture under her pillow; and how many many times did she kiss it, and weep and pray over it! A small kindness from those she loved made that timid heart grateful. Since her parting with George she had had no such joy and consolation.

At his new home Master George ruled like a lord: at dinner he invited the ladies to drink wine with the utmost coolness, and took off his champagne in a way which charmed his old grandfather. "Look at him," the old man would say, nudging his neighbour with a delighted purple face, "did you ever see such a chap? Lord, Lord! he'll be ordering a dressing-case next, and razors to shave with; I'm blessed if he won't."

The antics of the lad did not, however, delight Mr. Osborne's friends so much as they pleased the old gentleman. It gave Mr. Justice Coffin no pleasure to hear Georgy cut into the conversation and spoil his stories. Colonel Fogey was not interested in seeing the little boy half tipsy. Mr. Serjeant Toffy's lady felt no particular gratitude, when, with a twist of his elbow, he tilted a glass of port-wine over her yellow satin, and laughed at the disaster: nor was she better pleased, although old Osborne was highly delighted, when Georgy "whopped" her third boy (a young gentleman a year older than Georgy, and by chance home for the holidays from Dr. Tickleus's at Ealing School) in Russell Square. George's grandfather gave the boy a couple of sovereigns for that feat, and promised to reward him further for every boy above his own size and age whom he whopped in a similar manner. It is difficult to say what good the old man saw in these combats; he had a vague notion that quarrelling made boys hardy, and that tyranny was a useful accomplishment for them to learn. English youth have been so educated time out of mind, and we have hundreds of thousands of apologists and admirers of injustice, misery, and brutality, as perpetrated among children. Flushed with praise and victory over Master Toffy, George wished naturally to pursue his conquests further, and one day as he was strutting about in prodigiously dandyfied new clothes, near St. Pancras, and a young baker's boy made sarcastic comments upon his appearance, the youthful patrician pulled off his dandy jacket with great spirit, and giving it in charge to the friend who accompanied him (Master Todd, of Great Coram

Street, Russell Square, son of the junior partner of the house of Osborne and Co.)—George tried to whop the little baker. But the chances of war were unfavourable this time, and the little baker whopped Georgy: who came home with a rueful black eye and all his fine shirt frill dabbled with the claret drawn from his own little nose. He told his grandfather that he had been in combat with a giant; and frightened his poor mother at Brompton with long, and by no means authentic, accounts of the battle.

This young Todd, of Coram Street, Russell Square, was Master George's great friend and admirer. They both had a taste for painting theatrical characters; for hard-bake and raspberry tarts; for sliding and skating in the Regent's Park and the Serpentine, when the weather permitted; for going to the play, whither they were often conducted, by Mr. Osborne's orders, by Rowson, Master George's appointed body-servant; with whom they sate in great comfort in the pit.

In the company of this gentleman they visited all the principal theatres of the metropolis—knew the names of all the actors from Drury Lane to Sadler's Wells; and performed, indeed, many of the plays to the Todd family and their youthful friends, with West's famous characters, on their pasteboard theatre. Rowson, the footman, who was of a generous disposition, would not unfrequently, when in cash, treat his young master to oysters after the play, and to a glass of rum-shrub for a night-cap. We may be pretty certain that Mr. Rowson profited in his turn, by his young master's liberality and gratitude for the pleasures to which the footman inducted him.

A famous tailor from the West End of the town,—Mr. Osborne would have none of your City or Holborn bunglers, he said, for the boy (though a City tailor was good enough for *him*),—was summoned to ornament little George's person, and was told to spare no expense in so doing. So, Mr. Woolsey, of Conduit Street, gave a loose to his imagination, and sent the child home fancy trowsers, fancy waistcoats, and fancy jackets enough to furnish a school of little dandies. Georgy had little white waistcoats for evening parties and little cut velvet waistcoats for dinners, and

a dear little darling shawl dressing-gown, for all the world
like a little man. He dressed for dinner every day, "like
a regular West End Swell," as his grandfather remarked;
one of the domestics was affected to his special service,
attended him at this toilette, answered his bell, and brought
him his letters always on a silver tray.

Georgy, after breakfast, would sit in the arm-chair in
the dining-room, and read the *Morning Post*, just like a
grown-up man. "How he *du* dam and swear," the servants
would cry, delighted at his precocity. Those who remembered the Captain his father, declared Master George was
his Pa every inch of him. He made the house lively by
his activity, his imperiousness, his scolding, and his good-
nature.

George's education was confided to a neighbouring scholar
and private pedagogue who "prepared young noblemen and
gentlemen for the Universities, the senate, and the learned
professions: whose system did not embrace the degrading
corporal severities still practised at the ancient places of
education, and in whose family the pupils would find the
elegances of refined society and the confidence and affection
of a home." It was in this way that the Reverend Lawrence
Veal of Hart Street, Bloomsbury, and domestic Chaplain
to the Earl of Bareacres, strove with Mrs. Veal his wife
to entice pupils.

By thus advertising and pushing sedulously, the domestic
Chaplain and his Lady generally succeeded in having one
or two scholars by them: who paid a high figure: and
were thought to be in uncommonly comfortable quarters.
There was a large West Indian, whom nobody came to see,
with a mahogany complexion, a woolly head, and an exceedingly dandyfied appearance; there was another hulking
boy of three-and-twenty whose education had been neglected,
and whom Mr. and Mrs. Veal were to introduce into the
polite world: there were two sons of Colonel Bangles of
the East India Company's Service: these four sate down
to dinner at Mrs. Veal's genteel board, when Georgy was
introduced to her establishment.

Georgy was, like some dozen other pupils, only a day
boy; he arrived in the morning under the guardianship of

his friend Mr. Rowson, and if it was fine, would ride away in the afternoon on his pony, followed by the groom. The wealth of his grandfather was reported in the school to be prodigious.

The Rev. Mr. Veal used to compliment Georgy upon it personally, warning him that he was destined for a high station; that it became him to prepare, by sedulity and docility in youth, for the lofty duties to which he would be called in mature age; that obedience in the child was the best preparation for command in the man; and that he therefore begged George would not bring toffy into the school, and ruin the health of the Masters Bangles, who had everything they wanted at the elegant and abundant table of Mrs. Veal.

With respect to learning, "the Curriculum," as Mr. Veal loved to call it, was of prodigious extent: and the young gentlemen in Hart Street might learn a something of every known science. The Rev. Mr. Veal had an orrery, an electrifying machine, a turning lathe, a theatre (in the wash-house), a chemical apparatus, and what he called a select library of all the works of the best authors of ancient and modern times and languages. He took the boys to the British Museum, and descanted upon the antiquities and the specimens of natural history there, so that audiences would gather round him as he spoke, and all Bloomsbury highly admired him as a prodigiously well-informed man. And whenever he spoke (which he did almost always), he took care to produce the very finest and longest words of which the vocabulary gave him the use; rightly judging, that it was as cheap to employ a handsome, large, and sonorous epithet, as to use a little stingy one.

Thus he would say to George in school, "I observed on my return home from taking the indulgence of an evening's scientific conversation with my excellent friend Doctor Bulders—a true archæologian, gentlemen, a true archæologian—that the windows of your venerated grandfather's almost princely mansion in Russell Square were illuminated as if for the purposes of festivity. Am I right in my conjecture, that Mr. Osborne entertained a society of chosen spirits round his sumptuous board last night?"

Little Georgy, who had considerable humour, and used to mimic Mr. Veal to his face with great spirit and dexterity, would reply, that Mr. V. was quite correct in his surmise.

"Then those friends who had the honour of partaking of Mr. Osborne's hospitality, gentlemen, had no reason, I will lay any wager, to complain of their repast. I myself have been more than once so favoured. (By the way, Master Osborne, you came a little late this morning, and have been a defaulter in this respect more than once.) I myself, I say, gentlemen, humble as I am, have been found not unworthy to share Mr. Osborne's elegant hospitality. And though I have feasted with the great and noble of the world —for I presume that I may call my excellent friend and patron, the Right Honourable George Earl of Bareacres, one of the number—yet I assure you that the board of the British merchant was to the full as richly served, and his reception as gratifying and noble. Mr. Bluck, sir, we will resume, if you please, that passage of Eutropius, which was interrupted by the late arrival of Master Osborne."

To this great man George's education was for some time entrusted. Amelia was bewildered by his phrases, but thought him a prodigy of learning. That poor widow made friends of Mrs. Veal, for reasons of her own. She liked to be in the house, and see Georgy coming to school there. She liked to be asked to Mrs. Veal's *conversazioni,* which took place once a month (as you were informed on pink cards, with ΑΘΗΝΗ engraved on them), and where the professor welcomed his pupils and their friends to weak tea and scientific conversation. Poor little Amelia never missed one of these entertainments, and thought them delicious so long as she might have Georgy sitting by her. And she would walk from Brompton in any weather, and embrace Mrs. Veal with tearful gratitude for the delightful evening she had passed, when, the company having retired and Georgy gone off with Mr. Rowson, his attendant, poor Mrs. Osborne put on her cloaks and her shawls preparatory to walking home.

As for the learning which Georgy imbibed under this valuable master of a hundred sciences, to judge from the weekly reports which the lad took home to his grandfather, his progress was remarkable. The names of a score or more of desirable branches of knowledge were printed in a table, and the pupil's progress in each was marked by the professor. In Greek Georgy was pronounced aristos, in Latin optimus, in French *très bien,* and so forth; and everybody had prizes for everything at the end of the year. Even Mr. Swartz, the woolly-headed young gentleman, and half-brother to the Honourable Mrs. Mac Mull, and Mr. Bluck, the neglected young pupil of three-and-twenty from the agricultural districts, and that idle young scapegrace of a Master Todd before mentioned, received little eighteen-penny books, with "Athene" engraved on them, and a pompous Latin inscription from the professor to his young friends.

The family of this Master Todd were hangers-on of the house of Osborne. The old gentleman had advanced Todd from being a clerk to be a junior partner in his establishment.

Mr. Osborne was the godfather of young Master Todd (who in subsequent life wrote Mr. Osborne Todd on his cards, and became a man of decided fashion), while Miss Osborne had accompanied Miss Maria Todd to the font, and gave her *protégée* a prayer-book, a collection of tracts, a volume of very low church poetry, or some such memento of her goodness every year. Miss O. drove the Todds out in her carriage now and then: when they were ill, her footman, in large plush smalls and waistcoat, brought jellies and delicacies from Russell Square to Coram Street. Coram Street trembled and looked up to Russell Square indeed; and Mrs. Todd, who had a pretty hand at cutting out paper trimmings for haunches of mutton, and could make flowers, ducks, &c., out of turnips and carrots in a very creditable manner, would go to "the Square," as it was called, and assist in the preparations incident to a great dinner, without even so much as thinking of sitting down to the banquet. If any guest failed at the eleventh hour, Todd was asked to dine. Mrs. Todd and Maria came across in the evening, slipped in with a muffled knock, and were in the drawing-room by the time Miss Osborne and the ladies under her convoy reached that apartment; and ready to fire off duets

and sing until the gentlemen came up. Poor Maria Todd;
poor young lady! How she had to work and thrum at
these duets and sonatas in the Street, before they appeared
in public in the Square!

Thus it seemed to be decreed by fate, that Georgy was to
domineer over everybody with whom he came in contact,
and that friends, relatives, and domestics were all to bow
the knee before the little fellow. It must be owned that
he accommodated himself very willingly to this arrangement. Most people do so. And Georgy liked to play the
part of master, and perhaps had a natural aptitude for it.

In Russell Square everybody was afraid of Mr. Osborne,
and Mr. Osborne was afraid of Georgy. The boy's dashing
manners, and offhand rattle about books and learning, his
likeness to his father (dead unreconciled in Brussels yonder), awed the old gentleman, and gave the young boy the
mastery. The old man would start at some hereditary fea-
ture or tone unconsciously used by the little lad, and fancy
that George's father was again before him. He tried by
indulgence to the grandson to make up for harshness to the
elder George. People were surprised at his gentleness to
the boy. He growled and swore at Miss Osborne as usual:
and would smile when George came down late for breakfast.

Miss Osborne, George's aunt, was a faded old spinster,
broken down by more than forty years of dulness and coarse
usage. It was easy for a lad of spirit to master *her*. And
whenever George wanted anything from her, from the jam-
pots in her cupboards, to the cracked and dry old colours
in her paint-box (the old paint-box which she had had when
she was a pupil of Mr. Smee, and was still almost young
and blooming), Georgy took possession of the object of his
desire, which obtained, he took no further notice of his
aunt.

For his friends and cronies, he had a pompous old schoolmaster, who flattered him, and a toady, his senior, whom
he could thrash. It was dear Mrs. Todd's delight to leave
him with her youngest daughter, Rosa Jemima, a darling
child of eight years old. The little pair looked so well
together, she would say (but not to the folks in "the
Square," we may be sure),—"Who knows what might hap-

pen? Don't they make a pretty little couple?" the fond mother thought.

The broken-spirited, old, maternal grandfather was likewise subject to the little tyrant. He could not help respecting a lad who had such fine clothes, and rode with a groom behind him. Georgy, on his side, was in the constant habit of hearing coarse abuse and vulgar satire levelled at John Sedley, by his pitiless old enemy, Mr. Osborne. Osborne used to call the other the old pauper, the old coalman, the old bankrupt, and by many other such names of brutal contumely. How was little George to respect a man so prostrate? A few months after he was with his paternal grandfather, Mrs. Sedley died. There had been little love between her and the child. He did not care to show much grief. He came down to visit his mother in a fine new suit of mourning, and was very angry that he could not go to a play upon which he had set his heart.

The illness of that old lady had been the occupation and perhaps the safeguard of Amelia. What do men know about women's martyrdoms? We should go mad had we to endure the hundredth part of those daily pains which are meekly borne by many women. Ceaseless slavery meeting with no reward; constant gentleness and kindness met by cruelty as constant; love, labour, patience, watchfulness, without even so much as the acknowledgment of a good word; all this, how many of them have to bear in quiet, and appear abroad with cheerful faces as if they felt nothing. Tender slaves that they are, they must needs be hypocrites and weak.

From her chair Amelia's mother had taken to her bed, which she had never left: and from which Mrs. Osborne herself was never absent except when she ran to see George. The old lady grudged her even those rare visits; she, who had been a kind, smiling, good-natured mother once, in the days of her prosperity, but whom poverty and infirmities had broken down. Her illness or estrangement did not affect Amelia. They rather enabled her to support the other calamity under which she was suffering, and from the thoughts of which she was kept by the ceaseless calls of the invalid. Amelia bore her harshness quite gently;

smoothed the uneasy pillow; was always ready with a soft
answer to the watchful, querulous voice; soothed the sufferer with words of hope, such as her pious simple heart
could best feel and utter, and closed the eyes that had
once looked so tenderly upon her.

Then all her time and tenderness were devoted to the
consolation and comfort of the bereaved old father, who
was stunned by the blow which had befallen him, and
stood utterly alone in the world. His wife, his honour,
his fortune, everything he loved best had fallen away from
him. There was only Amelia to stand by and support with
her gentle arms the tottering, heart-broken, old man. We
are not going to write the history: it would be too dreary
and stupid. I can see Vanity Fair yawning over it
d'avance.

One day as the young gentlemen were assembled in the
study at the Rev. Mr. Veal's, and the domestic chaplain
to the Right Honourable the Earl of Bareacres was spout-
ing away as usual—a smart carriage drove up to the door
decorated with the statue of Athene, and two gentlemen
stepped out. The young Masters Bangles rushed to the
window, with a vague notion that their father might have
arrived from Bombay. The great hulking scholar of three-
and-twenty, who was crying secretly over a passage of
Eutropius, flattened his neglected nose against the panes,
and looked at the drag, as the *laquais de place* sprang from
the box and let out the persons in the carriage.

"It's a fat one and a thin one," Mr. Bluck said, as a
thundering knock came to the door.

Everybody was interested, from the domestic chaplain
himself, who hoped he saw the fathers of some future
pupils, down to Master Georgy, glad of any pretext for
laying his book down.

The boy in the shabby livery, with the faded copper-
buttons, who always thrust himself into the tight coat to
open the door, came into the study and said, "Two gentlemen want to see Master Osborne." The professor had had
a trifling altercation in the morning with that young gentleman, owing to a difference about the introduction of crackers

in school-time; but his face resumed its habitual expression of bland courtesy, as he said, "Master Osborne, I give you full permission to go and see your carriage friends,—to whom I beg you to convey the respectful compliments of myself and Mrs. Veal."

Georgy went into the reception-room, and saw two strangers, whom he looked at with his head up, in his usual haughty manner. One was fat, with mustachios, and the other was lean and long, in a blue frock-coat, with a brown face, and a grizzled head.

"My God, how like he is!" said the long gentleman, with a start. "Can you guess who we are, George?"

The boy's face flushed up, as it did usually when he was moved, and his eyes brightened. "I don't know the other," he said, "but I should think you must be Major Dobbin."

Indeed it was our old friend. His voice trembled with pleasure as he greeted the boy, and taking both the other's hands in his own, drew the lad to him.

"Your mother has talked to you about me—has she?" he said.

"That she has," Georgy answered, "hundreds and hundreds of times."

CHAPTER XXII

Eothen

IT was one of the many causes for personal pride with
which old Osborne chose to recreate himself, that Sedley, his ancient rival, enemy, and benefactor, was in
his last days so utterly defeated and humiliated, as to be
forced to accept pecuniary obligations at the hands of the
man who had most injured and insulted him. The successful man of the world cursed the old pauper, and relieved him from time to time. As he furnished George
with money for his mother, he gave the boy to understand by hints, delivered in his brutal, coarse way, that
George's maternal grandfather was but a wretched old
bankrupt and dependant, and that John Sedley might thank
the man to whom he already owed ever so much money,
for the aid which his generosity now chose to administer.
George carried the pompous supplies to his mother and the
shattered old widower whom it was now the main business of her life to tend and comfort. The little fellow
patronised the feeble and disappointed old man.

It may have shown a want of "proper pride" in Amelia
that she chose to accept these money benefits at the hands
of her father's enemy. But proper pride and this poor
lady had never had much acquaintance together. A disposition naturally simple and demanding protection; a long
course of poverty and humility, of daily privations, and
hard words, of kind offices and no returns, had been her lot
ever since womanhood almost, or since her luckless marriage with George Osborne. You who see your betters,
bearing up under this shame every day, meekly suffering
under the slights of fortune, gentle and unpitied, poor, and
rather despised for their poverty, do you ever step down
from your prosperity and wash the feet of these poor wearied

beggars? The very thought of them is odious and low.
"There must be classes—there must be rich and poor,"
Dives says, smacking his claret—(it is well if he even sends
the broken meat out to Lazarus sitting under the window).
Very true; but think how mysterious and often unaccountable it is—that lottery of life which gives to this man the
purple and fine linen, and sends to the other rags for garments and dogs for comforters.

So I must own, that without much repining, on the contrary with something akin to gratitude, Amelia took the
crumbs that her father-in-law let drop now and then, and
with them fed her own parents. Directly she understood it
to be her duty, it was this young woman's nature (ladies,
she is but thirty still, and we choose to call her a young
woman even at that age)—it was, I say, her nature to
sacrifice herself and to fling all that she had at the feet of
the beloved object. During what long thankless nights
had she worked out her fingers for little Georgy whilst at
home with her; what buffets, scorns, privations, poverties
had she endured for her father and mother! And in the
midst of all these solitary resignations and unseen sacrifices,
she did not respect herself any more than the world re-
pected her; but I believe thought in her heart that she was
a poor-spirited, despicable little creature, whose luck in life
was only too good for her merits. O you poor women! O
you poor secret martyrs and victims, whose life is a torture,
who are stretched on racks in your bedrooms, and who lay
your heads down on the block daily at the drawing-room
table; every man who watches your pains, or peers into
those dark places where the torture is administered to you,
must pity you—and—and thank God that he has a beard.
I recollect seeing, years ago, at the prisons for idiots and
madmen at Bicêtre, near Paris, a poor wretch bent down
under the bondage of his imprisonment and his personal
infirmity, to whom one of our party gave a halfpennyworth
of snuff in a *cornet* or "screw" of paper. The kindness
was too much for the poor epileptic creature. He cried in
an anguish of delight and gratitude: if anybody gave you
and me a thousand a year, or saved our lives, we could not
be so affected. And so, if you properly tyrannise over a

woman, you will find a halfp'orth of kindness act upon her, and bring tears into her eyes, as though you were an angel benefiting her.

Some such boons as these were the best which Fortune allotted to poor little Amelia. Her life, begun not unprosperously, had come down to this—to a mean prison and a long, ignoble bondage. Little George visited her captivity sometimes, and consoled it with feeble gleams of encouragement. Russell Square was the boundary of her prison: she might walk thither occasionally, but was always back to sleep in her cell at night; to perform cheerless duties; to watch by thankless sick-beds; to suffer the harassment and tyranny of querulous disappointed old age. How many thousands of people are there, women for the most part, who are doomed to endure this long slavery?—who are hospital nurses without wages,—sisters of Charity, if you like, without the romance and the sentiment of sacrifice,—who strive, fast, watch, and suffer, unpitied; and fade away ignobly and unknown.

The hidden and awful Wisdom which apportions the destinies of mankind is pleased so to humiliate and cast down the tender, good, and wise; and to set up the selfish, the foolish, or the wicked. Oh, be humble, my brother, in your prosperity! Be gentle with those who are less lucky, if not more deserving. Think, what right have you to be scornful, whose virtue is a deficiency of temptation, whose success may be a chance, whose rank may be an ancestor's accident, whose prosperity is very likely a satire.

They buried Amelia's mother in the churchyard at Brompton; upon just such a rainy, dark day, as Amelia recollected when first she had been there to marry George. Her little boy sate by her side in pompous new sables. She remembered the old pew-woman and clerk. Her thoughts were away in other times as the parson read. But that she held George's hand in her own, perhaps she would have liked to change places with . . . Then, as usual, she felt ashamed of her selfish thoughts, and prayed inwardly to be strengthened to do her duty.

So she determined with all her might and strength to try and make her old father happy. She slaved, toiled, patched, and mended, sang and played backgammon, read out the newspaper, cooked dishes, for old Sedley, walked him out sedulously into Kensington Gardens or the Brompton Lanes, listened to his stories with untiring smiles and affectionate hypocrisy, or sate musing by his side and communing with her own thoughts and reminiscences, as the old man, feeble and querulous, sunned himself on the garden benches and prattled about his wrongs or his sorrows.

What sad, unsatisfactory thoughts those of the widow were! The children running up and down the slopes and broad paths in the gardens, reminded her of George who was taken from her: the first George was taken from her: her selfish, guilty love, in both instances, had been rebuked and bitterly chastised. She strove to think it was right that she should be so punished. She was such a miserable wicked sinner. She was quite alone in the world.

I know that the account of this kind of solitary imprisonment is insufferably tedious, unless there is some cheerful or humorous incident to enliven it,—a tender gaoler, for instance, or a waggish commandant of the fortress, or a mouse to come out and play about Latude's beard and whiskers, or a subterranean passage under the castle, dug by Trenck with his nails and a toothpick: the historian has no such enlivening incident to relate in the narrative of Amelia's captivity. Fancy her, if you please, during this period, very sad, but always ready to smile when spoken to; in a very mean, poor, not to say vulgar position of life; singing songs, making puddings, playing cards, mending stockings, for her old father's benefit. So, never mind, whether she be a heroine or no; or you and I, however old, scolding, and bankrupt;—may we have in our last days a kind soft shoulder on which to lean, and a gentle hand to soothe our gouty old pillows.

Old Sedley grew very fond of his daughter after his wife's death; and Amelia had her consolation in doing her duty by the old man.

But we are not going to leave these two people long in such a low and ungenteel station of life. Better days, as far as worldly prosperity went, were in store for both. Perhaps the ingenious reader has guessed who was the stout gentleman who called upon Georgy at his school in company with our old friend Major Dobbin. It was another old acquaintance returned to England, and at a time when his presence was likely to be of great comfort to his relatives there.

Major Dobbin having easily succeeded in getting leave from his good-natured commandant to proceed to Madras, and thence probably to Europe, on urgent private affairs, never ceased travelling night and day until he reached his journey's end, and had directed his march with such celerity, that he arrived at Madras in a high fever. His servants who accompanied him, brought him to the house of the friend with whom he had resolved to stay until his departure for Europe in a state of delirium: and it was thought for many, many days that he would never travel farther than the burying-ground of the church of St. George's, where the troops should fire a salvo over his grave, and where many a gallant officer lies far away from his home.

Here, as the poor fellow lay tossing in his fever, the people who watched him might have heard him raving about Amelia. The idea that he should never see her again depressed him in his lucid hours. He thought his last day was come; and he made his solemn preparations for departure: setting his affairs in this world in order, and leaving the little property of which he was possessed to those whom he most desired to benefit. The friend in whose house he was located witnessed his testament. He desired to be buried with a little brown hair-chain which he wore round his neck, and which, if the truth must be known, he had got from Amelia's maid at Brussels, when the young widow's hair was cut off, during the fever which prostrated her after the death of George Osborne on the plateau at Mount St. John.

He recovered, rallied, relapsed again, having undergone such a process of blood-letting and calomel as showed the strength of his original constitution. He was almost a skeleton when they put him on board the Ramchunder East Indiaman, Captain Bragg, from Calcutta, touching at Madras; and so weak and prostrate, that his friend who had tended him through his illness, prophesied that the honest Major would never survive the voyage, and that he would pass some morning, shrouded in flag and hammock, over the ship's side, and carrying down to the sea with him the relic that he wore at his heart. But whether it was the sea air, or the hope which sprung up in him afresh, from the day that the ship spread her canvas and stood out of the roads towards *home,* our friend began to amend, and he was quite well (though as gaunt as a greyhound) before they reached the Cape. "Kirk will be disappointed of his majority this time," he said, with a smile: "he will expect to find himself gazetted by the time the regiment reaches home." For it must be premised that while the Major was lying ill at Madras, having made such prodigious haste to go thither, the gallant —th, which had passed many years abroad, which after its return from the West Indies had been baulked of its stay at home by the Waterloo campaign, and had been ordered from Flanders to India, had received orders home; and the Major might have accompanied his comrades had he chosen to wait for their arrival at Madras.

Perhaps he was not inclined to put himself in his exhausted state again under the guardianship of Glorvina. "I think Miss O'Dowd would have done for me," he said, laughingly, to a fellow-passenger, "if we had had her on board, and when she had sunk me, she would have fallen upon you, depend upon it, and carried you in as a prize to Southampton, Jos, my boy."

For indeed it was no other than our stout friend who was also a passenger on board the Ramchunder. He had passed ten years in Bengal.—Constant dinners, tiffins, pale ale and claret, the prodigious labour of cutchery, and the refreshment of brandy-pawnee which he was forced to take there, had their effect upon Waterloo Sedley. A voyage to Europe was pronounced necessary for him—and having served his full time in India, and had fine appointments which had enabled him to lay by a considerable sum of money, he was free to come home and stay with a good pension, or to return and resume that rank in the service to which his seniority and his vast talents entitled him.

He was rather thinner than when we last saw him, but had gained in majesty and solemnity of demeanour. He had resumed the mustachios to which his services at Waterloo entitled him, and swaggered about on deck in a magnificent velvet cap with a gold band, and a profuse ornamentation of pins and jewellery about his person. He took breakfast in his cabin, and dressed as solemnly to appear on the quarter-deck, as if he were going to turn out for Bond Street, or the Course at Calcutta. He brought a native servant with him, who was his valet and pipe-bearer; and who wore the Sedley crest in silver on his turban. That oriental menial had a wretched life under the tyranny of Jos Sedley. Jos was as vain of his person as a woman, and took as long a time at his toilette as any fading beauty. The youngsters among the passengers, Young Chaffers of the 150th, and poor little Ricketts, coming home after his third fever, used to draw out Sedley at the cuddy-table, and make him tell prodigious stories about himself and his exploits against tigers and Napoleon. He was great when he visited the Emperor's tomb at Longwood, when to these gentlemen and the young officers of the ship, Major Dobbin not being by, he described the whole battle of Waterloo, and all but announced that Napoleon never would have gone to Saint Helena at all but for him, Jos Sedley.

After leaving St. Helena he became very generous, disposing of a great quantity of ship stores, claret, preserved meats, and great casks packed with soda-water, brought out for his private delectation. There were no ladies on board: the Major gave the pas of precedency to the civilian, so that he was the first dignitary at table; and treated by Captain Bragg, and the officers of the Ramchunder, with the respect which his rank warranted. He disappeared rather in a panic during a two-days' gale, in which he had the portholes of his cabin battened down; and remained in his cot reading the "Washerwoman of Finchley Common," left on board the Ramchunder by the Right Honourable the Lady Emily Hornblower, wife of the Rev. Silas Horn-

blower, when on their passage out to the Cape, where the
Reverend gentleman was a missionary: but, for common
reading, he had brought a stock of novels and plays which
he lent to the rest of the ship, and rendered himself agreeable to all by his kindness and condescension.

Many and many a night as the ship was cutting through
the roaring dark sea, the moon and stars shining overhead,
and the bell singing out the watch, Mr. Sedley and the
Major would sit on the quarter-deck of the vessel talking
about home, as the Major smoked his cheroot, and the civilian puffed at the hookah which his servant prepared for him.

In these conversations it was wonderful with what perseverance and ingenuity Major Dobbin would manage to bring
the talk round to the subject of Amelia and her little boy.
Jos, a little testy about his father's misfortunes and uncere-
monious applications to him, was soothed down by the
Major, who pointed out the elder's ill fortunes and old age.
He would not perhaps like to live with the old couple:
whose ways and hours might not agree with those of a
younger man, accustomed to different society, (Jos bowed
at this compliment): but, the Major pointed out, how advantageous it would be for Jos Sedley to have a house of
his own in London, and not a mere bachelor's establishment
as before: how his sister Amelia would be the very person to
preside over it; how elegant, how gentle she was, and of
what refined good manners. He recounted stories of the
success which Mrs. George Osborne had had in former days
at Brussels, and in London, where she was much admired
by people of very great fashion: and he then hinted how
becoming it would be for Jos to send Georgy to a good
school and make a man of him; for his mother and her
parents would be sure to spoil him. In a word, this artful
Major made the civilian promise to take charge of Amelia
and her unprotected child. He did not know as yet what
events had happened in the little Sedley family: and how
death had removed the mother, and riches had carried off
George from Amelia. But the fact is, that every day and
always, this love-smitten and middle-aged gentleman was
thinking about Mrs. Osborne, and his whole heart was bent
upon doing her good. He coaxed, wheedled, cajoled, and

complimented Jos Sedley with a perseverance and cordiality of which he was not aware himself, very likely; but some men who have unmarried sisters or daughters even, may remember how uncommonly agreeable gentlemen are to the male relations when they are courting the females; and perhaps this rogue of a Dobbin was urged by a similar hypocrisy.

The truth is, when Major Dobbin came on board the Ramchunder, very sick, and for the three days she lay in the Madras Roads, he did not begin to rally, nor did even the appearance and recognition of his old acquaintance, Mr. Sedley, on board much cheer him, until after a conversation which they had one day, as the Major was laid languidly on the deck. He said then he thought he was doomed; he had left a little something to his godson in his will; and he trusted Mrs. Osborne would remember him kindly, and be happy in the marriage she was about to make. "Married? not the least," Jos answered: "he had heard from her: she made no mention of the marriage, and by the way, it was curious, she wrote to say that Major Dobbin was going to be married, and hoped that *he* would be happy." What were the dates of Sedley's letters from Europe? The civilian fetched them. They were two months later than the Major's; and the ship's surgeon congratulated himself upon the treatment adopted by him towards his new patient, who had been consigned to ship-board by the Madras practitioner with very small hopes indeed; for, from that day, the very day that he changed the draught, Major Dobbin began to mend. And thus it was that deserving officer, Captain Kirk, was disappointed of his majority.

After they passed St. Helena, Major Dobbin's gaiety and strength was such as to astonish all his fellow-passengers. He larked with the midshipmen, played single-stick with the mates, ran up the shrouds like a boy, sang a comic song one night to the amusement of the whole party assembled over their grog after supper, and rendered himself so gay, lively, and amiable, that even Captain Bragg, who thought there was nothing in his passenger, and considered he was a poor-spirited feller at first, was constrained to own that the Major was a reserved but well-informed and meritorious officer. "He ain't got distangy manners, dammy," Bragg observed to his first mate; "he wouldn't do at Government House, Roper, where his Lordship and Lady William was as kind to me, and shook hands with me before the whole company, and asking me at dinner to take beer with him, before the Commander-in-Chief himself; he ain't got manners, but there's something about him—" And thus Captain Bragg showed that he possessed discrimination as a man, as well as ability as a commander.

But a calm taking place when the Ramchunder was within ten days' sail of England, Dobbin became so impatient and ill-humoured as to surprise those comrades who had before admired his vivacity and good temper. He did not recover until the breeze sprang up again, and was in a highly excited state when the pilot came on board. Good God, how his heart beat as the two friendly spires of Southampton came in sight.

CHAPTER XXIII

Our Friend the Major

OUR Major had rendered himself so popular on board the Ramchunder, that when he and Mr. Sedley descended into the welcome shore-boat which was to take them from the ship, the whole crew, men and officers, the great Captain Bragg himself leading off, gave three cheers for Major Dobbin, who blushed very much, and ducked his head in token of thanks. Jos, who very likely thought the cheers were for himself, took off his gold-laced cap and waved it majestically to his friends, and they were pulled to shore and landed with great dignity at the pier, whence they proceeded to the Royal George Hotel.

Although the sight of that magnificent round of beef, and the silver tankard suggestive of real British home-brewed ale and porter, which perennially greet the eyes of the traveller returning from foreign parts, who enters the coffee-room of the George, are so invigorating and delightful, that a man entering such a comfortable snug homely English inn, might well like to stop some days there, yet Dobbin began to talk about a post-chaise instantly, and was no sooner at Southampton than he wished to be on the road to London. Jos, however, would not hear of moving that evening. Why was he to pass a night in a post-chaise instead of a great large undulating downy feather bed which was there ready to replace the horrid little narrow crib in which the portly Bengal gentleman had been confined during the voyage? He could not think of moving till his baggage was cleared, or of travelling until he could do so with his chillum. So the Major was forced to wait over that night, and despatched a letter to his family announcing his arrival; entreating from Jos a promise to write to his own friends. Jos promised, but didn't keep his promise. The Captain, the surgeon, and one or two passengers came and dined with our two gentlemen at the inn; Jos exerting himself in a sumptuous way in ordering the dinner: and promising to go to town the next day with the Major. The landlord said it did his eyes good to see Mr. Sedley take off his first pint of porter. If I had time and dared to enter into digressions, I would write a chapter about that first pint of porter drunk upon English ground. Ah, how good it is! It is worth while to leave home for a year, just to enjoy that one draught.

Major Dobbin made his appearance the next morning very neatly shaved and dressed, according to his wont. Indeed, it was so early in the morning, that nobody was up in the house except that wonderful Boots of an inn who never seems to want sleep: and the Major could hear the snores of the various inmates of the house roaring through the corridors as he creaked about in those dim passages. Then the sleepless Boots went shirking round from door to door, gathering up at each the Bluchers, Wellingtons, Oxonians, which stood outside. Then Jos's native servant arose and began to get ready his master's ponderous dressing apparatus, and prepare his hookah: then the maid servants got up, and meeting the dark man in the passages, shrieked, and mistook him for the devil. He and Dobbin stumbled over their pails in the passages as they were scouring the decks of the Royal George. When the first unshorn waiter appeared and unbarred the door of the inn, the Major thought that the time for departure was arrived, and ordered a post-chaise to be fetched instantly, that they might set off.

He then directed his steps to Mr. Sedley's room, and opened the curtains of the great large family bed wherein Mr. Jos was snoring. "Come, up! Sedley," the Major said, "it's time to be off; the chaise will be at the door in half an hour."

Jos growled from under the counterpane to know what the time was; but when he at last extorted from the blushing Major (who never told fibs, however they might be to his advantage) what was the real hour of the morning, he broke out into a volley of bad language, which we will not repeat here, but by which he gave Dobbin to understand that he would jeopardy his soul if he got up at that moment, that the Major might go and be hanged, that he would not travel with Dobbin, and that it was most unkind and ungentleman-like to disturb a man out of his sleep in that way; on which the discomfited Major was obliged to retreat, leaving Jos to resume his interrupted slumbers.

The chaise came up presently, and the Major would wait no longer.

If he had been an English nobleman travelling on a pleas-ure tour, or a newspaper courier bearing despatches (govern-ment messages are generally carried much more quietly), he could not have travelled more quickly. The post-boys wondered at the fees he flung amongst them. How happy and green the country looked as the chaise whirled rapidly from mile-stone to mile-stone, through neat country towns where landlords came out to welcome him with smiles and bows; by pretty road-side inns, where the signs hung on the elms, and horses and waggoners were drinking under the chequered shadow of the trees; by old halls and parks; rustic hamlets clustered round ancient grey churches—and through the charming friendly English landscape. Is there any in the world like it? To a traveller returning home it looks so kind—it seems to shake hands with you as you pass through it. Well, Major Dobbin passed through all this from Southampton to London, and without noting much beyond the mile-stones along the road. You see he was so eager to see his parents at Camberwell.

He grudged the time lost between Piccadilly and his old haunt at the Slaughters', whither he drove faithfully. Long years had passed since he saw it last, since he and George, as young men, had enjoyed many a feast, and held many a revel there. He had now passed into the stage of old-fellow-hood. His hair was grizzled, and many a passion and feeling of his youth had grown grey in that interval. There, however, stood the old waiter at the door, in the same greasy black suit, with the same double chin and flaccid face, with the same huge bunch of seals at his fob, rattling his money in his pockets as before, and receiving the Major as if he had gone away only a week ago. "Put the Major's things in twenty-three, that's his room," John said, exhibiting not the least surprise. "Roast fowl for your dinner, I suppose.

You ain't got married? They said you was married—the Scotch surgeon of yours was here. No, it was Captain Humbly of the thirty-third, as was quartered with the —th in Injee. Like any warm water? What do you come in a chay for—ain't the coach good enough?" And with this, the faithful waiter, who knew and remembered every officer who used the house, and with whom ten years were but as yesterday, led the way up to Dobbin's old room, where stood the great moreen bed, and the shabby carpet, a thought more dingy, and all the old black furniture covered with faded chintz, just as the Major recollected them in his youth.

He remembered George pacing up and down the room, and biting his nails, and swearing that the Governor must come round, and that if he didn't, he didn't care a straw, on the day before he was married. He could fancy him walking in, banging the door of Dobbin's room, and his own hard by—

"You ain't got young," John said, calmly surveying his friend of former days.

Dobbin laughed. "Ten years and a fever don't make a man young, John," he said. "It is you that are always young:—No, you are always old."

"What became of Captain Osborne's widow?" John said. "Fine young fellow that. Lord, how he used to spend his money. He never came back after that day he was married from here. He owes me three pound at this minute. Look here, I have it in my book. 'April 10, 1815, Captain Osborne: 3l.' I wonder whether his father would pay me," and so saying, John of the Slaughters pulled out the very morocco pocket-book in which he had noted his loan to the Captain, upon a greasy faded page still extant, with many other scrawled memoranda regarding the bygone frequenters of the house.

Having inducted his customer into the room, John retired with perfect calmness; and Major Dobbin, not without a blush and a grin at his own absurdity, chose out of his kit the very smartest and most becoming civil costume he possessed, and laughed at his own tanned face and grey hair, as he surveyed them in the dreary little toilet-glass on the dressing-table.

"I'm glad old John didn't forget me," he thought. "She'll know me, too, I hope." And he sallied out of the inn, bending his steps once more in the direction of Brompton.

Every minute incident of his last meeting with Amelia was present to the constant man's mind as he walked towards her house. The arch and the Achilles statue were up since he had last been in Piccadilly; a hundred changes had occurred which his eye and mind vaguely noted. He began to tremble as he walked up the lane from Brompton, that well-remembered lane leading to the street where she lived. Was she going to be married or not? If he were to meet her with the little boy—Good God, what should he do? He saw a woman coming to him with a child of five years old—was that she? He began to shake at the mere possibility. When he came up to the row of houses, at last, where she lived, and to the gate, he caught hold of it and paused. He might have heard the thumping of his own heart. "May God Almighty bless her, whatever has happened," he thought to himself. "Psha! she may be gone from here," he said, and went in through the gate.

The window of the parlour which she used to occupy was open, and there were no inmates in the room. The Major thought he recognised the piano, though, with the picture over it, as it used to be in former days, and his perturbations were renewed. Mr. Clapp's brass plate was still on the door, at the knocker of which Dobbin performed a summons.

A buxom-looking lass of sixteen, with bright eyes and purple cheeks, came to answer the knock, and looked hard at the Major as he leant back against the little porch.

He was as pale as a ghost, and could hardly falter out the words—"Does Mrs. Osborne live here?"

She looked him hard in the face for a moment—and then turning white too—said, "Lord bless me—it's Major Dobbin." She held out both her hands shaking—"Don't you remember me?" she said. "I used to call you Major Sugarplums." On which, and I believe it was for the first time that he ever so conducted himself in his life, the Major took the girl in his arms and kissed her. She began to laugh and cry hysterically, and calling out "Ma, Pa!" with all her voice, brought up those worthy people, who had already been surveying the Major from the casement of the ornamental kitchen, and were astonished to find their daughter in the little passage in the embrace of a great tall man in a blue frock-coat and white duck trowsers.

"I'm an old friend," he said—not without blushing though. "Don't you remember me, Mrs. Clapp, and those good cakes you used to make for tea?—Don't you recollect me, Clapp? I'm George's godfather, and just come back from India." A great shaking of hands ensued—Mrs. Clapp was greatly affected and delighted; she called upon heaven to interpose a vast many times in that passage.

The landlord and landlady of the house led the worthy Major into the Sedleys' room (whereof he remembered every single article of furniture, from the old brass ornamented piano, once a natty little instrument, Stothard maker, to the screens and the alabaster miniature tombstone, in the midst of which ticked Mr. Sedley's gold watch), and there, as he sat down in the lodger's vacant arm-chair, the father, the mother, and the daughter, with a thousand ejaculatory breaks in the narrative, informed Major Dobbin of what we know already, but of particulars in Amelia's history of which he was not aware—namely of Mrs. Sedley's death, of George's reconcilement with his grandfather Osborne, of the way in which the widow took on at leaving him, and of other particulars of her life. Twice or thrice he was going to ask about the marriage question, but his heart failed him. He did not care to lay it bare to these people. Finally, he was informed that Mrs. O. was gone to walk with her Pa in Kensington Gardens, whither she always went with the old gentleman (who was very weak and peevish now, and led her a sad life, though she behaved to him like an angel, to be sure,) of a fine afternoon, after dinner.

"I'm very much pressed for time," the Major said, "and have business to-night of importance. I should like to see Mrs. Osborne tho'. Suppose Miss Polly would come with me and show me the way."

Miss Polly was charmed and astonished at this proposal. She knew the way. She would show Major Dobbin. She had often been with Mr. Sedley when Mrs. O. was gone—was gone Russell Square way: and knew the bench where he liked to sit. She bounced away to her apartment, and appeared presently in her best bonnet and her mamma's yellow shawl and large pebble brooch, of which she assumed the loan in order to make herself a worthy companion for the Major.

That officer, then, in his blue frock-coat and buckskin gloves, gave the young lady his arm, and they walked away very gaily. He was glad to have a friend at hand for the scene which he dreaded somehow. He asked a thousand more questions from his companion about Amelia: his kind heart grieved to think that she should have had to part with her son. How did she bear it? Did she see him often? Was Mr. Sedley pretty comfortable now in a worldly point of view? Polly answered all these questions of Major Sugarplums to the very best of her power.

And in the midst of their walk an incident occurred which, though very simple in its nature, was productive of the greatest delight to Major Dobbin. A pale young man with feeble whiskers and a stiff white neckcloth came walking down the lane, *en sandwich*:—having a lady, that is, on each arm. One was a tall and commanding middle-aged female, with features and a complexion similar to those of the clergyman of the Church of England by whose side she marched, and the other a stunted little woman with a dark face, ornamented by a fine new bonnet and white ribbons, and in a smart pelisse, with a rich gold watch in the midst of her person. The gentleman, pinioned as he was by these two ladies, carried further a parasol, shawl, and basket, so that his arms were entirely engaged, and of course he was unable to touch his hat in acknowledgment of the curtsey with which Miss Mary Clapp greeted him.

He merely bowed his head in reply to her salutation, which the two ladies returned with a patronising air, and at the same time looking severely at the individual in the blue coat and bamboo cane who accompanied Miss Polly.

"Who's that?" asked the Major, amused by the group, and after he had made way for the three to pass up the lane. Mary looked at him rather roguishly.

"That is our curate, the Reverend Mr. Binny (a twitch from Major Dobbin), and his sister Miss B. Lord bless us,

how she did use to worret us at Sunday-school; and the other
lady, the little one with a cast in her eye, and the handsome
watch, is Mrs. Binny—Miss Grits that was; her Pa was a
grocer, and kept the Little Original Gold Tea Pot in Kensington Gravel Pits. They were married last month, and are
just come back from Margate. She's five thousand pound
to her fortune; but her and Miss B., who made the match,
have quarrelled already."

If the Major had twitched before, he started now, and
slapped the bamboo on the ground with an emphasis which
made Miss Clapp cry, "Law," and laugh too. He stood for a
moment silent with open mouth looking after the retreating
young couple, while Miss Mary told their history; but he did
not hear beyond the announcement of the reverend gentleman's marriage; his head was swimming with felicity. After
this rencontre he began to walk double quick towards the
place of his destination; and yet they were too soon (for he
was in a great tremor at the idea of a meeting for which
he had been longing any time these ten years)—through the
Brompton lanes, and entering at the little old portal in
Kensington Garden wall.

"There they are," said Miss Polly, and she felt him again
start back on her arm.

She was a confidante at once of the whole business.
She knew the story as well as if she had read it in one of
her favourite novel-books—"Fatherless Fanny," or the
"Scottish Chiefs."

"Suppose you were to run on and tell her," the Major
said. Polly ran forward, her yellow shawl streaming in
the breeze.

Old Sedley was seated on a bench, his handkerchief placed
over his knees, prattling away according to his wont, with
some old story about old times, to which Amelia had listened,
and awarded a patient smile many a time before. She could
of late think of her own affairs, and smile or make other
marks of recognition of her father's stories, scarcely hearing
a word of the old man's tales. As Mary came bouncing
along, and Amelia caught sight of her, she started up from
her bench. Her first thought was, that something had happened to Georgy; but the sight of the messenger's eager

and happy face dissipated that fear in the timorous mother's bosom.

"News! News!" cried the emissary of Major Dobbin. "He's come! He's come!"

"Who is come?" said Emmy, still thinking of her son.

"Look there," answered Miss Clapp, turning round and pointing; in which direction Amelia looking, saw Dobbin's lean figure and long shadow stalking across the grass. Amelia started in her turn, blushed up, and, of course, began to cry.

At all this simple little creature's fêtes, the *grandes eaux* were accustomed to play.

He looked at her—oh, how fondly—as she came running towards him, her hands before her, ready to give them to him. She wasn't changed. She was a little pale: a little stouter in figure. Her eyes were the same, the kind trustful eyes. There were scarce three lines of silver in her soft brown hair. She gave him both her hands as she looked up flushing and smiling through her tears into his honest homely face. He took the two little hands between his two, and held them there. He was speechless for a moment. Why did he not take her in his arms, and swear that he would never leave her? She must have yielded: she could not but have obeyed him.

"I—I've another arrival to announce," he said, after a pause.

"Mrs. Dobbin?" Amelia said, making a movement back— Why didn't he speak?

"No," he said, letting her hands go: "Who has told you those lies?—I mean, your brother Jos came in the same ship with me, and is come home to make you all happy."

"Papa, papa!" Emmy cried out, "here are news! My brother is in England. He is come to take care of you.— Here is Major Dobbin."

Mr. Sedley started up, shaking a great deal, and gathering up his thoughts. Then he stepped forward and made an old-fashioned bow to the Major, whom he called Mr. Dobbin, and hoped his worthy father, Sir William, was quite well. He proposed to call upon Sir William, who had done him the honour of a visit a short time ago. Sir William had not called upon the old gentleman for eight years—it was that visit he was thinking of returning.

"He is very much shaken," Emmy whispered, as Dobbin went up and cordially shook hands with the old man.

Although he had such particular business in London that evening, the Major consented to forego it upon Mr. Sedley's invitation to him to come home and partake of tea. Amelia put her arm under that of her young friend with the yellow shawl, and headed the party on their return homewards, so that Mr. Sedley fell to Dobbin's share. The old man walked very slowly, and told a number of ancient histories about himself and his poor Bessy, his former prosperity, and his bankruptcy. His thoughts, as is usual with failing old men, were quite in former times. The present, with the exception of the one catastrophe which he felt, he knew little about.

The Major was glad to let him talk on. His eyes were fixed upon the figure in front of him—the dear little figure always present to his imagination and in his prayers, and visiting his dreams wakeful or slumbering.

Amelia was very happy, smiling, and active all that evening; performing her duties as hostess of the little entertainment with the utmost grace and propriety, as Dobbin thought. His eyes followed her about as they sate in the twilight. How many a time had he longed for that moment, and thought of her far away under hot winds and in weary marches, gentle and happy, kindly ministering to the wants of old age, and decorating poverty with sweet submission— as he saw her now. I do not say that his taste was the highest, or that it is the duty of great intellects to be content with a bread-and-butter paradise, such as sufficed our simple old friend; but his desires were of this sort, whether for good or bad; and, with Amelia to help him, he was ready to drink as many cups of tea as Doctor Johnson.

Amelia seeing this propensity, laughingly encouraged it; and looked exceedingly roguish as she administered to him cup after cup. It is true she did not know that the Major had had no dinner, and that the cloth was laid for him at the Slaughters', and a plate laid thereon to mark that the table was retained, in that very box in which the Major and George had sate many a time carousing, when she was a child just come home from Miss Pinkerton's school.

The first thing Mrs. Osborne showed the Major was Georgy's miniature, for which she ran upstairs on her arrival at home. It was not half handsome enough of course for the boy, but wasn't it noble of him to think of bringing it to his mother? Whilst her papa was awake she did not talk much about Georgy. To hear about Mr. Osborne and Russell Square was not agreeable to the old man, who very likely was unconscious that he had been living for some months past mainly on the bounty of his richer rival; and lost his temper if allusion was made to the other.

Dobbin told him all, and a little more perhaps than all, that had happened on board the Ramchunder; and exaggerated Jos's benevolent dispositions towards his father, and resolution to make him comfortable in his old days. The truth is, that during the voyage the Major had impressed this duty most strongly upon his fellow-passenger and extorted promises from him that he would take charge of his sister and her child. He soothed Jos's irritation with regard to the bills which the old gentleman had drawn upon him, gave a laughing account of his own sufferings on the same score, and of the famous consignment of wine with which the old man had favoured him: and brought Mr. Jos, who was by no means an ill-natured person when well pleased and moderately flattered, to a very good state of feeling regarding his relatives in Europe.

And in fine I am ashamed to say that the Major stretched the truth so far as to tell old Mr. Sedley that it was mainly a desire to see his parent which brought Jos once more to Europe.

At his accustomed hour Mr. Sedley began to doze in his chair, and then it was Amelia's opportunity to commence her conversation, which she did with great eagerness;—it related exclusively to Georgy. She did not talk at all about her own sufferings at breaking from him, for indeed, this worthy woman, though she was half-killed by the separation from the child, yet thought it was very wicked in her to repine at losing him; but everything concerning him, his virtues, talents, and prospects, she poured out. She described his angelic beauty; narrated a hundred instances of his generosity and greatness of mind whilst living with her: how a Royal Duchess had stopped and admired him in Kensington Gardens; how splendidly he was cared for now, and how he had a groom and a pony; what quickness and cleverness he had, and what a prodigiously well-read and delightful person the Reverend Lawrence Veal was, George's master. "He knows *everything*," Amelia said. "He has the most delightful parties. You who are so learned yourself, and have read so much, and are so clever and accomplished—don't shake your head and say no—*He* always used say you were—you will be charmed with Mr. Veal's parties. The last Tuesday in every month. He says there is no place in the bar or the senate that Georgy may not aspire to. Look here," and she went to the piano-drawer and drew out a theme of Georgy's composition. This great effort of genius, which is still in the possession of George's mother, is as follows:

On Selfishness.—Of all the vices which degrade the human character, Selfishness is the most odious and contemptible. An undue love of Self leads to the most monstrous crimes; and occasions the greatest misfortune both in *States and Families*. As a selfish man will impoverish his family and often bring them to ruin: so a selfish king brings ruin on his people and often plunges them into war.

Example: The selfishness of Achilles, as remarked by the poet Homer, occasioned a thousand woes to the Greeks—μυρί᾿ Ἀχαιοῖς ἄλγε᾿ ἔθηκε—(Hom. Il. A. 2). The selfishness of the late Napoleon Bonaparte occasioned innumerable wars in Europe, and caused him to perish, himself, in a miserable island:—that of Saint Helena in the Atlantic Ocean.

We see by these examples that we are not to consult our own interest and ambition, but that we are to consider the interests of others as well as our own.

GEORGE S. OSBORNE.

Athenè House, 24 April, 1827.

"Think of him writing such a hand, and quoting Greek too, at his age," the delighted mother said. "O William," she added, holding out her hand to the Major—"what a treasure Heaven has given me in that boy! He is the comfort of my life—and he is the image of—of him that's gone!"

"Ought I to be angry with her for being faithful to him?" William thought. "Ought I to be jealous of my friend in the

grave, or hurt that such a heart as Amelia's can love only
once and for ever? Oh, George, George, how little you knew
the prize you had, though." This sentiment passed rapidly
through William's mind, as he was holding Amelia's hand,
whilst the handkerchief was veiling her eyes.

"Dear friend," she said, pressing the hand which held
hers, "how good, how kind you always have been to me!
See! Papa is stirring. You will go and see Georgy to-
morrow, won't you?"

"Not to-morrow," said poor old Dobbin. "I have business." He did not like to own that he had not as yet
been to his parents' and his dear sister Anne—a remissness
for which I am sure every well-regulated person will blame
the Major. And presently he took his leave, leaving his
address behind him for Jos, against the latter's arrival.
And so the first day was over, and he had seen her.

When he got back to the Slaughters', the roast fowl was of
course cold, in which condition he ate it for supper. And
knowing what early hours his family kept, and that it
would be needless to disturb their slumbers at so late an
hour, it is on record, that Major Dobbin treated himself to
half-price at the Haymarket Theatre that evening, where
let us hope he enjoyed himself.

CHAPTER XXIV

The Old Piano

THE Major's visit left old John Sedley in a great state of agitation and excitement. His daughter could not induce him to settle down to his customary occupations or amusements that night. He passed the evening fumbling amongst his boxes and desks, untying his papers with trembling hands, and sorting and arranging them against Jos's arrival. He had them in the greatest order— his tapes and his files, his receipts, and his letters with lawyers and correspondents; the documents relative to the Wine Project (which failed from a most unaccountable accident, after commencing with the most splendid prospects), the Coal Project (which only a want of capital prevented from becoming the most successful scheme ever put before the public), the Patent Saw-mills and Sawdust Consolidation Project, &c., &c.—All night, until a very late hour, he passed in the preparation of these documents, trembling about from one room to another, with a quivering candle and shaky hands.—Here's the wine papers, here's the sawdust, here's the coals; here's my letters to Calcutta and Madras, and replies from Major Dobbin, C.B., and Mr. Joseph Sedley to the same. "He shall find no irregularity about *me*, Emmy," the old gentleman said.

Emmy smiled. "I don't think Jos will care about seeing those papers, Papa," she said.

"You don't know anything about business, my dear," answered the sire, shaking his head with an important air. And it must be confessed, that on this point Emmy was very ignorant, and that is a pity, some people are so knowing. All these twopenny documents arranged on a side table, old Sedley covered them carefully over with a clean bandanna handkerchief (one out of Major Dobbin's lot), and enjoined the maid and landlady of the house, in the most solemn way,

284

not to disturb those papers, which were arranged for the
arrival of Mr. Joseph Sedley the next morning, "Mr. Joseph
Sedley of the Honourable East India Company's Bengal
Civil Service."

Amelia found him up very early the next morning, more
eager, more hectic, and more shaky than ever. "I didn't
sleep much, Emmy, my dear," he said. "I was thinking of
my poor Bessy. I wish she was alive, to ride in Jos's carriage once again. She kept her own, and became it very
well." And his eyes filled with tears, which trickled down
his furrowed old face. Amelia wiped them away, and smilingly kissed him, and tied the old man's neckcloth in a smart
bow, and put his brooch into his best shirt frill, in which, in
his Sunday suit of mourning, he sat from six o'clock in the
morning awaiting the arrival of his son.

There are some splendid tailors' shops in the High Street
of Southampton, in the fine plate-glass windows of which
hang gorgeous waistcoats of all sorts, of silk and velvet,
and gold and crimson, and pictures of the last new fashions
in which those wonderful gentlemen with quizzing glasses,
and holding on to little boys with the exceeding large eyes
and curly hair, ogle ladies in riding habits prancing by the
Statue of Achilles at Apsley House. Jos, although provided
with some of the most splendid vests that Calcutta could
furnish, thought he could not go to town until he was supplied with one or two of these garments, and selected a
crimson stain, embroidered with gold butterflies, and a black
and red velvet tartan with white stripes and a rolling collar,
with which, and a rich blue satin stock and a gold pin, con-
sisting of a five-barred gate with a horseman in pink enamel
jumping over it, he thought he might make his entry into
London with some dignity. For Jos's former shyness and
blundering blushing timidity had given way to a more candid
and courageous self-assertion of his worth. "I don't care
about owning it," Waterloo Sedley would say to his friends,
"I am a dressy man:" and though rather uneasy if the ladies
looked at him at the Government House balls, and though he
blushed and turned away alarmed under their glances, it was
chiefly from a dread lest they should make love to him, that
he avoided them, being averse to marriage altogether. But

there was no such swell in Calcutta as Waterloo Sedley, I
have heard say: and he had the handsomest turnout, gave
the best bachelor dinners, and had the finest plate in the
whole place.

To make these waistcoats for a man of his size and dignity
took at least a day, part of which he employed in hiring a
servant to wait upon him and his native; and in instructing
the agent who cleared his baggage, his boxes, his books,
which he never read; his chests of mangoes, chutney, and
currie-powders; his shawls for presents to people whom he
didn't know as yet; and the rest of his *Persicos apparatus.*

At length, he drove leisurely to London on the third day,
and in the new waistcoat: the native with chattering teeth,
shuddering in a shawl on the box by the side of the new
European servant; Jos puffing his pipe at intervals within,
and looking so majestic, that the little boys cried Hooray,
and many people thought he must be a Governor-General.
He, I promise, did not decline the obsequious invitation of
the landlords to alight and refresh himself in the neat
country towns.   Having partaken of a copious breakfast,
with fish, and rice, and hard eggs, at Southampton, he had
so far rallied at Winchester as to think a glass of sherry
necessary.   At Alton he stepped out of the carriage at his
servant's request, and imbibed some of the ale for which
the place is famous.   At Farnham he stopped to view the
Bishop's Castle, and to partake of a light dinner of stewed
eels, veal cutlets, and French beans, with a bottle of claret.
He was cold over Bagshot Heath, where the native chattered
more and more, and Jos Sahib took some brandy-and-water;
in fact, when he drove into town he was as full of wine,
beer, meat, pickles, cherry-brandy, and tobacco, as the
steward's cabin of a steam-packet.   It was evening when
his carriage thundered up to the little door in Brompton,
whither the affectionate fellow drove first, and before hieing
to the apartments secured for him by Mr. Dobbin at the
Slaughters'.

All the faces in the street were in the windows; the little
maid-servant flew to the wicket-gate, the Mesdames Clapp
looked out from the casement of the ornamented kitchen;
Emmy, in a great flutter, was in the passage among the hats

and coats, and old Sedley in the parlour inside, shaking all over. Jos descended from the post-chaise and down the creaking swaying steps in awful state, supported by the new valet from Southampton and the shuddering native, whose brown face was now livid with cold, and of the colour of a turkey's gizzard. He created an immense sensation in the passage presently, where Mrs. and Miss Clapp, coming perhaps to listen at the parlour door, found Loll Jewab shaking upon the hall-bench under the coats, moaning in a strange piteous way, and showing his yellow eyeballs and white teeth.

For, you see, we have adroitly shut the door upon the meeting between Jos and the old father, and the poor little gentle sister inside. The old man was very much affected: so, of course, was his daughter: nor was Jos without feeling. In that long absence of ten years, the most selfish will think about home and early ties. Distance sanctifies both. Long brooding over those lost pleasures exaggerates their charm and sweetness. Jos was unaffectedly glad to see and shake the hand of his father, between whom and himself there had been a coolness—glad to see his little sister, whom he remembered so pretty and smiling, and pained at the alteration which time, grief, and misfortune had made in the shattered old man. Emmy had come out to the door in her black clothes and whispered to him of her mother's death, and not to speak of it to their father. There was no need of this caution, for the elder Sedley himself began immediately to speak of the event, and prattled about it, and wept over it plenteously. It shocked the Indian not a little, and made him think of himself less than the poor fellow was accustomed to do.

The result of the interview must have been very satisfactory, for when Jos had reascended his post-chaise, and had driven away to his hotel, Emmy embraced her father tenderly, appealing to him with an air of triumph, and asking the old man whether she did not always say that her brother had a good heart?

Indeed, Joseph Sedley, affected by the humble position in which he found his relations, and in the expansiveness and overflowing of heart occasioned by the first meeting, declared that they should never suffer want or discomfort any more, that he was at home for some time at any rate, during which his house and everything he had should be theirs: and that Amelia would look very pretty at the head of his table—until she would accept one of her own.

She shook her head sadly, and had, as usual, recourse to the water-works. She knew what he meant. She and her young confidante, Miss Mary, had talked over the matter most fully, the very night of the Major's visit: beyond which time the impetuous Polly could not refrain from talking of the discovery which she had made, and describing the start and tremor of joy by which Major Dobbin betrayed himself when Mr. Binny passed with his bride, and the Major learned that he had no longer a rival to fear. "Didn't you see how he shook all over when you asked if he was married, and he said, 'Who told you those lies?' O Ma'am," Polly said, "he never kept his eyes off you: and I'm sure he's grown grey a-thinking of you."

But Amelia, looking up at her bed, over which hung the portraits of her husband and son, told her young *protégée,* never, never, to speak on that subject again; that Major Dobbin had been her husband's dearest friend, and her own and George's most kind and affectionate guardian; that she loved him as a brother—but that a woman who had been married to such an angel as that, and she pointed to the wall, could never think of any other union. Poor Polly sighed: she thought what she should do if young Mr. Tomkins, at the surgery, who always looked at her so at church, and who, by those mere aggressive glances had put her timorous little heart into such a flutter that she was ready to surrender at once,—what she should do if he were to die? She knew he was consumptive, his cheeks were so red, and he was so uncommon thin in the waist.

Not that Emmy, being made aware of the honest Major's passion, rebuffed him in any way, or felt displeased with him. Such an attachment from so true and loyal a gentleman could make no woman angry. Desdemona was not angry with Cassio, though there is very little doubt she saw the Lieutenant's partiality for her (and I for my part believe that many more things took place in that sad affair than the

worthy Moorish officer ever knew of); why, Miranda was
even very kind to Caliban, and we may be pretty sure for
the same reason. Not that she would encourage him in the
least,—the poor uncouth monster—of course not. No more
would Emmy by any means encourage her admirer, the
Major. She would give him that friendly regard, which
so much excellence and fidelity merited; she would treat him
with perfect cordiality and frankness until he made his proposals; and *then* it would be time enough for her to speak,
and to put an end to hopes which never could be realised.

She slept, therefore, very soundly that evening, after the
conversation with Miss Polly, and was more than ordinarily
happy, in spite of Jos's delaying. "I am glad he is not going
to marry that Miss O'Dowd," she thought. "Colonel O'Dowd
never could have a sister fit for such an accomplished man
as Major William." Who was there amongst her little circle,
who would make him a good wife? Not Miss Binny, she
was too old and and ill-tempered; Miss Osborne?—too old
too. Little Polly was too young. Mrs. Osborne could not
find anybody to suit the Major before she went to sleep.

However, when the postman made his appearance, the
little party were put out of suspense by the receipt of a
letter from Jos to his sister, who announced that he felt a
little fatigued after his voyage, and should not be able to
move on that day, but that he would leave Southampton
early the next morning, and be with his father and mother
at evening. Amelia, as she read out the letter to her
father, paused over the latter word; her brother, it was
clear, did not know what had happened in the family. Nor
could he: for the fact is that, though the Major rightly
suspected that his travelling companion never would be got
into motion in so short a space as twenty-four hours, and
would find some excuse for delaying, yet Dobbin had not
written to Jos to inform him of the calamity which had befallen the Sedley family; being occupied in talking with
Amelia until long after post-hour.

The same morning brought Major Dobbin a letter to the
Slaughters' Coffee House from his friend at Southampton:
begging dear Dob to excuse Jos for being in a rage when
awakened the day before (he had a confounded head-ache,

and was just in his first sleep), and entreating Dob to engage comfortable rooms at the Slaughters' for Mr. Sedley
and his servants. The Major had become necessary to
Jos during the voyage. He was attached to him, and hung
upon him. The other passengers were away to London.
Young Ricketts and little Chaffers went away on the coach
that day—Ricketts on the box, and taking the reins from
Botley; the Doctor was off to his family at Portsea; Bragg
gone to town to his co-partners: and the first mate busy in
the unloading of the Ramchunder. Mr. Jos was very
lonely at Southampton, and got the landlord of the George
to take a glass of wine with him that day; at the very hour
at which Major Dobbin was seated at the table of his father,
Sir William, where his sister found out (for it was impossible for the Major to tell fibs) that he had been to see
Mrs. George Osborne.

Jos was so comfortably situated in St. Martin's Lane, he
could enjoy his hookah there with such perfect ease, and
could swagger down to the theatres, when minded, so agree-
ably, that, perhaps, he would have remained altogether at
the Slaughters' had not his friend, the Major, been at his
elbow. That gentleman would not let the Bengalee rest
until he had executed his promise of having a home for
Amelia and his father. Jos was a soft fellow in anybody's
hands; Dobbin most active in anybody's concerns but his
own; the civilian was, therefore, an easy victim to the
guileless arts of this good-natured diplomatist, and was
ready to do, to purchase, hire, or relinquish whatever his
friend thought fit. Loll Jewab, of whom the boys about
St. Martin's Lane used to make cruel fun whenever he
showed his dusky countenance in the street, was sent back
to Calcutta in the Lady Kicklebury East Indiaman, in
which Sir William Dobbin had a share; having previously
taught Jos's European the art of preparing curries, pilaus,
and pipes. It was a matter of great delight and occupation to Jos to superintend the building of a smart chariot,
which he and the Major ordered in the neighbouring Long
Acre: and a pair of handsome horses were jobbed, with
which Jos drove about in state in the Park, or to call upon

his Indian friends. Amelia was not seldom by his side on these excursions, when also Major Dobbin would be seen in the back seat of the carriage. At other times old Sedley and his daughter took advantage of it: and Miss Clapp, who frequently accompanied her friend, had great pleasure in being recognised as she sate in the carriage, dressed in the famous yellow shawl, by the young gentleman at the surgery, whose face might commonly be seen over the window-blinds as she passed.

Shortly after Jos's first appearance at Brompton, a dismal scene, indeed, took place at that humble cottage, at which the Sedleys had passed the last ten years of their life. Jos's carriage (the temporary one, not the chariot under construction) arrived one day and carried off old Sedley and his daughter—to return no more. The tears that were shed by the landlady and the landlady's daughter at that event were as genuine tears of sorrow as any that have been outpoured in the course of this history. In their long acquaintanceship and intimacy they could not recall a harsh word that had been uttered by Amelia. She had been all sweetness and kindness, always thankful, always gentle, even when Mrs. Clapp lost her own temper, and pressed for the rent. When the kind creature was going away for good and all, the landlady reproached herself bitterly for ever having used a rough expression to her—how she wept, as they stuck up with wafers on the window, a paper notifying that the little rooms so long occupied were to let! They never would have such lodgers again, that was quite clear. After-life proved the truth of this melancholy prophecy: and Mrs. Clapp revenged herself for the deterioration of mankind by levying the most savage contributions upon the tea-caddies and legs of mutton of her *locataires*. Most of them scolded and grumbled; some of them did not pay: none of them stayed. The landlady might well regret those old, old friends, who had left her.

As for Miss Mary, her sorrow at Amelia's departure was such as I shall not attempt to depict. From childhood upwards she had been with her daily, and had attached herself so passionately to that dear good lady, that when the grand barouche came to carry her off into splendour,

she fainted in the arms of her friend, who was indeed
scarcely less affected than the good-natured girl. Amelia
loved her like a daughter. During eleven years the girl
had been her constant friend and associate. The separation was a very painful one indeed to her. But it was of
course arranged that Mary was to come and stay often at
the grand new house whither Mrs. Osborne was going; and
where Mary was sure she would never be so happy as she
had been in their humble cot, as Miss Clapp called it, in
the language of the novels which she loved.

Let us hope she was wrong in her judgment. Poor
Emmy's days of happiness had been very few in that humble cot. A gloomy Fate had oppressed her there. She
never liked to come back to the house after she had left it,
or to face the landlady who had tyrannised over her when
ill-humoured and unpaid, or when pleased had treated her
with a coarse familiarity scarcely less odious. Her servil-
ity and fulsome compliments when Emmy was in prosperity were not more to that lady's liking. She cast about
notes of admiration all over the new house, extolling every
article of furniture or ornament; she fingered Mrs. Osborne's dresses, and calculated their price. Nothing could
be too good for that sweet lady, she vowed and protested.
But in the vulgar sycophant who now paid court to her,
Emmy always remembered the coarse tyrant who had made
her miserable many a time, to whom she had been forced
to put up petitions for time, when the rent was overdue;
who cried out at her extravagance if she bought delicacies
for her ailing mother or father; who had seen her humble
and trampled upon her.

Nobody ever heard of these griefs, which had been part
of our poor little woman's lot in life. She kept them
secret from her father, whose improvidence was the cause
of much of her misery. She had to bear all the blame of
his misdoings, and indeed was so utterly gentle and humble as to be made by nature for a victim.

I hope she is not to suffer much more of that hard
usage. And, as in all griefs there is said to be some consolation, I may mention that poor Mary, when left at her
friend's departure in a hysterical condition, was placed

under the medical treatment of the young fellow from the surgery, under whose care she rallied after a short period. Emmy, when she went away from Brompton, endowed Mary with every article of furniture that the house contained: only taking away her pictures (the two pictures over the bed) and her piano—that little old piano which had now passed into a plaintive jingling old age, but which she loved for reasons of her own. She was a child when first she played on it: and her parents gave it her. It had been given to her again since, as the reader may remember, when her father's house was gone to ruin, and the instrument was recovered out of the wreck.

Major Dobbin was exceedingly pleased when, as he was superintending the arrangements of Jos's new house, which the Major insisted should be very handsome and comfortable, the cart arrived from Brompton, bringing the trunks and band-boxes of the emigrants from that village, and with them the old piano.

Amelia would have it up in her sitting-room, a neat little apartment on the second floor, adjoining her father's chamber: and where the old gentleman sate commonly of evenings.

When the men appeared then bearing this old music-box, and Amelia gave orders that it should be placed in the chamber aforesaid, Dobbin was quite elated. "I'm glad you've kept it," he said in a very sentimental manner. "I was afraid you didn't care about it."

"I value it more than anything I have in the world," said Amelia.

"*Do* you, Amelia?" cried the Major. The fact was, as he had bought it himself, though he never said anything about it, it never entered into his head to suppose that Emmy should think anybody else was the purchaser, and as a matter of course he fancied that she knew the gift came from him. "Do you, Amelia?" he said; and the question, the great question of all, was trembling on his lips, when Emmy replied—

"Can I do otherwise?—did not *he* give it me?"

"I did not know," said poor old Dob, and his countenance fell.

Emmy did not note the circumstance at the time, nor take immediate heed of the very dismal expression which honest Dobbin's countenance assumed; but she thought of it afterwards. And then it struck her, with inexpressible pain and mortification too, that it was William who was the giver of the piano; and not George, as she had fancied. It was not George's gift; the only one which she had received from her lover, as she thought—the thing she had cherished beyond all others—her dearest relic and prize. She had spoken to it about George; played his favourite airs upon it: sate for long evening hours, touching, to the best of her simple art, melancholy harmonies on the keys, and weeping over them in silence. It was not George's relic. It was valueless now. The next time that old Sedley asked her to play, she said it was shockingly out of tune, that she had a headache, that she couldn't play.

Then, according to her custom, she rebuked herself for her pettishness and ingratitude, and determined to make a reparation to honest William for the slight she had not expressed to him, but had felt for his piano. A few days afterwards, as they were seated in the drawing-room, where Jos had fallen asleep with great comfort after dinner, Amelia said with rather a faltering voice to Major Dobbin,—

"I have to beg your pardon for something."

"About what?" said he.

"About—about that little square piano. I never thanked you for it when you gave it me; many, many years ago, before I was married. I thought somebody else had given it. Thank you, William." She held out her hand; but the poor little woman's heart was bleeding; and as for her eyes, of course they were at their work.

But William could hold no more. "Amelia, Amelia," he said, "I did buy it for you. I loved you then as I do now. I must tell you. I think I loved you from the first minute that I saw you, when George brought me to your house, to show me the Amelia whom he was engaged to. You were but a girl, in white, with large ringlets; you came down singing—do you remember?—and we went to

Vauxhall. Since then I have thought of but one woman in the world, and that was you. I think there is no hour in the day has passed for twelve years that I haven't thought of you. I came to tell you this before I went to India, but you did not care, and I hadn't the heart to speak. You did not care whether I stayed or went."

"I was very ungrateful," Amelia said.

"No; only indifferent," Dobbin continued, desperately. "I have nothing to make a woman to be otherwise. I know what you are feeling now. You are hurt in your heart at the discovery about the piano; and that it came from me and not from George. I forgot, or I should never have spoken of it so. It is for me to ask your pardon for being a fool for a moment, and thinking that years of constancy and devotion might have pleaded with you."

"It is you who are cruel now," Amelia said with some spirit. "George is my husband, here and in heaven. How could I love any other but him? I am his now as when you first saw me, dear William. It was he who told me how good and generous you were, and who taught me to love you as a brother. Have you not been everything to me and my boy? Our dearest, truest, kindest friend and protector? Had you come a few months sooner perhaps you might have spared me that—that dreadful parting. O, it nearly killed me, William—but you didn't come, though I wished and prayed for you to come, and they took him too away from me. Isn't he a noble boy, William? Be his friend still and mine"—and here her voice broke, and she hid her face on his shoulder.

The Major folded his arms round her, holding her to him as if she was a child, and kissed her head. "I will not change, dear Amelia," he said. "I ask for no more than your love. I think I would not have it otherwise. Only let me stay near you, and see you often."

"Yes, often," Amelia said. And so William was at liberty to look and long: as the poor boy at school who has no money may sigh after the contents of the tart-woman's tray.

CHAPTER XXV

RETURNS TO THE GENTEEL WORLD

GOOD fortune now begins to smile upon Amelia. We are glad to get her out of that low sphere in which she has been creeping hitherto, and introduce her into a polite circle; not so grand and refined as that in which our other female friend, Mrs. Becky, has appeared, but still having no small pretensions to gentility and fashion. Jos's friends were all from the three presidencies, and his new house was in the comfortable Anglo-Indian district of which Moira Place is the centre. Minto Square, Great Clive Street, Warren Street, Hastings Street, Ochterlony Place, Plassy Square, Assaye Terrace ("Gardens" was a felicitous word not applied to stucco houses with asphalte terraces in front, so early as 1827)—who does not know these respectable abodes of the retired Indian aristocracy, and the quarter which Mr. Wenham calls the Black Hole, in a word? Jos's position in life was not grand enough to entitle him to a house in Moira Place, where none can live but retired Members of Council, and partners of Indian firms (who break after having settled a hundred thousand pounds on their wives, and retire into comparative penury to a country place and four thousand a year) : he engaged a comfortable house of a second or third-rate order in Gillespie Street, purchasing the carpets, costly mirrors, and handsome and appropriate planned furniture by Seddons, from the assignees of Mr. Scape, lately admitted partner into the great Calcutta House of Fogle, Fake, and Cracksman, in which poor Scape had embarked seventy thousand pounds, the earnings of a long and honourable life, taking Fake's place, who retired to a princely Park in Sussex, (the Fogles have been long out of the firm, and Sir Horace Fogle is about to be raised to the peerage as Baron Bandanna)—admitted, I say, partner into the great agency house of Fogle and Fake two years before it failed for a million, and plunged half the Indian public into misery and ruin.

Scape, ruined, honest, and broken-hearted at sixty-five years of age, went out to Calcutta to wind up the affairs of the house. Walter Scape was withdrawn from Eton, and put into a merchant's house. Florence Scape, Fanny Scape, and their mother faded away to Boulogne, and will be heard of no more. To be brief, Jos stepped in and bought their carpets and sideboards, and admired himself in the mirrors which had reflected their kind handsome faces. The Scape tradesmen, all honourably paid, left their cards, and were eager to supply the new household. The large men in white waistcoats, who waited at Scape's dinners, green-grocers, bank-porters, and milkmen in their private capacity, left their addresses, and ingratiated themselves with the butler. Mr. Chummy, the chimney-purifier, who had swep the last three families, tried to coax the butler and the boy under him, whose duty it was to go out covered with buttons and stripes down his trowsers, for the protection of Mrs. Amelia whenever she chose to walk abroad.

It was a modest establishment. The butler was Jos's valet also, and never was more drunk than a butler in a small family should be who has a proper regard for his master's wine. Emmy was supplied with a maid, grown on Sir William Dobbin's suburban estate; a good girl, whose kindness and humility disarmed Mrs. Osborne, who was at first terrified at the idea of having a servant to wait upon herself, who did not in the least know how to use one, and who always spoke to domestics with the most reverential politeness. But this maid was very useful in the family, in dexterously tending old Mr. Sedley, who kept almost entirely to his own quarter of the house, and never mixed in any of the gay doings which took place there.

Numbers of people came to see Mrs. Osborne. Lady Dobbin and daughters were delighted at her change of fortune, and waited upon her. Miss Osborne from Russell Square came in her grand chariot with the flaming hammer-cloth emblazoned with the Leeds arms. Jos was reported to be immensely rich. Old Osborne had no objection that Georgy should inherit his uncle's property as well as his own. "Damn it, we will make a man of the feller," he said; "and I'll see him in Parliament before I die. *You* may go and see his mother, Miss O., though I'll never set eyes on her:" and Miss Osborne came. Emmy, you may be sure, was very glad to see her, and so be brought nearer to George. That young fellow was allowed to come much more frequently than before to visit his mother. He dined once or twice a week in Gillespie Street, and bullied the servants and his relations there, just as he did in Russell Square.

He was always respectful to Major Dobbin, however, and more modest in his demeanour when that gentleman was present. He was a clever lad, and afraid of the Major. George could not help admiring his friend's simplicity, his good-humour, his various learning quietly imparted, his general love of truth and justice. He had met no such man as yet in the course of his experience, and he had an instinctive liking for a gentleman. He hung fondly by his godfather's side; and it was his delight to walk in the Parks and hear Dobbin talk. William told George about his father, about India and Waterloo, about everything but himself.

When George was more than usually pert and conceited, the Major made jokes at him, which Mrs. Osborne thought very cruel. One day, taking him to the play, and the boy declining to go into the pit because it was vulgar, the Major took him to the boxes, left him there, and went down himself to the pit. He had not been seated there very long, before he felt an arm thrust under him, and a dandy little hand in a kid-glove squeezing his arm. George had seen the absurdity of his ways, and come down from the upper region. A tender laugh of benevolence lighted up old Dobbin's face and eyes as he looked at the repentant little prodigal. He loved the boy, as he did everything that belonged to Amelia. How charmed she was when she heard of this instance of George's goodness! Her eyes looked more kindly on Dobbin than they ever had done. She blushed, he thought, after looking at him so.

Georgy never tired of his praises of the Major to his mother. "I like him, Mamma, because he knows such lots

of things; and he ain't like old Veal, who is always brag-
ging and using such long words, don't you know? The
chaps call him 'Longtail' at school. I gave him the name;
ain't it capital? But Dob reads Latin like English, and
French and that; and when we go out together he tells
me stories about my Papa, and never about himself; though
I heard Colonel Buckler, at Grandpapa's, say that he was
one of the bravest officers in the army, and had distinguished
himself ever so much. Grandpapa was quite surprised, and
said, 'That feller! why, I didn't think he could say Bo to a
goose'—but I know he could, couldn't he, Mamma?"

Emmy laughed: she thought it was very likely the Major
could do thus much.

If there was a sincere liking between George and the
Major, it must be confessed that between the boy and his
uncle no great love existed. George had got a way of
blowing out his cheeks, and putting his hands in his waistcoat pockets, and saying, "God bless my soul, you don't
say so," so exactly after the fashion of old Jos, that it was
impossible to refrain from laughter. The servants would
explode at dinner if the lad, asking for something which
wasn't at table, put on that countenance and used that
favourite phrase. Even Dobbin would shoot out a sudden
peal at the boy's mimicry. If George did not mimic his
uncle to his face, it was only by Dobbin's rebukes and
Amelia's terrified entreaties that the little scapegrace was
induced to desist. And the worthy civilian being haunted
by a dim consciousness that the lad thought him an ass,
and was inclined to turn him into ridicule, used to be
extremely timorous and, of course, doubly pompous and dignified in the presence of Master Georgy. When it was
announced that the young gentleman was expected in Gillespie Street to dine with his mother, Mr. Jos commonly
found that he had an engagement at the Club. Perhaps
nobody was much grieved at his absence. On those days
Mr. Sedley would commonly be induced to come out from
his place of refuge in the upper storeys; and there would
be a small family party, whereof Major Dobbin pretty generally formed one. He was the *ami de la maison;* old
Sedley's friend, Emmy's friend, Georgy's friend, Jos's coun-

sel and adviser. "He might almost as well be at Madras for anything *we* see of him," Miss Ann Dobbin remarked, at Camberwell. Ah! Miss Ann, did it not strike you that it was not *you* whom the Major wanted to marry?

Joseph Sedley then led a life of dignified otiosity such as became a person of his eminence. His very first point, of course, was to become a member of the Oriental Club; where he spent his mornings in the company of his brother Indians, where he dined, or whence he brought home men to dine.

Amelia had to receive and entertain these gentlemen and their ladies. From these she heard how soon Smith would be in Council; how many lacs Jones had brought home with him, how Thomson's House in London had refused the bills drawn by Thomson, Kibobjee, and Co., the Bombay House, and how it was thought the Calcutta House must go too: how very imprudent, to say the least of it, Mrs. Brown's conduct (wife of Brown of the Ahmednuggur Irregulars) had been with young Swankey of the Body Guard, sitting up with him on deck until all hours, and losing themselves as they were riding out at the Cape; how Mrs. Hardyman had had out her thirteen sisters, daughters of a country curate, the Rev. Felix Rabbits, and married eleven of them, seven high up in the service: how Hornby was wild because his wife would stay in Europe, and Trotter was appointed Collector at Ummerapoora. This and similar talk took place, at the grand dinners all round. They had the same conversation; the same silver dishes; the same saddles of mutton, boiled turkeys, and entrées. Politics set in a short time after dessert, when the ladies retired upstairs and talked about their complaints and their children.

Mutato nomine, it is all the same. Don't the barristers' wives talk about Circuit?—Don't the soldiers' ladies gossip about the Regiment?—don't the clergymen's ladies discourse about Sunday Schools, and who takes whose duty?—don't the very greatest ladies of all talk about that small clique of persons to whom they belong, and why should our Indian friends not have their own conversation?—only I admit it is slow for the laymen whose fate it sometimes is to sit by and listen.

Before long Emmy had a visiting book, and was driving about regularly in a carriage, calling upon Lady Bludyer (wife of Major-General Sir Roger Bludyer, K.C.B., Bengal Army) ; Lady Huff, wife of Sir G. Huff, Bombay ditto ; Mrs. Pice, the Lady of Pice the Director, &c. We are not long in using ourselves to changes in life. That carriage came round to Gillespie Street every day : that buttony boy sprang up and down from the box with Emmy's and Jos's visiting-cards; at stated hours Emmy and the carriage went for Jos to the Club, and took him an airing; or, putting old Sedley into the vehicle, she drove the old man round the Regent's Park. The lady's maid and the chariot, the visiting-book and the buttony page, became soon as familiar to Amelia as the humble routine of Brompton. She accommodated herself to one as to the other. If Fate had ordained that she should be a duchess, she would even have done that duty, too. She was voted, in Jos's female society, rather a pleasing young person—not much in her, but pleasing, and that sort of thing.

The men, as usual, liked her artless kindness and simple refined demeanour. The gallant young Indian dandies at home on furlough—immense dandies these—chained and moustached—driving in tearing cabs, the pillars of the theatres, living at West End hotels,—nevertheless admired Mrs. Osborne, liked to bow to her carriage in the Park, and to be admitted to have the honour of paying her a morning visit. Swankey of the Body Guard himself, that dangerous youth, and the greatest buck of all the Indian army now on leave, was one day discovered by Major Dobbin *tête-à-tête* with Amelia, and describing the sport of pig-sticking to her with great humour and eloquence; and he spoke afterwards of a d—d king's officer that's always hanging about the house—a long, thin, queer-looking, oldish fellow—a dry fellow though, that took the shine out of a man in the talking line.

Had the Major possessed a little more personal vanity he would have been jealous of so dangerous a young buck as that fascinating Bengal Captain. But Dobbin was of too simple and generous a nature to have any doubts about Amelia. He was glad that the young men should pay her

respect; and that others should admire her. Ever since
her womanhood almost, had she not been persecuted and
undervalued? It pleased him to see how kindness brought
out her good qualities, and how her spirits gently rose with
her prosperity. Any person who appreciated her paid a
compliment to the Major's good judgment—that is, if a
man may be said to have good judgment who is under the
influence of Love's delusion.

After Jos went to Court, which we may be sure he did as
a loyal subject of his Sovereign (showing himself in his
full court suit at the Club, whither Dobbin came to fetch
him in a very shabby old uniform) he who had always been
a staunch Loyalist and admirer of George IV., became
such a tremendous Tory and pillar of the State, that he was
for having Amelia to go to a Drawing-room, too. He somehow had worked himself up to believe that he was impli-
cated in the maintenance of the public welfare, and that the
Sovereign would not be happy unless Jos Sedley and his
family appeared to rally round him at St. James's.

Emmy laughed. "Shall I wear the family diamonds,
Jos?" she said.

"I wish you would let me buy you some," thought the
Major. "I should like to see any that were too good for
you."

CHAPTER XXVI

In Which Two Lights Are Put Out

THERE came a day when the round of decorous pleasures and solemn gaieties in which Mr. Jos Sedley's family indulged was interrupted by an event which happens in most houses. As you ascend the staircase of your house from the drawing towards the bed-room floors, you may have remarked a little arch in the wall right before you, which at once gives light to the stair which leads from the second storey to the third (where the nursery and servants' chambers commonly are) and serves for another purpose of utility, of which the undertaker's men can give you a notion. They rest the coffins upon that arch, or pass them through it so as not to disturb in any unseemly manner the cold tenant slumbering within the black ark.

That second-floor arch in a London house, looking up and down the well of the staircase, and commanding the main thoroughfare by which the inhabitants are passing; by which cook lurks down before daylight to scour her pots and pans in the kitchen; by which young master stealthily ascends, having left his boots in the hall, and let himself in after dawn from a jolly night at the Club; down which miss comes rustling in fresh ribbons and spreading muslins, brilliant and beautiful, and prepared for conquest and the ball; or Master Tommy slides, preferring the bannisters for a mode of conveyance, and disdaining danger and the stair; down which the mother is fondly carried smiling in her strong husband's arms, as he steps steadily step by step, and followed by the monthly nurse, on the day when the medical man has pronounced that the charming patient may go downstairs; up which John lurks to bed, yawning, with a sputtering tallow candle, and to gather up before sunrise the boots which are awaiting him in the passages;—that stair, up or down which babies are carried, old people are helped, guests are marshalled to the ball, the parson walks to the christening, the doctor to the sick-room, and the undertaker's men to the upper floor—what a memento of Life, Death, and Vanity it is, that arch and stair—if you choose to consider it, and sit on the landing, looking up and down the well! The doctor will come up to us too for the last time there, my friend in motley. The nurse will look in at the curtains, and you take no notice—and then she will fling open the windows for a little, and let in the air. Then they will pull down all the front blinds of the house and live in the back rooms—then they will send for the lawyer and other men in black, &c. —Your comedy and mine will have been played then, and we shall be removed, O how far, from the trumpets, and the shouting, and the posture-making. If we are gentle-folks they will put hatchments over our late domicile, with gilt cherubim, and mottoes stating that there is "Quiet in Heaven." Your son will new furnish the house, or perhaps let it, and go into a more modern quarter; your name will be among the "Members Deceased" in the lists of your clubs next year.

However much you may be mourned, your widow will like to have her weeds neatly made—the cook will send or come up to ask about dinner—the survivor will soon bear to look at your picture over the mantel-piece, which will presently be deposed from the place of honour, to make way for the portrait of the son who reigns.

Which of the dead are most tenderly and passionately deplored? Those who love the survivors the least, I believe. The death of a child occasions a passion of grief and frantic tears, such as your end, brother reader, will never inspire. The death of an infant which scarce knew you, which a week's absence from you would have caused to forget you, will strike you down more than the loss of your closest friend, or your first-born son—a man grown like yourself, with children of his own. We may be harsh and stern with Judah and Simeon—our love and pity gush out for Benjamin, the little one. And if you are old, as some reader of this may be or shall be—old and rich, or old and poor—you may one day be thinking for yourself—"These people are very good round about me; but they won't grieve too much when

I am gone. I am very rich, and they want my inheritance
—or very poor, and they are tired of supporting me."

The period of mourning for Mrs. Sedley's death was only
just concluded, and Jos scarcely had had time to cast off his
black and appear in the splendid waistcoats which he loved,
when it became evident to those about Mr. Sedley, that another event was at hand, and that the old man was about to
go seek for his wife in the dark land whither she had preceded him. "The state of my father's health," Jos Sedley
solemnly remarked at the Club, "prevents me from giving
any *large* parties this season: but if you will come in quietly
at half-past six, Chutney, my boy, and take a homely dinner
with one or two of the old set—I shall be always glad to
see you." So Jos and his acquaintances dined and drank
their claret among themselves in silence; whilst the sands of
life were running out in the old man's glass upstairs. The
velvet-footed butler brought them their wine; and they composed themselves to a rubber after dinner: at which Major
Dobbin would sometimes come and take a hand: and Mrs.
Osborne would occasionally descend, when her patient above
was settled for the night, and had commenced one of those
lightly troubled slumbers which visit the pillow of old age.

The old man clung to his daughter during this sickness.
He would take his broths and medicines from scarcely any
other hand. To tend him became almost the sole business
of her life. Her bed was placed close by the door which
opened into his chamber, and she was alive at the slightest
noise or disturbance from the couch of the querulous invalid.
Though, to do him justice, he lay awake many an hour, silent
and without stirring, unwilling to awaken his kind and
vigilant nurse.

He loved his daughter with more fondness now, perhaps,
than ever he had done since the days of her childhood. In
the discharge of gentle offices and kind filial duties, this
simple creature shone most especially. "She walks into the
room as silently as a sunbeam," Mr. Dobbin thought, as he
saw her passing in and out from her father's room; a cheerful sweetness lighting up her face as she moved to and
fro, graceful and noiseless. When women are brooding over
their children, or busied in a sick-room, who has not

seen in their faces those sweet angelic beams of love and pity?

A secret feud of some years' standing was thus healed: and with a tacit reconciliation. In these last hours, and touched by her love and goodness, the old man forgot all his grief against her, and wrongs which he and his wife had many a long night debated: how she had given up everything for her boy: how she was careless of her parents in their old age and misfortune, and only thought of the child: how absurdly and foolishly, impiously indeed, she took on, when George was removed from her. Old Sedley forgot these charges as he was making up his last account, and did justice to the gentle and uncomplaining little martyr. One night when she stole into his room, she found him awake, when the broken old man made his confession. "O Emmy, I've been thinking we were very unkind and unjust to you," he said, and put out his cold and feeble hand to her. She knelt down and prayed by his bedside, as he did too, having still hold of her hand. When our turn comes, friend, may we have such company in our prayers!

Perhaps as he was lying awake then, his life may have passed before him—his early hopeful struggles, his manly successes and prosperity, his downfall in his declining years, and his present helpless condition—no chance of revenge against Fortune, which had had the better of him —neither name nor money to bequeath—a spent-out, bootless life of defeat and disappointment, and the end here! Which, I wonder, brother reader, is the better lot, to die prosperous and famous, or poor and disappointed? To have, and to be forced to yield; or to sink out of life, having played and lost the game? That must be a strange feeling, when a day of our life comes and we say, "*To-morrow*, success or failure won't matter much: and the sun will rise, and all the myriads of mankind go to their work or their pleasure as usual, but I shall be out of the turmoil."

So there came one morning and sunrise, when all the world got up and set about its various works and pleasures, with the exception of old John Sedley, who was not to fight with fortune, or to hope or scheme any more: but to

go and take up a quiet and utterly unknown residence in
a churchyard at Brompton by the side of his old wife.

Major Dobbin, Jos, and Georgy followed his remains to
the grave, in a black cloth coach. Jos came on purpose
from the Star and Garter at Richmond, whither he retreated after the deplorable event. He did not care to
remain in the house, with the—under the circumstances,
you understand. But Emmy stayed and did her duty as
usual. She was bowed down by no especial grief, and
rather solemn than sorrowful. She prayed that her own
end might be as calm and painless, and thought with trust
and reverence of the words which she had heard from her
father during his illness, indicative of his faith, his resignation, and his future hope.

Yes, I think that will be the better ending of the two,
after all. Suppose you are particularly rich and well to
do, and say on that last day, "I am very rich; I am tolerably well known; I have lived all my life in the best society, and thank Heaven, come of a most respectable family. I have served my King and country with honour. I
was in Parliament for several years, where, I may say, my
speeches were listened to, and pretty well received. I
don't owe any man a shilling: on the contrary, I lent my
old college friend, Jack Lazarus, fifty pounds, for which
my executors will not press him. I leave my daughters
with ten thousand pounds a-piece—very good portions for
girls; I bequeath my plate and furniture, my house in
Baker Street, with a handsome jointure, to my widow for
her life; and my landed property, besides money in the
funds, and my cellar of well-selected wine in Baker Street,
to my son. I leave twenty pound a-year to my valet; and
I defy any man after I have gone to find anything against
my character." Or suppose, on the other hand, your swan
sings quite a different sort of a dirge, and you say, "I am a
poor blighted, disappointed old fellow, and have made an
utter failure through life. I was not endowed either with
brains or with good fortune; and confess that I have committed a hundred mistakes and blunders. I own to having
forgotten my duty many a time. I can't pay what I owe.
On my last bed I lie utterly helpless and humble: and I

pray forgiveness for my weakness, and throw myself with a contrite heart, at the feet of the Divine Mercy." Which of these two speeches, think you, would be the best oration for your own funeral? Old Sedley made the last; and in that humble frame of mind, and holding by the hand of his daughter, life and disappointment and vanity sank away from under him.

"You see," said old Osborne to George, "what comes of merit and industry, and judicious speculations, and that. Look at me and my banker's account. Look at your poor grandfather Sedley, and his failure. And yet he was a better man than I was, this day twenty years—a better man, I should say, by ten thousand pound."

Beyond these people and Mr. Clapp's family, who came over from Brompton to pay a visit of condolence, not a single soul alive ever cared a penny piece about old John Sedley, or remembered the existence of such a person.

When old Osborne first heard from his friend Colonel Buckler (as little Georgy has already informed us) how distinguished an officer Major Dobbin was, he exhibited a great deal of scornful incredulity, and expressed his surprise how ever such a feller as that should possess either brains or reputation. But he heard of the Major's fame from various members of his society. Sir William Dobbin had a great opinion of his son, and narrated many stories illustrative of the Major's learning, valour, and estimation of the world's opinion.

Finally, his name appeared in the lists of one or two great parties of the nobility: and this circumstance had a prodigious effect upon the old aristocrat of Russell Square.

The Major's position, as guardian to Georgy, whose possession had been ceded to his grandfather, rendered some meetings between the two gentlemen inevitable; and it was in one of these that old Osborne, a keen man of business, looking into the Major's accounts with his ward and the boy's mother, got a hint which staggered him very much, and at once pained and pleased him, that it was out of William Dobbin's own pocket that a part of the fund had been supplied upon which the poor widow and the child had subsisted.

When pressed upon the point, Dobbin, who could not tell lies, blushed and stammered a good deal, and finally confessed. "The marriage," he said, (at which his interlocutor's face grew dark,) "was very much my doing. I thought my poor friend had gone so far, that retreat from his engagement would have been dishonour to him, and death to Mrs. Osborne; and I could do no less, when she was left without resources, than give what money I could spare to maintain her."

"Major D.," Mr. Osborne said, looking hard at him, and turning very red—"you did me a great injury; but give me leave to tell you, sir, you are an honest feller. There's my hand, sir, though I little thought that my flesh and blood was living on you—" and the pair shook hands, with great confusion on Major Dobbin's part, thus found out in his act of charitable hypocrisy.

He strove to soften the old man, and reconcile him towards his son's memory. "He was such a noble fellow," he said, "that all of us loved him, and would have done anything for him. I, as a young man in those days, was flattered beyond measure by his preference for me; and was more pleased to be seen in his company than in that of the Commander-in-Chief. I never saw his equal for pluck and daring, and all the qualities of a soldier;" and Dobbin told the old father as many stories as he could remember regarding the gallantry and achievements of his son. "And Georgy is so like him," the Major added.

"He's so like him that he makes me tremble sometimes," the grandfather said.

On one or two evenings the Major came to dine with Mr. Osborne (it was during the time of the sickness of Mr. Sedley), and as the two sate together in the evening after dinner all their talk was about the departed hero. The father boasted about him according to his wont, glorifying himself in recounting his son's feats and gallantry, but his mood was at any rate better and more charitable than that in which he had been disposed until now to regard the poor fellow; and the Christian heart of the kind Major was pleased at these symptoms of returning peace and good will. On the second evening old Osborne called Dobbin, William, just as he used to do at the time when Dobbin and George were boys together: and the honest gentleman was pleased by that mark of reconciliation.

On the next day at breakfast when Miss Osborne, with the asperity of her age and character, ventured to make some remark reflecting slightly upon the Major's appearance or behaviour—the master of the house interrupted her. "You'd have been glad enough to git him for yourself, Miss O. But them grapes are sour. Ha! ha! Major William is a fine feller."

"That he is, Grandpapa," said Georgy, approvingly: and going up close to the old gentleman he took a hold of his large grey whiskers, and laughed in his face good-humouredly and kissed him. And he told the story at night to his mother; who fully agreed with the boy. "Indeed he is," she said. "Your dear father always said so. He is one of the best and most upright of men." Dobbin happened to drop in very soon after this conversation, which made Amelia blush perhaps: and the young scapegrace increased the confusion by telling Dobbin the other part of the story. "I say, Dob," he said, "there's such an uncommon nice girl wants to marry you. She's plenty of tin: she wears a front: and she scolds the servants from morning till night." "Who is it?" asked Dobbin. "It's aunt O.," the boy answered. "Grandpapa said so. And I say, Dob, how prime it would be to have you for my uncle." Old Sedley's quavering voice from the next room at this moment weakly called for Amelia, and the laughing ended.

That old Osborne's mind was changing, was pretty clear. He asked George about his uncle sometimes, and laughed at the boy's imitation of the way in which Jos said, "God-bless-my-soul," and gobbled his soup. Then he said, "It's not respectful, sir, of you younkers to be imitating of your relations. Miss O., when you go out a-driving to-day, leave my card upon Mr. Sedley, do you hear? There's no quarrel betwigst me and him anyhow."

The card was returned, and Jos and the Major were

asked to dinner,—to a dinner the most splendid and stupid
that perhaps ever Mr. Osborne gave; every inch of the
family plate was exhibited, and the best company was asked.
Mr. Sedley took down Miss O. to dinner, and she was very
gracious to him; whereas she hardly spoke to the Major,
who sat apart from her, and by the side of Mr. Osborne,
very timid. Jos said, with great solemnity, it was the
best turtle soup he had ever tasted in his life; and asked
Mr. Osborne where he got his Madeira?

"It is some of Sedley's wine," whispered the butler to
his master. "I've had it a long time, and paid a good
figure for it, too," Mr. Osborne said aloud, to his guest; and
then whispered to his right-hand neighbour how he had got
it "at the old chap's sale."

More than once he asked the Major about—about Mrs.
George Osborne—a theme on which the Major could be very
eloquent when he chose. He told Mr. Osborne of her sufferings—of her passionate attachment to her husband,
whose memory she worshipped still—of the tender and
dutiful manner in which she had supported her parents,
and given up her boy, when it seemed to her her duty to
do so. "You don't know what she endured, sir," said
honest Dobbin with a tremor in his voice; "and I hope
and trust you will be reconciled to her. If she took your
son away from you, she gave hers to you; and however
much you loved your George, depend on it, she loved hers
ten times more."

"By God, you are a good feller, sir," was all Mr.
Osborne said. It had never struck him that the widow
would feel any pain at parting from the boy, or that his
having a fine fortune could grieve her. A reconciliation
was announced as speedy and inevitable; and Amelia's
heart already began to beat at the notion of the awful meeting with George's father.

It was never, however, destined to take place. Old
Sedley's lingering illness and death supervened, after which
a meeting was for some time impossible. That catastrophe
and other events may have worked upon Mr. Osborne. He
was much shaken of late, and aged, and his mind was working inwardly. He had sent for his lawyers, and probably

changed something in his will. The medical man who looked in, pronounced him shaky, agitated, and talked of a little blood and the sea-side; but he took neither of these remedies.

One day when he should have come down to breakfast, his servant missing him, went into his dressing-room, and found him lying at the foot of the dressing-table in a fit. Miss Osborne was apprised; the doctors were sent for, Georgy stopped away from school; the bleeders and cuppers came. Osborne partially regained cognizance; but never could speak again, though he tried dreadfully once or twice, and in four days died. The doctors went down, and the undertaker's men went up the stairs; and all the shutters were shut towards the garden in Russell Square. Bullock rushed from the City in a hurry. "How much money had he left to that boy?—not half, surely? Surely share and share alike between the three?" It was an agitating moment.

What was it that poor old man tried once or twice in vain to say? I hope it was that he wanted to see Amelia, and be reconciled before he left the world to the dear and faithful wife of his son: it was most likely that; for his will showed that the hatred which he had so long cherished had gone out of his heart.

They found in the pocket of his dressing-gown the letter with the great red seal, which George had written him from Waterloo. He had looked at the other papers, too, relative to his son, for the key of the box in which he kept them was also in his pocket, and it was found the seals and envelopes had been broken—very likely on the night before the seizure—when the butler had taken him tea into his study, and found him reading in the great red family Bible.

When the will was opened, it was found that half the property was left to George, and the remainder between the two sisters. Mr. Bullock to continue, for their joint benefit, the affairs of the commercial house, or to go out, as he thought fit. An annuity of five hundred pounds, chargeable on George's property, was left to his mother, "the widow of my beloved son, George Osborne," who was to resume the guardianship of the boy.

"Major William Dobbin, my beloved son's friend," was appointed executor; "and as out of his kindness and bounty, and with his own private funds, he maintained my grandson and my son's widow, when they were otherwise without means of support," (the testator went on to say,) "I hereby thank him heartily for his love and regard for them: and beseech him to accept such a sum as may be sufficient to purchase his commission as a Lieutenant-Colonel, or to be disposed of in any way he may think fit."

When Amelia heard that her father-in-law was reconciled to her, her heart melted, and she was grateful for the fortune left to her. But when she heard how Georgy was restored to her, and knew how and by whom, and how it was William's bounty that supported her in poverty, how it was William who gave her her husband and her son—O, then she sank on her knees, and prayed for blessings on that constant and kind heart: she bowed down and humbled herself, and kissed the feet, as it were, of that beautiful and generous affection.

And gratitude was all that she had to pay back for such admirable devotion and benefits—only gratitude! If she thought of any other return, the image of George stood up out of the grave, and said, "You are mine, and mine only, now and for ever."

William knew her feelings: had he not passed his whole life in divining them?

When the nature of Mr. Osborne's will became known to the world, it was edifying to remark how Mrs. George Osborne rose in the estimation of the people forming her circle of acquaintance. The servants of Jos's establishment, who used to question her humble orders, and say they would "ask Master," whether or not they could obey, never thought now of that sort of appeal. The cook forgot to sneer at her shabby old gowns (which, indeed, were quite eclipsed by that lady's finery when she was dressed to go to church of a Sunday evening), the others no longer grumbled at the sound of her bell, or delayed to answer that summons. The coachman, who grumbled that his 'osses should be brought out, and his carriage made into a hospital for that old feller and Mrs. O., drove her with the utmost alacrity now, and trembling lest he should be superseded by Mr. Osborne's coachman, asked "what them there Russell Square coachmen

knew about town, and whether *they* was fit to sit on a box
before a lady?" Jos's friends, male and female, suddenly
became interested about Emmy, and cards of condolence
multiplied on her hall table. Jos himself, who had looked on
her as a good-natured harmless pauper, to whom it was his
duty to give victuals and shelter, paid her and the rich little
boy, his nephew, the greatest respect—was anxious that she
should have change and amusement after her troubles and
trials, "poor dear girl"—and began to appear at the break-
fast-table, and most particularly to ask how she would like
to dispose of the day.

In her capacity of guardian to Georgy, she, with the consent of the Major, her fellow-trustee, begged Miss Osborne
to live in the Russell Square house as long as ever she chose
to dwell there; but that lady, with thanks, declared that she
never could think of remaining alone in that melancholy
mansion, and departed in deep mourning to Cheltenham,
with a couple of her old domestics. The rest were liberally
paid and dismissed; the faithful old butler, whom Mrs.
Osborne proposed to retain, resigning and preferring to
invest his savings in a public-house, where, let us hope, he
was not unprosperous. Miss Osborne not choosing to live
in Russell Square, Mrs. Osborne also, after consultation,
declined to occupy the gloomy old mansion there. The house
was dismantled; the rich furniture and effects, the awful
chandeliers and dreary blank mirrors packed away and
hidden, the rich rosewood drawing-room suite was muffled
in straw, the carpets were rolled up and corded, the small
select library of well-bound books was stowed into two wine-
chests, and the whole paraphernalia rolled away in several
enormous vans to the Pantechnicon, where they were to lie
until Georgy's majority. And the great heavy dark plate-
chests went off to Messrs. Stumpy and Rowdy, to lie in the
cellars of those eminent bankers until the same period should
arrive.

One day Emmy with George in her hand and clad in deep
sables went to visit the deserted mansion which she had not
entered since she was a girl. The place in front was littered
with straw where the vans had been laden and rolled off.
They went into the great blank rooms, the walls of which

bore the marks where the pictures and mirrors had hung. Then they went up the great blank stone-staircases into the upper rooms, into that where grandpapa died, as George said in a whisper, and then higher still into George's own room. The boy was still clinging by her side, but she thought of another besides him. She knew that it had been his father's room as well as his own.

She went up to one of the open windows (one of those at which she used to gaze with a sick heart when the child was first taken from her), and thence as she looked out she could see, over the trees of Russell Square, the old house in which she herself was born, and where she had passed so many happy days of sacred youth. They all came back to her, the pleasant holidays, the kind faces, the careless, joyful past times: and the long pains and trials that had since cast her down. She thought of these and of the man who had been her constant protector, her good genius, her sole benefactor, her tender and generous friend.

"Look here, mother," said Georgy, "here's a G. O. scratched on the glass with a diamond; I never saw it before, *I* never did it."

"It was your father's room long before you were born, George," she said, and she blushed as she kissed the boy.

She was very silent as they drove back to Richmond where they had taken a temporary house: where the smiling lawyers used to come bustling over to see her (and we may be sure noted the visit in the bill): and where of course there was a room for Major Dobbin, too, who rode over frequently, having much business to transact on behalf of his little ward.

Georgy at this time was removed from Mr. Veal's on an unlimited holiday, and that gentleman was engaged to prepare an inscription for a fine marble slab, to be placed up in the Foundling under the monument of Captain George Osborne.

The female Bullock, aunt of Georgy, although despoiled by that little monster of one-half of the sum which she expected from her father, nevertheless showed her charitableness of spirit by being reconciled to the mother and the boy. Roehampton is not far from Richmond, and one day the chariot, with the golden bullocks emblazoned on the panels, and the flaccid children within, drove to Amelia's house at Richmond; and the Bullock family made an irruption into the garden, where Amelia was reading a book, Jos was in an arbour placidly dipping strawberries into wine, and the Major in one of his Indian jackets was giving a back to Georgy, who chose to jump over him. He went over his head, and bounded into the little advance of Bullocks, with immense black bows in their hats, and huge black sashes, accompanying their mourning mamma.

"He is just of the age for Rosa," the fond parent thought, and glanced towards that dear child, an unwholesome little Miss of seven years of age.

"Rosa, go and kiss your dear cousin," Mrs. Frederick said. "Don't you know me, George?—I am your aunt."

"*I* know you well enough," George said; "but I don't like kissing, please;" and he retreated from the obedient caresses of his cousin.

"Take me to your dear mamma, you droll child," Mrs. Frederick said; and those ladies accordingly met, after an absence of more than fifteen years. During Emmy's cares and poverty the other had never once thought about coming to see her; but now that she was decently prosperous in the world, her sister-in-law came to her as a matter of course.

So did numbers more. Our old friend, Miss Swartz, and her husband came thundering over from Hampton Court, with flaming yellow liveries, and was as impetuously fond of Amelia as ever. Miss Swartz would have liked her always if she could have seen her. One must do her that justice. But, *que voulez vous?*—in this vast town one has not the time to go and seek one's friends; if they drop out of the rank they disappear, and we march on without them. Who is ever missed in Vanity Fair?

But so, in a word, and before the period of grief for Mr. Osborne's death had subsided, Emmy found herself in the center of a very genteel circle, indeed; the members of which could not conceive that anybody belonging to it was not very lucky. There was scarce one of the ladies that

hadn't a relation a peer, though the husband might be a
dry-salter in the City. Some of the ladies were very blue
and well informed; reading Mrs. Somerville, and frequenting the Royal Institution; others were severe and Evan-
gelical, and held by Exeter Hall. Emmy, it must be owned,
found herself entirely at a loss in the midst of their clavers,
and suffered wofully on the one or two occasions on which
she was compelled to accept Mrs. Frederick Bullock's hospitalities. That lady persisted in patronising her, and determined most graciously to form her. She found Amelia's
milliners for her, and regulated her household and her
manners. She drove over constantly from Roehampton,
and entertained her friend with faint fashionable fiddle-
faddle and feeble Court slipslop. Jos liked to hear it, but
the Major used to go off growling at the appearance of this
woman, with her twopenny gentility. He went to sleep
under Frederick Bullock's bald head, after dinner, at one
of the banker's best parties, (Fred was still anxious that
the balance of the Osborne property should be transferred
from Stumpy and Rowdy's to them,) and whilst Amelia,
who did not know Latin, or who wrote the last crack article
in the Edinburgh, and did not in the least deplore, or
otherwise, Mr. Peel's late extraordinary tergiversation on
the fatal Catholic Relief Bill, sate dumb amongst the ladies
in the grand drawing-room, looking out upon velvet lawns,
trim gravel walks, and glistening hot-houses.

"She seems good-natured but insipid," said Mrs. Rowdy;
"that Major seems to be particularly *épris.*"

"She wants *ton* sadly," said Mrs. Hollyock. "My dear
creature, you never will be able to form her."

"She is dreadfully ignorant or indifferent," said Mrs.
Glowry, with a voice as if from the grave, and a sad shake
of the head and turban.—"I asked her if she thought that
it was in 1836, according to Mr. Jowls, or in 1839, according to Mr. Wapshot, that the Pope was to fall: and she
said—'Poor Pope! I hope not—What has he done?'"

"She is my brother's widow, my dear friends," Mrs.
Frederick replied, "and as such I think we're all bound
to give her every attention and instruction on entering
into the world. You may fancy there can be no *merce-*

nary motives in those whose *disappointments* are well known."

"That poor dear Mrs. Bullock," said Rowdy to Hollyock, as they drove away together—"she is always scheming and managing. She wants Mrs. Osborne's account to be taken from our house to hers—and the way in which she coaxes that boy, and makes him sit by that blear-eyed little Rosa, is perfectly ridiculous."

"I wish Glowry was choked with her Man of Sin and her Battle of Armageddon," cried the other; and the carriage rolled away over Putney Bridge.

But this sort of society was too cruelly genteel for Emmy; and all jumped for joy when a foreign tour was proposed.

CHAPTER XXVII

AM RHEIN

THE above every-day events had occurred, and a few
weeks had passed, when on one fine morning, Parliament being over, the summer advanced, and all the
good company in London about to quit that city for their
annual tour in search of pleasure or health, the Batavier
steamboat left the Tower-stairs laden with a goodly company of English fugitives. The quarter-deck awnings were
up, and the benches and gangways crowded with scores
of rosy children, bustling nurse-maids, ladies in the prettiest pink bonnets and summer dresses, gentlemen in travelling caps and linen jackets, whose mustachios had just
begun to sprout for the ensuing tour; and stout trim old
veterans with starched neckcloths and neat-brushed hats,
such as have invaded Europe any time since the conclusion of the war, and carry the national Goddem into every
city of the Continent. The congregation of hat-boxes, and
Bramah desks, and dressing-cases was prodigious. There
were jaunty young Cambridge-men travelling with their
tutor, and going for a reading excursion to Nonnenwerth
or Königswinter: there were Irish gentlemen, with the most
dashing whiskers and jewellery, talking about horses incessantly, and prodigiously polite to the young ladies on
board, whom, on the contrary, the Cambridge lads and
their pale-faced tutor avoided with maiden coyness: there
were old Pall Mall loungers bound for Ems and Wiesbaden, and a course of waters to clear off the dinners of
the season, and a little roulette and *trente-et-quarante* to
keep the excitement going: there was old Methuselah, who
had married his young wife, with Captain Papillon of the
Guards holding her parasol and guide-books: there was
young May who was carrying off his bride on a pleasure

tour (Mrs. Winter that was, and who had been at school
with May's grandmother) ; there was Sir John and my Lady
with a dozen children, and corresponding nursemaids; and
the great grandee Bareacres family that sate by themselves
near the wheel, stared at everybody, and spoke to no one.
Their carriages, emblazoned with coronets, and heaped with
shining imperials, were on the foredeck; locked in with a
dozen more such vehicles: it was difficult to pass in and
out amongst them: and the poor inmates of the fore-cabin
had scarcely any space for locomotion. These consisted of
a few magnificently attired gentlemen from Houndsditch,
who brought their own provisions, and could have bought
half the gay people in the grand saloon; a few honest fellows with mustachios and portfolios, who set to sketching
before they had been half-an-hour on board; one or two
French *femmes de chambre* who began to be dreadfully ill
by the time the boat had passed Greenwich; a groom or
two who lounged in the neighbourhood of the horse-boxes
under their charge, or leaned over the side by the paddle-
wheels, and talked about who was good for the Leger,
and what they stood to win or lose for the Goodwood
cup.

All the couriers, when they had done plunging about the
ship, and had settled their various masters in the cabins
or on the deck, congregated together and began to chatter
and smoke; the Hebrew gentlemen joining them and looking at the carriages. There was Sir John's great carriage
that would hold thirteen people; my Lord Methuselah's
carriage, my Lord Bareacres' chariot, britzska, and four-
gon, that anybody might pay for who liked. It was a
wonder how my Lord got the ready money to pay for the
expenses of the journey. The Hebrew gentlemen knew
how he got it. They knew what money his Lordship had
in his pocket at that instant, and what interest he paid
for it, and who gave it him. Finally there was a very
neat, handsome travelling carriage, about which the gentlemen speculated.

"*A qui cette voiture là?*" said one gentleman-courier
with a large morocco money-bag and ear-rings, to another
with ear-rings and a large morocco money-bag.

"C'est à Kirsch je bense—je l'ai vu toute à l'heure—qui! brenoit des sangviches dans la voiture," said the carrier in a fine German French.

Kirsch emerging presently from the neighbourhood of the hold, where he had been bellowing instructions intermingled with polyglot oaths to the ship's men engaged in secreting the passengers' luggage, came to give an account of himself to his brother interpreters. He informed them that the carriage belonged to a Nabob from Calcutta and Jamaica enormously rich, and with whom he was engaged to travel; and at this moment a young gentleman who had been warned off the bridge between the paddle-boxes, and who had dropped thence on to the roof of Lord Methuselah's carriage, from which he made his way over other carriages and imperials until he had clambered on to his own, descended thence and through the window into the body of the carriage, to the applause of the couriers looking on.

"Nous allons avoir une belle traversée, Monsieur George," said the courier with a grin, as he lifted his gold-laced cap.

"D— your French," said the young gentleman, "where's the biscuits, ay?" Whereupon, Kirsch answered him in the English language or in such an imitation of it as he could command,—for though he was familiar with all languages, Mr. Kirsch was not acquainted with a single one, and spoke all with indifferent volubility and incorrectness.

The imperious young gentleman who gobbled the biscuits (and indeed it was time to refresh himself, for he had breakfasted at Richmond full three hours before), was our young friend George Osborne. Uncle Jos and his mamma were on the quarter-deck with a gentleman of whom they used to see a good deal, and the four were about to make a summer tour.

Jos was seated at that moment on deck under the awning, and pretty nearly opposite to the Earl of Bareacres and his family, whose proceedings absorbed the Bengalee almost entirely. Both the noble couple looked rather younger than in the eventful year '15, when Jos remembered to have seen them at Brussels (indeed he always gave out in India that he was intimately acquainted with them). Lady Bareacres' hair which was then dark was

now a beautiful golden auburn, whereas Lord Bareacres'
whiskers, formerly red, were at present of a rich black
with purple and green reflections in the light. But changed
as they were, the movements of the noble pair occupied
Jos's mind entirely. The presence of a lord fascinated him,
and he could look at nothing else.

"Those people seem to interest you a good deal," said
Dobbin, laughing and watching him. Amelia too laughed.
She was in a straw bonnet with black ribbons, and otherwise dressed in mourning: but the little bustle and holiday
of the journey pleased and excited her, and she looked
particularly happy.

"What a heavenly day!" Emmy said, and added, with
great originality, "I hope we shall have a calm passage."

Jos waved his hand, scornfully glancing at the same
time under his eyelids at the great folks opposite. "If
you had made the voyages we have," he said, "you wouldn't
much care about the weather." But nevertheless, traveller
as he was, he passed the night direfully sick in his carriage,
where his courier tended him with brandy-and-water and
every luxury.

In due time this happy party landed at the quays of
Rotterdam, whence they were transported by another steamer
to the city of Cologne. Here the carriage and the family
took to the shore, and Jos was not a little gratified to see
his arrival announced in the Cologne newspapers as "Herr
Graf Lord von Sedley nebst Begleitung aus London." He
had his court dress with him: he had insisted that Dobbin
should bring his regimental paraphernalia: he announced
that it was his intention to be presented at some foreign
courts, and pay his respects to the Sovereigns of the countries which he honoured with a visit.

Wherever the party stopped, and an opportunity was
offered, Mr. Jos left his own card and the Major's upon
"Our Minister." It was with great difficulty that he could
be restrained from putting on his cocked hat and tights to
wait upon the English consul at the Free City of Juden-
stadt, when that hospitable functionary asked our travellers
to dinner. He kept a journal of his voyage, and noted
elaborately the defects or excellences of the various inns

at which he put up, and of the wines and dishes of which
he partook.

As for Emmy, she was very happy and pleased. Dobbin used to carry about for her her stool and sketch-book
and admired the drawings of the good-natured little artist,
as they never had been admired before. She sate upon
steamers' decks and drew crags and castles, or she mounted
upon donkeys and ascended to ancient robber-towers, attended by her two aides-de-camp, Georgy and Dobbin. She
laughed, and the Major did too, at his droll figure on don-
key-back, with his long legs touching the ground. He was
the interpreter for the party, having a good military knowledge of the German language; and he and the delighted
George fought the campaigns of the Rhine and the Pala-
tinate. In the course of a few weeks, and by assiduously conversing with Herr Kirsch on the box of the
carriage, Georgy made prodigious advance in the knowledge
of High Dutch, and could talk to hotel waiters and posti-
lions in a way that charmed his mother, and amused his
guardian.

Mr. Jos did not much engage in the afternoon excursions
of his fellow-travellers. He slept a good deal after dinner, or basked in the arbours of the pleasant inn-gardens.
Pleasant Rhine gardens! Fair scenes of peace and sunshine—noble purple mountains, whose crests are reflected
in the magnificent stream—who has ever seen you, that has
not a grateful memory of those scenes of friendly repose
and beauty? To lay down the pen, and even to think of
that beautiful Rhineland makes one happy. At this time
of summer evening, the cows are trooping down from the
hills, lowing and with their bells tinkling, to the old town,
with its old moats, and gates, and spires, and chestnut-
trees, with long blue shadows stretching over the grass;
the sky and the river below flame in crimson and gold; and
the moon is already out, looking pale towards the sunset.
The sun sinks behind the great castle-crested mountains,
the night falls suddenly, the river grows darker and darker,
lights quiver in it from the windows in the old ramparts, and
twinkle peacefully in the villages under the hills on the opposite shore.

So Jos used to go to sleep a good deal with his bandanna over his face and be very comfortable, and read all the English news, and every word of Galignani's admirable newspaper (may the blessings of all Englishmen who have ever been abroad rest on the founders and proprietors of that piratical print!) and whether he woke or slept his friends did not very much miss him. Yes, they were very happy. They went to the Opera often of evenings—to those snug, unassuming, dear old operas in the German towns, where the noblesse sits and cries, and knits stockings on the one side, over against the bourgeoisie on the other; and His Transparency the Duke and his Transparent family, all very fat and good-natured, come and occupy the great box in the middle; and the pit is full of the most elegant slim-waisted officers with straw-coloured moustachios, and twopence a-day on full pay. Here it was that Emmy found her delight, and was introduced for the first time to the wonders of Mozart and Cimarosa. The Major's musical taste has been before alluded to, and his performances on the flute commended. But perhaps the chief pleasure he had in these operas was in watching Emmy's rapture while listening to them. A new world of love and beauty broke upon her when she was introduced to those divine compositions: this lady had the keenest and finest sensibility, and how could she be indifferent when she heard Mozart? The tender parts of "Don Juan" awakened in her raptures so exquisite that she would ask herself when she went to say her prayers of a night, whether it was not wicked to feel so much delight as that with which "Vedrai Carino" and "Batti Batti" filled her gentle little bosom? But the Major, whom she consulted upon this head, as her theological adviser (and who himself had a pious and reverent soul), said that for his part, every beauty of art or nature made him thankful as well as happy; and that the pleasure to be had in listening to fine music, as in looking at the stars in the sky, or at a beautiful landscape or picture, was a benefit for which we might thank Heaven as sincerely as for any other worldly blessing. And in reply to some faint objections of Mrs. Amelia's (taken from certain theological works like the "Washerwoman of Finchley Common" and others of that

school, with which Mrs. Osborne had been furnished during
her life at Brompton) he told her an Eastern fable of the
Owl who thought that the sunshine was unbearable for the
eyes, and that the Nightingale was a most overrated bird.
"It is one's nature to sing and the other's to hoot," he said,
laughing, "and with such a sweet voice as you have yourself, you must belong to the Bulbul faction."

I like to dwell upon this period of her life, and to think
that she was cheerful and happy. You see she has not had
too much of that sort of existence as yet, and has not fallen
in the way of means to educate her tastes or her intelligence. She has been domineered over hitherto by vulgar
intellects. It is the lot of many a woman. And as every
one of the dear sex is the rival of the rest of her kind,
timidity passes for folly in their charitable judgments; and
gentleness for dulness; and silence—which is but timid
denial of the unwelcome assertion of ruling folks, and
tacit protestantism—above all, finds no mercy at the hands
of the female Inquisition. Thus, my dear and civilised
reader, if you and I were to find ourselves this evening in
a society of greengrocers, let us say; it is probable that our
conversation would not be brilliant; if, on the other hand,
a greengrocer should find himself at your refined and polite
tea-table, where everybody was saying witty things, and
everybody of fashion and repute tearing her friends to pieces
in the most delightful manner, it is possible that the stranger
would not be very talkative, and by no means interesting
or interested.

And it must be remembered, that this poor lady had never
met a gentleman in her life until this present moment.
Perhaps these are rarer personages than some of us think
for. Which of us can point out many such in his circle—
men whose aims are generous, whose truth is constant, and
not only constant in its kind but elevated in its degree:
whose want of meanness makes them simple: who can look
the world honestly in the face with an equal manly sympathy
for the great and the small? We all know a hundred whose
coats are very well made, and a score who have excellent
manners, and one or two happy beings who are what they
call, in the inner circles, and have shot into the very centre

and bull's eye of the fashion; but of gentlemen how many? Let us take a little scrap of paper and each make out his list.

My friend the Major I write, without any doubt, in mine. He had very long legs, a yellow face, and a slight lisp, which at first was rather ridiculous. But his thoughts were just, his brains were fairly good, his life was honest and pure, and his heart warm and humble. He certainly had very large hands and feet, which the two George Osbornes used to caricature and laugh at; and their jeers and laughter perhaps led poor little Emmy astray as to his worth. But have we not all been misled about our heroes, and changed our opinions a hundred times? Emmy, in this happy time, found that hers underwent a very great change in respect of the merits of the Major.

Perhaps it was the happiest time of both their lives indeed, if they did but know it—and who does? Which of us can point out and say that was the culmination—that was the summit of human joy? But at all events, this couple were very decently contented, and enjoyed as pleasant a summer tour as any pair that left England that year. Georgy was always present at the play, but it was the Major who put Emmy's shawl on after the entertainment; and in the walks and excursions the young lad would be on a-head, and up a tower-stair or a tree, whilst the soberer couple were below, the Major smoking his cigar with great placidity and constancy, whilst Emmy sketched the site or the ruin. It was on this very tour that I, the present writer of a history of which every word is true, had the pleasure to see them first, and to make their acquaintance.

It was at the little comfortable Ducal town of Pumpernickel (that very place where Sir Pitt Crawley had been so distinguished as an *attaché;* but that was in early, early days, and before the news of the battle of Austerlitz sent all the English diplomatists in Germany to the right about) that I first saw Colonel Dobbin and his party. They had arrived with the carriage and courier at the Erbprinz Hotel, the best of the town, and the whole party dined at the *table d'hôte*. Everybody remarked the majesty of Jos, and the knowing way in which he sipped, or rather sucked, the Johannisberger, which he ordered for dinner. The little boy, too, we observed, had a famous appetite, and consumed schinken, and braten, and kartoffeln, and cranberry jam, and salad, and pudding, and roast fowls, and sweetmeats, with a gallantry that did honour to his nation. After about fifteen dishes, he concluded the repast with dessert, some of which he even carried out of doors; for some young gentlemen at table, amused with his coolness and gallant free and easy manner, induced him to pocket a handful of macaroons, which he discussed on his way to the theatre, whither everybody went in the cheery social little German place. The lady in black, the boy's mamma, laughed and blushed, and looked exceedingly pleased and shy as the dinner went on, and at the various feats and instances of *espièglerie* on the part of her son. The Colonel—for so he became very soon afterwards—I remember joked the boy with a great deal of grave fun, pointing out dishes which he *hadn't* tried, and entreating him not to baulk his appetite, but to have a second supply of this or that.

It was what they call a *gast-rolle* night at the Royal Grand Ducal Pumpernickelisch Hof,—or Court theatre; and Madame Schroeder Devrient, then in the bloom of her beauty and genius, performed the part of the heroine in the wonderful opera of "Fidelio." From our places in the stalls we could see our four friends of the *table d'hôte,* in the loge which Schwendler of the Erbprinz kept for his best guests: and I could not help remarking the effect which the magnificent actress and music produced upon Mrs. Osborne, for so we heard the stout gentleman in the mustachios call her. During the astonishing Chorus of the Prisoners, over which the delightful voice of the actress rose and soared in the most ravishing harmony, the English lady's face wore such an expression of wonder and delight that it struck even little Fipps, the *blasé* attaché, who drawled out, as he fixed his glass upon her, "Gayd, it really does one good to see a woman caypable of that stayt of excaytement." And in the Prison Scene where Fidelio, rushing to her husband, cries, "Nichts, nichts, mein Florestan," she fairly lost herself and covered her face with her handkerchief. Every woman in the house was snivelling at the time: but I suppose it was because it was predestined that I was to write this particular lady's memoirs that I remarked her.

The next day they gave another piece of Beethoven, "Die Schlacht bei Vittoria." Malbrook is introduced at the beginning of the performance, as indicative of the brisk advance of the French army. Then come drums, trumpets, thunders of artillery, and groans of the dying, and at last in a grand triumphal swell, "God save the King" is performed.

There may have been a score of Englishmen in the house, but at the burst of that beloved and well-known music, every one of them, we young fellows in the stalls, Sir John and Lady Bullminster (who had taken a house at Pumpernickel for the education of their nine children), the fat gentleman with the mustachios, the long Major in white duck trousers, and the lady with the little boy upon whom he was so sweet: even Kirsch, the courier in the gallery, stood bolt upright in their places, and proclaimed themselves to be members of the dear old British nation. As for Tapeworm, the Chargé d'Affaires, he rose up in his box and bowed and simpered, as if he would represent the whole empire. Tapeworm was nephew and heir to old Marshal Tiptoff, who has been introduced in this story as General Tiptoff, just before Waterloo, who was Colonel of the —th regiment in which Major Dobbin served, and who died in this year full of honours, and of an aspic of plovers' eggs; when the regiment was graciously given by his Majesty to Colonel Sir Michael O'Dowd, K.C.B., who had commanded it in many glorious fields.

Tapeworm must have met with Colonel Dobbin at the house of the Colonel's Colonel, the Marshal, for he recognised him on this night at the theatre; and with the utmost condescension, his Majesty's minister came over from his own box, and publicly shook hands with his new-found friend.

"Look at that infernal sly-boots of a Tapeworm," Fipps whispered, examining his chief from the stalls. "Wherever there's a pretty woman he always twists himself in." And I wonder what were diplomatists made for but for that?

"Have I the honour of addressing myself to Mrs. Dobbin?"
asked the Secretary, with a most insinuating grin.

Georgy burst out laughing, and said, "By Jove, that *is*
a good 'un."—Emmy and the Major blushed: we saw them
from the stalls.

"This lady is Mrs. George Osborne," said the Major,
"and this is her brother, Mr. Sedley, a distinguished officer
of the Bengal Civil Service: permit me to introduce him to
your lordship!"

My lord nearly sent Jos off his legs with the most fascinating smile. "Are you going to stop in Pumpernickel?" he
said. "It is a dull place: but we want some nice people,
and we would try and make it *so* agreeable to you. Mr.—
Ahum—Mrs.—Oho. I shall do myself the honour of calling
upon you to-morrow at your inn."—And he went away with
a Parthian grin and glance which he thought must finish Mrs.
Osborne completely.

The performance over, the young fellows lounged about
the lobbies, and we saw the society take its departure.
The Duchess Dowager went off in her jingling old coach,
attended by two faithful and withered old maids of honour,
and a little snuffy spindle-shanked gentleman in waiting,
in a brown jasey and a green coat covered with orders—of
which the star and the grand yellow cordon of the order of
St. Michael of Pumpernickel were most conspicuous. The
drums rolled, the guards saluted, and the old carriage drove
away.

Then came his Transparency the Duke and Transparent
family, with his great officers of state and household. He
bowed serenely to everybody. And amid the saluting of
the guards, and the flaring of the torches of the running
footmen, clad in scarlet, the Transparent carriages drove
away to the old Ducal Schloss, with its towers and pinna-
cles standing on the Schlossberg. Everybody in Pumpernickel knew everybody. No sooner was a foreigner seen
there, than the Minister of Foreign Affairs, or some other
great or small officer of state, went round to the Erbprinz,
and found out the name of the new arrival.

We watched them, too, out of the theatre. Tapeworm
had just walked off, enveloped in his cloak, with which his

gigantic chasseur was always in attendance, and looking as
much as possible like Don Juan. The Prime Minister's
lady had just squeezed herself into her sedan, and her
daughter, the charming Ida, had put on her calash and
clogs: when the English party came out, the boy yawning
drearily, the Major taking great pains in keeping the shawl
over Mrs. Osborne's head, and Mr. Sedley looking grand,
with a crush opera-hat on one side of his head, and his
hand in the stomach of a voluminous white waistcoat. We
took off our hats to our acquaintances of the *table d'hôte;*
and the lady, in return, presented us with a little smile and
a curtsey, for which everybody might be thankful.

The carriage from the inn, under the superintendence of
the bustling Mr. Kirsch, was in waiting to convey the party;
but the fat man said he would walk, and smoke his cigar
on his way homewards; so the other three, with nods and
smiles to us, went without Mr. Sedley; Kirsch, with the
cigar-case, following in his master's wake.

We all walked together, and talked to the stout gentleman about the *agrémens* of the place. It was very agreeable
for the English. There were shooting-parties and battues;
there was a plenty of balls and entertainments at the
hospitable Court; the society was generally good; the theatre
excellent, and the living cheap.

"And our Minister seems a most delightful and affable
person," our new friend said. "With such a representative,
and—and a good medical man, I fancy the place to be most
eligible. Good-night, gentlemen." And Jos creaked up the
stairs to bedward, followed by Kirsch with a flambeau. We
rather hoped that nice-looking woman would be induced to
stay some time in the town.

CHAPTER XXVIII

In Which We Meet an Old Acquaintance

SUCH polite behaviour as that of Lord Tapeworm did not fail to have the most favourable effect upon Mr. Sedley's mind, and the very next morning, at breakfast, he pronounced his opinion that Pumpernickel was the pleasantest little place of any which he had visited on their tour. Jos's motives and artifices were not very difficult of comprehension; and Dobbin laughed in his sleeve, like a hypocrite as he was, when he found by the knowing air of the Civilian and the off-hand manner in which the latter talked about Tapeworm Castle, and the other members of the family, that Jos had been up already in the morning, consulting his travelling Peerage. Yes, he had seen the Right Honourable the Earl of Bagwig, his lordship's father; he was sure he had, he had met him at—at the Levee—didn't Dob remember? and when the Diplomatist called on the party, faithful to his promise, Jos received him with such a salute and honours as were seldom accorded to the little Envoy. He winked at Kirsch on his Excellency's arrival, and that emissary, instructed beforehand, went out and superintended an entertainment of cold meats, jellies, and other delicacies, brought in upon trays, and of which Mr. Jos absolutely insisted that his noble guest should partake.

Tapeworm, so long as he could have an opportunity of admiring the bright eyes of Mrs. Osborne (whose freshness of complexion bore daylight remarkably well) was not ill pleased to accept any invitation to stay in Mr. Sedley's lodgings; he put one or two dexterous questions to him about India and the dancing-girls there; asked Amelia about that beautiful boy who had been with her, and complimented the astonished little woman upon the prodigious sensation which she had made in the house; and tried to fascinate Dobbin by talking of the late war, and the exploits of the Pumpernickel contingent under the command of the Hereditary Prince, now Duke of Pumpernickel.

Lord Tapeworm inherited no little portion of the family gallantry, and it was his happy belief, that almost every woman upon whom he himself cast friendly eyes, was in love with him. He left Emmy under the persuasion that she was slain by his wit and attractions, and went home to his lodgings to write a pretty little note to her. She was not fascinated; only puzzled by his grinning, his simpering, his scented cambric handkerchief, and his high-heeled lacquered boots. She did not understand one half the compliments which he paid; she had never, in her small experience of mankind, met a professional ladies' man as yet, and looked upon my lord as something curious rather than pleasant; and if she did not admire, certainly wondered at him. Jos, on the contrary, was delighted. "How very affable his Lordship is," he said; "how very kind of his Lordship to say he would send his medical man! Kirsch, you will carry our cards to the Count de Schlüsselback directly: the Major and I will have the greatest pleasure in paying our respects at Court as soon as possible. Put out my uniform, Kirsch,—both our uniforms. It is a mark of politeness which every English gentleman ought to show to the countries which he visits, to pay his respects to the sovereigns of those countries as to the representatives of his own."

When Tapeworm's doctor came, Doctor von Glauber, Body Physician to H.S.H. the Duke, he speedily convinced Jos that the Pumpernickel mineral springs and the Doctor's particular treatment would infallibly restore the Bengalee to youth and slimness. "Dere came here last year," he said, "Sheneral Bulkeley, an English Sheneral, tvice so pic as you, Sir. I sent him back qvite tin after tree months, and he danced vid Baroness Glauber at the end of two."

Jos's mind was made up; the springs, the Doctor, the Court, and the Chargé d'Affaires convinced him, and he proposed to spend the autumn in these delightful quarters. —And punctual to his word, on the next day the Chargé d'Affaires presented Jos and the Major to Victor Aurelius

XVII., being conducted to their audience with that sovereign by the Count de Schlüsselback, Marshal of the Court.

They were straightway invited to dinner at Court, and their intention of staying in the town being announced, the politest ladies of the whole town instantly called upon Mrs. Osborne; and as not one of these, however poor they might be, was under the rank of a Baroness, Jos's delight was beyond expression. He wrote off to Chutney at the Club to say that the Service was highly appreciated in Germany, that he was going to show his friend, the Count de Schlüsselback, how to stick a pig in the Indian fashion, and that his august friends, the Duke and Duchess, were everything that was kind and civil.

Emmy, too, was presented to the august family, and as mourning is not admitted in Court on certain days, she appeared in a pink crape dress, with a diamond ornament in the corsage, presented to her by her brother, and she looked so pretty in this costume that the Duke and Court (putting out of the question the Major, who had scarcely ever seen her before in an evening dress, and vowed that she did not look five-and-twenty) all admired her excessively.

In this dress she walked a Polonaise with Major Dobbin at a Court-ball, in which easy dance Mr. Jos had the honour of leading out the Countess of Schlüsselback, an old lady with a hump back, but with sixteen good quarters of nobility, and related to half the royal houses of Germany.

Pumpernickel stands in the midst of a happy valley, through which sparkles—to mingle with the Rhine somewhere, but I have not the map at hand to say exactly at what point—the fertilising stream of the Pump. In some places the river is big enough to support a ferryboat, in others to turn a mill; in Pumpernickel itself, the last Transparency but three, the great and renowned Victor Aurelius XIV., built a magnificent bridge, on which his own statue rises, surrounded by water-nymphs and emblems of victory, peace, and plenty; he has his foot on the neck of a prostrate Turk—history says he engaged and ran a Janissary through the body at the relief of Vienna by Sobieski,—but, quite undisturbed by the agonies of that prostrate Mahometan, who writhes at his feet in the most ghastly manner, the Prince smiles blandly, and points with his truncheon in the direction of the Aurelius Platz, where he began to erect a new palace that would have been the wonder of his age, had the great-souled Prince but had funds to complete it. But the completion of Monplaisir (*Monblaisir* the honest German folks call it) was stopped for lack of ready money, and it and its park and garden are now in rather a faded condition, and not more than ten times big enough to accommodate the Court of the reigning Sovereign.

The gardens were arranged to emulate those of Versailles, and amidst the terraces and groves there are some huge allegorical water-works still, which spout and froth stupendously upon fête-days, and frighten one with their enormous aquatic insurrections. There is the Trophonius' cave in which, by some artifice, the leaden Tritons are made not only to spout water, but to play the most dreadful groans out of their lead conchs—there is the Nymph-bath and the Niagara cataract, which the people of the neighbourhood admire beyond expression, when they come to the yearly fair at the opening of the Chamber, or to the fêtes with which the happy little nation still celebrates the birth-days and marriage-days of its princely governors.

Then from all the towns of the Duchy which stretches for nearly ten miles,—from Bolkum, which lies on its western frontier bidding defiance to Prussia, from Grogwitz where the Prince has a hunting-lodge, and where his dominions are separated by the Pump river from those of the neighbouring Prince of Potzenthal; from all the little villages which, besides these three great cities, dot over the happy Principality—from the farms and the mills along the Pump, come troops of people in red petticoats and velvet head-dresses, or with three-cornered hats and pipes in their mouths, who flock to the Residenz and share in the pleasures of the fair and the festivities there. Then the theatre is open for nothing, then the waters of Monblaisir begin to play (it is lucky that there is company to behold them, for one would be afraid to see them alone)—then there come mountebanks and riding troops (the way in which his Transparency was fascinated by one of the

horse-riders is well known, and it is believed that *La Petite
Vivandière,* as she was called, was a spy in the French
interest), and the delighted people are permitted to march
through room after room of the Grand Ducal palace, and
admire the slippery floor, the rich hangings, and the spittoons
at the doors of all the innumerable chambers. There is one
Pavilion at Monblaisir which Aurelius Victor XV. had
arranged—a great Prince but too fond of pleasure—and
which I am told is a perfect wonder of licentious elegance.
It is painted with the story of Bacchus and Ariadne, and
the table works in and out of the room by means of a
windlass so that the company was served without any in-
tervention of domestics. But the place was shut up by
Barbara, Aurelius XV.'s widow, a severe and devout
Princess of the House of Bolkum and Regent of the Duchy
during her son's glorious minority, and after the death of
her husband, cut off in the pride of his pleasures.

The theatre of Pumpernickel is known and famous in
that quarter of Germany. It languished a little when the
present Duke in his youth insisted upon having his own
operas played there, and it is said one day, in a fury, from
his place in the orchestra, when he attended a rehearsal,
broke a bassoon on the head of the Chapel Master, who
was conducting, and led too slow; and during which time
the Duchess Sophia wrote domestic comedies which must
have been very dreary to witness. But the Prince executes
his music in private now, and the Duchess only gives away
her plays to the foreigners of distinction who visit her
kind little Court.

It is conducted with no small comfort and splendour.
When there are balls, though there may be four hundred
people at supper, there is a servant in scarlet and lace to
attend upon every four, and every one is served on silver.
There are festivals and entertainments going continually
on; and the Duke has his chamberlains and equerries, and
the Duchess her mistress of the wardrobe and ladies of
honour, just like any other and more potent potentates.

The Constitution is or was a moderate despotism,
tempered by a Chamber that might or might not be elected.
I never certainly could hear of its sitting in my time at

Pumpernickel. The Prime Minister had lodgings in a second floor; and the Foreign Secretary occupied the comfortable lodgings over Zwieback's Conditorey. The army consisted of a magnificent band that also did duty on the stage, where it was quite pleasant to see the worthy fellows marching in Turkish dresses with rouge on and wooden scimitars, or as Roman warriors with ophicleides and trombones,—to see them again, I say, at night, after one had listened to them all the morning in the Aurelius Platz, where they performed opposite the Café where we breakfasted. Besides the band, there was a rich and numerous staff of officers, and, I believe, a few men. Besides the regular sentries, three or four men, habited as hussars, used to do duty at the Palace, but I never saw them on horseback, and *au fait,* what was the use of cavalry in a time of profound peace?—and whither the deuce should the hussars ride?

Everybody—everybody that was noble of course, for as for the Bourgeois we could not quite be expected to take notice of *them*—visited his neighbour. H. E. Madame de Burst received once a week, H. E. Madame de Schnurrbart had her night—the theatre was open twice a week, the Court graciously received once, so that a man's life might in fact be a perfect round of pleasure in the unpretending Pumpernickel way.

That there were feuds in the place, no one can deny. Politics ran very high at Pumpernickel, and parties were very bitter. There was the Strumpff faction and the Lederlung party, the one supported by our Envoy and the other by the French Chargé d'Affaires, M. de Macabau. Indeed it sufficed for our Minister to stand up for Madame Strumpff, who was clearly the greater singer of the two, and had three more notes in her voice than Madame Lederlung, her rival—it sufficed, I say, for our Minister to advance *any* opinion to have it instantly contradicted by the French diplomatist.

Everybody in the town was ranged in one or other of these factions. The Lederlung was a prettyish little creature certainly, and her voice (what there was of it,) was very sweet, and there is no doubt that the Strumpff was not in her first youth and beauty, and certainly too stout; when she came on in the last scene of the "Sonnambula" for instance in her night-chemise with a lamp in her hand, and had to go out of the window, and pass over the plank of the mill, it was all she could do to squeeze out of the window, and the plank used to bend and creak again under her weight—but how she poured out the finale of the opera! and with what a burst of feeling she rushed into Elvino's arms—almost fit to smother him! Whereas the little Lederlung—but a truce to this gossip—the fact is, that these two women were the two flags of the French and the English party at Pumpernickel, and the society was divided in its allegiance to those two great nations.

We had on our side the Home Minister, the Master of the Horse, the Duke's Private Secretary, and the Prince's Tutor: whereas of the French party were the Foreign Minister, the Commander-in-chief's Lady, who had served under Napoleon and the Hof-Marschall and his wife, who was glad enough to get the fashions from Paris, and always had them and her caps by M. de Macabau's courier. The Secretary of his Chancery was little Grignac, a young fellow, as malicious as Satan, and who made caricatures of Tapeworm in all the albums of the place.

Their head-quarters and *table d'hôte* were established at the Pariser Hof, the other inn of the town; and though, of course, these gentlemen were obliged to be civil in public, yet they cut at each other with epigrams that were as sharp as razors, as I have seen a couple of wrestlers in Devonshire, lashing at each other's shins, and never showing their agony upon a muscle of their faces. Neither Tapeworm nor Macabau ever sent home a despatch to his government, without a most savage series of attacks upon his rival. For instance, on our side we would write, "The interests of Great Britain in this place, and throughout the whole of Germany, are perilled by the continuance in office of the present French envoy; this man is of a character so infamous that he will stick at no falsehood, or hesitate at no crime, to attain his ends. He poisons the mind of the Court against the English minister, represents the conduct of Great Britain in the most odious and atrocious light, and is unhappily backed by a

minister whose ignorance and necessities are as notorious as
his influence is fatal." On their side they would say, "M.
de Tapeworm continues his system of stupid insular arro-
gance and vulgar falsehood against the greatest nation in
the world. Yesterday he was heard to speak lightly of Her
Royal Highness Madame the Duchess of Berri: on a former
occasion he insulted the heroic Duke of Angoulême, and
dared to insinuate that H.R.H. the Duke of Orleans was
conspiring against the august throne of the lilies. His gold
is prodigated in every direction which his stupid menaces
fail to frighten. By one and the other, he has won over
creatures of the Court here,—and, in fine, Pumpernickel will
not be quiet, Germany tranquil, France respected, or Europe
content, until this poisonous viper be crushed under heel:"
and so on. When one side or the other had written any
particularly spicy despatch, news of it was sure to slip out.

Before the winter was far advanced it is actually on record
that Emmy took a night and received company with great
propriety and modesty. She had a French master who complimented her upon the purity of her accent and her facility
of learning; the fact is she had learned long ago, and
grounded herself subsequently in the grammar so as to be
able to teach it to George; and Madame Strumpff came to
give her lessons in singing, which she performed so well and
with such a true voice that the Major's windows, who had
lodgings opposite under the Prime Minister, were always
open to hear the lesson. Some of the German ladies, who
are very sentimental and simple in their tastes, fell in love
with her and began to call her *du* at once. These are trivial
details, but they relate to happy times. The Major made
himself George's tutor, and read Cæsar and mathematics
with him, and they had a German master and rode out of
evenings by the side of Emmy's carriage—she was always
too timid, and made a dreadful outcry at the slightest disturbance on horseback. So she drove about with one of her
dear German friends, and Jos asleep on the back-seat of the
barouche.

He was becoming very sweet upon the Gräfin Fanny de
Butterbrod, a very gentle, tender-hearted and unassuming
young creature, a Canoness and Countess in her own right,

but with scarcely ten pounds per year to her fortune, and
Fanny for her part declared that to be Amelia's sister was
the greatest delight that heaven could bestow on her, and
Jos might have put a Countess's shield and coronet by the
side of his own arms on his carriage and forks; when—
when events occurred, and those grand fêtes given upon the
marriage of the Hereditary Prince of Pumpernickel with
the lovely Princess Amelia of Humbourg-Schlippenschloppen
took place.

At this festival the magnificence displayed was such as
had not been known in the little German place since the
days of the prodigal Victor XIV. All the neighbouring
Princes, Princesses, and Grandees were invited to the feast.
Beds rose to half-a-crown per night in Pumpernickel, and
the army was exhausted in providing guards of honour for
the Highnesses, Serenities, and Excellencies, who arrived
from all quarters. The Princess was married by proxy, at
her father's residence, by the Count de Schlüsselback. Snuff-
boxes were given away in profusion (as we learned from the
Court jeweller, who sold and afterwards bought them again),
and bushels of the Order of Saint Michael of Pumpernickel
were sent to the nobles of the Court, while hampers of the
cordons and decorations of the Wheel of St. Catherine of
Schlippenschloppen were brought to ours. The French envoy got both. "He is covered with ribbons like a prize cart-
horse," Tapeworm said, who was not allowed by the rules
of his service to take any decorations: "Let him have the
cordons; but with whom is the victory?" The fact is, it was
a triumph of British diplomacy: the French party having
proposed and tried their utmost to carry a marriage with a
Princess of the House of Potztausend-Donnerwetter, whom,
as a matter of course, we opposed.

Everybody was asked to the fêtes of the marriage. Gar-
lands and triumphal arches were hung across the road to
welcome the young bride. The great Saint Michael's Fountain ran with uncommonly sour wine, while that in the
Artillery Place frothed with beer. The great waters played;
and poles were put up in the park and gardens for the
happy peasantry, which they might climb at their leisure,
carrying off watches, silver forks, prize sausages hung with

pink ribbon, &c., at the top. Georgy got one, wrenching it off, having swarmed up the pole to the delight of the spectators, and sliding down with the rapidity of a fall of water. But it was for the glory's sake merely. The boy gave the sausage to a peasant, who had very nearly seized it, and stood at the foot of the mast, blubbering, because he was unsuccessful.

At the French Chancellerie they had six more lampions in their illumination than ours had; but our transparency, which represented the young Couple advancing, and Discord flying away, with the most ludicrous likeness to the French ambassador, beat the French picture hollow; and I have no doubt got Tapeworm the advancement and the Cross of the Bath, which he subsequently attained.

Crowds of foreigners arrived for the fêtes: and of English of course. Besides the Court balls, public balls were given at the Town Hall and the Redoute, and in the former place there was a room for *trente-et-quarante* and *roulette* established, for the week of the festivities only, and by one of the great German companies from Ems or Aix-la-Chapelle. The officers or inhabitants of the town were not allowed to play at these games, but strangers, peasants, ladies were admitted, and any one who chose to lose or win money.

That little scapegrace Georgy Osborne amongst others, whose pockets were always full of dollars, and whose relations were away at the grand festival of the Court, came to the Stadthaus ball in company of his uncle's courier, Mr. Kirsch, and having only peeped into a play-room at Baden Baden when he hung on Dobbin's arm, and where, of course, he was not permitted to gamble, came eagerly to this part of the entertainment, and hankered round the tables where the croupiers and the punters were at work. Women were playing; they were masked, some of them; this license was allowed in these wild times of carnival.

A woman with light hair, in a low dress, by no means so fresh as it had been, and with a black mask on, through the eyelets of which her eyes twinkled strangely, was seated at one of the roulette-tables with a card and a pin, and a couple of florins before her. As the croupier called out the colour

and number, she pricked on the card with great care and
regularity, and only ventured her money on the colours after
the red or black had come up a certain number of times. It
was strange to look at her.

But in spite of her care and assiduity she guessed wrong,
and the last two florins followed each other under the
croupier's rake, as he cried out with his inexorable voice,
the winning colour and number. She gave a sigh, a shrug
with her shoulders, which were already too much out of her
gown, and dashing the pin through the card on to the table,
sat thrumming it for a while. Then she looked round her,
and saw Georgy's honest face staring at the scene. The
little scamp! what business had he to be there?

When she saw the boy, at whose face she looked hard
through her shining eyes and mask, she said, *"Monsieur
n'est pas joueur?"*

"Non, Madame," said the boy: but she must have known,
from his accent, of what country he was, for she answered
him with a slight foreign tone. "You have nevare played—
will you do me a littl' favor?"

"What is it?" said Georgy, blushing again. Mr. Kirsch
was at work for his part at the *rouge et noir,* and did not
see his young master.

"Play this for me, if you please; put it on any number,
any number." And she took from her bosom a purse, and
out of it a gold piece, the only coin there, and she put it
into George's hand. The boy laughed, and did as he was bid.

The number came up sure enough. There is a power
that arranges that, they say, for beginners.

"Thank you," said she, pulling the money towards her;
"thank you. What is your name?"

"My name's Osborne," said Georgy, and was fingering in
his own pockets for dollars, and just about to make a trial,
when the Major, in his uniform, and Jos, *en Marquis,* from
the Court ball, made their appearance. Other people finding
the entertainment stupid, and preferring the fun at the Stadthaus, had quitted the Palace ball earlier; but it is probable
the Major and Jos had gone home and found the boy's
absence, for the former instantly went up to him, and taking
him by the shoulder, pulled him briskly back from the place

of temptation. Then, looking around the room, he saw Kirsch employed as we have said, and going up to him, asked how he dared to bring Mr. George to such a place.

"Laissez-moi tranquille," said Mr. Kirsch, very much excited by play and wine. *"Il faut s'amuser, parbleu. Je ne suis pas au service de Monsieur."*

Seeing his condition the Major did not choose to argue with the man; but contented himself with drawing away George, and asking Jos if he would come away. He was standing close by the lady in the mask, who was playing with pretty good luck now; and looking on much interested at the game.

"Hadn't you better come, Jos," the Major said, "with George and me?"

"I'll stop and go home with that rascal, Kirsch," Jos said; and for the same reason of modesty, which he thought ought to be preserved before the boy, Dobbin did not care to remonstrate with Jos, but left him and walked home with Georgy.

"Did you play?" asked the Major, when they were out, and on their way home.

The boy said "No."

"Give me your word of honour as a gentleman, that you never will."

"Why?" said the boy: "It seems very good fun." And, in a very eloquent and impressive manner, the Major showed him why he shouldn't, and would have enforced his precepts by the example of Georgy's own father, had he liked to say anything that should reflect on the other's memory. When he had housed him he went to bed, and saw his light, in the little room outside of Amelia's, presently disappear. Amelia's followed half an hour afterwards. I don't know what made the Major note it so accurately.

Jos, however, remained behind, over the play-table; he was no gambler, but not averse to the little excitement of the sport now and then; and he had some Napoleons chinking in the embroidered pockets of his court waistcoat. He put down one over the fair shoulder of the little gambler before him, and they won. She made a little movement to make room for him by her side, and just took the skirt of her gown from a vacant chair there.

"Come and give me good luck," she said, still in a foreign accent, quite different from that frank and perfectly English "Thank you," with which she had saluted George's *coup* in her favour. The portly gentleman, looking round to see that nobody of rank observed him, sat down; he muttered—"Ah, really, well now, God bless my soul. I'm very fortunate; I'm sure to give you good fortune," and other words of compliment and confusion.

"Do you play much?" the foreign mask said.

"I put a Nap or two down," said Jos, with a superb air, flinging down a gold piece.

"Yes; a nap after dinner," said the mask, archly. But Jos looking frightened, she continued, in her pretty French accent, "You do not play to win. No more do I. I play to forget, but I cannot. I cannot forget old times, Monsieur. Your little nephew is the image of his father; and you—you are not changed—but yes, you are. Everybody changes, everybody forgets; nobody has any heart."

"Good God, who is it?" asked Jos in a flutter.

"Can't you guess, Joseph Sedley?" said the little woman, in a sad voice, and undoing her mask, she looked at him. "You have forgotten me."

"Good heavens! Mrs. Crawley!" gasped out Jos.

"Rebecca," said the other, putting her hand on his; but she followed the game still, all the time she was looking at him.

"I am stopping at the Elephant," she continued. "Ask for Madame de Raudon. I saw my dear Amelia to-day; how pretty she looked, and how happy! So do you! Everybody but me, who am wretched, Joseph Sedley." And she put her money over from the red to the black, as if by a chance movement of her hand, and while she was wiping her eyes with a pocket-handkerchief fringed with torn lace.

The red came up again, and she lost the whole of that stake. "Come away," she said. "Come with me a little—we are old friends, are we not, dear Mr. Sedley?"

And Mr. Kirsch having lost all his money by this time, followed his master out into the moonlight, where the illuminations were winking out, and the transparency over our mission was scarcely visible.

CHAPTER XXIX

A Vagabond Chapter

WE must pass over a part of Mrs. Rebecca Crawley's biography with that lightness and delicacy which the world demands—the moral world, that has, perhaps, no particular objection to vice, but an insuperable repugnance to hearing vice called by its proper name. There are things we do and know perfectly well in Vanity Fair, though we never speak of them: as the Ahrimanians worship the devil, but don't mention him: and a polite public will no more bear to read an authentic description of vice than a truly-refined English or American female will permit the word breeches to be pronounced in her chaste hearing. And yet, Madam, both are walking the world before our faces every day, without much shocking us. If you were to blush every time they went by, what complexions you would have! It is only when their naughty names are called out that your modesty has any occasion to show alarm or sense of outrage, and it has been the wish of the present writer, all through this story, deferentially to submit to the fashion at present prevailing, and only to hint at the existence of wickedness in a light, easy, and agreeable manner, so that nobody's fine feelings may be offended. I defy any one to say that our Becky, who has certainly some vices, has not been presented to the public in a perfectly genteel and inoffensive manner. In describing this syren, singing and smiling, coaxing and cajoling, the author, with modest pride, asks his readers all round, has he once forgotten the laws of politeness, and showed the monster's hideous tail above water? No!

Those who like may peep down under the waves that are pretty transparent, and see it writhing and twirling, diabolically hideous and slimy, flapping amongst bones, or curling around corpses; but above the water-line, I ask, has

344

not everything been proper, agreeable, and decorous, and has any the most squeamish immoralist in Vanity Fair a right to cry fie? When, however, the syren disappears and dives below, down among the dead men, the water of course grows turbid over her, and it is labour lost to look into it ever so curiously. They look pretty enough when they sit upon a rock, twanging their harps and combing their hair, and sing, and beckon to you to come and hold the looking-glass; but when they sink into their native element, depend on it those mermaids are about no good, and we had best not examine the fiendish marine cannibals, revelling and feasting on their wretched pickled victims. And so, when Becky is out of the way, be sure that she is not particularly well employed, and that the less that is said about her doings is in fact the better.

If we were to give a full account of her proceedings during a couple of years that followed after the Curzon Street catastrophe, there might be some reason for people to say this book was improper. The actions of very vain, heartless, pleasure-seeking people are very often improper (as are many of yours, my friend with the grave face and spotless reputation;—but that is merely by the way); and what are those of a woman without faith—or love—or character? And I am inclined to think that there was a period in Mrs. Becky's life, when she was seized, not by remorse, but by a kind of despair, and absolutely neglected her person, and did not even care for her reputation.

This *abattement* and degradation did not take place all at once: it was brought about by degrees, after her calamity, and after many struggles to keep up—as a man who goes overboard hangs on to a spar whilst any hope is left, and then flings it away and goes down, when he finds that struggling is in vain.

She lingered about London whilst her husband was making preparations for his departure to his seat of government: and it is believed made more than one attempt to see her brother-in-law, Sir Pitt Crawley, and to work upon his feelings, which she had almost enlisted in her favour. As Sir Pitt and Mr. Wenham were walking down to the House of Commons, the latter spied Mrs. Rawdon in a black

veil, and lurking near the palace of the legislature. She
sneaked away when her eyes met those of Wenham, and
indeed never succeeded in her designs upon the Baronet.

Probably Lady Jane interposed. I have heard that she
quite astonished her husband by the spirit which she exhibited in this quarrel, and her determination to disown Mrs.
Becky.

Of her own movement, she invited Rawdon to come
and stop in Gaunt Street until his departure for Coventry
Island, knowing that with him for a guard Mrs. Becky would
not try to force her door: and she looked curiously at the
superscriptions of all the letters which arrived for Sir
Pitt, lest he and his sister-in-law should be corresponding.
Not but that Rebecca could have written had she a mind:
but she did not try to see or to write to Pitt at his own house,
and after one or two attempts consented to his demand that
the correspondence regarding her conjugal differences should
be carried on by lawyers only.

The fact was, that Pitt's mind had been poisoned against
her. A short time after Lord Steyne's accident Wenham
had been with the Baronet; and given him such a biography
of Mrs. Becky as had astonished the member for Queens
Crawley. He knew everything regarding her: who her
father was; in what year her mother danced at the Opera;
what had been her previous history, and what her conduct
during her married life:—as I have no doubt that the greater
part of the story was false and dictated by interested malevo-
lence, it shall not be repeated here. But Becky was left with
a sad, sad reputation in the esteem of a country gentleman
and relative who had been once rather partial to her.

The revenues of the Governor of Coventry Island are
not large. A part of them were set aside by his Excellency
for the payment of certain outstanding debts and liabilities,
the charges incident on his high situation required considerable expense; finally, it was found that he could not
spare to his wife more than three hundred pounds a year,
which he proposed to pay to her on an undertaking that she
would never trouble him. Otherwise: scandal, separation,
Doctors' Commons would ensue. But it was Mr. Wenham's
business, Lord Steyne's business, Rawdon's, everybody's—to

get her out of the country, and hush up a most disagreeable affair.

She was probably so much occupied in arranging these affairs of business with her husband's lawyers, that she forgot to take any step whatever about her son, the little Rawdon, and did not even once propose to go and see him. That young gentleman was consigned to the entire guardianship of his aunt and uncle, the former of whom had always possessed a great share of the child's affection. His mamma wrote him a neat letter from Boulogne when she quitted England, in which she requested him to mind his book, and said she was going to take a Continental tour, during which she would have the pleasure of writing to him again. But she never did for a year afterwards, and not, indeed, until Sir Pitt's only boy, always sickly, died of whooping-cough and measles;—then Rawdon's mamma wrote the most affectionate composition to her darling son, who was made heir of Queen's Crawley by this accident, and drawn more closely than ever to the kind lady, whose tender heart had already adopted him. Rawdon Crawley, then grown a tall, fine lad, blushed when he got the letter. "Oh, Aunt Jane, you are my mother!" he said "and not—and not that one." But he wrote back a kind and respectful letter to Mrs. Rebecca, then living at a boarding-house at Florence.—But we are advancing matters.

Our darling Becky's first flight was not very far. She perched upon the French coast at Boulogne, that refuge of so much exiled English innocence; and there lived in rather a genteel, widowed manner, with a *femme de chambre* and a couple of rooms, at an hotel. She dined at the *table d'hôte*, where people thought her very pleasant, and where she entertained her neighbours by stories of her brother, Sir Pitt, and her great London acquaintance; talking that easy, fashionable slipslop, which has so much effect upon certain folks of small breeding. She passed with many of them for a person of importance; she gave little tea-parties in her private room, and shared in the innocent amusements of the place,—in sea-bathing, and in jaunts in open carriages, in strolls on the sands, and in visits to the play. Mrs. Burjoice, the printer's lady, who was boarding with her family at the hotel for the summer, and to whom her Burjoice came of a Saturday and Sunday, voted her charming, until that little rogue of a Burjoice began to pay her too much attention. But there was nothing in the story, only that Becky was always affable, easy, and good-natured — and with men especially.

Numbers of people were going abroad as usual at the end of the season, and Becky had plenty of opportunities of finding out by the behaviour of her acquaintances of the great London world the opinion of "society" as regarded her conduct. One day it was Lady Partlet and her daughters whom Becky confronted as she was walking modestly on Boulogne pier, the cliffs of Albion shining in the distance across the deep blue sea. Lady Partlet marshalled all her daughters round her with a sweep of her parasol, and retreated from the pier darting savage glances at poor little Becky who stood alone there.

On another day the packet came in. It had been blowing fresh, and it always suited Becky's humour to see the droll woe-begone faces of the people as they emerged from the boat. Lady Slingstone happened to be on board this day. Her ladyship had been exceedingly ill in her carriage, and was greatly exhausted and scarcely fit to walk up the plank from the ship to the pier. But all her energies rallied the instant she saw Becky smiling roguishly under a pink bonnet: and giving her a glance of scorn, such as would have shrivelled up most women, she walked into the Custom House quite unsupported. Becky only laughed: but I don't think she liked it. She felt she was alone, quite alone: and the far-off shining cliffs of England were impassable to her.

The behaviour of the men had undergone, too, I don't know what change. Grinstone showed his teeth and laughed in her face with a familiarity that was not pleasant. Little Bob Suckling, who was cap in hand to her three months before, and would walk a mile in the rain to see for her carriage in the line at Gaunt House, was talking to Fitzoof of the Guards (Lord Heehaw's son) one day upon the jetty, as Becky took her walk there. Little Bobby nodded to her over his shoulder, without moving his hat, and continued his conversation with the heir of Heehaw. Tom Raikes tried to walk into her sitting-room at the inn with a cigar in his mouth; but she closed the door upon him and would have locked it only that his fingers were inside. She began to feel that she was very lonely indeed. "If *he'd* been here," she said, "those cowards would never have dared to insult me." She thought about "him" with great sadness, and perhaps longing—about his honest, stupid, constant kindness and fidelity: his never-ceasing obedience; his good humour; his bravery and courage. Very likely she cried, for she was particularly lively, and had put on a little extra rouge when she came down to dinner.

She rouged regularly now: and—and her maid got Cognac for her besides that which was charged in the hotel bill.

Perhaps the insults of the men were not, however, so intolerable to her as the sympathy of certain women. Mrs. Crackenbury and Mrs. Washington White passed through Boulogne on their way to Switzerland. (The party were protected by Colonel Horner, young Beaumoris, and of course old Crackenbury, and Mrs. White's little girl.) *They* did not avoid her. They giggled, cackled, tattled, condoled, consoled, and patronised her until they drove her almost wild with rage. To be patronised by *them!* she thought, as they went away simpering after kissing her. And she heard Beaumoris's laugh ringing on the stair, and knew quite well how to interpret his hilarity.

It was after this visit that Becky, who had paid her weekly bills, Becky who had made herself agreeable to every body in the house, who smiled at the landlady, called the waiters "Monsieur," and paid the chambermaids in politeness and apologies, what far more than compensated for a little niggardliness in point of money (of which Becky never was free), that Becky, we say, received a notice to quit from the landlord, who had been told by some one that she was quite an unfit person to have at his hotel, where English ladies would not sit down with her. And she was forced to fly into lodgings, of which the dulness and solitude were most wearisome to her.

Still she held up, in spite of these rebuffs, and tried to make a character for herself, and conquer scandal. She went to church very regularly, and sang louder than anybody there. She took up the cause of the widows of the shipwrecked fishermen, and gave work and drawings for the Quashyboo Mission; she subscribed to the Assembly and *wouldn't* waltz. In a word, she did everything that was respectable, and that is why we dwell upon this part of her career with more fondness than upon subsequent parts of her history, which are not so pleasant. She saw people avoiding her, and still laboriously smiled upon them; you never could suppose from her countenance what pangs of humiliation she might be enduring inwardly.

Her history was after all a mystery. Parties were divided about her. Some people, who took the trouble to busy themselves in the matter, said that she was the criminal; whilst others vowed that she was as innocent as a lamb, and that her odious husband was in fault. She won over a good many by bursting into tears about her boy, and exhibiting the most frantic grief when his name was mentioned, or she saw anybody like him. She gained good Mrs. Alderney's heart in that way, who was rather the Queen of British Boulogne, and gave the most dinners and balls of all the residents there, by weeping when Master Alderney came from Dr. Swishtail's academy to pass his holidays with his mother. "He and her Rawdon were of the same age, and *so* like," Becky said, in a voice choking with agony; whereas there was five years' difference between the boys' ages, and no more likeness between them than between my respected reader and his humble servant. Wenham, when he was going abroad, on his way to Kissingen to join Lord Steyne, enlightened Mrs. Alderney on this point, and told her how he was much more able to describe little Rawdon than his mamma, who notoriously hated him, and never saw him; how he was thirteen years old, while little Alderney was but nine; fair, while the other darling was dark,—in a word, caused the lady in question to repent of her good humour.

Whenever Becky made a little circle for herself with incredible toils and labour, somebody came and swept it down rudely, and she had all her work to begin over again. It was very hard: very hard; lonely and disheartening.

There was Mrs. Newbright, who took her up for some time, attracted by the sweetness of her singing at church,

and by her proper views upon serious subjects, concerning
which in former days, at Queen's Crawley, Mrs. Becky had
had a good deal of instruction.—Well, she not only took
tracts, but she read them. She worked flannel petticoats for
the Quashyboos—cotton night-caps for the Cocoanut Indians
—painted handscreens for the conversion of the Pope and
the Jews—sate under Mr. Rowls on Wednesdays, Mr. Hug-
gleton on Thursdays, attended two Sunday services at
church, besides Mr. Bawler, the Darbyite, in the evening,
and all in vain. Mrs. Newbright had occasion to correspond
with the Countess of Southdown about the Warmingpan
Fund for the Feejee Islanders (for the management of which
admirable charity both these ladies formed part of a female
committee), and having mentioned her "sweet friend," Mrs.
Rawdon Crawley, the Dowager Countess wrote back such a
letter regarding Becky, with such particulars, hints, facts,
falsehoods, and general comminations, that intimacy between
Mrs. Newbright and Mrs. Crawley ceased forthwith: and
all the serious world of Tours, where this misfortune took
place, immediately parted company with the reprobate. Those
who know the English Colonies abroad know that we carry
with us our pride, pills, prejudices, Harvey-sauces, cayenne-
peppers, and other Lares, making a little Britain wherever we
settle down.

From one colony to another Becky fled uneasily. From
Boulogne to Dieppe, from Dieppe to Caen, from Caen to
Tours—trying with all her might to be respectable, and
alas! always found out some day or other, and pecked out
of the cage by the real daws.

Mrs. Hook Eagles took her up at one of these places:—
a woman without a blemish in her character, and a house
in Portman Square. She was staying at the hotel at Dieppe,
whither Becky fled, and they made each other's acquaintance
first at sea, where they were swimming together, and subsequently at the *table d'hôte* of the hotel. Mrs. Eagles had
heard,—who indeed had not?—some of the scandal of the
Steyne affair; but after a conversation with Becky, she pronounced that Mrs. Crawley was an angel, her husband a
ruffian, Lord Steyne an unprincipled wretch, as everybody
knew, and the whole case against Mrs. Crawley, an infamous

and wicked conspiracy of that rascal Wenham. "If you were a man of any spirit, Mr. Eagles, you would box the wretch's ears the next time you see him at the Club," she said to her husband. But Eagles was only a quiet old gentleman, husband to Mrs. Eagles, with a taste for geology, and not tall enough to reach anybody's ears.

Mrs. Eagles then patronised Mrs. Rawdon, took her to live with her at her own house at Paris, quarrelled with the ambassador's wife because she would not receive her *protégée,* and did all that lay in woman's power to keep Becky straight in the paths of virtue and good repute.

Becky was very respectable and orderly at first, but the life of humdrum virtue grew utterly tedious to her before long. It was the same routine every day, the same dulness and comfort, the same drive over the same stupid Bois de Boulogne, the same company of an evening, the same Blair's Sermon of a Sunday night—the same opera always being acted over and over again : Becky was dying of weariness, when, luckily for her, young Mr. Eagles came from Cambridge, and his mother, seeing the impression which her little friend made upon him, straightaway gave Becky warning.

Then she tried keeping house with a female friend; then the double *ménage* began to quarrel and get into debt. Then she determined upon a boarding-house existence, and lived for some time at that famous mansion kept by Madame de Saint Amour, in the Rue Royale, at Paris, where she began exercising her graces and fascinations upon the shabby dandies and fly-blown beauties who frequented her landlady's *salons.* Becky loved society, and, indeed, could no more exist without it than an opium-eater without his dram, and she was happy enough at the period of her boarding-house life. "The women here are as amusing as those in May Fair," she told an old London friend who met her—"only, their dresses are not quite so fresh. The men wear cleaned gloves, and are sad rogues, certainly, but they are not worse than Jack This, and Tom That. The mistress of the house is a little vulgar, but I don't think she is so vulgar as Lady ——" and here she named the name of a great leader of fashion that I would die rather than reveal. In fact, when you saw Madame de Saint Amour's rooms lighted up of a night, men with *plaques* and *cordons* at the *écarté* tables, and the women at a little distance, you might fancy yourself for a while in good society, and that Madame was a real Countess. Many people did so fancy: and Becky was for a while one of the most dashing ladies of the Countess's *salons*.

But it is probable that her old creditors of 1815 found her out and caused her to leave Paris, for the poor little woman was forced to fly from the city rather suddenly; and went thence to Brussels.

How well she remembered the place! She grinned as she looked up at the little *entresol* which she had occupied and thought of the Bareacres family, bawling for horses and flight, as their carriage stood in the *porte-cochère* of the hotel. She went to Waterloo and to Laeken, where George Osborne's monument much struck her. She made a little sketch of it. "That poor Cupid!" she said; "how dreadfully he was in love with me, and what a fool he was! I wonder whether little Emmy is alive. It was a good little creature: and that fat brother of hers. I have his funny fat picture still among my papers. They were kind, simple people."

At Brussels Becky arrived, recommended by Madame de Saint Amour to her friend, Madame la Comtesse de Borodino, widow of Napoleon's General, the famous Count de Borodino, who was left with no resource by the deceased hero but that of a *table-d'hôte* and an *écarté* table. Second rate dandies and *roués*, widow-ladies who always have a law-suit, and very simple English folks, who fancy they see "Continental society" at these houses, put down their money, or ate their meals, at Madame de Borodino's tables. The gallant young fellows treated the company round to champagne at the *table-d'hôte*, rode out with the women, or hired horses on country excursions, clubbed money to take boxes at the play or the Opera, betted over the fair shoulders of the ladies at the *écarté* tables, and wrote home to their parents, in Devonshire, about their felicitous introduction to foreign society.

Here, as at Paris, Becky was a boarding-house queen: and ruled in select *pensions*. She never refused the champagne, or the bouquets, or the drives into the country, or the private boxes; but what she preferred was the *écarté* at night,—and she played audaciously. First she played only for a little, then for five-franc pieces, then for Napoleons, then for notes: then she would not be able to pay her month's *pension:* then she borrowed from the young gentlemen: then she got into cash again, and bullied Madame de Borodino, whom she had coaxed and wheedled before: then she was playing for ten sous at a time, and in a dire state of poverty; then her quarter's allowance would come in, and she would pay off Madame de Borodino's score: and would once more take the cards against Monsieur de Rossignol, or the Chevalier de Raff.

When Becky left Brussels, the sad truth is, that she owed three months' *pension* to Madame de Borodino, of which fact, and of the gambling, and of the drinking, and of the going down on her knees to the Reverend Mr. Muff, Ministre Anglican, and borrowing money of him, and of her coaxing and flirting with Milor Noodle, son of Sir Noodle, pupil of the Rev. Mr. Muff, whom she used to take into her private room, and of whom she won large sums at *écarté*—of which fact, I say, and of a hundred of her other knaveries, the Countess de Borodino informs every English person who stops at her establishment, and announces that Madame Rawdon was no better than a *vipère*.

So our little wanderer went about setting up her tent in various cities of Europe, as restless as Ulysses or Bampfylde Moore Carew. Her taste for disrespectability grew more and more remarkable. She became a perfect Bohemian ere long, herding with people whom it would make your hair stand on end to meet.

There is no town of any mark in Europe but it has its little colony of English raffs—men whose names Mr. Hemp the officer reads out periodically at the Sheriffs' Court—young gentlemen of very good family often, only that the latter disowns them; frequenters of billiard-rooms and estaminets, patrons of foreign races and gaming-tables. They people the debtors' prisons—they drink and swagger—they fight and brawl—they run away without paying—they have duels with French and German officers—they cheat Mr. Spooney at *écarté*—they get the money, and drive off to

Baden in magnificent britzkas—they try their infallible mar-tingale, and lurk about the tables with empty pockets, shabby bullies, penniless bucks, until they can swindle a Jew banker with a sham bill of exchange, or find another Mr. Spooney to rob. The alternations of splendour and misery which these people undergo are very queer to view. Their life must be one of great excitement. Becky—must it be owned?—took to this life, and took to it not unkindly. She went about from town to town among these Bohemians. The lucky Mrs. Rawdon was known at every play-table in Germany. She and Madame de Cruchecassée kept house at Florence to-gether. It is said she was ordered out of Munich; and my friend Mr. Frederick Pigeon avers that it was at her house at Lausanne that he was hocussed at supper and lost eight hundred pounds to Major Loder and the Honourable Mr. Deuceace. We are bound, you see, to give some account of Becky's biography; but of this part, the less, perhaps, that is said the better.

They say, that when Mrs. Crawley was particularly down on her luck, she gave concerts and lessons in music here and there. There was a Madame de Raudon, who certainly had a *matinée musicale* at Wildbad, accompanied by Herr Spoff, premier pianist to the Hospodar of Wallachia, and my little friend Mr. Eaves, who knew everybody, and had travelled everywhere, always used to declare that he was at Strasburg in the year 1830, when a certain Madame Re-becque made her appearance in the opera of the "Dame Blanche," giving occasion to a furious row in the theatre there. She was hissed off the stage by the audience, partly from her own incompetency, but chiefly from the ill-advised sympathy of some persons in the *parquet*, (where the officers of the garrison had their admissions;) and Eaves was certain that the unfortunate *débutante* in question was no other than Mrs. Rawdon Crawley.

She was, in fact, no better than a vagabond upon this earth. When she got her money she gambled; when she had gambled it she was put to shifts to live; who knows how or by what means she succeeded? It is said that she was once seen at St. Petersburg, but was summarily dis-missed from that capital by the police, so that there cannot be any possibility of truth in the report that she was a Russian spy at Toplitz and Vienna afterwards. I have even been informed, that at Paris she discovered a relation of her own, no less a person than her maternal grandmother, who was not by any means a Montmorenci, but a hideous old box-opener at a theatre on the Boulevards. The meeting between them, of which other persons, as it is hinted elsewhere, seem to have been acquainted, must have been a very affecting interview. The present historian can give no certain details regarding the event.

It happened at Rome once, that Mrs. de Rawdon's half-year's salary had just been paid into the principal banker's there, and, as everybody who had a balance of above five hundred scudi was invited to the balls which this prince of merchants gave during the winter, Becky had the honour of a card, and appeared at one of the Prince and Princess Polonia's splendid evening entertainments. The Princess was of the family of Pompili, lineally descended from the second king of Rome, and Egeria of the house of Olympus, while the Prince's grandfather, Alessandro Polonia, sold wash-balls, essences, tobacco, and pocket-handkerchiefs, ran errands for gentlemen, and lent money in a small way. All the great company in Rome thronged to his saloons—Princes, Dukes, Ambassadors, artists, fiddlers, monsignori, young bears with their leaders—every rank and condition of man. His halls blazed with light and magnificence; were resplendent with gilt frames (containing pictures), and dubious antiques; and the enormous gilt crown and arms of the princely owner, a gold mushroom on a crimson field (the colour of the pocket-handkerchiefs which he sold), and the silver fountain of the Pompili family shone all over the roof, doors, and panels of the house, and over the grand velvet baldaquins prepared to receive Popes and Emperors.

So Becky, who had arrived in the diligence from Florence, and was lodged at an inn in a very modest way, got a card for Prince Polonia's entertainment, and her maid dressed her with unusual care, and she went to this fine ball leaning on the arm of Major Loder, with whom she happened to be travelling at the time—(the same man who shot Prince Ravoli at Naples the next year, and was caned by Sir John

Buckskin for carrying four kings in his hat besides those
which he used in playing at *écarté*)—and this pair went
into the rooms together, and Becky saw a number of old faces
which she remembered in happier days, when she was not
innocent, but not found out. Major Loder knew a great
number of foreigners, keen-looking whiskered men with dirty
striped ribbons in their buttonholes, and a very small display
of linen; but his own countrymen, it might be remarked,
eschewed the Major. Becky, too, knew some ladies here and
there—French widows, dubious Italian countesses, whose
husbands had treated them ill—faugh—what shall we say,
we who have moved among some of the finest company of
Vanity Fair, of this refuse and sediment of rascals? If we
play, let it be with clean cards, and not with this dirty
pack. But every man who has formed one of the innumerable army of travellers has seen these marauding irregulars hanging on, like Nym and Pistol, to the main force;
wearing the king's colours, and boasting of his commission,
but pillaging for themselves, and occasionally gibbeted by
the road-side.

Well, she was hanging on the arm of Major Loder, and
they went through the rooms together, and drank a great
quantity of champagne at the buffet, where the people, and
especially the Major's irregular corps, struggled furiously
for refreshments, of which when the pair had had enough,
they pushed on until they reached the Duchess's own pink
velvet saloon, at the end of the suite of apartments (where
the statue of the Venus is, and the great Venice looking-
glasses, framed in silver,) and where the princely family
were entertaining their most distinguished guests at a round
table at supper. It was just such a little select banquet
as that of which Becky recollected that she had partaken at
Lord Steyne's—and there he sat at Polonia's table, and she
saw him.

The scar cut by the diamond on his white, bald, shining
forehead, made a burning red mark; his red whiskers were
dyed of a purple hue, which made his pale face look still
paler. He wore his collar and orders, his blue ribbon and
garter. He was a greater prince than any there, though
there was a reigning duke and a royal highness, with their

princesses, and near his lordship was seated the beautiful
Countess of Belladonna, née de Glandier, whose husband
(the Count Paolo della Belladonna), so well known for his
brilliant entomological collections, had been long absent on
a mission to the Emperor of Morocco.

When Becky beheld that familiar and illustrious face,
how vulgar all of a sudden did Major Loder appear to her,
and how that odious Captain Rook did smell of tobacco!
In one instant she reassumed her fine-ladyship, and tried
to look and feel as if she were in May Fair once more.
"That woman looks stupid and ill-humoured," she thought;
"I am sure she can't amuse him.   No, he must be bored
by her—he never was by me."   A hundred such touching
hopes, fears, and memories palpitated in her little heart, as
she looked with her brightest eyes (the rouge which she
wore up to her eyelids made them twinkle) towards the
great nobleman.   Of a Star and Garter night Lord Steyne
used also to put on his grandest manner, and to look and
speak like a great prince, as he was.   Becky admired him
smilingly sumptuously, easy, lofty, and stately.   Ah, *bon
Dieu*, what a pleasant companion he was, what a brilliant
wit, what a rich fund of talk, what a grand manner!—and
she had exchanged this for Major Loder, reeking of cigars
and brandy-and-water, and Captain Rook with his horse-
jockey jokes, and prize-ring slang, and their like.   "I
wonder whether he will know me," she thought.   Lord
Steyne was talking and laughing with a great and illustrious lady at his side, when he looked up and saw Becky.

She was all over in a flutter as their eyes met, and she
put on the very best smile she could muster, and dropped
him a little timid, imploring curtsey.   He stared aghast
at her for a minute, as Macbeth might on beholding Banquo's
sudden appearance at his ball-supper; and remained looking
at her with open mouth, when that horrid Major Loder
pulled her away.

"Come away into the supper-room, Mrs. R.," was that
gentleman's remark: "seeing these nobs grubbing away has
made me peckish too.   Let's go and try the old governor's
champagne."   Becky thought the Major had had a great deal
too much already.

The day after she went to walk on the Pincian Hill—the
Hyde Park of the Roman idlers — possibly in hopes to
have another sight of Lord Steyne. But she met another
acquaintance there: it was Mr. Fiche, his lordship's confidential man, who came up nodding to her rather familiarly,
and putting a finger to his hat. "I knew that Madame was
here," he said; "I followed her from her hotel. I have some
advice to give Madame."

"From the Marquis of Steyne?" Becky asked, resuming
as much of her dignity as she could muster, and not a little
agitated by hope and expectation.

"No," said the valet; "it is from me. Rome is very
unwholesome."

"Not at this season, Monsieur Fiche,—not till after Easter."

"I tell Madame it is unwholesome now. There is always
malaria for some people. That cursed marsh wind kills
many at all seasons. Look, Madame Crawley, you were
always *bon enfant,* and I have an interest in you, *parole
d' honneur.* Be warned. Go away from Rome, I tell you—
or you will be ill and die."

Becky laughed, though in rage and fury. "What! assassi-
nate poor little me?" she said. "How romantic! Does my
lord carry bravos for couriers, and stilettos in the fourgons?
Bah! I will stay, if but to plague him. I have those who
will defend me whilst I am here."

It was Monsieur Fiche's turn to laugh now. "Defend
you," he said, "and who? The Major, the Captain, any
one of those gambling men whom Madame sees, would
take her life for a hundred louis. We know things about
Major Loder (he is no more a Major than I am my Lord
the Marquis) which would send him to the galleys or worse.
We know everything, and have friends everywhere. We
know whom you saw at Paris, and what relations you found
there. Yes, Madame may stare, but we do. How was it
that no minister on the Continent would receive Madame?
She has offended somebody: who never forgives—whose
rage redoubled when he saw you. He was like a madman
last night when he came home. Madame de Belladonna
made him a scene about you, and fired off in one of her
furies."

"O, it was Madame de Belladonna, was it?" Becky said, relieved a little, for the information she had just got had scared her.

"No—she does not matter—she is always jealous. I tell you it was Monseigneur. You did wrong to show yourself to him. And if you stay here you will repent it. Mark my words. Go. Here is my lord's carriage" — and seizing Becky's arm, he rushed down an alley of the garden as Lord Steyne's barouche, blazing with heraldic devices, came whirling along the avenue, borne by the almost priceless horses, and bearing Madame de Belladonna lolling on the cushions, dark, sulky, and blooming, a King Charles in her lap, a white parasol swaying over her head, and old Steyne stretched at her side with a livid face and ghastly eyes. Hate, or anger, or desire, caused them to brighten now and then still; but ordinarily, they gave no light, and seemed tired of looking out on a world of which almost all the pleasure and all the best beauty had palled upon the worn-out wicked old man.

"Monseigneur has never recovered the shock of that night, never," Monsieur Fiche whispered to Mrs. Crawley as the carriage flashed by, and she peeped out at it from behind the shrubs that hid her. "That was a consolation at any rate," Becky thought.

Whether my lord really had murderous intentions towards Mrs. Becky as Monsieur Fiche said—(since Monseigneur's death he has returned to his native country, where he lives much respected, and has purchased from his Prince the title of Baron Ficci),—and the factotum objected to have to do with assassination; or whether he simply had a commission to frighten Mrs. Crawley out of a city where his lordship proposed to pass the winter, and the sight of her would be eminently disagreeable to the great nobleman, is a point which has never been ascertained: but the threat had its effect upon the little woman, and she sought no more to intrude herself upon the presence of her old patron.

Everybody knows the melancholy end of that nobleman, which befell at Naples two months after the French Revolution of 1830: when the Most Honourable George Gustavus, Marquis of Steyne, Earl of Gaunt and of Gaunt Castle, in the Peerage of Ireland, Viscount Hellborough, Baron Pitchley and Grillsby, a Knight of the Most Noble Order of the Garter, of the Golden Fleece of Spain, of the Russian Order of Saint Nicholas of the First Class, of the Turkish Order of the Crescent, First Lord of the Powder Closet and Groom of the Back Stairs, Colonel of the Gaunt or Regent's Own Regiment of Militia, a Trustee of the British Museum, an Elder Brother of the Trinity House, a Governor of the White Friars, and D.C.L.,—died after a series of fits, brought on, as the papers said, by the shock occasioned to his lordship's sensibilities by the downfall of the ancient French monarchy.

An eloquent catalogue appeared in a weekly print, describing his virtues, his magnificence, his talents, and his good actions. His sensibility, his attachment to the illustrious House of Bourbon, with which he claimed an alliance, were such that he could not survive the misfortunes of his august kinsmen. His body was buried at Naples, and his heart—that heart which always beat with every generous and noble emotion—was brought back to Castle Gaunt in a silver urn. "In him," Mr. Wagg said, "the poor and the Fine Arts have lost a beneficent patron, society one of its most brilliant ornaments, and England one of her loftiest patriots and statesmen," &c., &c.

His will was a good deal disputed, and an attempt was made to force from Madame de Belladonna the celebrated jewel called the "Jew's-eye" diamond, which his lordship always wore on his forefinger, and which it was said that she removed from it after his lamented demise. But his confidential friend and attendant, Monsieur Fiche, proved that the ring had been presented to the said Madame de Belladonna two days before the Marquis's death; as were the bank-notes, jewels, Neapolitan and French bonds, &c., found in his lordship's secretaire, and claimed by his heirs from that injured woman.

CHAPTER XXX

Full of Business and Pleasure

THE day after the meeting at the play-table, Jos had himself arrayed with unusual care and splendour, and without thinking it necessary to say a word to any member of his family regarding the occurrences of the previous night, or asking for their company in his walk, he sallied forth at an early hour, and was presently seen making inquiries at the door of the Elephant Hotel. In consequence of the *fêtes* the house was full of company, the tables in the street were already surrounded by persons smoking and drinking the national small-beer, the public rooms were in a cloud of smoke, and Mr. Jos having, in his pompous way, and with his clumsy German, made inquiries for the person of whom he was in search, was directed to the very top of the house, above the first-floor rooms where some travelling pedlars had lived, and were exhibiting their jewelry and brocades; above the second-floor apartments occupied by the *état major* of the gambling firm; above the third-floor rooms, tenanted by the band of renowned Bohemian vaulters and tumblers; and so on to the little cabins of the roof, where, among students, bag-men, small tradesmen, and country-folks, come in for the festival, Becky had found a little nest;—as dirty a little refuge as ever beauty lay hid in.

Becky liked the life. She was at home with everybody in the place, pedlars, punters, tumblers, students and all. She was of a wild, roving nature, inherited from father and mother, who were both Bohemians, by taste and circumstance; if a lord was not by, she would talk to his courier with the greatest pleasure; the din, the stir, the drink, the smoke, the tattle of the Hebrew pedlars, the solemn, braggart ways of the poor tumblers, the *sournois* talk of the gambling-table officials, the songs and swagger of the students, and the general buzz and hum of the place had pleased and tickled the little woman, even when her luck was down, and she had not wherewithal to pay her bill. How pleasant was all the bustle to her now that her purse was full of the money which little Georgy had won for her the night before!

As Jos came creaking and puffing up the final stairs, and was speechless when he got to the landing, and began to wipe his face and then to look for No. 92, the room where he was directed to seek for the person he wanted, the door of the opposite chamber, No. 90, was open, and a student, in jack-boots and a dirty schlafrock, was lying on the bed smoking a long pipe; whilst another student in long yellow hair and a braided coat, exceeding smart and dirty too, was actually on his knees at No. 92, bawling through the key-hole supplications to the person within.

"Go away," said a well-known voice, which made Jos thrill, "I expect somebody; I expect my grandpapa. He mustn't see you there."

"Angel Engländerin!" bellowed the kneeling student with the whity-brown ringlets and the large finger-ring, "do take compassion upon us. Make an appointment. Dine with me and Fritz at the inn in the park. We will have roast pheasants and porter, plum-pudding and French wine. We shall die if you don't."

"That we will," said the young nobleman on the bed; and this colloquy Jos overheard, though he did not comprehend it, for the reason that he had never studied the language in which it was carried on.

"*Newmero kattervang dooze, si vous plait,*" Jos said in his grandest manner, when he was able to speak.

"*Quater fang tooce!*" said the student, starting up, and he bounced into his own room, where he locked the door, and where Jos heard him laughing with his comrade on the bed.

The gentleman from Bengal was standing disconcerted by this incident, when the door of the 92 opened of itself, and Becky's little head peeped out full of archness and mischief. She lighted on Jos. "It's you," she said, coming out. "How I have been waiting for you! Stop! not yet—in one minute you shall come in." In that instant she put a rouge-pot, a brandy bottle, and a plate of broken meat into the bed, gave one smooth to her hair, and finally let in her visitor.

She had, by way of morning robe, a pink domino, a trifle faded and soiled, and marked here and there with pomatum; but her arms shone out from the loose sleeves of the dress very white and fair, and it was tied round her little waist, so as not ill to set off the trim little figure of the wearer. She led Jos by the hand into her garret. "Come in," she said. "Come, and talk to me. Sit yonder on the chair;" and she gave the Civilian's hand a little squeeze, and laughingly placed him upon it. As for herself, she placed herself on the bed —not on the bottle and plate, you may be sure—on which Jos might have reposed, had he chosen that seat; and so there she sate and talked with her old admirer.

"How little years have changed you," she said, with a look of tender interest. "I should have known you anywhere. What a comfort it is amongst strangers to see once more the frank honest face of an old friend!"

The frank honest face, to tell the truth, at this moment bore any expression but one of openness and honesty: it was, on the contrary, much perturbed and puzzled in look. Jos was surveying the queer little apartment in which he found his old flame. One of her gowns hung over the bed, another depending from a hook of the door: her bonnet obscured half the looking-glass, on which, too, lay the prettiest little pair of bronze boots; a French novel was on the table by the bed-side, with a candle, not of wax. Becky thought of popping that into the bed, too, but she only put in the little paper night-cap with which she had put 'the candle out on going to sleep.

"I should have known you anywhere," she continued, "a woman never forgets some things. And you were the first man I ever—I ever saw."

"Was I, really?" said Jos. "God bless my soul, you—you don't say so."

"When I came with your sister from Chiswick, I was scarcely more than a child," Becky said. "How is that dear love? Oh, her husband was a sad wicked man, and of course it was of me that the poor dear was jealous. As if I cared about him, heigho! when there was somebody—but no—don't let us talk of old times;" and she passed her handkerchief with the tattered lace across her eyelids.

"Is not this a strange place," she continued, "for a woman, who has lived in a very different world, too, to be found in? I have had so many griefs and wrongs, Joseph Sedley, I have been made to suffer so cruelly, that I am almost made mad sometimes. I can't stay still in any place, but wander about always restless and unhappy. All my friends have been false to me—all. There is no such thing as an honest man in the world. I was the truest wife that ever lived, though I married my husband out of pique, because somebody else—but never mind that. I was true, and he trampled upon me, and deserted me. I was the fondest mother. I had but one child, one darling, one hope, one joy, which I held to my heart with a mother's affection, which was my life, my prayer, my—my blessing; and they—they tore it from me—tore it from me;" and she put her hand to her heart with a passionate gesture of despair, burying her face for a moment on the bed.

The brandy-bottle inside clinked up against the plate which held the cold sausage. Both were moved, no doubt, by the exhibition of so much grief. Max and Fritz were at the door listening with wonder to Mrs. Becky's sobs and cries. Jos, too, was a good deal frightened and affected at seeing his old flame in this condition. And she began, forthwith, to tell her story—a tale so neat, simple, and artless, that it was quite evident from hearing her, that if ever there was a white-robed angel escaped from heaven to be subject to the infernal machinations and villainy of fiends here below, that spotless being—that miserable unsullied martyr, was present on the bed before Jos—on the bed, sitting on the brandy-bottle.

They had a very long, amicable, and confidential talk there; in the course of which, Jos Sedley was somehow made aware (but in a manner that did not in the least scare or offend him) that Becky's heart had first learned to beat at his enchanting presence: that George Osborne had certainly paid an unjustifiable court to *her*, which might account for Amelia's jealousy, and their little rupture; but that Becky never gave the least encouragement to the unfortunate officer, and that she had never ceased to think about Jos from the very first day she had seen him, though, of course, her duties as a married woman were paramount—duties which she had always preserved, and would, to her dying day, or until the proverbially bad climate in which Colonel Crawley was living should release her from a yoke which his cruelty had rendered odious to her.

Jos went away, convinced that she was the most virtuous, as she was one of the most fascinating of women, and revolving in his mind all sorts of benevolent schemes for her welfare. Her persecutions ought to be ended: she ought to return to the society of which she was an ornament. He would see what ought to be done. She must quit that place, and take a quiet lodging. Amelia must come and see her, and befriend her. He would go and settle about it, and consult with the Major. She wept tears of heartfelt gratitude as she parted from him, and pressed his hand as the gallant stout gentleman stooped down to kiss hers.

So Becky bowed Jos out of her little garret with as much grace as if it was a palace of which she did the honours; and that heavy gentleman having disappeared down the stairs, Max and Fritz came out of their hole, pipe in mouth, and she amused herself by mimicking Jos to them as she munched her cold bread and sausage and took draughts of her favourite brandy-and-water.

Jos walked over to Dobbin's lodgings with great solemnity, and there imparted to him the affecting history with which he had just been made acquainted, without, however, mentioning the play-business of the night before. And the two gentlemen were laying their heads together, and consulting as to the best means of being useful to Mrs. Becky, while she was finishing her interrupted *déjeuner à la fourchette*.

How was it that she had come to that little town? How was it that she had no friends and was wandering about alone? Little boys at school are taught in their earliest Latin book, that the path of Avernus is very easy of descent. Let us skip over the interval in the history of her downward progress. She was not worse now than she had been in the days of her prosperity:—only a little down on her luck.

As for Mrs. Amelia, she was a woman of such a soft and foolish disposition, that when she heard of anybody unhappy, her heart straightway melted towards the sufferer; and as she had never thought or done anything mortally guilty herself, she had not that abhorrence for wickedness which distinguishes moralists much more knowing. If she spoiled everybody who came near her with kindness and compliments, —if she begged pardon of all her servants for troubling them to answer the bell,—if she apologised to a shop-boy who showed her a piece of silk, or made a curtsey to a street-sweeper with a complimentary remark upon the elegant state of his crossing—and she was almost capable of every one of these follies—the notion that an old acquaintance was miserable was sure to soften her heart; nor would she hear of anybody's being deservedly unhappy. A world under such legislation as hers would not be a very orderly place of abode; but there are not many women, at least not of the rulers, who are of her sort. This lady, I believe, would have abolished all gaols, punishments, handcuffs, whippings, poverty, sickness, hunger, in the world; and was such a mean-spirited creature, that—we are obliged to confess it—she could even forget a mortal injury.

When the Major heard from Jos of the sentimental adventure which had just befallen the latter, he was not, it must be owned, nearly as much interested as the gentleman from Bengal. On the contrary, his excitement was quite the reverse from a pleasurable one; he made use of a brief but improper expression regarding a poor woman in distress, saying, in fact,—"the little minx, has she come to light again?" He never had had the slightest liking for her; but had heartily mistrusted her from the very first moment when her green eyes had looked at, and turned away from, his own.

"That little devil brings mischief wherever she goes," the Major said, disrespectfully. "Who knows what sort of life she has been leading? and what business has she here abroad and alone? Don't tell me about persecutors and enemies; an honest woman always has friends, and never is separated from her family. Why has she left her husband? He may have been disreputable and wicked, as you say. He always was. I remember the confounded blackleg, and the way in which he used to cheat and hoodwink poor George. Wasn't there a scandal about their separation? I think I heard something," cried out Major Dobbin, who did not care much about gossip; and whom Jos tried in vain to convince that

Mrs. Becky was in all respects a most injured and virtuous female.

"Well, well; let's ask Mrs. George," said that arch-diplomatist of a Major. "Only let us go and consult *her*. I suppose you will allow that *she* is a good judge at any rate, and knows what is right in such matters."

"Hm! Emmy is very well," said Jos, who did not happen to be in love with his sister.

"Very well? by Gad, sir, she's the finest lady I ever met in my life," bounced out the Major. "I say at once, let us go and ask her if this woman ought to be visited or not—I will be content with her verdict." Now this odious, artful rogue of a Major was thinking in his own mind that he was sure of his case. Emmy, he remembered, was at one time cruelly and deservedly jealous of Rebecca, never mentioned her name but with a shrinking and terror—a jealous woman never forgives, thought Dobbin: and so the pair went across the street to Mrs. George's house, where she was contentedly warbling at a music-lesson with Madame Strumpff.

When that lady took her leave, Jos opened the business with his usual pomp of words. "Amelia, my dear," said he, "I have just had the most extraordinary—yes—God bless my soul! the most extraordinary adventure—an old friend—yes, a most interesting old friend of yours, and I may say in old times, has just arrived here, and I should like you to see her."

"Her!" said Amelia, "who is it? Major Dobbin, if you please not to break my scissors." The Major was twirling them round by the little chain from which they sometimes hung to their lady's waist, and was thereby endangering his own eye.

"It is a woman whom I dislike very much," said the Major, doggedly; "and whom you have no cause to love."

"It is Rebecca, I'm sure it is Rebecca," Amelia said, blushing, and being very much agitated.

"You are right; you always are," Dobbin answered. Brussels, Waterloo, old, old times, griefs, pangs, remembrances, rushed back into Amelia's gentle heart, and caused a cruel agitation there.

"Don't let me see her," Emmy continued. "I couldn't see her."

"I told you so," Dobbin said to Jos.

"She is very unhappy, and—and that sort of thing," Jos urged. "She is very poor and unprotected: and has been ill —exceedingly ill—and that scoundrel of a husband has deserted her."

"Ah!" said Amelia.

"She hasn't a friend in the world," Jos went on, not undexterously; "and she said she thought she might trust in you. She's so miserable, Emmy. She has been almost mad with grief. Her story quite affected me:—'pon my word and honour, it did—never was such a cruel persecution borne so angelically, I may say. Her family has been most cruel to her."

"Poor creature!" Amelia said.

"And if she can get no friend, she says she thinks she'll die," Jos proceeded, in a low tremulous voice.—"God bless my soul! do you know that she tried to kill herself? She carries laudanum with her—I saw the bottle in her room— such a miserable little room—at a third-rate house, the Elephant, up in the roof at the top of all. I went there."

This did not seem to affect Emmy. She even smiled a little. Perhaps she figured Jos to herself panting up the stair.

"She's beside herself with grief," he resumed. "The agonies that woman has endured are quite frightful to hear of. She had a little boy, of the same age as Georgy."

"Yes, yes, I think I remember," Emmy remarked. "Well?"

"The most beautiful child ever seen," Jos said, who was very fat, and easily moved, and had been touched by the story Becky told; "a perfect angel, who adored his mother. The ruffians tore him shrieking out of her arms, and have never allowed him to see her."

"Dear Joseph," Emmy cried out, starting up at once, "let us go and see her this minute." And she ran into her adjoining bed-chamber, tied on her bonnet in a flutter, came out with her shawl on her arm, and ordered Dobbin to follow.

He went and put her shawl—it was a white Cashmere, consigned to her by the Major himself from India—over her shoulders. He saw there was nothing for it but to obey; and she put her hand into his arm, and they went away.

"It is number 92, up four pair of stairs," Jos said, perhaps not very willing to ascend the steps again; but he placed himself in the window of his drawing-room, which commands the place on which the Elephant stands, and saw the pair marching through the market.

It was as well that Becky saw them too from her garret; for she and the two students were chattering and laughing there; they had been joking about the appearance of Becky's grandpapa—whose arrival and departure they had witnessed —but she had time to dismiss them, and have her little room clear before the landlord of the Elephant, who knew that Mrs. Osborne was a great favourite at the Serene Court, and respected her accordingly, led the way up the stairs to the roof-story, encouraging Miladi and the Herr Major as they achieved the ascent.

"Gracious lady, gracious lady!" said the landlord, knocking at Becky's door; he had called her Madame the day before, and was by no means courteous to her.

"Who is it?" Becky said, putting out her head, and she gave a little scream. There stood Emmy in a tremble, and Dobbin, the tall Major, with his cane.

He stood still watching, and very much interested at the scene; but Emmy sprang forward with open arms towards Rebecca, and forgave her at that moment, and embraced her and kissed her with all her heart. Ah, poor wretch, when was your lip pressed before by such pure kisses?

CHAPTER XXXI

AMANTIUM IRÆ

FRANKNESS and kindness like Amelia's were likely to touch even such a hardened little reprobate as Becky. She returned Emmy's caresses and kind speeches with something very like gratitude, and an emotion which, if it was not lasting, for a moment was almost genuine. That was a lucky stroke of hers about the child "torn from her arms shrieking." It was by that harrowing misfortune that Becky had won her friend back, and it was one of the very first points, we may be certain, upon which our poor simple little Emmy began to talk to her new-found acquaintance.

"And so they took your darling child from you?" our simpleton cried out. "Oh, Rebecca, my poor dear suffering friend, I know what it is to lose a boy, and to feel for those who have lost one. But please Heaven yours will be restored to you, as a merciful merciful Providence has brought me back mine."

"The child, my child? Oh, yes, my agonies were frightful," Becky owned, not perhaps without a twinge of conscience. It jarred upon her, to be obliged to commence instantly to tell lies in reply to so much confidence and simplicity. But that is the misfortune of beginning with this kind of forgery. When one fib becomes due as it were, you must forge another to take up the old acceptance; and so the stock of your lies in circulation inevitably multiplies, and the danger of detection increases every day.

"My agonies," Becky continued, "were terrible (I hope she won't sit down on the bottle) when they took him away from me; I thought I should die; but I fortunately had a brain fever, during which my doctor gave me up, and—and I recovered, and—and here I am, poor and friendless."

"How old is he?" Emmy asked.

"Eleven," said Becky.

"Eleven!" cried the other. "Why, he was born the same year with Georgy, who is—"

"I know, I know," Becky cried out, who had in fact quite forgotten all about little Rawdon's age. "Grief has made me forget so many things, dearest Amelia. I am very much changed: half wild sometimes. He was eleven when they took him away from me. Bless his sweet face; I have never seen it again."

"Was he fair or dark?" went on that absurd little Emmy, "Show me his hair."

Becky almost laughed at her simplicity. "Not to-day, love, —some other time, when my trunks arrive from Leipzig, whence I came to this place,—and a little drawing of him, which I made in happy days."

"Poor Becky, poor Becky!" said Emmy. "How thankful, how thankful I ought to be;" (though I doubt whether that practice of piety inculcated upon us by our womankind in early youth, namely, to be thankful because we are better off than somebody else, be a very rational religious exercise;) and then she began to think as usual, how her son was the handsomest, the best, and the cleverest boy in the whole world.

"You will see my Georgy," was the best thing Emmy could think of to console Becky. If anything could make her comfortable that would.

And so the two women continued talking for an hour or more, during which Becky had the opportunity of giving her new friend a full and complete version of her private history. She showed how her marriage with Rawdon Crawley had always been viewed by the family with feelings of the utmost hostility; how her sister-in-law (an artful woman) had poisoned her husband's mind against her; how he had formed odious connections, which had estranged his affections from her; how she had borne everything—poverty, neglect, coldness, from the being whom she most loved—and all for the sake of her child; how, finally, and by the most flagrant outrage, she had been driven into demanding a separation from her husband. when the wretch did not scruple to ask that she should sacrifice her own fair fame so that he might procure advancement through the means of a very great and powerful but unprincipled man—the Marquis of Steyne, indeed. The atrocious monster!

This part of her eventful history Becky gave with the utmost feminine delicacy, and the most indignant virtue. Forced to fly her husband's roof by this insult, the coward had pursued his revenge by taking her child from her. And thus Becky said she was a wanderer, poor, unprotected, friendless, and wretched.

Emmy received this story, which was told at some length, as those persons who are acquainted with her character may imagine that she would. She quivered with indignation at the account of the conduct of the miserable Rawdon and the unprincipled Steyne. Her eyes made notes of admiration for every one of the sentences in which Becky described the persecutions of her aristocratic relatives, and the falling away of her husband. (Becky did not abuse him. She spoke rather in sorrow than in anger. She had loved him only too fondly: and was he not the father of her boy?) And as for the separation-scene from the child, while Becky was reciting it, Emmy retired altogether behind her pocket-hand-kerchief, so that the consummate little tragedian must have been charmed to see the effect which her performance produced on her audience.

Whilst the ladies were carrying on their conversation, Amelia's constant escort, the Major (who, of course, did not wish to interrupt their conference, and found himself rather tired of creaking about the narrow stair passage of which the roof brushed the nap from his hat), descended to the ground-floor of the house and into the great room common to all the frequenters of the Elephant, out of which the stair led. This apartment is always in a fume of smoke, and liberally sprinkled with beer. On a dirty table stand scores of corresponding brass-candlesticks with tallow candles for the lodgers, whose keys hang up in rows over the candles. Emmy had passed blushing through the room anon, where all sorts of people were collected; Tyrolese glove-sellers and Danubian linen-merchants, with their packs; students recruiting themselves with butter-brods and meat; idlers, playing cards or dominoes on the sloppy, beery tables; tumblers refreshing during the cessation of their performances;

—in a word, all the *fumum* and *strepitus* of a German inn in fair time. The waiter brought the Major a mug of beer, as a matter of course; and he took out a cigar, and amused himself with that pernicious vegetable and a newspaper until his charge should come down to claim him.

Max and Fritz came presently downstairs, their caps on one side, their spurs jingling, their pipes splendid with coats-of-arms and full-blown tassels, and they hung up the key of No. 90 on the board, and called for the ration of butterbrod and beer. The pair sate down by the Major and fell into a conversation of which he could not help hearing somewhat. It was mainly about "Fuchs" and "Philister," and duels and drinking-bouts at the neighbouring University of Schoppen-hausen, from which renowned seat of learning they had just come in the Eilwagen, with Becky, as it appeared, by their side, and in order to be present at the bridal fêtes at Pumpernickel.

"The little Engländerin seems to be *en bays de gonnois-ance*," said Max, who knew the French language, to Fritz, his comrade. "After the fat grandfather went away, there came a pretty little compatriot. I heard them chattering and whimpering together in the little woman's chamber."

"We must take the tickets for her concert," Fritz said.

"Hast thou any money, Max?"

"Bah," said the other, "the concert is a concert *in nubibus*. Hans said that she advertised one at Leipzig: and the Bur-schen took many tickets. But she went off without singing. She said in the coach yesterday that her pianist had fallen ill at Dresden. She cannot sing, it is my belief: her voice is as cracked as thine, O thou beer-soaking Renowner!"

"It is cracked; *I* hear her trying out of her window a schrecklich English ballad, called 'De Rose upon de Balgony.'"

"*Saufen* and *singen* go not together," observed Fritz with the red nose, who evidently preferred the former amusement, "No, thou shalt take none of her tickets. She won money at the *trente* and *quarante* last night. I saw her: she made a little English boy play for her. We will spend thy money there or at the theatre, or we will treat her to French wine or Cognac in the Aurelius Garden, but the tickets we will

not buy. What sayest thou? Yet, another mug of beer?"
and one and another successively having buried their blond
whiskers in the mawkish draught, curled them and swaggered
off into the fair.

The Major, who had seen the key of No. 90 put up on its
hook, and had heard the conversation of the two young
University bloods, was not at a loss to understand that their
talk related to Becky. "The little devil is at her old tricks,"
he thought, and he smiled as he recalled old days, when he
had witnessed the desperate flirtation with Jos, and the
ludicrous end of that adventure. He and George had often
laughed over it subsequently, and until a few weeks after
George's marriage, when he also was caught in the little
Circe's toils, and had an understanding with her which his
comrade certainly suspected, but preferred to ignore. William was too much hurt or ashamed to ask to fathom that
disgraceful mystery, although once, and evidently with remorse on his mind, George had alluded to it. It was on the
morning of Waterloo, as the young men stood together in
front of their line, surveying the black masses of Frenchmen
who crowned the opposite heights, and as the rain was coming
down, "I have been mixing in a foolish intrigue with a
woman," George said. "I am glad we were marched away.
If I drop, I hope Emmy will never know of that business.
I wish to God it had never been begun!" And William was
pleased to think, and had more than once soothed poor
George's widow with the narrative, that Osborne, after quitting his wife, and after the action of Quatre Bras, on the
first day, spoke gravely and affectionately to his comrade of
his father and his wife. On these facts, too, William had
insisted very strongly in his conversations with the elder
Osborne: and had thus been the means of reconciling the
old gentleman to his son's memory, just at the close of the
elder man's life.

"And so this devil is still going on with her intrigues,"
thought William. "I wish she were a hundred miles from
here. She brings mischief wherever she goes." And he was
pursuing these forebodings and this uncomfortable train of
thought, with his head between his hands, and the "Pumpernickel Gazette" of last week unread under his nose, when

somebody tapped his shoulder with a parasol, and he looked up and saw Mrs. Amelia.

This woman had a way of tyrannising over Major Dobbin (for the weakest of all people will domineer over somebody), and she ordered him about, and patted him, and made him fetch and carry just as if he was a great Newfoundland dog. He liked, so to speak, to jump into the water if she said "High, Dobbin!" and to trot behind her with her reticule in his mouth. This history has been written to very little purpose if the reader has not perceived that the Major was a spooney.

"Why did you not wait for me, sir, to escort me downstairs?" she said, giving a little toss of her head, and a most sarcastic curtsey.

"I couldn't stand up in the passage," he answered, with a comical deprecatory look; and, delighted to give her his arm, and to take her out of the horrid smoky place, he would have walked off without even so much as remembering the waiter, had not the young fellow run after him and stopped him on the threshold of the Elephant, to make him pay for the beer which he had not consumed. Emmy laughed: she called him a naughty man, who wanted to run away in debt: and, in fact, made some jokes suitable to the occasion and the small-beer. She was in high spirits and good humour, and tripped across the market-place very briskly. She wanted to see Jos that instant. The Major laughed at the impetuous affection Mrs. Amelia exhibited; for, in truth, it was not very often that she wanted her brother "that instant."

They found the Civilian in his saloon on the first-floor; he had been pacing the room, and biting his nails, and looking over the market-place towards the Elephant a hundred times at least during the past hour, whilst Emmy was closeted with her friend in the garret, and the Major was beating the tattoo on the sloppy tables of the public room below, and he was, on his side, too, very anxious to see Mrs. Osborne.

"Well?" said he.

"The poor dear creature, how she has suffered!" Emmy said.

"God bless my soul, yes," Jos said, wagging his head so that his cheeks quivered like jellies.

"She may have Payne's room; who can go upstairs," Emmy continued. Payne was a staid English maid and personal attendant upon Mrs. Osborne, to whom the courier, as in duty bound, paid court, and whom Georgy used to "lark" dreadfully with accounts of German robbers and ghosts. She passed her time chiefly in grumbling, in ordering about her mistress, and in stating her intention to return the next morning to her native village of Clapham. "She may have Payne's room," Emmy said.

"Why, you don't mean to say you are going to have that woman into the *house?*" bounced out the Major jumping up.

"Of course we are," said Amelia in the most innocent way in the world. "Don't be angry, and break the furniture, Major Dobbin. Of course we are going to have her here."

"Of course, my dear," Jos said.

"The poor creature, after all her sufferings," Emmy continued: "her horrid banker broken and run away: her husband—wicked wretch—having deserted her and taken her child away from her" (here she doubled her two little fists and held them in a most menacing attitude before her, so that the Major was charmed to see such a dauntless virago), "the poor dear thing! quite alone and absolutely forced to give lessons in singing to get her bread—and not have her here!"

"Take lessons, my dear Mrs. George," cried the Major, "but don't have her in the house. I implore you, don't."

"Pooh," said Jos.

"You who are always good and kind; always used to be at any rate: I'm astonished at you, Major William," Amelia cried. "Why what is the moment to help her but when she is so miserable? Now is the time to be of service to her. The oldest friend I ever had, and not—"

"She was not always your friend, Amelia," the Major said, for he was quite angry. This allusion was too much for Emmy, who, looking the Major almost fiercely in the face, said, "For shame, Major Dobbin!" and after having fired this shot, she walked out of the room with a most majestic air, and shut her own door briskly on herself and her outraged dignity.

"To allude to *that!*" she said, when the door was closed. "Oh, it was cruel of him to remind me of it," and she looked up at George's picture, which hung there as usual, with the portrait of the boy underneath. "It was cruel of him. If I had forgiven it, ought he to have spoken? No. And it is from his own lips that I know how wicked and groundless my jealousy was; and that you were pure—Oh yes, you were pure, my saint in heaven!"

She paced the room trembling and indignant. She went and leaned on the chest of drawers over which the picture hung, and gazed and gazed at it. Its eyes seemed to look down on her with a reproach that deepened as she looked.

The early dear, dear memories of that brief prime of love rushed back upon her. The wound which years had scarcely cicatrised bled afresh, and oh, how bitterly! She could not bear the reproaches of the husband there before her. It couldn't be. Never, never!

Poor Dobbin; poor old William! That unlucky word had undone the work of many a year—the long laborious edifice of a life of love and constancy—raised, too, upon what secret and hidden foundations, wherein lay buried passions, uncounted struggles, unknown sacrifices—a little word was spoken, and down fell the fair palace of hope—one word, and away flew the bird which he had been trying all his life to lure!

William, though he saw by Amelia's looks that a great crisis had come, nevertheless continued to implore Sedley in the most energetic terms, to beware of Rebecca: and he eagerly, almost frantically, adjured Jos not to receive her. He besought Mr. Sedley to inquire at least regarding her: told him how he had heard that she was in the company of gamblers and people of ill repute; pointed out what evil she had done in former days: how she and Crawley had misled poor George into ruin: how she was now parted from her husband, by her own confession, and, perhaps. for good reason. What a dangerous companion she would be for his sister, who knew nothing of the affairs of the world! William implored Jos, with all the eloquence which he could bring to bear, and a great deal more energy than this quiet

gentleman was ordinarily in the habit of showing, to keep
Rebecca out of his household.

Had he been less violent, or more dexterous, he might
have succeeded in his supplications to Jos; but the Civilian
was not a little jealous of the airs of superiority which the
Major constantly exhibited towards him, as he fancied (indeed, he had imparted his opinions to Mr. Kirsch, the
courier, whose bills Major Dobbin checked on this journey,
and who sided with his master), and he began a blustering
speech about his competency to defend his own honour, his
desire not to have his affairs meddled with, his intention, in
fine, to rebel against the Major, when the colloquy—rather
a long and stormy one—was put an end to in the simplest
way possible, namely, by the arrival of Mrs. Becky, with a
porter from the Elephant Hotel, in charge of her very mea-
gre baggage.

She greeted her host with affectionate respect, and made
a shrinking, but amicable, salutation to Major Dobbin, who,
as her instinct assured her at once, was her enemy, and had
been speaking against her; and the bustle and clatter conse-
quent upon her arrival brought Amelia out of her room.
Emmy went up and embraced her guest with the greatest
warmth, and took no notice of the Major, except to fling him
an angry look—the most unjust and scornful glance that
had perhaps ever appeared in that poor little woman's face
since she was born.

But she had private reasons of her own, and was bent
upon being angry with him. And Dobbin, indignant at the
injustice, not at the defeat, went off, making her a bow
quite as haughty as the killing curtsey with which the little
woman chose to bid him farewell.

He being gone, Emmy was particularly lively and affectionate to Rebecca, and bustled about the apartments and
installed her guest in her room with an eagerness and activity seldom exhibited by our placid little friend. But when an
act of injustice is to be done, especially by weak people, it is
best that it should be done quickly; and Emmy thought she
was displaying a great deal of firmness and proper feeling
and veneration for the late Captain Osborne in her present
behaviour.

Georgy came in from the fêtes for dinner-time, and found four covers laid as usual; but one of the places was occupied by a lady, instead of by Major Dobbin. "Hullo! where's Dob?" the young gentleman asked, with his usual simplicity of language. "Major Dobbin is dining out, I suppose," his mother said: and, drawing the boy to her, kissed him a great deal, and put his hair off his forehead, and introduced him to Mrs. Crawley. "This is my boy, Rebecca." Mrs. Osborne said—as much as to say—can the world produce anything like that? Becky looked at him with rapture, and pressed his hand fondly. "Dear boy!" she said —"he is just like my——" Emotion choked her further utterance; but Amelia understood, as well as if she had spoken, that Becky was thinking of her own blessed child. However, the company of her friend consoled Mrs. Crawley, and she ate a very good dinner.

During the repast, she had occasion to speak several times, when Georgy eyed her and listened to her. At the dessert Emmy was gone out to superintend further domestic arrangements: Jos was in his great chair dozing over *Galignani*s Georgy and the new arrival sat close to each other: he had continued to look at her knowingly more than once, and at last, he laid down the nut-crackers.

"I say," said Georgy.

"What do you say?" Becky said, laughing.

"You're the lady I saw in the mask at the Rouge et Noir."

"Hush! you little sly creature," Becky said, taking up his hand and kissing it. "Your uncle was there, too, and mamma mustn't know."

"Oh no—not by no means," answered the little fellow.

"You see we are quite good friends already," Becky said to Emmy, who now re-entered; and it must be owned that Mrs. Osborne had introduced a most judicious and amiable companion into her house.

William, in a state of great indignation, though still unaware of all the treason that was in store for him, walked about the town wildly until he fell upon the Secretary of Legation, Tapeworm, who invited him to dinner. As they were discussing that meal, he took occasion to ask the Secretary whether he knew anything about a certain Mrs. Rawdon Crawley, who had, he believed, made some noise in London; and then Tapeworm, who of course knew all the London gossip, and was besides a relative of Lady Gaunt, poured out into the astonished Major's ears such a history about Becky and her husband as astonished the querist, and supplied all the points of this narrative, for it was at that very table years ago that the present writer had the pleasure of hearing the tale. Tufto, Steyne, the Crawleys, and their history—everything connected with Becky and her previous life passed under the record of the bitter diplomatist. He knew everything and a great deal besides, about all the world;—in a word, he made the most astounding revelations to the simple-hearted Major. When Dobbin said that Mrs. Osborne and Mr. Sedley had taken her into their house, Tapeworm burst into a peal of laughter which shocked the Major, and asked if they had not better send into the prison, and take in one or two of the gentlemen in shaved heads and yellow jackets, who swept the streets of Pumpernickel, chained in pairs, to board and lodge, and act as tutor to that little scapegrace Georgy.

This information astonished and horrified the Major not a little. It had been agreed in the morning (before meeting with Rebecca) that Amelia should go to the Court ball that night. There would be the place where he should tell her. The Major went home and dressed himself in his uniform, and repaired to Court, in hopes to see Mrs. Osborne. She never came. When he returned to his lodgings all the lights in the Sedley tenement were put out. He could not see her till the morning. I don't know what sort of a night's rest he had with this frightful secret in bed with him.

At the earliest convenient hour in the morning he sent his servant across the way with a note, saying, that he wished very particularly to speak with her. A message came back to say, that Mrs. Osborne was exceedingly unwell, and was keeping her room.

She, too, had been awake all that night. She had been thinking of a thing which had agitated her mind a hundred times before. A hundred times on the point of yielding, she had shrunk back from a sacrifice which she felt was too much for her. She couldn't, in spite of his love and constancy, and her own acknowledged regard, respect, and gratitude. **What are benefits, what is constancy, or merit?** One curl of a girl's ringlet, one hair of a whisker, will turn the scale against them all in a minute. They did not weigh with Emmy more than with other women. She had tried them; wanted to make them pass; could not; and the pitiless little woman had found a pretext, and determined to be free.

When at length, in the afternoon, the Major gained admission to Amelia, instead of the cordial and affectionate greeting, to which he had been accustomed now for many a long day, he received the salutation of a curtsey, and of a little gloved hand, retracted the moment after it was accorded to him.

Rebecca, too, was in the room, and advanced to meet him with a smile and an extended hand. Dobbin drew back rather confusedly. "I—I beg your pardon, ma'am," he said; "but I am bound to tell you that it is not as your friend that I am come here now."

"Pooh! damn; don't let us have this sort of thing!" Jos cried out, alarmed, and anxious to get rid of a scene.

"I wonder what Major Dobbin has to say against Rebecca?" Amelia said in a low, clear voice with a slight quiver in it, and a very determined look about the eyes.

"I will *not* have this sort of thing in my house," Jos again interposed. "I say I will not have it: and Dobbin, I beg, sir, you'll stop it." And he looked round trembling and turning very red, and gave a great puff, and made for his door.

"Dear friend!" Rebecca said with angelic sweetness, "do hear what Major Dobbin has to say against me."

"I will *not* hear it, I say," squeaked out Jos at the top of his voice, and, gathering up his dressing-gown, he was gone.

"We are only two women," Amelia said. "You can speak now, sir."

"This manner towards me is one which scarcely becomes you, Amelia," the Major answered haughtily; "nor I believe am I guilty of habitual harshness to women. It is not a pleasure to me to do the duty which I am come to do."

"Pray proceed with it quickly, if you please, Major Dobbin," said Amelia, who was more and more in a pet. The expression of Dobbin's face, as she spoke in this imperious manner, was not pleasant.

"I came to say—and as you stay, Mrs. Crawley, I must say it in your presence—that I think you—you ought not to form a member of the family of my friends. A lady who is separated from her husband, who travels not under her own name, who frequents public gaming-tables—"

"It was to the ball I went," cried out Becky.

"—is not a fit companion for Mrs. Osborne and her son," Dobbin went on: "and I may add that there are people here who know you, and who profess to know that regarding your conduct, about which I don't even wish to speak before— before Mrs. Osborne."

"Yours is a very modest and convenient sort of calumny, Major Dobbin," Rebecca said. "You leave me under the weight of an accusation which, after all, is unsaid. What is it? Is it unfaithfulness to my husband? I scorn it, and defy anybody to prove it—I defy you, I say. My honour is as untouched as that of the bitterest enemy who ever maligned me. Is it of being poor, forsaken, wretched, that you accuse me? Yes, I am guilty of those faults, and punished for them every day. Let me go, Emmy. It is only to suppose that I have not met you, and I am no worse to-day than I was yesterday. It is only to suppose that the night is over and the poor wanderer is on her way. Don't you remember the song we used to sing in old, dear old days? I have been wandering ever since then—a poor castaway, scorned for being miserable, and insulted because I am alone. Let me go: my stay here interferes with the plans of this gentleman."

"Indeed it does, madam," said the Major. "If I have any authority in this house—"

"Authority, none!" broke out Amelia. "Rebecca, you stay with me. *I* won't desert you, because you have been persecuted, or insult you, because—because Major Dobbin chooses to do so. Come away, dear." And the two women made towards the door.

William opened it. As they were going out, however, he took Amelia's hand, and said—"Will you stay a moment and speak to me?"

"He wishes to speak to you away from me," said Becky, looking like a martyr. Amelia gripped her hand in reply.

"Upon my honour it is not about you that I am going to speak," Dobbin said. "Come back, Amelia," and she came. Dobbin bowed to Mrs. Crawley, as he shut the door upon her. Amelia looked at him, leaning against the glass: her face and her lips were quite white.

"I was confused when I spoke just now," the Major said, after a pause; "and I misused the word authority."

"You did," said Amelia, with her teeth chattering.

"At least I have claims to be heard," Dobbin continued.

"It is generous to remind me of our obligations to you," the woman answered.

"The claims I mean, are those left me by George's father," William said.

"Yes, and you insulted his memory. You did yesterday. You know you did. And I will never forgive you. Never!" said Amelia. She shot out each little sentence in a tremor of anger and emotion.

"You don't mean that, Amelia?" William said, sadly. "You don't mean that these words, uttered in a hurried moment, are to weigh against a whole life's devotion? I think that George's memory has not been injured by the way in which I have dealt with it, and if we are come to bandying reproaches, I at least merit none from his widow and the mother of his son. Reflect, afterwards when—when you are at leisure, and your conscience will withdraw this accusation. It does even now," Amelia held down her head.

"It is not that speech of yesterday," he continued, "which moves you. That is but the pretext, Amelia, or I have loved you and watched you for fifteen years in vain. Have I not learned in that time to read all your feelings, and look into your thoughts? I know what your heart is capable of: it can cling faithfully to a recollection, and cherish a fancy; but it can't feel such an attachment as mine deserves to mate with, and such as I would have won from a woman more generous than you. No, you are not worthy of the love which I have devoted to you. I knew all along that the prize I had set my life on was not worth the winning; that I was a fool, with fond fancies, too, bartering away my all of truth and ardour against your little feeble remnant of love. I will bargain no more. I withdraw. I find no fault with you. You are very good-natured, and have done your best; but you couldn't —you couldn't reach up to the height of the attachment which I bore you, and which a loftier soul than yours might have been proud to share. Good-bye, Amelia! I have watched your struggle. Let it end. We are both weary of it."

Amelia stood scared and silent as William thus suddenly broke the chain by which she held him, and declared his independence and superiority. He had placed himself at her feet so long that the poor little woman had been accustomed to trample upon him. She didn't wish to marry him, but she wished to keep him. She wished to give him nothing, but that he should give her all. It is a bargain not unfrequently levied in love.

William's sally had quite broken and cast her down. *Her* assault was long since over and beaten back.

"Am I to understand then,—that you are going—away,—William?" she said.

He gave a sad laugh. "I went once before," he said, "and came back after twelve years. We were young then, Amelia. Good-bye. I have spent enough of my life at this play."

Whilst they had been talking, the door into Mrs. Osborne's room had opened ever so little; indeed, Becky had kept a hold of the handle, and had turned it on the instant when Dobbin quitted it; and she heard every word of the conversation that had passed between these two. "What a noble heart that man has," she thought, "and how shamefully that woman plays with it!" She admired Dobbin; she bore him no rancour for the part he had taken against her. It was an open move in the game, and played fairly. "Ah!" she thought, "if I could have had such a husband as that—a man with a heart and brains, too! I would not have minded his large feet;" and running into her room, she absolutely bethought herself of something, and wrote him a note, beseeching him to stop for a few days—not to think of going—and that she could serve him with A.

The parting was over. Once more poor William walked to the door and was gone; and the little widow, the author

of all this work, had her will, and had won her victory,
and was left to enjoy it as she best might. Let the ladies
envy her triumph.

At the romantic hour of dinner, Mr. Georgy made his
appearance, and again remarked the absence of "Old Dob."
The meal was eaten in silence by the party. Jos's appetite
not being diminished, but Emmy taking nothing at all.

After the meal, Georgy was lolling in the cushions of
the old window, a large window, with three sides of glass
abutting from the gable, and commanding on one side the
Market Place, where the Elephant is, his mother being busy
hard by, when he remarked symptoms of movement at the
Major's house on the other side of the street.

"Hullo!" said he, "there's Dob's trap—they are bringing it out of the court-yard." The "trap" in question was
a carriage which the Major had bought for six pounds
sterling, and about which they used to rally him a good
deal.

Emmy gave a little start but said nothing.

"Hullo!" Georgy continued, "there's Francis coming out
with the portmanteaus, and Kunz, the one-eyed postilion,
coming down the market with three schimmels. Look at
his boots and yellow jacket,—ain't he a rum one? Why
—they're putting the horses to Dob's carriage. Is he going
anywhere?"

"Yes," said Emmy, "he is going on a journey."

"Going on a journey; and when is he coming back?"

"He is—not coming back," answered Emmy.

"Not coming back!" cried out Georgy, jumping up.
"Stay here, sir," roared out Jos. "Stay, Georgy," said his
mother, with a very sad face. The boy stopped; kicked
about the room; jumped up and down from the window-
seat with his knees, and showed every symptom of uneasiness and curiosity.

The horses were put to. The baggage was strapped on.
Francis came out with his master's sword, cane, and umbrella tied up together, and laid them in the well, and his
desk and old tin cocked-hat case, which he placed under
the seat. Francis brought out the stained old blue cloak
lined with red camlet, which had wrapped the owner up

any time these fifteen years, and had *manchen Sturm erlebt,*
as a favourite song of those days said. It had been new
for the campaign of Waterloo, and had covered George and
William after the night of Quatre Bras.

Old Burcke, the landlord of the lodgings, came out, then
Francis, with more packages—final packages—then Major
William,—Burcke wanted to kiss him. The Major was
adored by all people with whom he had to do. It was
with difficulty he could escape from this demonstration of
attachment.

"By Jove, I *will* go!" screamed out George. "Give him
this," said Becky, quite interested, and put a paper into
the boy's hand. He had rushed down the stairs and flung
across the street in a minute—the yellow postilion was
cracking his whip gently.

William had got into the carriage, released from the
embraces of his landlord. George bounded in afterwards
and flung his arms round the Major's neck (as they saw
from the window), and began asking him multiplied questions. Then he felt in his waistcoat-pocket and gave him a
note. William seized at it rather eagerly, he opened it
trembling, but instantly his countenance changed, and he
tore the paper in two, and dropped it out of the carriage.
He kissed Georgy on the head, and the boy got out, doubling
his fists into his eyes, and with the aid of Francis. He
lingered with his hand on the panel. Fort, Schwager!
The yellow postilion cracked his whip prodigiously, up
sprang Francis to the box, away went the schimmels, and
Dobbin with his head on his breast. He never looked up
as they passed under Amelia's window: and Georgy, left
alone in the street, burst out crying in the face of all the
crowd.

Emmy's maid heard him howling again during the night,
and brought him some preserved apricots to console him.
She mingled her lamentations with his. All the poor, all
the humble, all honest folks, all good men who knew him,
loved that kind-hearted and simple gentleman.

As for Emmy, had she not done her duty? She had her
picture of George for a consolation.

CHAPTER XXXII

Which Contains Births, Marriages, and Deaths

WHATEVER Becky's private plan might be by which Dobbin's true love was to be crowned with success, the little woman thought that the secret might keep, and indeed, being by no means so much interested about anybody's welfare as about her own, she had a great number of things pertaining to herself to consider, and which concerned her a great deal more than Major Dobbin's happiness in this life.

She found herself suddenly and unexpectedly in snug comfortable quarters: surrounded by friends, kindness, and good-natured simple people such as she had not met with for many a long day; and, wanderer as she was by force and inclination, there were moments when rest was pleasant to her. As the most hardened Arab that ever careered across the Desert over the hump of a dromedary, likes to repose sometimes under the date-trees by the water, or to come into the cities, walk into the bazaars, refresh himself in the baths, and say his prayers in the Mosques, before he goes out again marauding, so Jos's tents and pilau were pleasant to this little Ishmaelite. She picketed her steed, hung up her weapons, and warmed herself comfortably by his fire. The halt in that roving, restless life, was inexpressibly soothing and pleasant to her.

So, pleased herself, she tried with all her might to please everybody; and we know that she was eminent and successful as a practitioner in the art of giving pleasure. As for Jos, even in that little interview in the garret at the Elephant Inn, she had found means to win back a great deal of his good-will.

In the course of a week, the Civilian was her sworn slave and frantic admirer. He didn't go to sleep after dinner, as his custom was, in the much less lively society of Amelia.

388

He drove out with Becky in his open carriage. He asked little parties and invented festivities to do her honour.

Tapeworm, the Chargé d'Affaires, who had abused her so cruelly, came to dine with Jos, and then came every day to pay his respects to Becky. Poor Emmy, who was never very talkative, and more glum and silent than ever after Dobbin's departure, was quite forgotten when this superior genius made her appearance. The French Minister was as much charmed with her as his English rival. The German ladies, never particularly squeamish as regards morals, especially in English people, were delighted with the cleverness and wit of Mrs. Osborne's charming friend; and though she did not ask to go to Court, yet the most august and Transparent Personages there heard of her fascinations, and were quite curious to know her. When it became known that she was noble, of an ancient English family, that her husband was a Colonel of the Guard, Excellenz and Governor of an island, only separated from his lady by one of those trifling differences which are of little account in a country where "Werther" is still read, and the "Wahlverwandtschaften" of Goethe is considered an edifying moral book, nobody thought of refusing to receive her in the very highest society of the little Duchy; and the ladies were even more ready to call her *du,* and to swear eternal friendship for her, than they had been to bestow the same inestimable benefits upon Amelia. Love and Liberty are interpreted by those simple Germans in a way which honest folks in Yorkshire and Somersetshire little understand; and a lady might, in some philosophic and civilized towns, be divorced ever so many times from her respective husbands, and keep her character in society. Jos's house never was so pleasant since he had a house of his own, as Rebecca caused it to be. She sang, she played, she laughed, she talked in two or three languages; she brought everybody to the house; and she made Jos believe that it was his own great social talents and wit which gathered the society of the place round about him.

As for Emmy, who found herself not in the least mistress, of her own house, except when the bills were to be paid, Becky soon discovered the way to soothe and please her. She talked to her perpetually about Major Dobbin sent about

his business, and made no scruple of declaring her admiration
for that excellent, high-minded gentleman, and of telling
Emmy that she had behaved most cruelly regarding him.
Emmy defended her conduct, and showed that it was dictated
only by the purest religious principles; that a woman once,
&c., and to such an angel as him to whom she had had the
good fortune to marry, was married for ever; but she had
no objection to hear the Major praised as much as ever
Becky chose to praise him; and indeed brought the conversation round to the Dobbin subject a score of times
every day.

Means were easily found to win the favour of Georgy
and the servants. Amelia's maid, it has been said, was
heart and soul in favour of the generous Major. Having
at first disliked Becky for being the means of dismissing
him from the presence of her mistress, she was reconciled
to Mrs. Crawley subsequently, because the latter became
William's most ardent admirer and champion. And in those
nightly conclaves in which the two ladies indulged after
their parties, and while Miss Payne was "brushing their
'airs," as she called the yellow locks of the one, and the
soft brown tresses of the other, this girl always put in her
word for that dear good gentleman Major Dobbin. Her
advocacy did not make Amelia angry any more than Rebecca's admiration of him. She made George write to him
constantly, and persisted in sending Mamma's kind love in
a postscript. And as she looked at her husband's portrait
of nights, it no longer reproached her—perhaps she reproached it, now William was gone.

Emmy was not very happy after her heroic sacrifice.
She was very *distraite*, nervous, silent, and ill to please.
The family had never known her so peevish. She grew
pale and ill. She used to try to sing certain songs ("Ein-
sam bin ich nicht alleine," was one of them; that tender
love-song of Weber's, which, in old-fashioned days, young
ladies, and when you were scarcely born, showed that those
who lived before you knew too how to love and to sing);
—certain songs, I say, to which the Major was partial; and
as she warbled them in the twilight in the drawing-room,
she would break off in the midst of the song, and walk into

her neighbouring apartment, and there, no doubt, take refuge in the miniature of her husband.

Some books still subsisted, after Dobbin's departure, with his name written in them; a German Dictionary, for instance, with "William Dobbin, —th Reg.," in the flyleaf; a guide-book with his initials, and one or two other volumes which belonged to the Major. Emmy cleared these away, and put them on the drawers, where she placed her work-box, her desk, her Bible, and Prayer-book, under the pictures of the two Georges. And the Major, on going away, having left his gloves behind him, it is a fact that Georgy, rummaging his mother's desk some time afterwards, found the gloves neatly folded up, and put away in what they call the secret-drawers of the desk.

Not caring for society, and moping there a great deal, Emmy's chief pleasure in the summer evenings was to take long walks with Georgy (during which Rebecca was left to the society of Mr. Joseph), and then the mother and son used to talk about the Major in a way which even made the boy smile. She told him that she thought Major William was the best man in all the world; the gentlest and the kindest, the bravest and the humblest. Over and over again, she told him how they owed everything which they possessed in the world to that kind friend's benevolent care of them; how he had befriended them all through their poverty and misfortunes; watched over them when nobody cared for them: how all his comrades admired him though he never spoke of his own gallant actions; how Georgy's father trusted him beyond all other men, and had been constantly befriended by the good William. "Why, when your papa was a little boy," she said, "he often told me that it was William who defended him against a tyrant at the school where they were; and their friendship never ceased from that day until the last, when your dear father fell."

"Did Dobbin kill the man who killed papa?" Georgy said. "I'm sure he did, or he would if he could have caught him; wouldn't he, mother? When I'm in the army, won't I hate the French?—that's all."

In such colloquies the mother and the child passed a great deal of their time together. The artless woman had

made a confidante of the boy. He was as much William's
friend as everybody else who knew him well.

By the way, Mrs. Becky, not to be behind-hand in sentiment, had got a miniature, too, hanging up in her room, to
the surprise and amusement of most people, and the delight
of the original, who was no other than our friend Jos. On
her first coming to favour the Sedleys with a visit, the little
woman, who had arrived with a remarkably small shabby kit,
was perhaps ashamed of the meanness of her trunks and
band-boxes, and often spoke with great respect about her
baggage left behind at Leipzig, which she must have from
that city. When a traveller talks to you perpetually about
the splendour of his luggage, which he does not happen to
have with him; my son, beware of that traveller! He is,
ten to one, an impostor.

Neither Jos nor Emmy knew this important maxim. It
seemed to them of no consequence whether Becky had a
quantity of very fine clothes in invisible trunks; but as her
present supply was exceedingly shabby, Emmy supplied her
out of her own stores, or took her to the best milliner in the
town, and there fitted her out. It was no more torn collars
now, I promise you, and faded silks trailing off at the
shoulder. Becky changed her habits with her situation in life
—the rouge-pot was suspended—another excitement to which
she had accustomed herself was also put aside, or at least
only indulged in in privacy; as when she was prevailed on
by Jos of a summer evening, Emmy and the boy being absent
on their walks, to take a little spirit-and-water. But if she
did not indulge—the courier did: that rascal Kirsch could
not be kept from the bottle; nor could he tell how much he
took when he applied to it. He was sometimes surprised
himself at the way in which Mr. Sedley's Cognac diminished.
Well, well; this is a painful subject. Becky did not very
likely indulge so much as she used before she entered a
decorous family.

At last the much-bragged-about boxes arrived from Leipzig;—three of them not by any means large or splendid;—
nor did Becky appear to take out any sort of dresses or ornaments from the boxes when they did arrive. But out of one,

which contained a mass of her papers (it was that very box which Rawdon Crawley had ransacked in his furious hunt for Becky's concealed money), she took a picture with great glee, which she pinned up in her room, and to which she introduced Jos. It was the portrait of a gentleman in pencil, his face having the advantage of being painted up in pink. He was riding on an elephant away from some cocoa-nut trees, and a pagoda: it was an Eastern scene.

"God bless my soul, it is my portrait," Jos cried out. It was he indeed, blooming in youth and beauty, in a nankeen jacket of the cut of 1804. It was the old picture that used to hang up in Russell Square.

"I bought it," said Becky, in a voice trembling with emotion; "I went to see if I could be of any use to my kind friends. I have never parted with that picture—I never will."

"Won't you?" Jos cried, with a look of unutterable rapture and satisfaction. "Did you really now value it for my sake?"

"You know I did, well enough," said Becky; "but why speak,—why think,—why look back! It is too late now!"

That evening's conversation was delicious for Jos. Emmy only came in to go to bed very tired and unwell. Jos and his fair guest had a charming *tête-à-tête,* and his sister could hear, as she lay awake in her adjoining chamber, Rebecca singing over to Jos the old songs of 1815. He did not sleep, for a wonder, that night, any more than Amelia.

It was June, and, by consequence, high season in London; Jos, who read the incomparable *Galignani* (the exile's best friend) through every day, used to favour the ladies with extracts from his paper during their breakfast. Every week in this paper there is a full account of military movements, in which Jos, as a man who had seen service, was especially interested. On one occasion he read out—"Arrival of the —th regiment.—Gravesend, June 20.—The Ramchunder, East Indiaman, came into the river this morning, having on board 14 officers, and 132 rank and file of this gallant corps. They have been absent from England fourteen years, having been embarked the year after Waterloo, in which glorious conflict they took an active part, and having subsequently distinguished themselves in the Burmese war. The veteran colonel, Sir Michael O'Dowd, K.C.B., with his lady and sister, landed here yesterday, with Captains Posky, Stubble, Macraw, Malony; Lieutenants Smith, Jones, Thompson, F. Thomson; Ensigns Hicks and Grady; the band on the pier playing the national anthem, and the crowd loudly cheering the gallant veterans as they went into Wayte's hotel, where a sumptuous banquet was provided for the defenders of Old England.

During the repast, which we need not say was served up in Wayte's best style, the cheering continued so enthusiastically that Lady O'Dowd and the Colonel came forward to the balcony and drank the healths of their fellow-countrymen in a bumper of Wayte's best claret."

On a second occasion Jos read a brief announcement— Major Dobbin had joined the —th regiment at Chatham; and subsequently he promulgated accounts of the presentations at the Drawing-room, of Colonel Sir Michael O'Dowd, K.C.B., Lady O'Dowd (by Mrs. Molloy Malony of Bally-malony, and Miss Glorvina O'Dowd (by Lady O'Dowd). Almost directly after this, Dobbin's name appeared among the Lieutenant-Colonels: for old Marshal Tiptoff had died during the passage of the —th from Madras, and the Sovereign was pleased to advance Colonel Sir Michael O'Dowd to the rank of Major-General on his return to England, with an intimation that he should be Colonel of the distinguished regiment which he had so long commanded.

Amelia had been made aware of some of these movements. The correspondence between George and his guardian had not ceased by any means: William had even written once or twice to her since his departure, but in a manner so unconstrainedly cold, that the poor woman felt now in her turn that she had lost her power over him, and that, as he had said, he was free. He had left her, and she was wretched. Her memory of his almost countless services, and lofty and affectionate regard, now presented itself to her, and rebuked her day and night. She brooded over those recollections according to her wont: saw the purity and beauty of the affection with which she had trifled, and reproached herself for having flung away such a treasure.

It was gone indeed. William had spent it all out. He loved her no more, he thought, as he had loved her. He never could again. That sort of regard, which he had proffered to her for so many faithful years can't be flung down and shattered and mended so as to show no scars. The little heedless tyrant had so destroyed it. No, William thought again and again, "It was myself I deluded, and persisted in cajoling; had she been worthy of the love I gave her, she would have returned it long ago. It was a fond mistake. Isn't the whole course of life made up of such? and suppose I had won her, should I not have been disenchanted the day after my victory? Why pine, or be ashamed of my defeat?" The more he thought of this long passage of his life, the more clearly he saw his deception. "I'll go into harness again," he said, "and do my duty in that state of life in which it has pleased Heaven to place me. I will see that the buttons of the recruits are properly bright, and that the sergeants make no mistakes in their accounts. I will dine at mess, and listen to the Scotch surgeon telling his stories. When I am old and broken, I will go on half-pay, and my old sisters shall scold me. I have 'geliebt und gelebet' as the girl in Wallenstein says. I am done.—Pay the bills and get me a cigar: find out what there is at the play to-night, Francis; to-morrow we cross by the 'Batavier.' " He made the above speech, whereof Francis only heard the last two lines, pacing up and down the Boompjes at Rotterdam. The "Batavier" was lying in the basin. He could see the place on the quarter-deck, where he and Emmy had sate in the happy voyage out. What had that little Mrs. Crawley to say to him? Psha; to-morrow we will put to sea, and return to England, home, and duty!

After June all the little Court Society of Pumpernickel used to separate, according to the German plan, and make for a hundred watering-places, where they drank at the wells; rode upon donkeys; gambled at the *redoutes,* if they had money and a mind; rushed with hundreds of their kind to gourmandise at the *tables-d'hôte;* and idled away the summer. The English diplomatists went off to Toeplitz and Kissingen, their French rivals shut up their *Chan-*

cellerie and whisked away to their darling Boulevard de
Gand. The Transparent reigning family took too to the
waters, or retired to their hunting lodges. Everybody went
away having any pretension to politeness, and of course,
with them, Doctor von Glauber, the Court Doctor, and his
Baroness. The seasons for the baths were the most productive periods of the Doctor's practice—he united business
with pleasure, and his chief place of resort was Ostend,
which is much frequented by Germans, and where the
Doctor treated himself and his spouse to what he called a
"dib" in the sea.

His interesting patient, Jos, was a regular milch cow to
the Doctor, and he easily persuaded the Civilian, both for
his own health's sake and that of his charming sister,
which was really very much shattered, to pass the summer
at that hideous seaport town. Emmy did not care where
she went much. Georgy jumped at the idea of a move.
As for Becky, she came as a matter of course in the fourth
place inside of the fine barouche Mr. Jos had bought: the
two domestics being on the box in front. She might have
some misgivings about the friends whom she should meet
at Ostend, and who might be likely to tell ugly stories—
but bah! she was strong enough to hold her own. She
had cast such an anchor in Jos now, as would require a
strong storm to shake. That incident of the picture had
finished him. Becky took down her elephant, and put it
into the little box which she had had from Amelia ever so
many years ago. Emmy also came off with her Lares,—
her two pictures,—and the party, finally, were lodged in
an exceedingly dear and uncomfortable house at Ostend.

There Amelia began to take baths, and get what good she
could from them, and though scores of people of Becky's
acquaintance passed her and cut her, yet Mrs. Osborne,
who walked about with her, and who knew nobody, was not
aware of the treatment experienced by the friend whom
she had chosen so judiciously as a companion; indeed,
Becky never thought fit to tell her what was passing under
her innocent eyes.

Some of Mrs. Rawdon Crawley's acquaintances, however,
acknowledged her readily enough,—perhaps more readily

than she would have desired. Among those were Major
Loder (unattached), and Captain Rook (late of the Rifles),
who might be seen any day on the Dyke, smoking and
staring at the women, and who speedily got an introduction to the hospitable board and select circle of Mr. Joseph
Sedley. In fact they would take no denial; they burst
into the house whether Becky was at home or not, walked
into Mrs. Osborne's drawing-room, which they perfumed
with their coats and mustachios, called Jos "Old buck,"
and invaded his dinner-table, and laughed and drank for
long hours there.

"What can they mean?" asked Georgy, who did not
like these gentlemen. "I heard the Major say to Mrs.
Crawley yesterday, 'No, no, Becky, you shan't keep the old
buck to yourself. We must have the bones in, or, dammy,
I'll split.' What could the Major mean, mamma?"

"Major! don't call _him_ Major!" Emmy said. "I'm sure
I can't tell what he meant." His presence and that of
his friend inspired the little lady with intolerable terror
and aversion. They paid her tipsy compliments; they leered
at her over the dinner-table. And the Captain made her
advances that filled her with sickening dismay, nor would
she ever see him unless she had George by her side.

Rebecca, to do her justice, never would let either of
these men remain alone with Amelia; the Major was dis-
engaged, too, and swore he would be the winner of her.
A couple of ruffians were fighting for this innocent creature, gambling for her at her own table; and though she
was not aware of the rascals' designs upon her, yet she
felt a horror and uneasiness in their presence, and longed
to fly.

She besought, she entreated Jos to go. Not he. He
was slow of movement, tied to his Doctor, and perhaps to
some other leading-strings. At least Becky was not anxious
to go to England.

At last she took a great resolution—made the great
plunge. She wrote off a letter to a friend whom she had
on the other side of the water; a letter about which she
did not speak a word to anybody, which she carried herself to the post under her shawl, nor was any remark made

about it: only that she looked very much flushed and agitated
when Georgy met her; and she kissed him, and hung over
him a great deal that night. She did not come out of
her room after her return from her walk. Becky thought
it was Major Loder and the Captain who frightened her.

"She mustn't stop here," Becky reasoned with herself.
"She must go away, the silly little fool. She is still
whimpering after that gaby of a husband—dead (and served
right!) these fifteen years. She shan't marry either of
these men. It's too bad of Loder. No; she shall marry
the bamboo-cane, I'll settle it this very night."

So Becky took a cup of tea to Amelia in her private
apartment, and found that lady in the company of her
miniatures, and in a most melancholy and nervous condition. She laid down the cup of tea.

"Thank you," said Amelia.

"Listen to me, Amelia," said Becky, marching up and
down the room before the other, and surveying her with a
sort of contemptuous kindness. "I want to talk to you.
You must go away from here and from the impertinences
of these men. I won't have you harassed by them: and
they will insult you if you stay. I tell you they are rascals;
men fit to send to the hulks. Never mind how I know them.
I know everybody. Jos can't protect you, he is too weak,
and wants a protector himself. You are no more fit to live
in the world than a baby in arms. You must marry, or
you and your precious boy will go to ruin. You must have
a husband, you fool; and one of the best gentlemen I ever
saw offered you a hundred times, and you have rejected
him, you silly, heartless, ungrateful little creature!"

"I tried—I tried my best, indeed I did, Rebecca," said
Amelia, deprecatingly, "but I couldn't forget—;" and she
finished the sentence by looking up at the portrait.

"Couldn't forget *him!*" cried out Becky, "that selfish
humbug, that low-bred cockney dandy, that padded booby,
who had neither wit, nor manners, nor heart, and was no
more to be compared to your friend with the bamboo cane,
than you are to Queen Elizabeth. Why, the man was weary
of you, and would have jilted you, but that Dobbin forced
him to keep his word. He owned it to me. He never

cared for you. He used to sneer about you to me, time
after time; and made love to me the week after he married you."

"It's false! It's false! Rebecca," cried out Amelia,
starting up.

"Look there, you fool," Becky said, still with provoking
good humour, and taking a little paper out of her belt, she
opened it and flung it into Emmy's lap. "You know his
handwriting. He wrote that to me—wanted me to run
away with him—gave it me under your nose, the day
before he was shot—and served him right!" Becky repeated.

Emmy did not hear her; she was looking at the letter.
It was that which George had put into the bouquet and
given to Becky on the night of the Duchess of Richmond's
ball. It was as she said: the foolish young man had asked
her to fly.

Emmy's head sank down, and for almost the last time
in which she shall be called upon to weep in this history,
she commenced that work. Her head fell to her bosom,
and her hands went up to her eyes; and there for a while,
she gave way to her emotions, as Becky stood on and regarded her. Who shall analyse those tears, and say
whether they were sweet or bitter? Was she most grieved,
because the idol of her life was tumbled down and shivered
at her feet, or indignant that her love had been so despised,
or glad because the barrier was removed which modesty
had placed between her and a new, a real affection?
"There is nothing to forbid me now," she thought. "I may
love him with all my heart now. O, I will, I will, if he will
but let me and forgive me." I believe it was this feeling
rushed over all the others which agitated that gentle little
bosom.

Indeed, she did not cry so much as Becky expected—
the other soothed and kissed her—a rare mark of sympathy
with Mrs. Becky. She treated Emmy like a child, and
patted her head. "And now let us get pen and ink, and
write to him to come this minute," she said.

"I—I wrote to him this morning," Emmy said, blushing
exceedingly. Becky screamed with laughter—*"Un biglietto,"*

she sang out with Rosina, *"eccolo quà!"*—the whole house echoed with her shrill singing.

Two mornings after this little scene, although the day was rainy and gusty, and Amelia had had an exceedingly wakeful night, listening to the wind roaring, and pitying all travellers by land and by water, yet she got up early, and insisted upon taking a walk on the Dyke with Georgy; and there she paced as the rain beat into her face, and she looked out westward across the dark sea line, and over the swollen billows which came tumbling and frothing to the shore. Neither spoke much, except now and then, when the boy said a few words to his timid companion, indicative of sympathy and protection.

"I hope he won't cross in such weather," Emmy said.

"I bet ten to one he does," the boy answered. "Look, mother, there's the smoke of the steamer." It was that signal, sure enough.

But though the steamer was under way, he might not be on board; he might not have got the letter; he might not choose to come.—A hundred fears poured one over the other into the little heart, as fast as the waves on to the Dyke.

The boat followed the smoke into sight. Georgy had a dandy telescope, and got the vessel under view in the most skilful manner. And he made appropriate nautical comments upon the manner of the approach of the steamer as she came nearer and nearer, dipping and rising in the water. The signal of an English steamer in sight went fluttering up to the mast on the pier. I dare say Mrs. Amelia's heart was in a similar flutter.

Emmy tried to look through the telescope over George's shoulder, but she could make nothing of it. She only saw a black eclipse bobbing up and down before her eyes.

George took the glass again and raked the vessel. "How she does pitch!" he said. "There goes a wave slap over her bows. There's only two people on deck besides the steersman. There's a man lying down, and a—chap in a—cloak with a—Hooray!—It's Dob, by Jingo!" He clapped to the telescope, and flung his arms round his mother. As

for that lady: let us say what she did in the words of
a favourite poet—Δαχρνοεν γελασασα. She was sure it was
William. It could be no other. What she had said about
hoping that he would not come was all hypocrisy. Of
course he would come: what could he do else but come?
She knew he would come.

The ship came swiftly nearer and nearer. As they went
in to meet her at the landing-place at the Quay, Emmy's
knees trembled so that she scarcely could run. She would
have liked to kneel down and say her prayers of thanks
there. Oh, she thought, she would be all her life saying
them!

It was such a bad day that as the vessel came alongside
of the Quay there were no idlers abroad; scarcely even a
commissioner on the look-out for the few passengers in the
steamer. That young scapegrace George had fled, too: and
as the gentleman in the old cloak lined with red stuff
stepped on to the shore, there was scarcely any one present
to see what took place, which was briefly this:

A lady in a dripping white bonnet and shawl, with her
two little hands out before her, went up to him, and in the
next minute she had altogether disappeared under the folds
of the old cloak, and was kissing one of his hands with all
her might; whilst the other, I suppose, was engaged in
holding her to his heart (which her head just about reached)
and in preventing her from tumbling down. She was
murmuring something about—forgive—dear William—
dear, dear, dearest friend—kiss, kiss, kiss, and so forth—
and in fact went on under the cloak in an absurd manner.

When Emmy emerged from it, she still kept tight hold
of one of William's hands, and looked up in his face. It
was full of sadness and tender love and pity. She understood its reproach, and hung down her head.

"It was time you sent for me, dear Amelia," he said.

"You will never go again, William?"

"No, never," he answered: and pressed the dear little
soul once more to his heart.

As they issued out of the Custom-house precincts, Georgy
broke out on them, with his telescope up to his eye, and a
loud laugh of welcome; he danced round the couple, and

performed many facetious antics as he led them up to the house. Jos wasn't up yet; Becky not visible (though she looked at them through the blinds). Georgy ran off to see about breakfast. Emmy, whose shawl and bonnet were off in the passage in the hands of Mrs. Payne, now went to undo the clasp of William's cloak, and—we will, if you please, go with George, and look after breakfast for the Colonel. The vessel is in port. He has got the prize he has been trying for all his life. The bird has come in at last. There it is with its head on his shoulder, billing and cooing close up to his heart, with soft, outstretched, fluttering wings. This is what he has asked for every day and hour for eighteen years. This is what he pined after. Here it is— the summit, the end—the last page of the third volume. Good-bye, Colonel—God bless you, honest William!—Fare- well, dear Amelia—Grow green again, tender little parasite, round the rugged old oak to which you cling!

Perhaps it was compunction towards the kind and simple creature, who had been the first in life to defend her, per- haps it was a dislike to all such sentimental scenes,—but Rebecca, satisfied with her part in the transaction, never presented herself before Colonel Dobbin and the lady whom he married. "Particular business," she said, took her to Bruges, whither she went; and only Georgy and his uncle were present at the marriage ceremony. When it was over, and Georgy had rejoined his parents, Mrs. Becky returned (just for a few days) to comfort the solitary bachelor, Joseph Sedley. He preferred a continental life, he said, and declined to join in housekeeping with his sister and her husband.

Emmy was very glad in her heart to think that she had written to her husband before she read or knew of that letter of George's. "I knew it all along," William said; "but could I use that weapon against the poor fellow's memory? It was that which made me suffer so when you——"

"Never speak of that day again," Emmy cried out, so contrite and humble, that William turned off the conversa- tion, by his account of Glorvina and dear old Peggy O'Dowd, with whom he was sitting when the letter of recall reached

2

him. "If you hadn't sent for me," he added with a laugh, "who knows what Glorvina's name might be now?"

At present it is Glorvina Posky (now Mrs. Major Posky); she took him on the death of his first wife, having resolved never to marry out of the regiment. Lady O'Dowd is also so attached to it that, she says, if anything were to happen to Mick, bedad she'd come back and marry some of 'em. But the Major-General is quite well, and lives in great splendour at O'Dowdstown, with a pack of beagles, and (with the exception of perhaps their neighbour, Hoggarty of Castle Hoggarty) he is the first man of his county.

Her Ladyship still dances jigs, and insisted on standing up with the Master of the Horse at the Lord Lieutenant's last ball. Both she and Glorvina declared that Dobbin had used the latter *sheamfully,* but Posky falling in, Glorvina was consoled, and a beautiful turban from Paris appeased the wrath of Lady O'Dowd.

When Colonel Dobbin quitted the service, which he did immediately after his marriage, he rented a pretty little country place in Hampshire, not far from Queen's Crawley, where, after the passing of the Reform Bill, Sir Pitt and his family constantly resided now. All idea of a Peerage was out of the question, the Baronet's two seats in Parliament being lost. He was both out of pocket and out of spirits by that catastrophe, failed in his health, and prophesied the speedy ruin of the Empire.

Lady Jane and Mrs. Dobbin became great friends—there was a perpetual crossing of pony-chaises between the Hall and the Evergreens, the Colonel's place (rented of his friend Major Ponto, who was abroad with his family). Her Ladyship was godmother to Mrs. Dobbin's child, which bore her name, and was christened by the Rev. James Crawley, who succeeded his father in the living: and a pretty close friendship subsisted between the two lads, George and Rawdon, who hunted and shot together in the vacations, were both entered of the same college at Cambridge, and quarrelled with each other about Lady Jane's daughter, with whom they were both, of course, in love. A match between George and that young lady was long a favourite scheme of both the matrons, though I have heard that Miss Crawley herself inclined towards her cousin.

Mrs. Rawdon Crawley's name was never mentioned by either family. There were reasons why all should be silent regarding her. For wherever Mr. Joseph Sedley went, she travelled likewise; and that infatuated man seemed to be entirely her slave.

The Colonel's lawyers informed him that his brother-in-law had effected a heavy insurance upon his life, whence it was probable that he had been raising money to discharge debts. He procured prolonged leave of absence from the East India House, and indeed his infirmities were daily increasing.

On hearing the news about the insurance, Amelia, in a good deal of alarm, entreated her husband to go to Brussels, where Jos then was, and inquire into the state of his affairs. The Colonel quitted home with reluctance (for he was deeply immersed in his "History of the Punjaub," which still occupies him, and much alarmed about his little daughter, whom he idolizes, and who was just recovering from the chicken-pox) and went to Brussels and found Jos living at one of the enormous hotels in that city. Mrs. Crawley, who had her carriage, gave entertainments, and lived in a very genteel manner, occupied another suite of apartments in the same hotel.

The Colonel, of course, did not desire to see that lady, or even think proper to notify his arrival at Brussels, except privately, to Jos by a message through his valet. Jos begged the Colonel to come and see him that night, when Mrs. Crawley would be at a *soirée,* and when they could meet *alone.* He found his brother-in-law in a condition of pitiable infirmity; and dreadfully afraid of Rebecca, though eager in his praises of her. She tended him through a series of unheard-of illnesses, with a fidelity most admirable. She had been a daughter to him. "But—but—oh, for God's sake, do come and live near me, and—and—see me sometimes," whimpered out the unfortunate man.

The Colonel's brow darkened at this.

"We can't, Jos," he said. "Considering the circumstances, Amelia can't visit you."

"I swear to you—I swear to you on the Bible," gasped
out Joseph, wanting to kiss the book, "that she is as innocent as a child, as spotless as your own wife."

"It may be so," said the Colonel, gloomily; "but Emmy
can't come to you. Be a man, Jos: break off this disreputable connection. Come home to your family. We hear
your affairs are involved."

"Involved!" cried Jos. "Who has told such calumnies?
All my money is placed out most advantageously. Mrs.
Crawley—that is—I mean,—it is laid out to the best
interest."

"You are not in debt, then? Why did you insure your
life?"

"I thought—a little present to her—in case anything happened; and you know my health is so delicate—common
gratitude you know—and I intend to leave all my money
to you—and I can spare it out of my income, indeed I can,"
cried out William's weak brother-in-law.

The Colonel besought Jos to fly at once—to go back to
India, whither Mrs. Crawley could not follow him; to do
anything to break off a connection which might have the
most fatal consequences to him.

Jos clasped his hands, and cried,—"He would go back
to India. He would do anything: only he must have time:
they mustn't say anything to Mrs. Crawley:—she'd—she'd
kill me if she knew it. You don't know what a terrible
woman she is," the poor wretch said.

"Then, why not come away with me?" said Dobbin in
reply; but Jos had not the courage. "He would see Dobbin
again in the morning; he must on no account say that he
had been there. He must go now. Becky might come in."
And Dobbin quitted him full of forebodings.

He never saw Jos more. Three months afterwards
Joseph Sedley died at Aix-la-Chapelle. It was found that
all his property had been muddled away in speculations,
and was represented by valueless shares in different bubble
companies. All his available assets were the two thousand
pounds for which his life was insured, and which were left
equally between his beloved "sister Amelia, wife of, &c.,
and his friend and invaluable attendant during sickness,

Rebecca, wife of Lieutenant Colonel Rawdon Crawley, C.B.," who was appointed administratrix.

The solicitor of the Insurance Company swore it was the blackest case that ever had come before him; talked of sending a commission to Aix to examine into the death, and the Company refused payment of the policy. But Mrs., or Lady Crawley, as she styled herself, came to town at once (attended with her solicitors, Messrs. Burke, Thurtell, and Hayes, of Thavies Inn), and dared the Company to refuse the payment. They invited examination, they declared that she was the object of an infamous conspiracy, which had been pursuing her all through life, and triumphed finally. The money was paid, and her character established, but Colonel Dobbin sent back his share of the legacy to the Insurance Office, and rigidly declined to hold any communication with Rebecca.

She never was Lady Crawley, though she continued so to call herself. His Excellency Colonel Rawdon Crawley died of yellow fever at Coventry Island, most deeply beloved and deplored, and six weeks before the demise of his brother, Sir Pitt. The estate consequently devolved upon the present Sir Rawdon Crawley, Bart.

He, too, has declined to see his mother, to whom he makes a liberal allowance; and who, besides, appears to be very wealthy. The Baronet lives entirely at Queen's Crawley, with Lady Jane and her daughter; whilst Rebecca, Lady Crawley, chiefly hangs about Bath and Cheltenham, where a very strong party of excellent people consider her to be a most injured woman. She has her enemies. Who has not? Her life is her answer to them. She busies herself in works of piety. She goes to church, and never without a footman. Her name is in all the Charity Lists. The Destitute Orange-girl, the Neglected Washerwoman, the Distressed Muffin-man, find in her a fast and generous friend. She is always having stalls at Fancy Fairs for the benefit of these hapless beings. Emmy, her children, and the Colonel, coming to London some time back, found themselves suddenly before her at one of these fairs. She cast down her eyes demurely and smiled as they started away from her; Emmy skurrying off on the arm of George (now grown a dashing young gentleman) and the Colonel seizing up his little Janey, of whom he is fonder than of anything in the world—fonder even than of his "History of the Punjaub."

"Fonder than he is of me," Emmy thinks, with a sigh. But he never said a word to Amelia that was not kind and gentle; or thought of a want of hers that he did not try to gratify.

Ah! *Vanitas Vanitatum!* which of us is happy in this world? Which of us has his desire? or, having it, is satisfied?—come, children, let us shut up the box and the puppets, for our play is played out.